WE MOVED OUT OF THE JET—SO FAR SO GOOD.

Down the long tunnel where no airport-type personnel were. I knew we weren't really at an airport, but we'd taxied to a hangar and the ramp had attached to our plane just like at any advanced airport. There should have been someone or something to indicate we weren't enemies entering this area. But there was nothing and no one. So far so very creepy.

"Is it always devoid of personnel? Anybody could waltz in here."

"No." Christopher sounded worried. "Normally there are checkpoints." He had a gun in his pocket and his hand on the gun. His other hand was on his suitcase. "Take my arm," he said quietly.

I did. I could feel his muscles, and they were tensed. "Should I be scared?"

"Do you work better scared?"

"Sadly, yes."

"Then be scared."

I didn't want to think about the fact that Martini was in the lead. Adrenaline wasn't any good for bullet wounds.

Martini turned a corner, then the others did, too. Just as Christopher and I reached it, I heard what sounded like a lot of shouting. And then what sounded like an explosion....

"It's all great fun, with lots of quirky characters, witty dialogue, a bit of romance, some hot sex, and oodles of action . . . thoroughly diverting."
                                                                —*Locus*

ALIEN
TANGO

GINI KOCH

DAW BOOKS, INC.
DONALD A. WOLLHEIM, FOUNDER
375 Hudson Street, New York, NY 10014

ELIZABETH R. WOLLHEIM
SHEILA E. GILBERT
PUBLISHERS
http://www.dawbooks.com

First Printing, December 2010
2   3   4   5   6   7   8   9

To Mary, Lisa and Veronica,
for reams of paper, hours of time,
and consistently brutal honesty.

ACKNOWLEDGMENTS

Many thanks to Cherry Weiner and Sheila Gilbert, still the best agent and editor anyone could hope to have.

Same again to Lisa Dovichi for all the crit partnering and then some, and to Mary Fiore for all the beta reading and then some. Couldn't do it without you.

Thanks again to everyone I thanked last time, anyone I might have missed last time, and everyone else added into the "family" along the way, for all you do and keep on doing—you know who you are and why I love and appreciate you. Extra shout outs to Adrian Payne for constant boosting and being the first person to preorder *Touched by an Alien*, to Mary Rehak for a whole lot of help and support, and to Helen King, for all the marketing and promotion ideas I didn't even dream of along with those very needed long lunches and even more needed laughs. Much love to Joe, Kenne, Pauline, and Sydney for throwing the best book signing parties in the world.

Special thanks to authors Erin Quinn and David Boop for guidance, encouragement, and mentoring through all the publication and promotion stages.

Finally, as before and always, the biggest thanks and all my love to my husband, Steve, and my daughter, Veronica. *Might* be able to do it without you two, but it wouldn't be worth it.

ALIENS WALK AMONG US.

Six months ago, that line would have totally freaked me out. Now, I'm living with thousands of them and dating one—if you define dating as spending almost every waking hour together and pretty much every sleeping hour together, too, while still maintaining separate living quarters.

Aliens do walk among us—it helps that they're here to protect the Earth, and they're all gorgeous, too. They also run at hyperspeed, have talents humans don't, and really have the edge in terms of stamina, seeing as they all have two hearts. From my vast but specialized experience, they're also godlike in bed.

However, they can't handle human machinery like cars or planes, and they can't lie to save their or anyone else's lives. So humans have nothing to worry about. At least, not from the ones who live here.

From the others out there in space? Oh, yeah, worry. Worry a lot.

But then, remind yourself that "our" aliens are watching over you, protecting the Earth and its citizens from danger.

And if that doesn't make you feel all secure, this should. I'm watching over you, too.

Huh. I sort of expected more than the "Sounds of Silence." Tough room.

CHAPTER 1

"**A**RE YOU SURE SHE CAN DO THIS,** Captain Tucker?"

"Absolutely, Commander Martini." Jerry chuckled. "Like lickin' butter off a knife."

"Jeff, I've done it already."

"Yeah, don't remind me." I could hear him talking to someone in the background. "Christopher says you shouldn't brag about your first landing."

"He should talk. It was like five months ago. I've landed plenty of times since then."

"With Jerry's help." He was worried. It was cute. Annoying, but cute.

"Jerry's helping me again."

"Jerry's not in the plane." Martini sounded really stressed.

"I'm right next to her, Commander. She'll be fine." I looked to my right to see Jerry passing me the "he's really bugging me" sign. I passed the same right back.

"Jeff? I love you. Now, shut up. I do need to concentrate." This was true. I was landing a supersonic jet for the second time by myself. The first time had been a lot more exciting, and I define exciting to mean survival was nowhere close to a given.

"Kitty, I'll be right here, but I'm not talking you through anything. You ready?" Jerry didn't sound worried. But then, that was part of his charm.

"Yep." I relaxed and did what Jerry had spent the better part of the last four months teaching me—how to fly and, most importantly, how to land. We were part of the new Airborne Division, created pretty much because of me. Not that I was some sort of great flier—certainly not five months ago—but because I'd managed air support so well during Operation Fugly.

Well, that's what I called it. Most everyone else referred to it as The Big Engagement or something equally impressive. I suppose when you take down Public Superbeing Enemy Number One and all his cronies, it does deserve an impressive title. They were just big, fugly monsters to me, but then again, I'm not from Alpha Centauri.

It had been a shock to discover the Roswell UFO rumors had been based in a lot of truth. But now I was living in the Dulce Science Center, routinely trained out of Home Base, aka Area 51, and most of my friends and co-workers were aliens, or A-Cs, as they called themselves. You could spot them easily—they were the drop-dead gorgeous ones in black and white Armani.

I was allowed the Armani outfit, too, but I spent most of my time in jeans and whichever concert T-shirt struck my fancy. Today, in honor of the big solo event, I was in my newest Aerosmith shirt. Steven, Joe, and the rest of my boys had never let me down, after all.

Jerry was a great teacher, and one of the things he'd stressed was making this all seem second nature, like driving a car or killing a newly formed parasitic superbeing. So, while I was nervous, I tried to put myself into a relaxed state.

Didn't work.

"Wow, that was an impressive 'made you look' moment," Martini said as I pulled up to avoid slamming into the dirt. "I think my heartbeats should go back to normal in a few minutes."

"I went down too fast."

"Baby, I've never thought that was a problem of yours."

"Jeff!" Of course, he was right. And one to talk.

"Commander Martini? Could you keep the chatter and romantic innuendos down? I really want Kitty to concentrate." I was back up next to Jerry, and he shook his head at me. "Too slow at the start, too fast at the end."

"Okay, you all said it was stupid, but I want what I asked for."

"It'll wreck your concentration," Jerry said flatly.

"It'll help it."

"Oh, give her what she wants. Girlfriend, gimme the song cue." Thank God. James Reader—human, former top international male supermodel, coolest guy in the room, and, somehow, the person in my "new life" I was closest to—was finally on the radio. I'd have been in trouble if he weren't gay, since Martini wasn't a man open to the idea of sharing.

"James, we're going with something a little off the standard path."

"Not Tears for Fears. Please." I heard a lot of groaning.

"How many of you are on the intercom?"

"Your entire team, Alpha Team, and HQ. But no pressure," Reader chuckled. "Now, what song?"

"Elton John's 'Rocket Man.'" Lots of groans. "Or we could go for John Mayer's 'Bigger Than My Body.'"

"Elton John!" Ah, the chorus of male voices choosing their lesser of two evils.

"Why not Aerosmith?" Reader asked.

"Because I need to slow down, not break the sound barrier. Follow it up with his 'I've Seen the Saucers.' I think it's going to be a two-song landing."

"Sir Elton coming right up."

"You're the best."

The music started, and I truly relaxed. I ran through a few loops and maneuvers to clear out the aborted landing attempt. It took most of 'Rocket Man' for me to feel ready. Then I started down again, from a bit higher than before. The next song came on, perfect for landing, at least as far as I was concerned. I even touched down to the beat.

"Great job, Kitty!" Jerry was landing now.

"She does have a great singing voice." Tim Crawford, my team's official driver. We'd sort of bonded over music during Operation Fugly. I still didn't know what he actually listened to, but he controlled my car iPod now and was getting really good at picking out what songs to play in tense situations.

I finished helping Elton on the high notes. "Thanks, Tim, you're a prince." Reader was a sweetie and put "Crocodile Rock" on while I taxied and parked my jet.

"Kitty? You can get out now." This was Matt Hughes, one of my flyboys.

"Laaaaaa . . . la la la laaaaaa." The song wasn't over. The music stopped, mid-la. "Oh, fine." Spoilsports.

"Love your voice, Kitty." This from Chip Walker, one of my other flyboys. "Just need you out of the jet."

"Liar." I climbed out. Jerry was waiting for me. He, like all our pilots and drivers, was human, so while he was cute, he wasn't up to A-C standards. Though I'd told him he could grow it out, he still kept his blond hair in a crew cut. All the pilots assigned to me had been at the Top Gun school before joining us during Operation Fugly, and they all maintained their Navy attitudes, even though they were now officially part of Centaurion Division, the American government's name for what I thought of as the Alien Protection Organization.

Jerry grinned. "You make it look easy, Commander Katt." We were back on the ground and so back to formality. In the air, he was in charge. On the ground, I was. More than one person had mentioned that this was truly frightening.

"It's a gift, my love. And I have the best teacher around." Okay, he was back to formality. Me, not so much.

We headed toward the main headquarters building. As we got nearer, a tall man with broad shoulders, rather wide features over a strong chin, light brown eyes, and dark, wavy hair left the building and came toward us. He was in Armani and, as always, looked beyond drool-worthy. He spotted us and then was next to me before I could blink.

"Nice to see you, Commander Martini, I'll just leave you two alone. Enjoy." Jerry gave Martini a quick salute, shot me a wink where Martini couldn't see it, and trotted off to the main building.

Martini grunted at Jerry, then pulled me into his arms

and kissed me. This definitely made it all worthwhile. His lips were soft, like down pillows, and his tongue could do things I'd never imagined before I met him. I wrapped my arms around his back and enjoyed how he pulled me even closer against him. But I could feel his hearts, and they were pounding.

He ended our kiss. "You know, I thought you were going to die. I don't know if I can run fast enough to pull you out of an exploding jet."

I leaned against his chest. "Jeff, I was okay. I have to be able to do this."

"Why?" I didn't answer. He sighed. "I don't get kidnapped every week, you know."

"Once was enough for me." I could still see him, on his knees, hands bound behind him, being tortured and almost killed.

"Baby, don't dwell on that," he said softly.

"I don't." Well, not all the time. There were whole days I'd gotten through without that memory surfacing and suggesting I might not be so lucky next time. Because there was always a next time.

"You may be human and able to lie to me, but not about your emotions."

"I know, Mr. Empath. I just . . . " I sighed. "I just want to be able to do everything I can. Not only for you, but for our missions. If I can't fly, then I've got one less weapon in my arsenal."

His turn to sigh. "Okay. You did great the second time. I'm really proud of you."

"James tell you to say that?"

Martini grinned. "Yeah. Did I do it right?"

"You always do it right."

"Nice to know." He put his arm around my shoulders, I put mine around his waist, and we walked to the main building. "So, are we going to your high school reunion?"

"Jeff, I don't know why you want to go." This wasn't completely true. As an A-C born on Earth, he'd been schooled within their community. They were a tight-knit group, all related somewhere back there in the generations, so every day was a reunion of some sort for them. I could understand Martini's interest in how the other half had done it, but I still didn't want to attend.

"They're supposed to be fun, romantic, exciting."

"You are watching way too much Lifetime Channel. And why, may I ask?"

"Helps me relate to you."

"Hardly."

"You don't think I relate to you well?" I could hear a little bit of hurt in his voice.

"No, I think that, as the super empath, you, more than any other man I've ever known, relate to me just fine. However, I don't think you watching *Mother, May I Sleep With Danger* again will give you more relatability to me."

"Tori Spelling's really an underrated actress."

"So's Shannen Doherty, you've told me. I'm impressed. Join their fan clubs. I miss your *Fantasy Island* fixation."

"I'll stop watching Lifetime if we go to your reunion."

"Wow, you can't even lie if I'm not looking directly at your face."

The door opened before we got to the entrance, and Christopher White came out. He looked upset. "Jeff, we have a problem."

CHAPTER 2

CHRISTOPHER DIDN'T REALLY LOOK LIKE his cousin. Where Martini was well over six feet and extremely muscular in a non-body-builder way, Christopher was a head shorter and more lean and wiry. He was fairer, with green eyes and lighter straight brown hair. They were both gorgeous—I still hadn't met an A-C who wasn't—but Christopher resembled his late mother, and I'd been told Martini resembled his father, so you had to know them to realize they were closely related.

Christopher also had glaring down to an art form, and we were being treated to patented Glare #1. "What did I do now?" Martini asked.

"Why am I the one who has to field every communication from your parents?"

Oh, this one again. I tried to slip away, but Martini had a firm grasp on me.

"Because, like everyone else, they like you better."

"I like you better, Jeff."

"Thanks, baby. You're about the only one."

Christopher rolled his eyes. "If I have to tell Aunt Lucinda one more time that you're tied up in an important meeting, I'm going to kill you."

Martini rubbed his forehead. "What did she want this time?"

Christopher didn't answer and looked at me. "Great landing, Kitty."

"Your mother wants to know why you haven't dumped me yet and married a nice A-C girl or boy like you're supposed to." A-Cs didn't have hang-ups about same-sex relationships. They just had them about interspecies and interreligious ones.

Christopher flushed. Got it in one! "It's not like that," he muttered, but he was now looking at his shoes.

"And you wonder why I'm dodging her calls?" Martini hugged me. "Let's get inside."

"Jeff, it's not Christopher's fault." It was mine, for being human and falling in love with her son, at least, as far as I'd picked up. Or Martini's, for doing the same with me. The whole "saved his life" thing didn't seem to factor in for Martini's parents. "Maybe if I met them—"

"Not a great idea!" both Christopher and Martini chorused.

"How bad can they be? I mean, Christopher, your father seems to think I'm okay." Richard White was the Sovereign Pontifex for the A-Cs, or, as I thought of it, their Pope with Benefits.

"My father thinks you're great."

"But I'm not his son's girlfriend." Both of them winced, because that had been a close call, and the three of us normally did our best not to bring it up. So, my bad, as pretty much always. Maybe Martini was right to keep me away from his parents.

"Let's talk about this later." Martini sounded tired and depressed. Which made me worry. "Don't stress out, baby." The positive of being with the strongest empath on Earth was that he was really in tune with how I was feeling. The downside was that I couldn't hide anything from him emotionally, even when I wanted to.

Paul Gower joined us in the doorway. He was built like Martini, only black and bald. His father had married an African-American human. I often found myself wondering how happy she was, but I hadn't asked. Yet.

"We have a bigger issue than your parents," Gower shared, looking tense and sounding tenser. "Clustered activity."

Martini and Christopher both flipped into what I considered Commander Mode. "Where?" Martini asked briskly as we all trotted inside.

"Paraguay."

"Paraguay?" Christopher sounded shocked. Martini grimaced.

"Why not Paraguay?" I'd been all over the world by now, killing forming fuglies and keeping the world safe from becoming superbeing sushi. South America was hit as frequently as everywhere else, though in overall superbeing activity, the U.S.A. was still number one with a bullet.

"In the Chaco," Gower added.

"Of course," Martini muttered.

I grabbed my purse from Hughes, told him that he and the rest of my flyboys were off duty but on standby, and then we headed for the nearest bank of gates. The gates were alien technology that allowed us to move freely about the world by leaping from one gate to another. The majority of the gates were located in the restrooms of all the world's airports. Having visited more men's rooms than I cared to remember, by now I could attest to their placement being both effective and gross at the same time. But we could go from Nevada to New York in about three seconds.

"There are airports there," I reminded them, as I tried to pull up how rainy or dry Paraguay was and failed.

"True," Martini acknowledged. "But we're not going there."

"We're not?" I wasn't overly disappointed. We had dinner with my parents planned, and superbeing-extermination trips tended to wreck any schedule.

Reader joined us. "They're right on the line." He sounded worried, and the other men looked tense. I felt nothing other than confusion—this was a new one.

"Excuse me?"

We reached the gate, and Gower calibrated. As always when any A-C did this, his hand was a blur. and I couldn't watch. Not that staring at alien technology that still looked more like an airport metal detector than anything else to me was a thrill in the first place. "Going through single. Sorry, Kitty," he added with an apologetic smile. "We're in an emergency situation.

Martini didn't look happy, but he didn't argue, either, so I chose to be a big girl and not whine. Gower went through, I took a deep breath, then I followed.

Going through a gate was like being in a movie where they speed up the film to show the passage of time quickly. Only you were in said movie live, with no Dramamine. The gates had made me sick to my stomach from day one and continued their work unabated. It took no more than a second and a half for the step that moved me from Area 51 to the Dulce Science Center but it was a year in terms of nausea.

Out just before I barfed, like always. Martini and the others were right behind me. We were on what I call the Bat Cave level of the Science Center—it looked like the most high-tech command-type center ever conceived. I tended to ignore most of the equipment on the grounds that it made me dizzy, and if I ignored it, I could pretend it wasn't there.

We trotted to Batman's Inner Sanctum, or what Martini and Christopher called Field and Imageering Central Command. Well, Reader and I trotted. Martini, Christopher, and Gower all used hyperspeed, meaning to our human eyes they disappeared. Hyperspeed for humans was slightly better than the gates in terms of nausea, but only a little, so I was glad to move at boring old human levels.

"What did you mean by 'the line,' James?"

"The Tropic of Capricorn crosses through Paraguay, that's what we mean by the line."

"Why is that good, bad, or indifferent?"

He shook his head. "For whatever reasons, when superbeings form along the Tropics of Cancer or Capricorn, they're stronger."

"Stronger than the ones that were able to control the transfer?"

"No. Differently stronger."

I wanted to share that this wasn't clearing anything up for me, but we were in the Inner Sanctum, and things were in a very controlled form of chaotic activity. There were actually two rooms that made up this section, one for Field, one for Imageering. By the time Reader and I arrived, Christopher had presumably raced off to his room, and Martini was settled in front of the huge bank of screens that were the focus of the Field side.

By settled, I mean he was standing in front of them as images flashed on the screen. There were easily fifty screens on the main wall, and while the peripheral ones had areas I knew weren't in Paraguay, the majority were showing what I assumed was the Tropic of Capricorn.

It looked like a flat, marshy part of Paraguay with a lot of superbeings in it. The Paraguay portion of our Must Watch Horrorvision was rather pretty. The superbeings made up for that, though. All twelve of them.

CHAPTER 3

IN THE OLDEN DAYS OF the mid-twentieth century, the parasites that created superbeings when joined with an unsuspecting human host arrived in ones and twos at irregular intervals. After Mephistopheles, the Big Bad of Operation Fugly, had established himself on Earth, they came with a lot of regularity, building up to lots and lots all the time.

However, clustering—where several superbeings manifested at the same time and in one area—had happened in the past only when an in-control superbeing was getting ready to hit the town. Since we'd destroyed all the in-control ones, it was unsettling to have a cluster, especially one of a dozen.

The parasites were attracted to rage. How they'd found twelve angry people out in what looked like the middle of nowhere was beyond me.

Every superbeing manifested differently based, as far as we knew, more on the parasite than its human host. These were no exception, though I saw similarities among them. They were all along the Insect of Your Nightmares variety, though insects that weren't from anywhere around here. Then again, I didn't know what kinds of bugs Paraguay specialized in. However, I tended to doubt their bugs were between six and ten feet tall and loaded with an amazing array of horrifically shaped, yet seemingly razor-sharp, extremities, mandibles, and so forth.

I could see a great number of droolingly handsome men in Armani suits dashing about on the screens, meaning we had a lot of A-Cs on the scene. All field teams consisted of an empath and an imageer. Depending on what was going on, they might have a human along to drive or fly, and usually no more than two additional A-Cs. The teams in Paraguay had all that and more. It didn't look like a normal setup at all.

Martini was giving orders, and he was doing it at normal speed for an A-C, meaning a lot faster than humans could hear, at least if we were interested in silly things like comprehension. Like so many other aspects of hyperspeed, this made me sick.

A random A-C handed me a set of wireless headphones, which I put on gratefully. Since I'd joined up and pointed out that having your human teammates barfing when you were trying to save the day was a bad plan, the A-Cs had added their version of translation headsets to the Inner Sanctum supply closet.

So I could now hear Martini's orders and not pass out. I was hearing them at least five minutes after he'd said them, but I considered this a huge improvement over fainting. I made sure I didn't look at his mouth moving—the few times I had, it was like watching a badly dubbed foreign film. Right after barfing or passing out, I'd discovered no one liked me cracking up during Inner Sanctum sessions, Martini least of all.

"Do we need Airborne involved?" I asked Reader, who was putting his own headset on.

He shook his head. "Jeff's handling it."

I decided not to argue or whine about this. My division was still very new, and while I had utmost confidence in my team, they were all still at Home Base, and even with a gate transfer, shipping military jets took some time. Hopefully it'd all be over before they could get there, so why send them. Besides, Martini seemed intent, and I didn't want to throw off his groove.

I listened for a while, but after a few minutes it became boring and frustrating. Frustrating because I was now used to being in the action, and I wasn't a fan of sitting around watching others getting to kick butt.

Martini was sending various A-C teams to different parts of Paraguay, calling in military support from both Brazil and Argentina, and giving a variety of directions to those directly engaged with these particular manifestations. I should have been paying rapt attention, learning how to do this myself.

But it was all done in extreme military-speak, which got dull fast. I hadn't yet mastered the lingo and jargon, and situations like this never made learning seem worthwhile. And watching international politics fade in the face of extreme danger had stopped being a thrill months ago. I'd learned that when it came to hanging around kibitzing, I preferred watching the imageers work.

While Martini brought in tanks and artillery, I slunk over to Christopher's half of the Sanctum.

The Imageering side had a similar setup to the Field half—lots of screens, computer terminals, and so forth. There were also a variety of monitors, and every one of them had an A-C in front of it, hands on the screen, expressions in varying stages of concentration.

Empaths felt emotions but couldn't manipulate them. They were the ones who spotted superbeing trouble most of the time, because the superbeings were attracted to rage and when they formed, the human host's brain and emotions went haywire.

Martini, the most powerful empath on Earth, was able to feel what the other empaths did, almost like short-wave radio, passed from the teams in the Field on back, as needed. He could turn it on and off—apparently they all could—due to drugs and training, but it meant that while he was ordering everyone around, he was also monitoring who was in the most emotional need.

It was impressive to the extreme and one of the main reasons he was the man in charge of pretty much all A-C operations that weren't religiously based, but it wasn't something I was actually able to share or experience myself.

Imageers, by contrast, couldn't feel anything unless they were touching an image—any kind of image. Once touched, they knew everything about that person. Christopher said it was because photos and the like captured a copy of the person's mind and soul as well as their physical image.

Imageers could also manipulate images, and that's what they were all doing—altering what the cameras in Paraguay were catching and changing it into something far less terrifying than the Attack of the Intergalactic Dirty Dozen.

So the screens on the wall showed what was really going on, and the monitors showed what the A-Cs were changing the various camera feeds into. Christopher had tried to explain it to me, and I'd done better with it than learning all the military blah, blah, blah Martini had shared with me. I wasn't clear on how it all worked, of course, but the bottom line was that the more cameras, cell phones, video cameras, and satellites that were trained on a superbeing incident, the more imageers needed.

From the number of bodies in the room, there were a lot more cameras in this part of Paraguay than I'd have thought there would be. The area I was looking at on the big screen didn't seem overly populated.

Christopher had the biggest monitor, and he was altering footage while barking orders. Unlike Martini, he was barking them at human speeds. And also unlike Martini's side of the house, I got to see what those orders translated into.

"I want all the cell phone feeds altered to blurred images," Christopher snapped. "Video and film footage altered to show native folk dancing and similar. Go for stock footage."

The imageers handling the cell phones had it easy, as far as I could tell. The images on their monitors blurred until they looked like nothing so much as someone with serious palsy taking pictures of the inside of an enthusiastic squirrel.

I was interested to discover that the term "stock footage" was used by the whole galaxy, at least those parts of it present on Earth. There was a wide variety of choices filtering through—some I recognized from a couple of National Geographic specials, some I didn't. But they all had the canned look of people performing their native dances for the cameras—it was clear these shots weren't Live at the Scene.

An A-C ran in from the Field side. "Commander White, Commander Martini says the C.I.A. on the scene are creating problems."

"Like always," Christopher growled. "What do they want?"

The A-C gulped. "They want to control these superbeings, not kill them."

"What?" Christopher exploded. "Are they crazy? This is their stated goal?"

"No, sir. Commander Martini was able to determine this based on their emotional reactions." The A-C coughed. "The rest of us were able to determine based on their telling our field teams to go away and let them handle it."

"How *Aliens* of them." I shrugged at the confused look Christopher shot me. I always forgot—the A-Cs never went in for science fiction movies of any kind, presumably on the belief they were documentaries they lived every day. "It's a real common theme in the movies. Governmental bad guys want to control the evil, almost unstoppable monsters, small band of good guys manages to save the day, blah, blah, blah. Want me to talk to them?" I asked brightly.

"No, and I'm sure Jeff doesn't, either." Christopher looked at the messenger. "What does Commander Martini want to do?"

Before anyone could reply, the superbeings on screen all blew up. The images shifted to either the native dances ending, fireworks displays, or the palsied squirrels going dormant, depending.

Martini walked in. "Now that our friends from Argentina used some stinger missiles and stopped the immediate problem, I want to go to C.I.A. headquarters and deal with the ongoing one."

CHAPTER 4

"GREAT!" I'd been dying to go to C.I.A. headquarters for quite a while now. Based on the A-Cs' levels of hierarchy, the only people allowed to interact with the top C.I.A. bigwigs were Martini and Christopher. The Pontifex, Gower, and Reader weren't even allowed over there. I hadn't been, either, and this looked like my big chance.

"Not just no, but hell no," Martini said calmly. I started to pout, and he shook his head. "You don't need to see what we're going to do over there, and we don't need them getting any better idea of what you can and can't do than they already have."

Reader joined us. "Jeff, I just got off with your favorite guy. He insists this wasn't an official C.I.A. plan and wants you and Christopher over there immediately."

Martini growled. "They don't give us orders."

Christopher's expression said this wasn't actually true. I thought back to Operation Fugly—the traitorous side had certainly had the C.I.A. on speed dial, and despite what my parents had said about government control of Centaurion Division, I wasn't fully convinced they were right. In the few months I'd been here, it seemed as though every government agency in the U.S. and at least half of them worldwide felt they had a stake in Centaurion.

But no amount of whining and complaining changed Martini's mind. I still wasn't getting to hang with the C.I.A.

He and Christopher cleaned up, gave some orders, then they and Reader headed for the main launch area. I tagged along, of course, on the off chance I could still weasel an opportunity out of Martini.

"You're not going," he said as we walked along, his arm around my shoulders and mine around his waist. He sounded relaxed but felt tense.

"Who're you going to see?"

"No one you need to worry about."

"What's his name?"

"None of your business."

"I'm the head of Airborne. I think it *is* my business."

"Nope." He kissed the top of my head. "See, I'm still in charge, baby. You haven't been on board long enough to know how to deal with these people, the new head guy in particular."

"So, he's new to the job? Maybe we'd have that in common, a bonding sort of thing."

Christopher snorted. "No one's as new as you, Kitty."

"He's had the position for about a year and a half," Martini said. "But he's been dealing with us for several years. Got promoted due to his ability to 'understand' us." Martini wasn't snarling, but it was close.

"Why don't you like him?"

"Because I don't trust him. I don't trust anyone in the C.I.A." Martini shrugged. "Your mother excluded."

At the same time I'd discovered real live aliens were living on Earth, I'd also discovered that my mother had been living a secret life. She wasn't a consultant, she was a former Mossad agent who was now the head of antiterrorism for an elite agency that reported directly to the President of the United States.

"My mother's not in the C.I.A. She's the head of the P.T.C.U."

"It's really part of the C.I.A., girlfriend," Reader explained. "It's above them, and considered a separate unit, does report directly to the President. But the paychecks come out of Langley."

"I hate bureaucracy."

"But we're all so good at it." Reader grinned. "Stop

sulking. There'll be plenty of time to harangue Jeff about this later."

We reached the gates, and someone calibrated. I ignored it while Martini kissed me good-bye. As always, even though it wasn't long, it was great. "Behave," he said with a smile. He looked over to the gate agent. "No one, not even Commander Katt, is to go where we're going."

"Yes, sir." This particular A-C was one of the Security types. They were all bigger than Martini and had that bored but focused way about them. I wasn't going anywhere, at least nowhere near the C.I.A.

We were at a larger gate, and they went through together. We watched them slowly fade away. I controlled myself from tossing cookies or trying to pull them back, and then Reader and I headed back to the Bat Cave level.

No sooner had we exited than Queen's "My Best Friend" came on my cell phone. "You haven't changed that yet?" Reader asked as I dug my phone out of my purse.

"No reason to, any more than I can't hang around you. You two are my best guy friends, and he's my oldest friend, too. Nothing more."

Reader shook his head. "Jeff doesn't like it."

"I don't like not getting to go to visit the C.I.A. It evens out." I moved away from him as I answered. "Hi, Chuckie, what's up?"

"You okay?" He sounded worried. Of course, he'd sounded worried for the last several months, ever since I started being evasive about where I was, what I was doing, and who I was doing it with.

"On top of the world. Why?"

"Just curious. You going to the class reunion?"

"Are you high?"

He snorted. "No major lifestyle changes over here."

"Okay, good. And, of course I'm not going." I considered. "Were you planning to?" I couldn't imagine why. Chuckie had been, and still was, the most brilliant guy in any room. High school had been four years of torture for him. I still wasn't sure why he hadn't just taken the tests and headed for college when we were both freshmen, but he'd stuck it out.

Of course, he could win either the Least Likely to Succeed or the Class Hero awards now. Possibly both. He'd gone from short, acne-suffering, thick-glasses-wearing geek to six-foot-plus, clear-skinned, contact-lens-wearing handsome guy by the middle of our freshman year at Arizona State University. He'd also become a multimillionaire twice over. And had somehow remained the same sweet, cool, fun, supportive, and protective person he'd always been.

"Not really." He sounded evasive. "Thought I might if you were going, though."

"Well, if I change my mind somehow, I'll let you know." Or rather, if Martini changed my mind, but the chances were slim and I didn't want to mention the possibility. Because I hadn't told Chuckie about Martini yet. I hadn't even told him I was seriously involved with anyone. Because he'd want to meet my new guy, and there was no way I could lie to Chuckie face-to-face about anything, let alone about aliens really being on the planet. Martini knew this and didn't care for it. At all. Not that he wanted me to out him to Chuckie, but that Chuckie knew me so well and I was keeping them away from each other bothered Martini in the extreme.

"Sounds good. So, how's work?" He sounded like he wasn't expecting me to be truthful at all.

"Fine." Well, this was true. Sure, I wasn't working as a marketing manager any more, but still, I was being truthful about liking what I did now. "Busy. How's stock trading going?"

"Fine. Busy." He chuckled. "You know how it is."

"Not really, but I'll trust you on it."

He was quiet for a moment. "Yeah. I'll trust you on yours, too. Kitty?"

"Yes?"

"Promise me that if you get into something you can't handle, if you're in danger you really can't get out of, trapped in a situation you feel you can't escape from, or if you're unhappy for any reason, that you'll call me right away and let me help you."

This was both totally in character and weird at the same

time. Chuckie had always been there for me, since the first day of high school, and I'd been there for him. But this request had come out of nowhere.

"Dude, you know I don't go to frat parties and drink from the open tub of Jungle Juice any more."

"So you claim. I want your promise, Kitty." Chuckie's voice was in his "won't take no for an answer" tone, meaning he meant business.

I swallowed hard—I got into trouble on a regular basis these days, sometimes on an hourly basis. Sure, I'd always handled it, or Martini had been there to save me. But still, in the past, I'd called Chuckie when I was in over my head.

An almost overwhelming desire to tell him what was going on washed over me. He'd been called Conspiracy Chuck by everyone but me when we were in high school and by half of everyone we knew in college. In part because he'd always believed aliens were on the planet. He was my oldest friend, and I wanted so badly to let him know he'd been right all this time.

But I had a scary-high security clearance for a reason, and that clearance didn't allow me to tell Chuckie anything about what I did now. I took a deep breath, let it out, and shoved the guilt and desire down and away. "I promise. Same for you, you know. If you need me, let me know and I'll be there." Okay, I pushed the desire to tell away. The guilt seemed to enjoy hanging on.

He sighed. "I hope so." He cleared his throat. "You be careful."

"You, too. Chuckie?"

"Yeah?"

"You'll always be my friend, right?"

I could hear the smile in his voice. "Right."

"Then everything's right with my world."

"Mine too, Kitty," he said slowly. "Mine too."

CHAPTER 5

WE HUNG UP, and I felt worried for no good reason. It was close to time to go to my parents', and I had no idea how long Martini was going to be.

On cue my phone rang. "You're really stressed," Martini said, in a low voice. "Why?" I got the impression he wasn't alone and didn't want this call broadcast.

"Oh, just wondering if we're going to be late for dinner." I wondered if he could pick up that I was lying from this far away and prayed he couldn't.

"Right." He didn't sound like he'd bought it. Damn. "Our contact held us up calling his girlfriend," Martini snarled. "So we're going to be here longer."

"You're calling your girlfriend," I pointed out. Not that I had any idea of why I felt defending the nameless C.I.A. bigwig mattered. An interesting thought occurred. "Ooooh. Is he married and do you think he was calling his mistress?"

"This isn't *Desperate Housewives*," Martini snapped. "And no, to my knowledge, he's not married. Looking to trade up?"

"I've got the leader of the A-C pack. No need to make roster changes at this time." Let alone to some likely old, paunchy, balding guy who probably resembled a mangy ferret. At least, if I took how Martini and Christopher tended to describe anyone and everyone at the C.I.A. as an example.

"I'm so relieved." Martini's sarcasm meter was already at full. I felt bad for Mr. C.I.A. Dude.

"Jeff, relax. What's our status for tonight?"

He sighed. "Go ahead to your parents' without me, baby."

"You sure I shouldn't wait for you?"

"I'll be there as soon as I can, but trust me, it's going to take either a floater gate or hyperspeed."

"Okay! I'll head right over now. Can I take my car?"

"Sure. I love you."

"I love you, too, Jeff."

"Good to know." He sounded happier as we hung up than when he'd called, which was good.

I had my purse, and my parents didn't stand on ceremony, so no need to change. I headed for the top level, where, among other things, the motor pool was stored. The top level at the Science Center was actually the ground floor—the Center went down fifteen stories. The A-Cs had really done wondrous things with simulated lighting—it always seemed like proper daylight when it was supposed to.

I retrieved my car—a black Lexus IS300, stick shift, leather interior, turned on a dime, zero to sixty in a lot faster than I'd ever admit to a cop or my father. I loved my car. It stood out in the motor pool, too. Almost every vehicle the A-Cs had was a shade of gray. They'd never explained why, and the answer was still low on my long list of things to find out.

Had to do the slow, horrible gate transfer from Dulce to Caliente Base. I'd long ago stopped trying to be macho about it and closed my eyes the moment it started. I could always tell when it was over—my stomach settled down.

Caliente Base was smaller than the Science Center, but it was still a typical A-C base, meaning the top floor was ground level and everything else went down from there. Of course, "smaller" was a relative term. I had no clear idea of how huge the Science Center really was, but I'd been there for five months and knew I hadn't explored every part of every floor yet—and not because I wasn't interested. Because I always got lost. I had the distinct impression it was the equivalent of fifteen Pentagons, maybe more.

Caliente Base was merely very, very large. It was built on a supposed alien crash site. I tried not to think of Chuckie and failed. We'd hiked around here when we were younger, searching for said site, but hadn't found the entrance. I assumed it had been cloaked—the A-Cs had alien technology that would have made the *Star Trek* people sue for copyright infringement if they'd ever found out about it.

Like the Science Center and every other A-C base, the motor pool was on the ground level. I waved merrily and headed out for real daylight. It felt the same as A-C light.

I enjoyed the drive to my parents' house. It almost felt alien, to drive myself through the streets of Pueblo Caliente at a normal rate of speed. No gates, no hyperspeed, no limo with someone else acting as driver.

My phone rang. Happily, one of the many A-C bells and whistles that had been added onto my car was a hands-free system. It resided on automatic answer. "Hello?"

"Hey, Kit-Kat! How's things back in the 'burg?" It was Caroline, my sorority roommate. We still used our sorority nicknames because, well, they fit.

"Yo, Caro Syrup! Sunny and smiling, as always. What's up?"

"I got the job!" she squealed.

I squealed back. Then reality hit. "Um . . . what job?"

She laughed. "With the senator. I told you about it." I thought frantically. She had. Caroline was a lot better with the written correspondence than I was. She sent notes to every girl in our pledge class, her sister-line up and down, and anyone else from the sorority she'd liked, which was pretty much everyone, at least once a quarter. Individual notes. Handwritten. And somehow, she found time to work, eat, and sleep.

"Oh, right. That's great. When do you start?"

"This week. Had my orientation and everything."

"Make sure no one turns you into the Lurid Intern Story of the Week."

She snorted. "Our senator's not like that. He's a sweetie and very protective, and his wife's really involved. She's awesome. And a sister," she added a tad reproachfully.

Sluggish memory reared its head. Our sorority had a lot

of successful alumnae, and one of them had indeed married the senior senator from Arizona. "Great that she helped you land the job."

"Oh, your mom and Chuck helped, too. I saw him for lunch, by the way. He's looking great."

"The senator?" What was my mother doing helping anyone get a job? She'd never helped *me* get a job. I assumed Caroline had used Chuckie for a reference. References from rich, brilliant guys were always good to have.

"Wow, are you in the middle of something?"

"Only driving."

"Well, pull over and pay attention. I see the senator every day now. No, I had lunch with Chuck."

"Oh." A thought occurred. "Are you two dating?"

"No, you have nothing to worry about," she said with a laugh.

"Huh?"

She sighed. "You know what I love most about you?"

"My musical tastes?"

"Yes, but no. You never change."

"I think I should resent that."

"Don't. I have to go. Give my love to your parents, and tell your mom thanks."

"Will do. Keep me posted on stuff."

"Will do. Chuck looks *great*," she added.

"Good to hear. He's in D.C.?" This was normally the part of the year when Chuckie was in Australia most or all of the time.

"Yes." The way she said it, I could hear the "duh."

"Well, you could've been in Australia."

Caroline laughed. "Or in Paraguay."

"Hold that thought and don't hang up!" I pulled over and parked. "What do you mean about Paraguay?"

"Oh, there was a military action there today. The government's concerned. It seems to be under control, but it's the usual 'do we need to get involved' stuff. The senator might be sent down there as part of an investigative committee. He says it's a waste of time, but if he goes, I get to go, too, so I'm sort of hoping it happens."

"Keep me in the loop on that, will you?"

"It's kind of classified. I probably shouldn't have told you this much."

"I already knew about it."

She was quiet for a moment. "News travels fast."

"You have no idea. Just keep me apprised of what you can, okay? As a sort of sister favor?"

She sighed. "Will do." Well, it was something. Maybe I finally had a Washington "insider" on my speed dial. "Now I really have to go. Catch you later, Kit-Kat!"

"Talk to you in a few, Caro Syrup!"

We hung up. and I sat there for a few minutes. I wasn't hooked into the governmental stuff like Martini and Christopher were. For all I knew, the U.S. government always "got concerned' when we had superbeing activity and those in the know did the whole "it's no biggie" thing. Which would indicate that our senator was in the know. Which begged the "who all is in the know" question.

Well, I was having dinner with the right people to ask.

CHAPTER 6

I GOT BACK ON THE ROAD and pulled up in front of my parents' house in a few minutes. I stared at it. I'd grown up here—standard middle-class tract home. Two stories, two-car garage, about twenty-five hundred square feet. Not tiny but not huge, either. Typical desert landscaping out front consisting of river rocks and a variety of cacti.

For most of my life I'd figured I'd end up living in a similar type of house. Maybe a little bigger or smaller, maybe in a different city, even, but similar. Where I lived and what I did was in no way similar. But I liked it.

My father was playing catch with our four dogs in the backyard. I didn't have to see it—I could hear it. Our dogs lived to bark, and they had different barks for everything. They were clearly on, "Toy! Toy! Throw the toy!" as opposed to "Dangerous Intruder" or "Kitty is home, time to slobber!" I was grateful. I loved my dogs, but I wasn't in the mood to shower.

I found Mom in the kitchen. "Hi, kitten, where's Jeff?" One of our cats, Sugarfoot, was sitting on the counter helping her, or at least mooching food. He purred as I came in, and I slung him over my shoulder.

"Held up at C.I.A. headquarters. He'll be here as soon as he can." I gave her a peck. "What's for dinner?"

"I made a rib roast in honor of your first solo."

"Yum." Our other two cats, Candy and Kane, came in for pets. I so petted and was rewarded with a lot of purring.

One drawback to living in the Science Center was the No Pets Long-Term rule. I missed having the critters around all the time. "Caroline called."

"How is she?"

"Excited. She got the job with the senator, asked me to thank you."

Mom smiled. "Good, she's a very capable girl."

"So, you helped her get a job but not me?"

"You have a job."

"You know what I mean. She said Chuckie helped her, too." Come to think of it, Chuckie had never helped me get a job, either. Apparently my nearest and dearest either though I was Ms. Capable or didn't want their reputations sullied by referring me for anything. Sadly, I voted with option number two.

"I'm sure he did. Charles is very fond of all of your sorority sisters."

True. Unlike in high school, most of my college friends had liked him a lot, my sorority sisters in particular. We all did a lot better in school because Chuckie was very willing to tutor anyone at the sorority who needed it, and he was always willing to be available for whoever needed an escort. "Yeah, that was one worry of his that was needless."

Mom shrugged. "Your college friends were more... perceptive than your high school ones."

"I suppose. Amy and Sheila never needed tutoring, of course."

"Your sorority sisters liked Charles for more reasons than that."

"True enough. Caroline says Chuckie's looking good."

"Good to hear. How was the rest of your day?" It was a legitimate question and Mom sounded casual, but I figured she was asking for a reason.

"Fine." Of course, Mom also had that scary-high security clearance and, unlike Chuckie, she knew aliens were on the planet and what they did with their time. "Coincidentally, we had a cluster of forming superbeings. In Paraguay of all places."

Mom jerked and looked up from the potatoes she was mashing. "Paraguay?"

"Yeah. Jeff called in military support from Argentina and Brazil, and the Argentineans blew up the superbeings. But apparently the C.I.A. was on the scene and wanted the superbeings intact."

Mom's eyes narrowed. "Any idea why?"

I snorted. "To use as supersoldiers would be my guess."

"Is that why Jeff's in Langley? To verify?"

"Per what little I got, the head C.I.A. guy over Centaurion said he wasn't involved and wanted a briefing."

Mom looked relieved for a moment, then turned back to the potatoes.

"Caroline also said she might be going to Paraguay."

Mom was prepared, so she didn't react as much, though the potatoes got a slightly more vicious mashing. "Interesting."

Before I could ask her why she cared about this—Paraguay, Caroline possibly going there, and that the head C.I.A. guy over Centaurion was at least pretending not to be involved—Dad and the dogs came in, and I was buried under the tide of canines for a while.

Dogs appeased, I got a hug and kiss from Dad. "You getting enough to eat? Exercise?"

"Yes, Dad. Plenty of both."

"Sol, I forgot to get the Martinelli's. Would you get a few bottles?" A-Cs weren't allowed alcohol, supposedly for religious reasons. We'd discovered, however, that the real reason was that they were deadly allergic to the stuff. I hadn't had an alcoholic drink for months. This was a celebration, so since champagne was out, we were making do with what the kiddies drink on New Year's Eve.

"Sure." Dad gave Mom a kiss and a knowing look and headed for the garage.

I considered this. Mom wasn't given to forgetting anything, let alone that she'd need some nonalcoholic bubbly for tonight. I gave her a long look. "What will I find if I open the pantry or the fridge?"

Mom grinned. "You're getting good at this. Yes, I wanted

to speak with you when your father wasn't here. And when Jeff wasn't here. Your father and I are going to Washington tomorrow, and this opportunity appeared sooner than I thought it would, so why pass it up?"

"So, what's the big deal that requires girls only-ness?"

Mom shrugged. "You and Jeff are getting closer." I nodded. This wasn't exactly news. "I just want you to be sure that you've . . . considered all your options."

"Mom, for God's sake, Christopher and I would not work out on any kind of long-term basis."

"I don't mean just Christopher." Mom gave me a look I was familiar with—her "you're so dense" look.

"Then who? I don't recall a lot of other options I've been excited about for anything long term."

Mom sighed. "Are you going to your high school reunion?"

"Did the reunion committee send a desperate plea I missed? Chuckie asked me that today, too. And Jeff's been whining about going. And, no, even with all that, I'm still not planning on it."

"I think you should go."

I stared at her, trying to see if she was making a joke. She sure looked serious. "Um, why, exactly? I don't think Amy or Sheila are planning to go, and Chuckie said he'd only consider it if I was going. High school was fine, but I don't feel some strong urge to reminisce with people I don't see or speak to at all anymore."

"You might enjoy it."

"Or I might not." I considered all the potential reasons she was suggesting this. "You want me to show Jeff off or something?" That had real possibilities. There was no way in the world anyone else had landed someone that gorgeous, unless they were dating a male model or an A-C.

"Or something." Mom sighed again. "What else did you and Charles talk about?"

"How do you know we talked?"

Her eyes rolled. "You told me he'd said he'd go to the reunion if you would." She shook her head. "He'd do anything you wanted, you know that, right?"

"Yeah." My turn to sigh. "He sounded worried but okay."

"Have you seen him recently?"

"No."

Mom glared. "So, you've abandoned the man who's always been there for you?"

Where was this coming from? "No. Mom, Chuckie's still one of my two best guy friends. It's just . . . I can't tell him about my life now. And he knows when I lie. I just . . . I don't want to lie to his face, okay?"

Mom's expression softened. "I understand. But maybe you should see him anyway. The reunion would be neutral ground."

"Neutral ground? You mean we'd be joined together against the forces trying to kill us, at least if it's anything like high school was. We haven't had a fight or anything, it's not like we need to kiss and make up."

I got another shot of the "dense" look. "Kitten, I just want you to be sure you've considered all your options."

"Mom, I'm in a serious relationship with, last time I checked, a guy you and Dad both like. What's wrong with Jeff that you don't want me with him suddenly?"

"Nothing's wrong with *Jeff*."

I considered this. "But . . . ?"

"But . . . what does his family think of you?"

Ah. This suddenly made sense. My turn to sigh. "No idea. He won't let me meet them. And, it doesn't matter, right? Because there's no interspecies mating allowed. That's what this is about, right?"

"For the most part, yes. Mixing families is hard enough when both sides are enthusiastic about it. When they're not . . . "

"Yeah. Well, I've been trying to meet them. I'll keep on trying."

"Keep on thinking about your options, too," Mom said seriously. "Your father and I both love Jeff, but we want you happy, and disapproving in-laws aren't a recipe for happiness."

"I will, but Jeff can pick it up." And he didn't like me

considering other men as romantic options almost as much as he didn't like that I still talked to Chuckie regularly and hadn't changed his ringtone. Martini's jealousy was almost as impressive as his bedroom skills.

"A little competition now and then is good for him, I'm sure."

"As soon as I identify this supposed competition, I'll be sure to let you know."

Mom sighed. "You are *so* dense sometimes."

"It's a gift."

CHAPTER 7

MARTINI ARRIVED JUST AS THE roast was coming
out of the oven. He looked pissed. "I hate dealing with
the C.I.A.," he said by way of hello. "Any way we can get
rid of them?"

"Not that anyone's ever discovered," Mom said dryly as
the cats all started purring and sashayed over to Martini for
petting. He had one cat on either shoulder and one in his
arms in a matter of moments.

The dogs heard Martini's voice and shrieked their demands to see him. Our dogs loved us, but they adored Martini. The dogs' and cats' love of Martini carried great weight
with my parents for some reason. Funny, but true—they
took the animals' opinions as more important than mine.

As the cats leaped for safety, Dotty, our Dalmatian,
reached him first, but Duke, the black lab, and Duchess,
our pit bull, were right there, too. Our Great Dane, Dudley,
actually took his time, but that was so he could monopolize
Martini by putting his paws up onto his shoulders and giving him a face wash.

Standard animal greetings over, Martini went to clean
up, and we got dinner on the table. Routine chitchat en-
sued, until the subject of my high school reunion somehow
surfaced. My parents and Martini all tried to convince me
attending was a great idea. To avoid running screaming into
the street, I strove for distraction.

"So, why are you guys going to Washington tomorrow?"

Mom sighed. "We have some politicians making problems."

"What kind of problems?"

"High-level security problems," Mom said pointedly.

"High-Level Security Girl, here. Spill it."

Mom glared at me. "No."

I looked at Dad. He looked uncomfortable. "Oh. It's about Centaurion."

Martini's eyes narrowed. "What now?"

Mom sighed again. "Not about Centaurion all that much. Though the incident in Paraguay is worrisome for a variety of reasons. We have various pressures coming at us from a variety of sources. Several House and Senate subcommittees are dealing with issues that either directly or indirectly affect Centaurion Division."

"Wow, that was a lot of confuse-speak."

Now I got the mother-glare. "What part of 'I'm not telling you' isn't coming through?"

"All of it. What part of 'tell me anyway' aren't you catching?"

She rolled her eyes. "Why me?"

"Like mother, like daughter," Martini offered. "I'm interested, too, of course."

Mom snorted. "And as you're the head of all A-C military operations, which means the head of the A-C government, I'm not at liberty to tell you, Jeff."

He shook his head. "Richard is the leader of our people."

"Religious leader, yes," Mom agreed. "However, when it comes down to it, who gives the orders to shoot or cease fire, who gives the orders to fight or not, who gives the orders for what scientific research is done or ignored? You do."

Martini shrugged. "Christopher does some, too. So does my father, honestly. And Richard does as well."

I coughed. "And yet, when it all comes down to it, the person whom those three people have to obey is . . . you."

He looked embarrassed. "I suppose."

Dad cleared his throat. "It's not quite that simple." We all looked at him, and he shrugged. "It's not. I've actually studied the Centaurion agreements with the United States government. The ranks are set up, yes, but there's a check and a balance."

"Jeff and Christopher are the check and Richard's the balance?"

Dad smiled at me. "Pretty much, yes. Scientific research, though, is more of a general bailiwick. However," he added to my mother's glare, "if Jeff were to say that a project should or shouldn't be done, then it would or wouldn't happen."

Martini nodded. "Same with Richard, though. And there are some things Christopher and I have no influence over." He looked embarrassed and upset suddenly and took a fast interest in his food.

It didn't require genius to come up with why. "In all social and religious situations, what the Pontifex says goes, right?"

Martini sighed. "Yes. And he's got more than just what he wants to do to consider."

This also wasn't new news. "I know. The older A-C generation isn't into that whole 'intermix with humans' idea."

"Some of the younger ones aren't either," Dad said quietly.

"Since when?" All the younger A-Cs I knew certainly were, or weren't against it.

"I meet different A-Cs than you do, kitten. And some of them are, oh, call it more orthodox than the others. Not the majority, mind you. Most are hoping things will change and they'll be allowed to marry humans. Some would be okay with it if said humans converted to the A-C religion. But just like not all the older A-Cs are against interbreeding, not all the younger ones are for it."

Well, this topic had somehow gotten more unpleasant than the high school reunion one. I tried for another idea change—either it'd help or I'd achieve the hat trick in terms of bad dinner conversation. "So, Mom, which politicians are you seeing?"

"The President and his closer advisers," she said quickly. I got the impression she was all for us getting onto a mutual enemy kind of discussion. "Then some of the more influential senators and representatives." She made a face. "And, of course, some of the more repugnant ones."

"Like who?" I was all over the gossip. I never met these people, so it was like listening to E! D.C. Edition. "Any dirty affairs going on?"

Mom started laughing and almost spit her apple cider out. Martini and Dad were having a good chuckle, too. "Kitty, that's what Washington *is*, dirty affairs of one kind or another."

"Just making a joke," I muttered. Well, at least everyone else was laughing. "Just thought it'd be interesting to hear about what the politicians you're dealing with are like. I mean, I know you like the President, but I figured there could be bits of info you could share." Like who was zooming who, but I let that one stay unasked.

"Pray you never run into the ones I'm dealing with right now," Mom said.

"Like Reid," Dad agreed. Mom shot him a look and he clamped his mouth shut.

"Which subcommittees?" Martini asked before I could ask who Reid was and why we wanted to avoid him or her. I got the feeling Martini was trying to avert a domestic dispute, and, realistically, if anyone would know when people were upset, he'd be the one. I let my curiosity pass.

"House South American Policy, Joint National Security, and House Immigration."

Oh, sure, I ask, I get jokes. Martini asks, and she tells him everything. "Why would any of those be something you couldn't discuss with us?" Okay, I let my curiosity about this Reid person, like what the full name was, pass.

Everyone gave me the "duh" look. I gave it more thought and reminded myself that Chuckie had spent years teaching me how to be suspicious of anyone and anything. "We just had superbeing action in Paraguay, that'll be nasty no matter who knows what. Security and superbeings go hand-in-hand." I looked at Martini. "And I guess we do have a large immigrant population that'd fit right in with the rest of America's melting pot."

Mom nodded. "Yes. It's nice to see some of the money we spent on your education wasn't wasted on keggers, comics, CDs, and football games only."

"Don't forget sorority fees. Speaking of which, will Caroline be okay?"

"Yes, and that's all we're discussing. At least right now." A look of worry flashed across her face, but then she smiled. "Chocolate cake for dessert." She got up and went into the kitchen.

I started to get up, but Dad cleared his throat softly. "Let it be, kitten. Trust me."

Martini nodded. "I'm sure we'll find out soon enough."

I stared at him. He looked a little too casual and didn't seem upset in the least. "In other words, you're confident you already know, and one day maybe I'll get to find out."

Martini grinned. "I love smart women."

CHAPTER 8

THE REST OF THE EVENING was uneventful. We left
shortly after dessert, since my parents had to pack for
their mysterious trip everyone knew the details of other
than me. I drove us back to Caliente Base while Martini
lounged in the passenger seat and refused to tell me anything. I was fairly sure he liked me losing my mind. He had
to move the seat back as far as it would go, but he claimed
to love my car anyway. Which was a good thing, since I
wasn't giving it up. Ever.

The gate transfer back to the Science Center was better
because I could look at Martini until my stomach forced me
to close my eyes, and he held my hand so I could squeeze
his as hard as I needed to.

No amount of whining, begging, or cajoling worked, so
after several hours of mind-blowing sex, we finally went to
sleep. A-Cs had incredibly fast healing and regenerative
powers, which fact Martini reminded me of on a happily
regular basis.

My first day as a licensed or close-enough-for-A-C-work
pilot was dull. Nothing much was going on at all, on a worldwide basis. A couple of superbeings, but they manifested in
rural parts of California and France and were dealt with
quickly, no Head of Anything required.

I wasn't used to Alpha Team having absolutely nothing
to do. It made me feel jumpy.

"Baby, relax," Martini said for the tenth time as we and

the rest of Alpha Team wandered around the Control Center at Home Base, just because we'd already toured all of the "action" parts of the Science Center where no action was happening. "We're allowed quiet days." He looked and sounded as relaxed as if we were on vacation.

This made me more tense. The rest of the team was wandering away from us, presumably because my tension was ruining their Zen or something. "Calm before the storm. We need to be ready."

He sighed. "No reason to. We get ready in seconds. We don't need to be on edge." He stopped walking and moved me so I was in front of him. Then he started to massage my shoulders. "You're unbelievably worried. Why?"

I was about to answer when Freddie Mercury started singing. I dug through my purse while Martini growled. I chose cowardice as the better part of valor and moved away. Martini's expression said he'd lost that relaxed feeling and was indeed instantly ready—to pound Chuckie into pulp. I decided they really didn't need to meet any time soon.

"Hi," I said as quietly as I could without sounding like I was trying to talk softly. "What's up?"

"Are you okay?" Chuckie sounded worried and freaked. "Yes, why?"

"There's some . . . weird stuff on the news." He sounded vague, like he wanted to tell me something but couldn't.

"There's always weird stuff on the news." There was. And Chuckie had made weird stuff his hobby since before I'd ever met him. "Is there something weirder than normal on the news?"

"Yes."

"Can you tell me what it is, or are we playing a game and I just don't know it?"

He made an exasperated sound. "Just be careful, okay?"

"I'm always careful."

Chuckie snorted so loudly I figured Martini could hear him. "You're never careful that I've ever seen."

I couldn't argue this—he did know me very well. "Fine. I'll be careful. What, exactly, should I be careful of?"

"Everything and everyone."

"Oh. Business as usual."

"It should be, yeah."

"You worry me, Chuckie."

"Feeling's mutual, Kitty. I . . . ," his voice softened, "I just don't want anything to happen to you."

"I don't want anything to happen to you, either." I tried to figure out what I could tell him that would ease his concerns, even just a little. "I'm training in kung fu again."

"Oh, good. I feel much better."

"Sarcasm is an ugly trait."

"Yeah? As far as I know, you love it." This, sadly, was true. He sighed. "Just watch out, and really don't take anything, anything at all, for granted."

"Okay, I'll be as suspicious of things as it's possible for me to be."

"I'd prefer it if you were as suspicious of things as it's possible for *me* to be."

"Ah, but you're the Conspiracy King, and I your mere lowly subject."

He laughed. "Never lowly. Never mere, either."

"Well, that's good to know." Martini caught my eye. He was still glaring. "I need to go."

"Okay. Kitty, remember—if you get into something you can't handle, call me."

"Will do, I promise."

We hung up, and I headed back to Martini. "How was your private chat with Mr. My Best Friend?" he growled.

"Fine. You can relax about it—" I would have continued talking, but Martini jerked and spun around. As he did, I saw people starting to act like something was wrong. Some I knew to be humans were running, and many expressions were grim. "What's going on?"

"I don't know." Martini sounded as he did when there were too many emotions going at once—confused and worried.

More people were running now. Toward Martini. I knew what that meant—something very bad was going on. Reader reached us first, holding a cell phone. "Jeff, your dad just called me."

"Why did he call James instead of you?"

Martini sighed. "I have my phone turned off."

This was unheard of in the A-C world—all phones on at all times, in case someone needed you, top dudes in particular. "Why?"

Christopher appeared before us out of nowhere. I jumped while I reminded myself that he'd obviously used hyperspeed. "Because he's still avoiding Aunt Lucinda," he snapped.

Martini shrugged. "It was a quiet day."

"Not any more." Reader gave Martini a commiserating smile as he held out the phone. "Your dad said to try to ignore your mother and please call him back."

Martini sighed, took the phone, and dialed. "Yeah, it's me. Uh-huh. What?" He spun around and walked a few paces away. "You're sure? Yeah, that's bad. Yes, we'll be there. Yes, I mean Kitty, too, she's the head of Airborne. Oh, really? Thanks. No, I mean it, thanks. Yeah, it'll be nice to see you, too." He hung up and turned back to us, all business. "We need Alpha Team assembled, now. There's a situation in Florida."

Christopher and Reader both looked freaked. They took off, presumably to alert the rest of Alpha team that we were traveling. I was in the dark. "What's going on?"

"My father works at Cape Canaveral. They've got a situation there. We need to make sure we don't have a major manifestation."

I looked around. Everyone was moving at hyperspeed or a run, depending on whether they were A-C or human. "How bad is this likely to be? Do my guys need to get into the air?"

Gower came over. "We don't need Airborne, so far, but I've put your boys on alert." He shook his head. "Richard doesn't want me to go on this one."

"Why not?" Martini's eyes narrowed. "What's going on?"

"Political issue on top of everything else. Richard doesn't want it to seem like Centaurion Division is getting involved."

"So why is Alpha Team going, then?" Alpha Team was a hybrid, the heads of each active division—Field, which was Martini, Image Control, which was Christopher, Airborne, so me, and Recruitment, which was Gower. Reader was also part of Alpha, the designated driver and pilot, and because of my addition to the team, Tim was on Alpha now as well. White, as the Sovereign Pontifex, went along frequently, too. To have Gower being told to stay behind was odd, to say the least.

Gower handed me a folder. "Make sure you all read this before you get there."

"This is like an inch thick, Paul. I'm a fast reader, but not this fast."

"You're not using a gate, you're flying. In a regular plane."

"What?" Martini sounded as shocked as I felt.

"I told you, it's political." Gower didn't look happy.

"Crap. This means I have to wear a suit, doesn't it? And heels."

"You clean up nice, so let's take care of that." Martini took my hand and we headed toward a gate anyway.

"Jeff, you have to leave right now."

Martini spun around. "No. If we have to leave now, we use a gate. I'm the damned head of the Field and you're telling me I have to send our highest-ranking team via public air, which is like asking Tiger Woods to use a miniature golf club to win the Masters. So we're packing for a trip, and if that means we miss taking Slower-Than-Dirt Airlines, then we'll just use a gate and get there before it's all over."

He spun back, dragging me along with him. "We'll pack fast," I shouted to Gower.

We reached a gate, and Martini calibrated. I ignored it on the grounds that nausea wasn't going to be helpful right now.

Reader and Tim came racing up. "Thank God you're letting us pack, Jeff," Reader said. "What the hell's going on?"

"No idea, he's *your* boyfriend." Martini seemed to realize what he'd said. "Wait a minute—Paul didn't tell you what's going on, either?"

Reader shook his head. "No. He's really not happy about whatever it is, though."

I held up the file. "Here, you live for the light reading."

The gate was ready, and Martini picked me up. Him

holding me was always my preferred way to travel. Normally in a rush situation we'd have gone singly, but he was angry. I didn't mind—burying my face in Martini's neck helped a lot with the nausea.

He stepped us through, I buried my face, he held me tighter. It was comforting. At least something was normal.

We landed at the Bat Cave level in the Science Center. Things were only slightly less hectic here. We raced to the elevator banks and went down, Reader and Tim to the eighth floor, which was Transient Housing, and me and Martini to the fifteenth, which was forensics, some utility, meeting space for top security, and what I called Martini's Human Lair, which was where I also happened to live. Technically, Martini had a room on the Transient level as well as an apartment somewhere around East Base. But they were mostly for show and to let me lie to myself that we weren't living together yet. I knew it was a lie, but it was one I still needed to hang onto for some reason.

We trotted through the living room area into the bedroom. The bed was made, which was a perk of living at the Science Center. Martini still hadn't told me who or how this got done, nor other oddities, like the right sized clothing being where you needed it when you needed it, and I hadn't been able to discover how it worked on my own.

However, it was working again. There were two small rolling bags waiting for us on the bed. I went to the closet and Martini went to the dresser, and we started packing what we'd need. "You want me in the standard issue outfit or one of my own suits?"

He considered this while I selected a couple of concert T-shirts to go along with a clean pair of jeans. I might have to look official but if we were staying for any length of time, I was going to have the means to be comfortable with me or die.

"Wear that blue suit of yours, the really sexy one."

"Jeff, am I meeting either one of your parents on this trip?"

"Probably my father." He wasn't looking at me, busying himself with his suitcase.

"Why that suit, then?"

Martini looked at me. "He's male. You look even sexier in that suit than you do in our women's standard issue, and you look damned sexy in that."

"I don't want to make your father think I'm hot, I want him to like me."

He looked down. "I wouldn't hold out hope for that." His voice was low and I heard the depression again. And he'd been so relaxed only a few minutes earlier.

Martini was normally pretty cheerful, unless we were having a spat, so all of this made my worry go supernova. He felt it, of course, and reached out and pulled me into his arms. He held me tightly, without speaking, for quite a while. I relaxed against him—it always felt good to be in his arms.

"I'm sorry my parents just aren't as ... accepting as yours," he said at last.

"My parents have actually met you. Maybe that's all it'll need, Jeff. Maybe you're worrying too much."

He sighed. "We'll see." He kissed the top of my head. "Let's finish getting ready and get the ordeal started."

I left his embrace and started taking my clothes off. I was in my underwear when his arms wrapped around me from behind. He nuzzled my ear and I melted back against him. "Don't we have to hurry?" He started to stroke my stomach, radiating out from my navel in ever-widening circles. My breathing got ragged.

"Maybe," he whispered in my ear, his breath hot. I moaned. He leaned my head back and to the side. "Maybe not." Then he kissed me.

CHAPTER 9

WE WOULD HAVE BEEN MAKING love like bunnies if the intercom hadn't gone off. "Commanders Martini and Katt, situation has been escalated. Please finish packing and head to Launch level immediately."

Martini sighed, and stopped the wonderful things he was doing to my breasts while he held me in his arms and I had my legs wrapped around his waist. "Fine, Gladys. Thanks for the hurry it up reminder."

"I live to serve." The intercom went dead. I'd never met Gladys, and I wasn't sure I wanted to.

Martini set me down, and I pulled my underwear back on. "We'll just finish that conversation later."

"Yeah." He stroked the back of my neck. "I'm going into the living room—I can't see you naked and not want to make love to you."

I spun around and kissed him. "Fine. I can't see you clothed and not feel the same way."

He laughed. "Good to know." He patted my bottom and then sauntered out with our suitcases. He seemed much more relaxed than when we'd first arrived in our rooms.

I dressed quickly, brushed my hair, threw everything I could think I might need into my purse, including hairbrush and hairspray, slipped my heels on, and I was ready to go.

Martini was sitting on the couch, reading something. I'd given the file to Reader, so it wasn't information about our mission. I sat next to him. "I'm ready. What's that?"

He handed it to me. It was the latest "why haven't you registered yet?" letter about my reunion. Why everyone wanted me to attend this event was beyond me—I'd been on the track team, in the chess club, thanks to Chuckie, and had plenty of friends while I was in high school. It had still been high school, and I hadn't ever missed it once I was gone.

Why Martini, of all people, wanted to go was further beyond me. I assumed my mother wanted me to compare my life to my peers, maybe Chuckie wanted to lord success over the creeps who'd made his life hellish and wanted backup for it, but Martini wanting to go was plain weird, wanting to see how the other half lived or not.

However, I knew my parents did things for each other they wouldn't have done for themselves—it was part of why they felt they had a great marriage. And Martini never complained about my being a comics geek-girl or a throwback feminist in an age of celebutants and reality TV. He'd even read the Feminist Manifesto without too much begging on my part.

"Okay, we'll go."

"Really?" He looked so happy, I just wanted to cuddle him.

"Yes, really. I'll make the reservations as soon as we're back."

The intercom went live again. "Oh, Commander Martini? Just wanted you to know the Princess Resort called. Your suite is confirmed." The Princess Resort was where my reunion was being held.

Martini tried to look surprised. "The Princess Resort?"

"Yes," Gladys said, and I could have sworn she was smirking. "You're booked there for three nights next month. Under the Desert Sun High School Reunion room block."

"Oh, uh, thanks." He looked both guilty and panicked.

"So, you made these reservations, when?"

"Well, you can cancel them twenty-four hours prior. I just figured you'd end up wanting to go and then all the rooms would be gone." He couldn't even look at my face.

Which was okay, because I wasn't angry. I hated to admit it, but I thought it was kind of cute.

He picked it up, and looked at me now. "You're not mad at me?"

I hugged him. "No, I'm not mad at you. I know how much you want to go. So, we'll go. Though I don't know how we can afford a suite at the Princess."

"We have plenty of money." This was true. I had no idea how they got this money, but I'd never seen any A-C or human agent short of cash. Martini gave me money every week, like an allowance, but he never asked how I spent it. Which was a good thing.

"So, I'll register when we're back." He was quiet. I thought about it. "Okay, what names did you register us under?"

He sighed. "Katherine Katt and Jeffrey Martini. Not what I wanted but . . . "

"But it's the truth." And since I didn't have an engagement, let alone wedding, ring, the far wiser choice. But I knew better than to say so. Martini was ready to get married at the drop of a shoe, but I wasn't, and more than me, as last night's dinner conversation had indicated, the rest of the A-Cs weren't ready to okay our official union. The few who'd been allowed to marry humans had done so as part of a genetics experiment the older generation of A-Cs felt had been a failure. I didn't, but I hadn't made the headway within the Pontifex's office that I'd hoped. Yet.

I kissed Martini. "It's okay. I should be mad, but I'm not. Again, because it means so much to you. You'll regret it, I'm sure, but we'll go."

"Speaking of going, we'd better get up to Launch level." Martini got up and pulled me to my feet. We each took a bag, and he took my free hand in his, and we went to the elevators.

I loved being in the elevator with him—we made out the entire way up. I wanted to do a lot more, and I was sure he did as well, but duty called. Besides, I wasn't sure if Gladys could intercom us in there or not and had no desire to find out that she could.

We reached the top level of the Science Center and
saw Reader and Tim there already. Gower was nowhere
around, which shocked me to my core. We'd never left on a
mission without Gower coming to say good-bye to Reader.

While Martini handled some issues, I grabbed Reader
and pulled him aside. "Is everything okay?"

He grimaced. "No idea, girlfriend. We weren't fighting
or anything before this. But Paul's really upset. I'm not sure
if he's not here because he wants to go or doesn't want the
rest of us to go."

I hugged him. "I'm sorry."

He laughed and kept his arm around my shoulders. "No
problem. If he's still acting funny when we get back, I'll just
tell him I've decided to go straight and take you away from
all this."

It was our joke that wasn't all that much of a joke.
Being together would make our lives so much simpler, and
Reader was easily as gorgeous as Martini, one of the few
humans who could pass as an A-C. I never said the wrong
thing to him, either. Plus his parents would be thrilled if he
turned straight. So, winner all the way around. Of course,
he was gay and in love with Gower, and I was a lot more in
love with Martini than I liked to admit even to myself, but
still, we joked about it all the time. Martini never found it
funny, though.

I heard a familiar throat clear behind us. "Mine, thanks."
Martini grabbed my hand and pulled me away from Reader.

"You worry too much, Jeff," Reader said, shooting us
both his cover-boy grin.

Martini grunted. "Right. We're ready to go." Christopher had joined us while I was talking to Reader. Like the
rest of us, he had a small rolling bag.

"Go where?" I didn't see a plane.

"Gate to Saguaro International, we're catching a plane
there." The way he said it you'd have thought we were
going to have our vital organs removed at the same time.

Since we were carting luggage, we had to go through
single-file. Martini went first, then me, followed by Christopher and Reader, with Tim bringing up the rear. I stepped
through, and the whooshing race through time and space

started, as did my nausea, right on cue. I exited the gate as per normal—wanting to barf my guts out.

Sadly, I didn't get that luxury. I had to move out of the toilet stall to see just how many men were already in the restroom waiting to gape at me in horror. Oh, good. A lot of them. Including, lucky me, a policeman. And being the wrong sex in the bathroom was a big deal in Arizona.

CHAPTER 10

THE COP LOOKED AT ME, and I reached into my purse. He went for his gun. Martini moved so fast I couldn't see it, but the cop was on the floor, knocked cold.

"Jeff, what the hell?" Christopher asked, as he pulled me to the side.

"Oh, that's not going to be easy to explain," Reader said as he exited the stall of wonder.

"Yeah," Tim echoed as he joined us. "Why'd you knock him out?"

There were a lot of other men in the bathroom, all frozen in what looked like terror and all wanting, clearly, to know the same answer.

A-Cs really couldn't lie, even when they'd worked at it for years, as Martini had. It was, as was always the case in our bathroom escapades, up to me.

"Federal officer," I barked. "Nobody move." The men complied; most of them hadn't been moving anyway. I jerked my head toward the cop. "Let's get him out of here." Martini nodded and hefted the cop over his shoulder. A-Cs were strong as well as fast. I managed to keep myself from drooling—every time Martini did something I considered overwhelmingly manly I wanted to have my way with him immediately, regardless of the situation.

I looked around and gave the men an icy stare. At least, I hoped it was icy. I'd been practicing, and in the mirror it was intimidating. Reader and Martini had, so far, only laughed at it. "Gentlemen, you're lucky. I'd suggest you all do your best to forget this little incident ever happened." I stalked out, with the rest of my guys following. My icy glare worked on strangers, at least.

We got out of the bathroom, and I turned so we were at a waiting area that, happily, had no plane leaving or arriving for a while, so it was fairly empty. Martini dropped the cop onto a seat.

"You could be a bit nicer to him," Reader said.

"He was going to shoot Kitty," Martini snapped.

"Well, he was probably going for his gun. But that doesn't mean he was going to fire."

"No," Martini looked right at me. "He was going to shoot you. I felt it. He panicked and thought you were going for a gun. He was going to shoot to kill and ask questions later." Martini had kept his tone level, but his eyes were flashing.

"It's okay," I said softly. "You were there."

I pulled out what I'd been going for in the first place and used it to slap the cop awake. Martini had both of the cop's arms held behind his back. "Yo, Rambo, you want to maybe not think about killing a federal officer the next time?" I opened the thin wallet and held it in front of his face.

"P.T.C.U.?" he asked, sounding fuzzy.

"Presidential Terrorism Control Unit. You might want to learn these letters, son. Or I'll make sure you spend the rest of your days in Nome, Alaska."

He nodded. "Sorry, ma'am. You just startled me."

"You're lucky you're young and I'm somewhat forgiving." I looked up at Martini. "Let him go."

He did, reluctantly, and the cop rubbed his wrists. "Look, please don't tell my superiors. I'll get reprimanded."

Martini lost it. He grabbed the cop by the back of his neck and flung him against the wall. He was in the cop's face within a moment, one hand holding the cop by the throat and off the floor. "You were going to kill her," he growled. "You'd better pray that all you get is a reprimand when I'm through with you."

Christopher jumped over the seats and grabbed Martini's arm. "Jeff, not now and not here."

Reader was on his cell, talking urgently. Tim was moving

people away, telling them this was police business. And I
had no idea what to do.

The cop was panicked, and I saw his hand moving toward his gun again. "Kid, you really want to die, don't
you?" I asked softly.

His eyes met mine. "He's gonna kill me."

"No," Gower's voice came from behind me. At least
Reader had had the brains to call for backup. "He's not.
However, I'm going to have your badge pulled. Jeff, take
his gun and let him go."

Martini wasn't moving. "Jeff . . . please," I said softly.

He stood there for another few seconds, then he nodded
and let go, pulling the cop's gun so fast I didn't see him do
it. He handed the gun to Gower, he didn't look away from
the cop to do it.

The cop took a shaky breath. "Thanks," he said to
Gower.

"No, don't thank me," Gower said, his voice like ice.
"I'll be the last person you want to thank when my report's
in." He looked behind him, and I did, too. There were four
A-Cs waiting. "Take him back to Home Base." They nodded, grabbed the cop, took his gun from Gower, and went
off, back into the bathroom.

Martini hadn't moved. I went to him. "Jeff, it's okay."
I stroked his arm. Christopher and I exchanged worried
glances. This really wasn't like Martini, and Christopher
looked as confused by it as I was.

Martini shook his head. "No. It's not." He turned to
Gower. "Thanks."

Gower nodded. "Since I'm here, let's get the five of you
onto your plane."

We moved on, but I kept my badge out. "Since when
are you a federal agent?" Reader asked me quietly, while
Martini and Gower strode on ahead of us, both radiating a
lot of anger. Christopher stayed on my other side, and Tim
was to our rear.

"My mother thought it would be a good idea and a useful tool."

"Oh, you're *not* a federal officer, just playing one on
TV." Reader chuckled.

"Whatever works. Besides, Mom gave it to me."

"I suppose if the head of the P.T.C.U. gives you a badge, you're allowed to use it. Even if it's illegal," Christopher said thoughtfully.

"Um, what we did with that cop's illegal."

Reader shrugged. "They'll take him back and do a short-term memory wipe."

"How, by knocking him out?"

"No, we have the technology to do that."

"Love your planning," I said to Christopher.

Reader coughed. "No, that's American government technology, girlfriend. Our brothers from another planet hate using it, but it comes in handy when something goes down like it just did." Christopher gave me a rather smug look.

"Good point. Any idea of what's wrong with Jeff?"

"No more than what's wrong with Paul."

"Christopher? You're not nearly as pissed off as those two. What's going on?"

"No idea. I haven't seen Jeff this mad in a long time."

I remembered the last time I'd seen him that mad—it was when Christopher and I had sort of made out while Martini was unconscious. I didn't want to be the reason for that kind of anger ever again.

"Sucks to be us, I guess." I didn't know what else to say.

"Maybe it'll calm down once we're in Florida." Christopher didn't sound as though he believed it, but then, neither did I.

I was going to ask why going to Florida was such a big deal—I mean, both sets of my grandparents had lived there for a while and seemed unscathed by the experience—but we reached our intended gate.

Martini and Gower went to talk to someone who looked official, and I looked at the flight information board. The plane going to Florida had been delayed. For two hours. I sidled up to hear what the others were talking about.

". . . been holding this plane for you for over two hours," the official airport employee said, sounding more than annoyed. "The other passengers are still on board."

Gower nodded, and Martini didn't argue. But before I'd

joined up with the boys from A-C, I'd been a marketing manager, and I'd done a lot of traveling. And this was making what Martini called my feminine intuition nervous.

"Excuse me, are you saying that you've held a full commercial flight for five passengers?"

The woman looked at me. "Yes," she snapped. "And I've had to field an unbelievable number of complaints about it, too."

"Sorry. And, sorry to ask, but are we in first class?"

"No."

"So, um, why did you hold this particular plane? Is it the last one going to Florida today?" I knew it wasn't—it was just after noon. There would be at least a dozen choices between now and midnight, probably more.

"No, we have three more going before nine this evening. One's already left, but I wasn't able to move any of this plane's passengers to it." She seemed frustrated and frazzled.

"Wow, that sucks. They didn't let you move them? After everyone was screaming at you? No one bothered to think how that was affecting you?"

She gave me a grateful smile. "No. They never do."

"That sucks more. So, the other plane wasn't full, and they made you keep everyone on this one? For us? I mean, clearly, we're not important enough for that." I nudged Martini with my foot, hoping he'd try to help me here.

He picked it up and gave her what I thought of as his killer grin. She visibly melted. Yeah, I did that too, every time. "You know, I'm so sorry," he said smoothly. "We'll just get on and get out of your hair."

"Um, no," I said quickly. They both looked at me. "I'm kind of wondering who's made these decisions that are making," quick look at her name tag, "Alicia's life so miserable. I want to be able to complain to someone—this was wrong, and wrong for them to make her handle it alone." I gave her a commiserating smile. "I know what it's like to get bossed around," I waggled my eyebrows toward Martini and Gower.

She smiled. "Yeah, I'm sure." She hit some buttons on her computer screen. "My bosses weren't happy about it either," she said. "The person who approved this was a Mr. Leventhal."

I looked over to Gower. "Know him?"

He looked confused. "No. Not at all."

I nodded. "Alicia, I think we have a situation." I showed her my badge. "Presidential Terrorism Control Unit. We're working undercover, and I think that cover's been blown."

She looked frightened. "What do you want me to do?"

"Nothing yet. But I don't want the plane going anywhere, okay?" She nodded and I pulled Martini and Gower away. "Something's wrong. Very wrong."

Gower started to argue, but Martini stopped him. "She's human, you're not."

I dug my phone out of my purse. "Do nothing, I need to call someone."

CHAPTER 11

I DIALED AND, HAPPILY, got her on the second ring. "Hi, Mom, I need your help."

"Kitty, what's wrong? You sound stressed."

"Mom, are you still in town by any chance?"

"No, kitten, you know Dad and I are in D.C. already. We had an early flight."

I figured they'd been on something other than a commercial jet, but we didn't have the time for me to ask. "I need someone to get over to Saguaro International, fast, someone from your team. Got anyone in the vicinity?"

"Sure, Kevin Lewis, he's my main field operative, and he lives locally. What's going on?"

"I think something big, but I'm not positive. But someone who has real authority to wave a P.T.C.U. badge around needs to get here fast. I'm about to start what'll be a huge incident."

"Hang on." I heard her call to my dad, get his cell, and make a call. "Where are you at?"

"Terminal Three, departures, Gate Twenty-Nine."

She spoke some more on the other line. "Okay, he'll be there pronto. You want to tell me what's going on?"

"Alpha Team was called to a situation in Florida."

"So?"

"So, note that we're at Saguaro International, not Miami? We're being told we have to take a regular jet, not a gate or one of the A-C planes."

She was quiet for a few moments. "So, maybe there's a political reason."

"Yeah, that's what we were told. However, the flight we're booked on, booked in coach, I might add, has been held up two hours waiting for us. The plane's full other than the five of us going, and they let another plane going to the same destination, which was not full, go. The gal working the gate wasn't allowed to pull anyone off our plane and let them go on the other jet."

"What do you think it is?"

This was a test question. I knew Mom knew already. "I think there's a bomb on it that's supposed to ensure that Alpha Team is wiped out." I didn't add that this would mean all the innocents on board would be wiped out, too. I'd had firsthand experience with how evil people could be five months ago.

"Yes, there is. You have a plan?"

"Yeah, actually, I do."

"Okay, call me if you need me. Roll your plan now. Kevin will be there fast to back you."

"Will do. Love you, Mom, and love to Dad." I hung up and looked at Gower. "Glad you're here. Trust me when I say that if you don't back me, right here and right now, I'll make sure you regret it."

I didn't wait for his response, just went back over to Alicia. "Okay, we have a situation. I need this terminal cleared. I want nothing off that plane yet, particularly the luggage, and I don't want the passengers or crew off, either. I want no one on the plane notified of what's going on yet. I will also want to see every single person who's worked on that plane since it got here today."

She nodded and looked freaked out. I reached across the counter and put my hand on her arm. "I'll be taking the full responsibility for this. Whatever we need to tell your superiors, we'll tell them, okay? You'll either be a hero or you'll be blameless, I promise."

Relief washed over her face. "Thanks, Miz Katt."

"Kitty." She tried to keep from smiling. "No problem, it's funny."

She chuckled. "But cute."

"Just what my parents thought. Now, let's get this fun-filled panic attack over, shall we? I'll take care of clearing the terminal, you get all the maintenance personnel in here, and we'll deal with the passengers and luggage once that's taken care of."

She got onto her phone and I went to my team. "I want every passenger cleared out of here. I'd like them moving calmly and happily, and I'd like them in baggage claim or somewhere else really safe."

Gower opened his mouth, to argue I figured. I put my hand up. "Paul, I haven't read the file. But I promise you, this is a setup. I don't want to die, particularly not right now. So, again, you either help me, or I make your life a living hell."

He heaved a sigh. "Fine. I don't know what's going on, but I'll back you."

"It's hallucination time, boys. Let's hurry it up, too."

Martini nodded and he looked at Christopher. "All planes delayed, free food and drink in baggage claim, non-essential Security told it's an approved publicity stunt?"

Christopher grinned. "Sure, why not?"

They both looked as though they were concentrating. Among the many new things I'd learned was that there were gases natural to Earth that the A-Cs used to cause mass hallucinations. Those A-Cs who worked in the field had something implanted into their brains that helped them manipulate the gases to create whatever hallucination they wanted to.

The human operatives were given monthly injections to keep us immune to any hallucinations. These were administered to our necks via an alien injection device. It looked like a hand can opener without any blades, but it did the trick and happily didn't hurt. It didn't work for everything, though, as I'd had to learn the hard way. Some things, like adrenaline, had to be done via hypodermics, and in the case of Martini's adrenaline needs, it meant using a hypodermic that looked a lot more like a harpoon than a sewing needle. The case I had to carry looked more like a gun case than medical supplies.

One by one and in groups, the passengers cleared until

there were just a handful who apparently weren't hungry or thirsty.

"What do you want us to do about them?" Martini asked me.

"I want them strip searched."

"What?" Wow. Five men all yelling that in unison. The sound was impressive.

"She's right," a voice I didn't know said from behind me. I turned to see a tall, handsome black man. Human, but I only knew that because he wasn't wearing Armani. He looked like an athlete. I wondered how quickly I could find his underwear ad. He put his hand out to me. "Agent Lewis. Here to help." He flashed me a smile that was close to rivaling Martini's. "Angela said you were in charge," he added with a wink. "Oh, and call me Kevin."

"I'm Kitty." I managed not to giggle. Geez, I hadn't acted like a teenager when I'd met Martini or Reader. This was embarrassing. But Kevin had bags of charisma. I introduced him to the rest of the team and noted Reader was checking him out as much as I was.

Martini, Gower, and Christopher were all glaring at Kevin. It dawned on me that Reader and I were both being a little obvious in our drooling.

"How much info on our situation has my mother given you?"

Kevin smiled again. He had great teeth. "I know all about Centaurion Division. And," he added, looking to the other men, "I'd like to thank you. If your agents hadn't acted when they did, my wife and children would have been killed during the engagement with Al Dejahl."

Darn. Married. Oh, well. I saw Reader have a similar reaction. No matter that Martini's expression was genial, I figured he was probably mad at me.

He gave Kevin a big grin. "Kids, huh? How many?"

"Two. Boy and girl."

"Got any pictures?"

"Sure. Happy to show 'em off when this is done. They're the best." Kevin looked back to me. "So, how do you want to do this?"

"I want those still sitting here searched and then put somewhere in a holding area, just in case."

"What do you think we're looking for?" Reader asked me. "Everything would have gone through airport security already."

I'd been giving this a lot of thought, in between admiring Kevin and trying to keep said admiration from Martini. "Two options. In the first, we'll discover one of the maintenance personnel has slipped a bomb into the belly of the plane. In the second, it'll be more than one, perhaps several. Put together they'll have the components to create a bomb, but separately each component will be harmless."

Kevin looked impressed. "You're Angela's daughter, that's for sure." He sighed. "I'm calling in all Security personnel. This'll be too much for us to handle alone."

"Works for me, do whatever it is the P.T.C.U. does best. But make it big—lots of fuss, lots of manpower, bomb sniffing dogs if at all possible, the works."

He laughed and pulled out a cell phone, moved a couple of feet away and started talking. I pulled my guys into a huddle. "Okay, I'm betting on option number two."

"Why?" Gower asked. "Maintenance seems easier."

"They held the plane," Christopher added. "So maintenance or checked luggage would seem to be the way to assume."

"No. They wouldn't let the passengers off. Half the time if you change planes like this your checked bags won't make it with you anyway. They'll fly out before or after you. In a standard delay situation, they'd move as many people to the next flight as they could, probably taking the first class passengers and then those with connecting flights."

"They held it for us. We're important." Christopher sounded frustrated.

Tim laughed. "Christopher, only *we* know we're important."

"Tim's right. We're a freaking covert operation. Commercial jets aren't held for covert ops. They fly in their own damn planes, like we normally do. Jeff was ready to pop a vessel over this, and, Paul, you know you don't like it. Think, dammit. It's a setup."

Reader had the file out and was skimming it. "Who did our girl Alicia say was the one who gave the order?"

"Leventhal. No first name."

"Oh." Reader was quiet for a moment, staring at the folder. "Ten to one that would be Leventhal Reid, head of the House Subcommittee on Terrorism." He looked up from the file. "And, for the record, he knows about us and hates our guts."

I wondered if this was the same Reid my parents had mentioned at dinner and bet that it was. "Is he also on the House South American Policy, Joint National Security, and House Immigration committees?"

Reader nodded. "He's got a lot of clout, in a lot of areas, all of which affect us."

"Figures." I'd never heard of him before last night, but this didn't surprise me all that much. I was more of a pop culture, as opposed to political, follower. I knew what Brad and Angelina were up to, not so much what was going on in areas that actually affected me. My mother wasn't the only one who found this more than a little annoying. "What agency asked us to come out to Florida in this odd manner?" I asked Gower.

"Richard wouldn't tell me," he admitted. "But I think it was high enough up that he had to acquiesce. And this arrangement was their idea, not Richard's."

"Reid's got a lot of influence," Reader said. "I'd bet he used it to do this."

"Why would he?" Kevin was back and had heard this exchange. "Not saying he wouldn't, by the way. He's a nasty piece of work. But it seems risky."

"Not if we'd blown up."

"We have to prove a threat first," Martini said. "We have nothing if there's nothing wrong other than Kitty being overly suspicious."

"Good point. Here's what we're going to do. We'll search each person, pilots and crew included. We'll line up—James, Paul, and me on the left, Tim, Christopher, and Kevin on the right—and we'll have them walk between us."

"What'll I be doing, knitting?" Martini sounded peeved.

"No, you'll be standing behind us, looking genial."

"Why?"

"Because the six of us will be looking carefully at each person. Tim and James will pull out the obvious suspects. Christopher and Paul will pull out some that might be and some just to make everyone else nervous. And Kevin and I will look over those who make it to us very closely, and we'll pull out people, too. Jeff, I want you to monitor the emotions. Everyone's going to be scared, of course."

Kevin looked at me closely. "You want to find, what? The ones who are relieved to make it past us?"

Martini grinned. "No. She wants to spot the ones who feel guilty or triumphant."

Gorgeous *and* smart. And mine. Okay, Kevin could stay happily married.

CHAPTER 12

AIRPORT SECURITY WAS THERE IN DROVES, as well as the Pueblo Caliente Bomb Squad, complete with several dogs, and a SWAT team. It was a big deal, and Kevin made sure it looked even bigger. I kept Alicia calm; Martini had already scanned her emotions, and he didn't think she was involved at all. I found myself hoping someone was indeed trying to kill us—the explanation if we found nothing would be worse than defusing a bomb.

We did our test-run strip searches—nothing. The few folks who hadn't moved to baggage claim were sent there with an escort. The entire wing of the terminal was emptied.

Maintenance crew was next. We found three illegal aliens from the exotic locales of Mexico and Guatemala. These were released into the baggage claim holding area and told to get a green card. None of us felt it was right to be too hard on them—they were here to work, not to try to kill innocent people.

We also found a couple of younger maintenance kids who had drugs stashed, another couple having sex on company time, and one asleep. All reprimanded, all clean, so to speak, all sent to baggage claim.

I really didn't think the bomb was going to be in the checked bags, and if it was, we wanted the passengers off the plane anyway, so we had them file through first.

Alicia was great. She explained we were looking for a terrorist, just as I'd told her to. She sounded frightened because she was, and we'd encouraged her not to try to remain calm and so ensured that the passengers and crew would be in a higher state of anxiety than normal.

This was going to be hard on Martini—there were a lot of things that wore his blocks and empathic synapses down. I learned new ones it seemed like every week. Running this kind of job without his filters up was probably going to be a new example, but we couldn't risk him missing something. Besides, I had the adrenaline harpoon case in my purse, so if it got too bad I could revive him. In five months I'd had to do it enough that I was a pro. I didn't like this skill, but it kept him alive, so it was worth it.

Martini had four burly human security guards assigned to him, and Gower had called in a complement of ten more A-Cs working as backup as well. Anyone Martini indicated was going to be considered the highest-level threat, and we didn't want them escaping or grabbing a hostage.

The passengers filed out. We let them keep their bags—if we could identify who the terrorists were, we could dispense with a full-on bag search. Whatever was happening in Florida was going to be done and handled before we ever arrived, but I felt our getting there alive was the preferable option.

Our only change was that there were two bomb dogs and their handlers next to Tim and Reader. The Bomb Squad had insisted on this, and no one had any objection. The rest of the dogs were in the section we'd set aside for main suspects. We had another holding area for passengers we thought were clean. All of this was still within view of our main gate area.

It was a big plane, and there were a lot of passengers. Tim and Reader pulled some obvious choices aside, and the searching began. We weren't providing a great deal of privacy—there were screens set up for men and women, but they were right in the same area we were. I didn't care about lawsuits—mass hallucinations had a great way of changing what people thought they'd gone through. Besides, once we found the means to make a bomb, most of the other passengers would be complaining they'd sat in the plane too long, not that we'd searched them later.

We kept on, pulling some men, a few women. I studied

everyone who went by. Kevin and I were playing the baddest of our three sets of bad cops, and I made sure I didn't look friendly.

An elderly couple moved through our line. My first reaction was to smile in a kindly manner and then to ignore them. Especially after the little old lady patted Tim's hand and thanked him for protecting them.

But there was something wrong about them. I wasn't sure what bothered me, but I examined them more closely than anyone else who'd gone past so far. They gave me weak smiles and kept on staggering through our line.

They still bothered me, to the point where I turned around to watch them. Martini caught my eye and gave me an almost imperceptible nod. They moved past him, and he gave a signal to his security gaggle. The oldsters were stopped.

And instantly started protesting. Loudly. The woman in particular was making quite the scene. They were taken over with our other suspects and separated. The woman was wailing about how she was being manhandled. She garnered a lot of sympathetic looks from the passengers who weren't corralled with our main suspects.

The next one to have his suspicions raised was Kevin. A young man came out, wearing his iPod headphones and seeming to be just sort of bouncing to the beat. He didn't look dangerous, and our first two lines let him through. Kevin grabbed him, flung him to the ground, and ripped the iPod and headphones off. "Check these, right now," he barked to one of the Bomb Squad.

Kevin let the kid up, but he kept the guy's arm twisted behind his back. An officer came over and slammed handcuffs onto the young man. "Yep," he said to Kevin, then dragged our boy over to our confirmed suspects area.

"What was in the iPod?" I asked him quietly, while more passengers crept through.

"Probably a plastic of some kind."

"How'd you spot him?"

"He was trying too hard."

That was it. I spun around and went over to Martini. "There's something really wrong with those old people."

He nodded. "Not sure what, but boy did they feel like they'd won the lottery when they got past you." He gave me a half-smile. "Your new boyfriend seems to be working out well."

"Oh, stop it."

Martini grinned. "Amazingly, I'm not jealous."

"Yeah, he's happily married."

"Nah. I liked that you were proud of me for knowing what you were thinking. Made up for your panting after the Fed." He nodded toward the line. "Back to work, baby. More are coming."

I returned to my post and more filtered through. A couple of the flight attendants came out now, one blonde, one brunette. The dogs started barking at the blonde's bag. She seemed freaked. The brunette tried to move past, but Reader grabbed her. Both of them were moved to the holding area.

I looked over my shoulder; Martini was talking to one of our spare A-Cs who then went and talked to the bomb guys.

And so it went. A few more suspects, then the plane was supposedly empty. Christopher took three A-Cs inside to do the cabin search. And came out with a little guy who looked like a weasel. "He was in the bathroom," Christopher said, as he dragged him to Martini.

"I had to go!" The guy was shorter than me, and I really figured I could take him easy, best two out of three. He was slight, poorly dressed, and looked like a smoker, if his teeth were any indication.

Martini shrugged. "We'll find out." He looked over to the security guards. "Someone gets the unenviable task of looking to see what he got rid of in the toilet."

"Urine!" He sounded panicked. "I'm not kidding, I couldn't hold it anymore, we sat there for hours waiting for you guys."

Martini looked at me and we both smiled. "What's your name, sir?" I asked him.

"Shannon."

"Isn't that a girl's name?" Tim asked.

"It's traditionally male," Shannon huffed.

"True. So, Shannon, let me put it this way . . . you can tell us what part in this you played, or we can use you as the example for your cronies of what we're going to do if they don't spill."

"What're you talking about?" he gasped. "I don't know what's going on."

"Then . . . how did you know the plane was waiting for *us*?" I let that one sink in while watching Shannon's eyes dart around frantically.

Martini chuckled. "He knew because he's absolutely in on it." He pulled me to him. "Use him as the litmus test for who his pals are?" he whispered in my ear.

"Mmmm . . . yeah." I had to control myself from rubbing up against him. There was something about being in these high-stress, dangerous situations that made me want to jump Martini's bones more than normal.

"You're an adrenaline junkie," he whispered. "But that's okay. I think it's sexy."

I managed to keep it together, mostly because Shannon's pitiful excuses wrenched me back to the reality of our situation. I went back to the rest of our team. "Let's start figuring out who has what. Oh, and Shannon? You'll talk, or we'll each take turns seeing how hard we can hit your face."

"Not in the face," he gasped. I didn't know why, a broken nose might be an improvement for him.

Kevin knew. He wrenched Shannon's jaws open—and pulled out his teeth.

CHAPTER 13

"**PLASTICS**," Kevin said as he handed the dentures to the Bomb Squad guy who'd raced over.

Reader pulled out a couple of wipes from his inner suit pocket. "Here you go, that has to be gross."

"Thanks," Kevin gave Reader a friendly smile. Reader grinned back, and I saw Gower's eyes narrow. Reader and I were going to be in trouble with our respective mates when we were alone, that was clear. Because even if Martini was okay with my drooling over Kevin, I knew he'd find a way to make me pay for it. Of course, it would be a way I'd enjoy to the point of wanting to self-destruct from pleasure. I hoped Reader's punishment would be similar. It wasn't like we could help it—Kevin really had bags and bags of charisma.

Shannon was dragged off to our main suspects area, still protesting that he just needed dentures.

"How stupid is that guy? I mean, who would get dentures that look like crap?"

"He seems pretty stupid, but that could just be an act." Kevin sighed. "We don't have enough with his teeth and the iPod. We're missing the trigger, at least. I'd guess we have at least five others involved, maybe more. And we also need to identify what group managed to find this many willing suicidals."

I thought about this as we walked to the main suspects holding area. "The old folks. There's something really wrong about them."

"Well, that's going to be tough, they're really creating a scene." Kevin didn't look happy.

As we reached them, the old lady started up again. "This is just like what they did in Uganda! They separated the Jews and then tried to kill them!"

My mother was an Italian-American former Catholic who had somehow been the only non-Israeli, non-Jew to ever join the Mossad. She'd met my very Jewish-American father in Tel Aviv. I had my father's fair coloring but I favored my mother otherwise, so I didn't "look" Jewish. But I was. And they weren't. But they were pretending to be.

"Why would you be insinuating that we're trying to separate Jews from the other passengers?" I asked her.

She started wailing. "It's what always happens!"

"Not in America." Kevin wasn't buying it now, either. I already knew Martini wasn't.

Martini gave her his most winning smile, usually reserved for my parents. "Ma'am, now, why would you think a nice Jewish boy like me would do that to you?"

She gave him a baleful look. "You're not Jewish."

He grinned. "You're right. And you're not an old lady." He reached out and yanked her hair. It came off in his hand. Revealing short, blonde hair, clearly dyed.

"Ick."

Martini dropped the wig. "We may want that checked out. Full search, her and her 'husband.'"

The supposedly old man with her started to protest. "That's not my wife! Help, they've switched my wife!"

"These are some of the worst actors I've ever seen in my life." It was like dinner theater, only without food.

Reader reached out and pulled the hair on the old man's mostly bald head. It came off along with the bald skullcap, revealing a head of plastered-down hair.

The searches of the two supposed old people—both of whom refused to tell us their names, real or fake—the young man, and Shannon the Toothless Weasel took a few minutes. While Pueblo Caliente's finest did the searches, Kevin, Martini, Christopher, and I went through their wallets and the "old lady's" purse. Reader, Tim, and Gower rechecked everything, just in case. The men were going a lot faster than I was—this chick had a lot of membership cards, and going through them was taking forever.

We were able to identify our suspects easily since they all had driver's licenses. Shannon's last name was O'Rourke, explaining the commitment on his parents' part to ensure he'd have a horrible life at American schools. The younger dude was Curtis Lee; he had a card listing him as a direct descendant of Robert E. Lee—I felt sure the South was okay with losing this particular son. The woman's name was Maureen Thompson, and since the guy playing her husband was named Robert Thompson, it was a good guess they were married.

"What are we looking for?" I asked as I looked at Maureen's fiftieth membership card.

"Anything that links them." Kevin sounded frustrated. "This is too big, too well organized."

"And the four we've identified are all too stupid."

"Yeah," Martini said. "So they didn't plan this, someone else did." I stared at him. "What? I can think, too."

"Yeah, that wasn't what made me look at you. It just dawned on me that you didn't say Reid, just someone else."

He shrugged. "We don't know it's Reid, yet."

"Right." My brain was kicking at me. I looked back at what I was holding, a Club 51 card. "James, is there some big warehouse store called Club 51?"

"No, not that I know of. But, you know . . . that sounds familiar."

"Well, we hang in Area 51," Tim said with a laugh.

Well, duh. Chuckie was beyond into UFO stuff. Because of him, I knew all the names and most of the rumors, many of which I'd been confirming as fact for the past five months. I shoved the guilt about not telling him anything away—we didn't have time for it.

"Okay, search the rest of their stuff for a card that looks like this." I showed them the Club 51 card. It was paper, punched out from a bigger sheet, not a really official-looking card at all. The name was printed on by hand, under the line where Maureen had signed.

They dug through—every one of them had one. "So, um, what?" Christopher asked. "I mean, if it's a local club, what's the big deal?"

"It's a club, but it's not just local." I was pulling this one up from way back—Chuckie hadn't liked these people, and he hadn't discussed them too much. "I need to ask someone about this." I pulled my phone out.

"Oh, great, she's calling Mr. My Best Friend again," Martini muttered. "Haven't you talked to him enough recently?"

"Best guy friend since ninth grade. Best friends talk to each other, sometimes a lot. Really, learn to accept it."

Martini's growl showed acceptance wasn't coming any time soon. I considered calling, but Martini was undoubtedly getting overtaxed, and me talking to Chuckie always upset him. Texting meant that when he asked me what was going on and I lied, he'd have a harder time proving it.

He replied immediately and took my evasiveness in better stride for this conversation than he had when we were speaking, so I congratulated myself on my wise decision-making. I tried to shove the standard pangs of guilt and remorse aside again—this wasn't really the way you were supposed to treat your best friends, but I'd become a pro at it by now, and a part of me hated myself for it.

Martini felt the guilt. "National security, baby," he said softly. "Your parents have managed all these years, remember."

"True enough." I cleared my throat and stomped down on the guilt. Back to the business of saving the world. Again. "Per Chuckie, this is a group who firmly believe that aliens walk among us."

"And?" Christopher sounded annoyed, which was natural for him, at least in my experience.

"And they don't like it. They're anti-alien, not pro. Most of the conspiracy theorists want there to be aliens here, want to know them, want to discover that new worlds do exist. Or they want to prove the government's lying. But they're positively spun toward aliens." I couldn't blame them. I was quite positive toward mine.

"Okay, so Club 51 people don't like the idea of aliens?" Kevin didn't sound convinced.

"Right, to an extreme level. Think of them as the skinheads of the UFO community."

This was met by blank stares from Martini, Gower, and Christopher. Tim and Reader, however, were nodding. Kevin still didn't look convinced. "So, skinheads beat people up. They don't do suicide missions."

"These people are lunatics."

"Aliens exist," Martini said. "In case you'd forgotten."

I rolled my eyes. "Yes, I know. But the general public does not. You're considered a crackpot, at best, if you believe aliens are really here." God knew, Chuckie had been saddled with the nickname of Conspiracy Chuck mainly because of his UFO fascination. "So, it stands to reason someone involved in a huge anti-alien underground organization would be more whacko than your average UFO whacko."

"True." Thank God, Reader was backing me. "Unless you know for sure that the Roswell rumors are real, it's sort of crazy to believe in them. We could call them more passionate, if we didn't want to use crazy, since they're right."

"Do these people believe or just want to believe? Jeff, can you tell?"

He closed his eyes. "Not . . . really. The four we have pulled aside are hating on us all right now."

"Hate, not fear?"

He nodded. "Hate. There are some others who are hating on us, too."

"Let's pull those out of the lineup and search them. Oh, I want everyone on the plane, whether we thought they were suspicious or not, searched for a Club 51 card."

"Okay, I'll get that started." Kevin moved off.

I grabbed Martini before he could follow. "You point them out to Kevin and then come right back. I want you staying with me. You too," I said to the rest of them. "I want to do my own tests."

"Just what are those going to be?" Martini asked.

"Trust me."

"Oh, God. I hate it when you say that."

CHAPTER 14

WE WENT OVER TO WHERE our confirmed suspects were. I got rid of the human police officers, and Gower brought some more A-Cs over. Our four little friends were surrounded, and they didn't look happy.

I wanted someone cracking, and while I thought Shannon would be the easiest, where was the fun in that? Besides, I really didn't like Maureen.

I had Reader and Tim slam Thompson into a chair, with the other three behind him. "I don't know what this is all about," he protested.

"Oh, I think you do." I made sure my voice was low, like I talked to Martini when we were leading up to ripping each other's clothes off. I sashayed over and ran my hands over his shoulders. "I think you know exactly . . . what . . . we are."

His eyes widened. "Keep away from me." His voice was shaking. Yep, either they thought we were all aliens or he really thought I was a troll. I had Martini, the gorgeous sex-god, to tell me otherwise, so I went with alien.

"You can tell us who your mastermind is, willingly. Or . . . well, we have ways of making you talk." I saw Reader working to keep himself from cracking up. Hey, I hadn't used an accent.

"I don't know anything." His eyes were shifting all over. He couldn't lie any better than the A-Cs could.

I could see Maureen, and she looked angry. Good.

I swung one leg over and sat in his lap, facing him. This meant I could see the others easily. I was almost flattered that Shannon looked jealous. Lee looked freaked. "Oh, I really think I can make you talk. You'll like it, too." I ran my hands over his head and through his hair. It was gross, but, you know, anything for the cause. I was just glad I couldn't see Martini or Christopher, who were thankfully standing behind me now.

"I . . . I . . . " Thompson was starting to sweat. And, other things.

"You know you want to walk on the wild side," I said in my best Mae West impersonation. I grabbed his hair at the scalp and yanked his head back, as though I were a vampire and going to bite him. I hoped Maureen would crack soon—I had no more intention of putting my mouth on this guy than I had of cleaning the men's room with my tongue.

However, I pretended. As I moved my mouth nearer to the guy's throat, I looked up at our other three suspects. I made eye contact with Shannon. "You're next." He looked as if he didn't know whether to cry or celebrate. I looked at Lee. "Then you, stud." He gulped, but I noted he was looking less freaked and a little more willing.

Then I made eye contact with Maureen and gave her a smirk. "You'll just get to watch."

That did it. "Get away from him, you alien bitch!" She lunged toward me.

Gower reached out, grabbed her by the back of her neck, and lifted her off the ground. "No human touches our leader." Ooooh, he was getting into it. Good.

I kept the smirk on my face. "I'll let him go, and the others. *If* you tell us what we want to know."

"Just read our minds," she snarled. "I know you can."

We couldn't, but why let them know that? "This way is . . . more fun." A little part of me felt bad about doing this—I'd lived through someone threatening Martini's life in front of me already, and it seemed wrong to do it to someone else. Then again, these someone else's wanted to kill Martini and the rest of us, along with a planeload of innocent people. I decided my moral quandary was over. Nice while it lasted.

I thrust my stomach at Thompson. This looked to her like I was doing a bump and grind on him, while allowing me to actually not have to rub my body against his. She clawed and struggled, but she was so short that she couldn't land anything, not even a kick, on Gower.

"You can tell me . . . or I can ruin him for any other woman. Once you go alien, you never go back." This was true, at least in my experience.

"It's okay," Thompson called out. "I can fight it."

Maureen went nuts. "You bastard, you *want* to sleep with her! I'll kill you both!"

I smirked at her again. "You want to tell me what's going on? Or you want to watch me do all three of them in front of you? So you can know they'll never look at you again?"

Maureen looked as though she was ready to talk. "No, don't tell her!" Shannon shouted. "We'll be strong, Maureen, I swear. Let her do her worst to us, we won't crack."

Reader and Tim had to move behind the suspects because they were laughing so hard they were leaning on each other and trying to do it without making a sound. Gower was grinning at me, but he was managing to keep the laughter at bay.

"What's it going to be, Maureen? The information the easy way, or," I pulled Thompson's head back even farther and ran the fingers of my other hand down his throat and chest, "the fun way?"

"I'll talk, just get off him," she snarled.

"Talk, and maybe I'll get off him." I couldn't wait to get off this guy. My legs were getting tired since I was using my thighs to keep my body off of his. He was enjoying his alien lap dance far more than you'd have expected from someone who wanted to wipe ETs off the planet.

"I'll be good," he whispered to me. "I've seen the error of my ways."

I stood up, still straddling him. It felt great to stand. "Tell me what I want to know."

He was staring at my chest. "We answer to a man called Howard."

"That's it? That's the information you think's going to keep me from doing what I want with you?"

His eyes were still glued to my female assets. "Maybe you could, you know, question me in private?"

That did it. Martini moved at hyperspeed and knocked the guy out of his chair. Thompson flew five feet and landed, but Martini grabbed him by the neck and started to squeeze. "Maybe you could, you know, tell us what we want to know before I break your neck."

I looked at Maureen. "You want to give us something better than Howard?" She looked sullen again. "Babe, let's be real. All three of your boys here want to do me. My men get a little jealous, but they answer to me. And ruining your little boys here for any other woman sounds like a lot of fun. Now, you can protect some other man who we both know would want to do me if he were here, or you can help yourself by being the one to cooperate. Your choice."

I avoided looking at Martini. Because in my view, he'd again done something manly, protective, and possessive, and he was the only person I wanted to interrogate with my clothes off. Right now. I wondered if there was a private room somewhere in the airport we could find.

"Don't kill me," Thompson gasped out. "We'll talk."

"She can talk, and then I can kill you," Martini growled. Oh, man, he needed to stop. I was ready to have my way with him here in front of everyone. We probably should have ignored Gladys back at the Lair. It wasn't as if we'd have missed any of this.

I sighed and dragged myself away from my fantasies of joining the Mile High Club with Martini and forced my mind back to the matter at hand. "So, Maureen? What's it going to be?"

"Howard Taft is our Supreme Leader."

"You're joking, right?"

Maureen shook her head. "No, he's really named after the late President."

I almost asked who would name their kid after Taft but then realized the answer was a crackpot and needed no further clarification. "Put her on her feet," I said to Gower. "But don't let go."

Once she was standing, Maureen shared some more.

"We have a large organization. They won't let you get away with this."

"Maureen, you're all part of Club 51, which means you have a large organization of loons. While loons can be dangerous, I think your current predicament proves your organization's planning skills leave something to be desired. Now, give me the full details or watch me do your men here with a lot of skill and nastiness."

Shannon moaned quietly. Martini, still holding Thompson off the ground by his neck, moved and grabbed Shannon's neck with his free hand. Now both of them were off the ground. I wondered if Martini was doing this just to turn me into a puddle. It was working, intentional or not.

"Oh," I added. "Let's also remember that you're going to need a fabulous lawyer to have a hope of staying out of jail for a goodly portion of your remaining life span. You're part of a terrorist conspiracy, and believe me, we've got the proof." As I said this, Kevin brought in both stewardesses who'd been identified by the bomb dogs and a couple of businessmen. "The only chance you've got is cooperation."

Maureen heaved a sigh. "Fine."

Before she could say anything else, the brunette stewardess spoke. "What's this all about?"

"Oh, please. Club 51. Now, shut up or spill. Period. These are the only options. I'm getting seriously bored." And beyond horny. Martini was pretty much doing barbell lifts with Thompson and Shannon. I knew he was doing it to get me, but I was well past caring. The part of me that was concerned about him losing emotional control was being overruled by the part of me that just wanted to rip his clothes off.

Our four new arrivals all contrived to look innocent, but I'd spent a lot of time in the last few months with people who really couldn't lie, and my internal lie detector was working on all cylinders. We had eight, two of whom were crew, and that should mean Kevin and the Bomb Squad could make a complete bomb out of what these folks had brought aboard.

Maureen spoke quickly now. I assumed she didn't want

anyone else to get the lighter sentence. "There are a lot of Club 51 chapters. Howard Taft is the head of all of Club 51. He's based out of Florida." Oh? Interesting. "He knows all about you aliens, and he has powerful friends in the government."

"One named Leventhal?"

Maureen, Thompson, Shannon, and Lee looked blank. So did the two businessmen and the blonde stewardess. The brunette one, however, wiped her face of emotion. I pointed to her. "Take her away into solitary. That's our group leader."

Maureen turned as much as Gower would let her. The brunette was protesting and struggling as one of our A-Cs removed her. "Yeah, that's Casey Jones. She's our chapter head." Who had named these people? Of course, I was Kitty Katt, so, really, I was in no position to judge.

"Casey's going to have more information than you, Maureen. Now, how much more can you give us?"

Maureen looked resigned. "I'll give you everything I know." I got the feeling she wasn't lying.

CHAPTER 15

I LEFT THE REST OF the interrogation to Kevin. I'd had
enough. The bags were pulled off the plane, and our
eight conspirators' luggage was pulled aside and searched
thoroughly.

Reader was running checks on this Howard Taft and his
connections within Washington, including Leventhal Reid.
Gower, after he and Christopher both lost an argument
with the Pontifex about using gates, was making arrangements to get one of the A-C private jets out to us. There was
no way any of us were going commercial. Christopher was
managing the other A-Cs in attendance. And I was guarding Martini. It was the tough job, but I felt ready for it.

Martini still wanted to take a gate, and being overruled
about it made him very unhappy. Added to this, he was on
the phone with his mother. I wasn't trying to listen, which
meant I was listening as hard as I could while pretending to
be fascinated by the bomb dogs who were giving everyone
on the plane another once-over, just in case.

"Yeah, delayed because some anti-alien group tried to
kill us. Yes. No. Yes, you heard right, she's the one who figured out what was going on. Yes, she's smart, that's part of
why I'm with her. Amazingly, no, she doesn't think I'm an
idiot. No, this doesn't make her stupid or easy to please. Of
course we're still going to Florida, if there's any reason to.
No, I didn't kill a policeman. Of course I would have. Why?

Did you even hear the full story or are you just getting this from the rumor mill?"

Long pause while Martini rolled his eyes, looked up as if asking God to take him now, and ground his teeth. "Of course it didn't happen like that. But why am I not surprised you believe someone other than me. Fine, I'll tell you about it when we get there, whenever that ends up being. Good, so glad the emergency's not going anywhere, I'd hate to miss it. Yes, that was sarcasm. No, I don't think it's her influence. I was sarcastic before, you just didn't notice."

Another long pause, during which he had his eyes closed and looked as if he were having a migraine. "Yes, you're right, I did like living with Aunt Terry better. She died twenty years ago, glad you're not still carrying the resentment. No, honestly, I don't want to come for a big family dinner. Ever. Right. Yes, fine, so we'll see you sometime after we handle the situation. No, not tonight. At this rate, it'll be tomorrow at the soonest. Great. Please remember I hate meat loaf. Oh, of course, naturally, I see you maybe three times a year, God forbid you'd cook something I like. Yes, I know, your meat loaf is famous on two worlds. I'm sure I'll like it this time."

Longer pause. "Yes, fine, I know. Yes, of course, Christopher, too. I wouldn't let him miss this for the world. Paul and James are with us as well, and Tim, human agent you don't know. Yes, of course, I'll bring them all along—no one should miss the meat loaf. Love you, too." He hung up and gently banged his head against the wall.

I stroked his back. "Jeff, you okay?"

"Please promise me you'll still want to be around me after you meet them." He sounded stressed and depressed again.

"You know I will."

He shook his head. "No. I don't. I can't imagine that you would." He rubbed his forehead. "Maybe I can die heroically handling this situation."

"I don't want you to die." I tried to hide it, but him acting like this was really worrying me.

Martini picked it up, of course. He pulled me into his arms and held me tightly. I leaned my head against his chest and rubbed his back some more. "I'm so sorry," he said finally. "It's going to be miserable, and I don't know how to protect you from them."

I nuzzled his chest. "In college, I briefly dated a guy whose family were the biggest neo-Nazis you could ever imagine. I didn't know it until he took me home to meet them. My Uncle Mort, the Marine, literally had to come get me with a complement of his leathernecks because I was that afraid of being killed by those people once they discovered I was Jewish. I truly can't imagine your family could be worse than them."

"Well, true. I don't think anyone in my family's going to try to kill you."

"See? So it'll be fine."

"God, I love your optimism."

"How are you doing, talentwise?" This was my veiled way of determining if I needed to have the adrenaline harpoon ready or not.

Martini sighed. "Not all that great, but I think I'll be fine."

"I'd hoped all this activity wouldn't have drained you." Worry crashed over me, as it always did when he was heading toward an empathic crash.

"It's not that, baby." Martini hugged me tighter. "Honestly, dealing with my parents, my mother particularly, is harder than any work we ever do."

"Well, parents can be like that."

"Yours aren't."

"Mine have accepted what I do and who I'm with." I studiously contemplated the image of flowers. Sometimes that worked to keep things from Martini. Flowers didn't suggest I should be considering options, after all.

"Mine merely love to show me how much they can't stand me." Martini sounded despondent. I hoped it wasn't that he'd gotten anything from me.

"I'm sure that's not true, Jeff. If they didn't love you, why would they care who you married?"

"To ensure I'm miserable?"

I tried another avenue. "What about your mother being jealous of Terry? Jealousy's not because of hatred, it's usually because of love. Or something."

"I point out that we're having meat loaf whenever we arrive. I think my mother just hates to lose, and if I was happier with Aunt Terry, then she's lost."

"Maybe. But if she's still jealous that you were with Terry, and that Terry was able to take care of you while she wasn't, then maybe it's not losing but loss, you know?"

"Maybe. But nothing she's ever done would give me that impression. Or Christopher." He heaved a sigh. "I hate going home. I'd rather have blown up in that plane than visit my parents' house."

"How are you going to handle being there?" If this was what he was like across the country from his mother, I didn't think I had enough adrenaline for this upcoming visit. The entire Science Center might not have enough adrenaline.

"I have very . . . strong . . . blocks up when I'm home. Aunt Terry taught me how to do it. It'll be okay, baby. I hope."

Kevin came over before the conversation spiraled even more downward, and we pulled apart. "Okay, we have enough components. For certain they could have fashioned a small but effective bomb from what they had, especially since they had two of the flight attendants in on it."

"What was their plan—the stewardesses would pick up the components from each conspirator as they went through getting trash, and then one of them would put it together in the galley while the other kept watch?"

Kevin gave me a long look. "Yeah, that was exactly their plan. Does Angela drill you on this stuff or something?"

"I just think like psychos, I guess." What a great skill. No wonder Martini's mother wasn't thrilled.

"Why were they willing to die?" Martini asked.

"Taft seems to have them convinced that they're immune to dying." Kevin shook his head. "They were all positive the bomb wouldn't have killed any of them."

"Just them or everyone?"

Kevin shrugged. "Don't know."

"Let's go talk to the weasel."

We went to where Shannon was being held. I got up close. "What do you want?" he asked, as he eyed Martini nervously. There were still red fingerprint marks on his throat.

"I want to know why you were willing to die for this cause." He shook his head, so I grabbed his chin and forced him to look at me. "I'll let him take out all his frustrations on you," I jerked my head toward Martini. "And, believe me, he has a lot of them right now."

Shannon looked frightened but still resistant. "What's in it for me?"

"Not dying," Martini snarled.

"We don't need you, Shannon. We have the head of your chapter. She has the real info. The best you're going to get is a reduced sentence if you help us. If you don't . . . well, I know what someone your size, who also happens to lack teeth, has to look forward to in prison."

Shannon gulped. "Okay. It'll help me stay out of jail?" I nodded. After all, it might. "Taft told us all about your psychic and telekinetic abilities."

"Come again?" What did these people think we were, the X-Men?

"We were going to blow up the plane to prove you were here on Earth. Everyone knows you're invulnerable. We also know you can hold things together with your minds. If several of you were on the plane and part of it blew up, you'd all do your psychic thing and save the plane. Then we'd have the proof, and you couldn't deny it."

I let go of Shannon's jaw. "And, at no time did you ask yourself if this was, say, true?" They *did* think we were the X-Men. Wow.

"Well, aliens exist. I mean, you're here." He had a point, but I was going to take it away from him.

"No, they don't. We're human undercover operatives for an antiterrorism branch of the federal government. We've targeted your little Club 51 because it's encouraging terrorist behavior."

Shannon shook his head. "I don't believe you. No one in Club 51 will ever believe that. We know you're here, and we know you're evil and need to be wiped off the face of the Earth."

CHAPTER 16

I WOULD HAVE LOVED TO have spent more time with Shannon learning about what else the scary people in Club 51 thought aliens could do, but we still had to get to Florida. Sometime. But not, as it turned out, any time soon.

Kevin had called in a whole bunch of federal agents. They seemed to take direction from him willingly. My mother wasn't pretending—she *did* outrank everyone.

The conspirators were taken away, handcuffed and heavily guarded. Their belongings went with them. The rest of the passengers had been triple-searched—no more bomb elements, no additional Club 51 cards.

True to my word, I made sure Alicia got a tremendous amount of credit. Kevin was prepping her for what to say and not to say when the reporters were allowed in, which would be as soon as the innocent passengers were released. She was dazed, to the point where Tim was holding her up. I got the impression Tim was being chivalrous because he thought she was cute. Alicia wasn't protesting about his arm around her waist.

Reader noticed, too. "Not every day we stop a huge terrorism plot and one of our team gets to make a love connection. Last time was when you joined up, girlfriend."

"We could rename ourselves the Love Team."

"Gag." Martini rubbed the back of my neck. "When can we get out of here?"

"We have to wait at least three hours for our jet to get here and get prepped," Reader replied. "I want only our own guys doing it, and it has to fly here, not use the Dome or a floater."

The Crash Site Dome was essentially the main gate hub. It was located where the original aliens, the Ancients, had first crash-landed in the U.S., so it had a lot of residual power. Larger equipment either went to the Dome and then to their final destination, or a floater gate was created. I still had no idea how that worked, and Christopher insisted I wouldn't want to know.

"Can we arrive at the Space Center at night?" Martini's fingers felt great. I was having to control myself from arching into his hand.

Martini shook his head. "No one will be there. It would make sense for us to gate over right now, while we could still deal with something today."

Reader sighed. "I'm with you, Jeff."

"Anyone know why Richard's still dead set against it?" I waited to hear, "It's political."

"No idea," Reader said. Well, maybe I was the only one making the political connection. "Paul doesn't know, but he's insisted on coming with us now." Gower had gone to pack but was expected back with us shortly.

"You sure Richard won't keep him there?" Martini asked.

"Positive. Paul's really pissed."

"Whatever's going on, the pressure on him has to be incredible. I mean, his son and nephew were just targeted for death, and he's still insisting we have to fly via jet." A thought occurred. "Hang on." I dug through my purse, pulled out my phone, and dialed. "Hey, Mom."

"How's it going? Were you right?"

"Dead on right. Kevin's awesome, by the way."

"Yeah. Hope you and James didn't embarrass yourselves." Geez, Mom was never fooled by anything.

"Um, sort of."

"I'll bet. So, what's the plan now?"

"We're still heading for Florida. Richard's insisting we have to arrive by jet, not gate."

"Don't take a commercial flight."

"Ahead of you." For once. "One of our jets is coming.

James is making sure only Centaurion Division are touching it."

"Good." She sighed. "You want to know what's going on, don't you?"

"Yeah. Spill. It's got something to do with you and Dad being in D.C., doesn't it?"

"In a way. There's a lot of pressure to use Centaurion Division as a full military unit, especially since the parasitic threat seems to be decreasing in the last few months."

"Because we took out the main fugly who was calling them here. However, I don't call a twelve-superbeing cluster slowing activity."

"Really? Before that and today, what's the superbeing activity been like?"

I didn't have to think about it. "Slowing. Getting slower the longer I've been with Centaurion."

"Exactly. They're running out of legitimate things to do. And that means we have governmental pressure to put them to better use."

"That's not what they're here for."

"I know. And I don't agree with this suggestion. However, it does bear discussion, and that's what we're doing. Right now, Centaurion Division needs to appear as human as possible, though."

Ah, that made sense. "So, we show up in a jet, with people watching us exit said jet, and we get to say, 'See? We travel like you.' Of course, someone's using this to try to wipe us out."

"Not everyone likes the idea of aliens living here with us."

"That reminds me. Leventhal Reid, you know him?"

"Know and loathe."

"Was he the Reid you and Dad were talking about at dinner last night?"

"Yes. Why?"

"I think he masterminded this terrorism attempt."

Mom was quiet for a few moments. "I'll check things out."

"Also, check out some guy named Howard Taft. He's the Supreme Leader of Club 51, the anti-alien underground organization that's responsible for this aborted terrorist attack."

"Supreme Leader?"

"I know, they're loons." Correct, in their way, but still loons.

"I'll check him and the organization out, too. What has James found so far?"

I handed the phone to Reader. "Please synchronize watches with my mother."

Reader took the phone with a grin. "Angela, great to hear your voice. Uh-huh. Yeah, checked that already. That too. Yep. We have proof of a connection to a man called Leventhal who gave the order to hold the commercial jet, but that's the only thing, and it's not enough. Right. Yeah." He laughed. "Probably. Yeah, we know, he's married." He laughed again. "No problem, but I'll keep it in mind. Yeah, nothing on Taft yet. I'm betting it's a fake name. Uh-huh. Yeah, I'll check those and run them by Kitty. Okay, great. Talk to you soon." He handed the phone back to me.

"I wish he were straight," Mom sighed. "That's a son-in-law I'd love."

I focused on the flowers again. "In a way, me too. However, what's going on?"

"James and I just made sure we weren't duplicating effort. Anyway, let me know when you get to Florida. I imagine you're heading down there because of the shuttle issues."

"No idea. No one's told me yet, and we've been a little busy."

"Well, find out, and keep me posted." I heard Dad's voice in the background. "Your father sends his love and reminds me we're late."

"Dinner at the White House?"

"Already did that. We're late for a reception, and I'm not dressed so, love you, gotta go."

"Love you too, Mom. Give my best to the Pres and the rest of the politicos."

I hung up and considered how different my life was from six months ago. Pretty much completely.

Kevin came back. "I think we want to be somewhere else when the press are allowed in."

"Good point. But can we just leave Alicia alone?"

"True. If you're okay leaving him here, Tim can handle it. He's been helping me get her ready."

"He's human, so a good choice. You don't want to be here for the press?"

Kevin shook his head. "We prefer to be a little more shadowy if at all possible." He grinned. "Besides, I'm having food brought in, and it'd be a shame to miss it."

CHAPTER 17

DINNER WAS NICE, not to mention long and drawn out. We had a lot of time to kill.

Kevin had catering brought in from one of my favorite local Italian restaurants, and we were given an entire room that I wouldn't have known existed in the airport but was apparently part of the security setup. The Feds were still all over the place, but the only non-Centaurion operative with us was Kevin.

"Not that this isn't great, but why don't we just go back to the Science Center?" I asked with my mouth full of cannelloni.

"I've suggested it," Gower said. "More than once. Richard would prefer we stay here." Martini growled and grumbled, but he didn't say anything. This was clearly one of those times when the Office of the Pontifex was trumping Field and Imageering.

"Why?"

Gower heaved a sigh. "We need to continue to appear 'regular.' "

"By spending the night in the airport?" By any standards, this seemed like Plan Inconvenient and Dumb.

Christopher and Martini exchanged glances. Reader chuckled. "Richard knows that if he lets us go back, Jeff'll enact a protocol that will send us via a gate."

"We have protocols?" Truly, no one ever told me anything.

"Some," Martini allowed. "I think Richard's trying to avoid a fight. Besides," he sighed, "as long as we leave somewhere in the early hours, we'll get there in the morning."

"Oh. Good." I wasn't what anyone would call a morning person. "We could go to my parents' house."

All the men shook their heads. "We need to remain here," Kevin said. "If Centaurion leaves the area, jurisdiction will shift. And we don't want that."

I gave up. "How are we going to sleep?"

"In shifts," Martini said. "If at all."

Tim and Alicia joined us for food before I could whine any more. He got some looks for bringing her, but I couldn't blame him—she looked wiped, and she knew most of what was going on, anyway.

"The press get their story?" Christopher asked meaningfully.

Tim nodded while he piled lasagna onto his plate. "All clear. Alicia did a great job, said exactly what Kevin told her to."

She smiled weakly. "I'm too tired to be creative."

"How are we getting Alicia home?" I asked Kevin quietly.

"We're not." He smiled at my shocked expression. "She'd prefer to avoid reporters, so she's staying here with us until we leave. Then I'll have her escorted home."

Alicia heard us. "Agent Lewis, could that be after my shift tomorrow? I've got morning duty, so I might as well not waste a sick day." I got the impression Alicia wanted to hang out with us, Tim in particular, for as long as she could.

"Sure thing." Kevin stood and stretched. "I'm going to check on things. It's fine if you want to wander, just don't leave this terminal, and make sure everyone has an idea of where you are if you do wander." He left the room. Some of our random A-Cs stretched out as much as they could and, as near as I could tell, went to sleep. A-Cs were big on napping whenever it was safe to do so.

Martini stroked the back of my neck. "So, we have time to kill?"

"Yep." Reader gave us both a knowing grin. "You two

want to go wander around, look at the gift shops? I think some of them are still open."

"What a great idea," Martini said. "Yeah, we're going to disappear for a bit."

Reader winked at me. "Enjoy. I'll call you when we're ready if you're not back yet."

We took our bags with us; it made us look less obvious. At least, so I told myself. "Where are we going?"

"Don't care. Just away from all this." Martini squeezed my hand. "You know this place better than I do."

This was true. But I'd never needed a private room before. "I know the elevator alarms go off if you stop one between floors."

"Damn."

"We could sneak back to the Science Center."

"No, I don't feel like getting into anything with Richard. Or Gladys interrupting us again."

"Does she do that on purpose?"

"Sometimes. Not always. She can't see us, and she can't hear us unless she's talking to us via the 'com."

Thank God. We walked by the food and gift areas. Not exactly private. However, there was a door between the last shop and the parking area. I led us over there—it said "Maintenance," but it was locked. It was also very out of the way, and the noise from the parking lot was loud, meaning it would drown out any suspicious noises.

Martini walked us out to the parking area, reached into his inner jacket pocket and pulled out a thin case. As he opened it, I realized it was a set of lock-picking tools. "You're trained to pick locks?" Why wasn't I trained to pick locks?

"Yep." He looked at me out of the corner of his eye. "I'll teach you once you're done learning to fly."

"Promise?"

"Of course. Now, wait here. I'm going to disable the camera for this area, open the door, get you in there, and then get the camera back up so we don't get inquisitive visitors."

"Check the soundproofing."

He grinned, left his rolling bag with me and disappeared. I counted and listened hard. He was back in eight seconds, grabbed me and the bags, and whooshed me off into the room. While my stomach settled, he disappeared again, was back in three seconds, door closed behind him.

"Sure you weren't spotted?" Now that he was back, I took a look around. It was a somewhat spacious utility closet, with toilet paper, paper towels, cleaning supplies, and similar items stocked inside.

Martini snorted. "No, I checked." Hyperspeed was a wonderful thing. "And I shouted a lot. Hear anything?"

"Not a sound."

"Good." Martini locked the door and also hooked our suitcases and my purse under the handle. Then he turned around, a very sexy half-smile on his face. He unbuttoned his jacket, his eyes smoldering. Just looking at him made my breathing get heavy. "C'mere, baby."

CHAPTER 18

MARTINI REACHED OUT AND PULLED me into his arms. One hand hooked into my hair, the other slid down my back. He kissed me, strong and almost predatory. I melted against him. He leaned against the only open wall space in the room and slid one leg between mine. I ground against his thigh.

"You were a bad girl," he said, as he moved my head and ran his tongue over my neck. I tried to protest, but my neck was one of my main erogenous zones, and he knew it. "Lusting after other men."

"No," I managed to gasp out. "I wasn't." It was a lie, but that was part of the fun.

He pulled my head back as I'd done to Thompson, but gently. "Liar." He ran his teeth over the front of my neck, as if he were going to rip my throat out. My breathing went ragged, my hands clawed at his chest, and my thighs locked around his leg.

He undid my jacket with his other hand. I wore a spaghetti-strap shelf-bra top under this particular suit. He slid the shelf portion from under my breasts, and then his mouth moved from my throat to my chest, while he kept my head pulled back.

Martini teased one breast and then the other with his lips, tongue, and teeth. He was the only man to ever bring me to orgasm at second base, and he was still batting a thousand. I was glad he'd checked the soundproofing, because I was howling.

He let my head up, and I ripped his shirt open. The sight of his incredible pecs, rippling torso and truly rock-hard abs, dusted with just the right amount of hair, did to me what it always did. I lunged at his chest—I had to have my mouth on it, all over it.

He gave a low, purrlike growl. "That's a good girl. But you haven't been good enough yet." He ran his fingers through my hair and directed my head. His other hand spent its time alternating between stroking my neck and my breast.

I slid my hands down his body to his pants. These I undid slowly while he thrust against me. While my tongue lapped at the hollow between his pecs, my hands found what I had come to consider the greatest appendage in the history of the world. He was hard as steel and felt like velvet against my skin. I ran my hands over him until my whole body was shaking with desire.

He pulled my head away from his body. His eyes were half-closed and he shook his head with a low chuckle. "Bad girls don't get what they want right away." He slid his hands down my arms and pulled my hands away, putting them behind my back. He held my wrists in one hand, while he toyed with my breasts with the other.

I moaned. "I'll . . . be good." His hand slid down my body and then moved my skirt up. His fingers stroked my thighs. "Jeff . . . please . . . "

"Please what?" His smile was wider, but still predatory. His fingers slid beneath my underwear. I couldn't talk, almost couldn't breathe. I could wail, and I did, as my eyes rolled back while he stroked and teased me. His fingers moved so fast and expertly, this orgasm crashed fast and hard. "Mmmm, that's nice. Almost makes me willing to punish you a little more."

"Oh, God, please Jeff . . . please . . . "

"Please what?" His voice was low and silky. "What do you want, baby?"

There was only one thing in the world I wanted right now. He knew, of course, but he liked to make me tell him aloud. "I need you ... inside me. Please, Jeff ... " His fingers started up again. It was wonderful, but tormenting, because the part of him inside me wasn't what my body craved.

"How badly do you want it?"

"More ... than anything." This was true. When he had me like this, there was nothing I wanted more than to have him deep inside of me. Of course, I wanted the same thing when I wasn't at the edge of sexual insanity, too, but that wasn't important now.

His mouth covered mine, and his tongue slid in as his fingers slid out and moved around to my back. Martini let go of my wrists, slipped both hands down, cupped my bottom and lifted me up. As my legs released his, he stripped my underwear off. He spun us around, so my back was against the wall. His fingers kneaded my flesh as I kicked my shoes off.

I wrapped my arms around his shoulders and legs around his waist. He growled and pulled me closer to him while his mouth moved back to my neck. I managed to moan his name and grind my pelvis against his.

"That's what I want," he whispered against my neck. I writhed against him; his tongue and teeth were on a spot that turned me incoherent. Then his hands guided me onto him—the fireworks went off in my brain, and coherency wasn't something I was concerned about any more.

My hands clutched at him and my mouth was open, but this orgasm was so intense I couldn't make a sound. His mouth covered mine again as he wrapped his arms around me. His thrusts were hard and fast and kept my orgasm going.

Our kiss got deeper and more intense as my latest climax subsided. I ran my hands through his hair and rocked my hips to keep Martini as deep inside me as possible. We slammed into each other over and over.

My whole body felt like an erogenous zone—any place it touched his tingled and burned. Martini's chest rubbed against my breasts while his hands roamed my backside, causing shock waves of pleasure to course through me. I slid my legs down and pushed against his behind to help him go deeper. Our movements were frenzied, and I screamed into his kiss, as another orgasm crashed over me.

His head reared back, and he roared as he exploded inside me. The room spun as my orgasm spiked in time to his—I buried my face in his neck and sobbed from erotic overload as our bodies throbbed together.

After what seemed like hours, our bodies began to calm, the throbbing diminished to weak pulsation, then slowed to gradual stop. Martini kissed my head, and I managed to move so he could reach my mouth. His kiss was tender and soft, and my body relaxed as he guided me to the floor, still kissing me.

I didn't want this to end, but then, I never did. However, duty called and I had to figure, out of the way and soundproofed or not, someone was going to bang on the door soon to determine just how a cat in heat had gotten locked inside.

Martini smiled against my mouth. "You worry too much."

"Mmmm, you always give me good reason."

"As long as it's always good."

"Always." He kissed me deeply again, and I decided to push worrying off for another long while.

CHAPTER 19

MARTINI PULLED AWAY FROM ME slowly and stroked my face. "I love you."

"I love you too, Jeff."

He shook his head. "Nothing in this world matters more to me than you. Your happiness, your safety. I'd lock you up at the Science Center to keep you out of this situation, but I know you'd get out somehow."

"I would, because I won't let anything happen to you, either."

He gave me a small grin. "I know. That's what I tell myself every time we're in danger—at least I'm there to catch you when you fall." He meant this literally—there had been more times than I could count now where he'd just managed to catch me before I'd splatted onto the ground.

"Someone has to keep your hearts beating." Also meant literally. I'd plunged the adrenaline harpoon into his hearts the second day we'd known each other. It was almost romantic, sort of "our thing"—he'd catch me, I'd stab him with a huge needle. Maybe we *were* adrenaline junkies, the Sid and Nancy of Centaurion Division.

He slid my top back up, taking time to stroke my breasts. I would have zipped his pants, but we'd learned that any time I did this we somehow ended up with fewer clothes on. I was willing to take the risk, but before I could suggest it, my phone rang.

I sighed and went to the door. Martini slipped my underwear back on me while I rummaged through my purse. He also took a moment to rub himself against me but stopped when I answered the phone. I was going to hate whoever was calling me.

"Girlfriend, hope you're dressed, because it's time to go."

"I hate you, James."

He laughed. "I'm sure. Just hustle, we need to be in the air yesterday."

Reader gave me the gate number, we hung up, and I traded my phone for my brush. "James says we have to hurry."

Martini smoothed my skirt down, taking the opportunity to rub up against me again. "I can't find your shoe." He handed me one of them.

"I kicked them off."

"Yeah, you really did. This one was stuck in the ceiling."

"Not my fault it's a stiletto."

"No complaints from me. Just saying I can't find the other one."

I finished brushing my hair and took a look around. "Oh, there it is." It was stabbed into a roll of toilet paper.

He pulled it out. "How did you get it stuck in there?"

"No idea. I wasn't paying attention to anything but you."

"Well, that's how it should be." He knelt down and slipped the shoe onto my foot. He looked up, and his expression was hard to read. He looked as though he wanted to tell me something. Or maybe ask me something. My heart started beating faster. I didn't know if I was ready for what he might suggest, but at the same time, I didn't know if I wasn't any longer.

Martini took a deep breath, but before he could say anything the lock turned and someone pushed against the door. He closed his eyes, and I could see disappointment flit across his face. Then he stood up and pulled me behind him.

He put his hand against the door. A-Cs were stronger than humans, so the door stayed shut. Martini handed me my purse and slid my bag to me. He moved his away also, then looked over his shoulder. "It's a human and doesn't feel like a threat. You want to handle it?"

This was the male way of admitting I'd handle any situation that required lying better. "Sure." I let him keep the illusion he was generously giving me a chance to take the lead as opposed to mentioning that he needed me to and I'd take it anyway. My mother hadn't raised a total idiot.

Martini opened the door, and we were greeted by the sight of a very nervous maintenance worker with an empty cart. His eyes widened when he saw us. "What . . . what are you doing in here?"

"Hi!" I moved from behind Martini, grabbed several rolls of toilet paper, and barreled out the door. The maintenance man moved back to let us out. "Sorry about that. Can you believe they told us to get more toilet paper for the flight ourselves? The cost-cutting is incredible when they make a pilot do this sort of thing, don't you think?" I jerked my head toward Martini, who caught on, grabbed a couple of rolls, and stalked out behind me.

"I went to flight school for this," he muttered, not looking at the maintenance man.

To me, this indicated Martini's still almost-total lack of ability to lie. To the maintenance man, however, it showed Martini's shame. "Oh, man, that sucks. Here, wait a sec." The maintenance man went inside, grabbed a full carton of TP, and handed it to us. He took the single rolls back. "You guys just take that whole box. Maybe you won't have to stock up next flight."

Martini gave me a "what now?" look. "Great. Jeff, can you carry the box all by yourself?"

I got the "I may love you but I really hate you right now" look. "Sure." He hoisted it easily. The man could lift me with one hand, a carton of rolled paper wasn't going to pose a challenge. "Thanks," he added to the maintenance man.

I gave the man a quick hug. "You're the greatest."

We left him smiling and shaking his head over how bad things in the airline industry were. "What the hell am I going to do with this box?" Martini asked me as we rounded the corner.

"Um, take it with us. Our new friend won't say a thing if he never sees the box again. But if he spots it dumped somewhere, then he might mention this to someone else."

"I hate my life."

"I think I could take that personally."

"Other than you. And other than at this moment."

"Think we were spotted coming out of the closet?"

"Maybe. There are no alarms going off, so maybe your toilet paper ploy will mean I don't have to have Christopher alter footage."

"See? My plans always work."

He snorted. "Right."

We went to the appropriate gate and caught up with the others. The looks on their faces were priceless. I knew Martini was going to make me pay for them later.

"Wow, glad you two think of everything," Reader said with a huge grin.

"You trying to tell us something?" Christopher asked.

"I went already," Tim added.

Gower shook his head. "And, somehow, you've been in charge of all Field operations for almost ten years."

"You never want to run out," I reminded them.

"I hate each and every one of you," Martini said. "Can we get going?"

"Gee," Kevin said from behind us, "I didn't think my coming along would necessitate the need for extra supplies."

"Everyone's a comedian," Martini muttered.

"You're coming with us?" I wasn't disappointed, and I could see Reader wasn't either.

He nodded. "The situation's under control here, but from what Paul told me, I think it'll be a help if I go along for the next event. If that's okay with you," he said to Martini.

"Sure," Martini sighed. "The more the merrier." He tossed the box to Tim, who just managed to catch it. "Oh, I just remembered—you report to me."

"Technically," Tim said, voice muffled by the box, "I report to Kitty."

"In a field situation," I recited from memory, "we all report to Jeff." I'd never followed this particular rule, but I was willing to pretend, especially since I knew it was taking effort for Martini to remain genial toward Kevin for a variety of reasons, my finding Kevin a hunk and a half being only one of them.

Our gray, mostly unmarked jet was docked and ready. Alicia was with us to say good-bye, and she escorted us down the ramp. I saw her slip a piece of paper into Tim's inner jacket pocket. Then he moved the box, and I couldn't see their faces. However, Alicia was blushing and looking really girlish as we dragged Tim onto the plane. She waved to us, and then the door closed, and we were back in action.

Reader and Tim were handling the flying and navigation, respectively, so the rest of us got to relax. The plane was the same one I'd ridden in the first day I'd discovered we had real live aliens on the planet. It was designed with comfort in mind—the seats were wide and cushy, and there was enough leg room so Martini could stretch out without issue.

The plane also had a nice galley and a bedroom that doubled as a medical bay. As much as I wanted to earn Mile High Miles with Martini, I didn't want to do it with everyone else inside the cabin. Even if I could manage to make love to him silently—so far a feat never accomplished—they'd still know. I felt it might affect my performance, so instead of dragging him to the back, I settled in the seat next to him. The others spread out behind us, one to a set of two seats.

The seats reclined, so as soon as we were up in the air, Christopher handed out full-sized pillows and blankets, and everyone leaned back. It was after midnight—the snores were immediate. I looked around—Kevin was following suit and looked asleep.

I moved the armrest between me and Martini up and snuggled next to him. He put his arm around me and tucked the blanket. My hand strayed below his belt. He caught it in his, brought it up to his lips and kissed my fingers. "Bad girl," he murmured, with a very cat-satisfied look on his face.

"Can't blame a girl for trying."

He put my hand onto his shoulder, then slid his finger under my chin and tilted my head. He kissed me deeply, then cuddled me closer. "Sleep time."

"Okay." I leaned against his chest, and dozed off.

Some turbulence woke me up. It seemed like nothing, but I wasn't sleepy any more. Martini's breathing was rhythmical. I closed my eyes. Nothing. And if I wasn't sleepy, being cuddled next to Martini didn't make me tired—it made me horny.

I moved slowly out of his embrace, tucked the blankets around him, and stroked his hair. He heaved a contented sigh. I kissed his forehead and moved into the aisle. Everyone was snoozing. I resisted the impulse to tuck the blanket around Christopher—there was never going to be a good reason to put either one of us into a situation that could be remotely taken for romantic. Martini had been very clear—I'd made my one and only allowable romantic mistake already. If I made another one, Martini was out of my life forever.

The mere thought of that made my stomach clench. My mother might want me looking at options, but I wasn't really open to the idea. I hurried into the galley—I wanted a soda.

"Coca-Colas." I opened the fridge and there they were, any variety I might want, all frosty cold. I closed the door. "How about some Mountain Dew and Dr Pepper?" Opened the fridge again and, sure enough, now there was Dew and Dr Pepper there, as cold as if they'd been in there for hours.

I played this game a bit more, choosing regional and hard to find soft drinks. Every single time, whatever it was I wanted showed up. The how of this drove me crazy, but Martini refused to give me the tiniest hint as to how this worked.

I took a Cactus Cooler and closed the fridge. It worked

the same for food, but I wasn't all that hungry for some reason. We'd had a great dinner, but it was heading toward breakfast time. But no hunger pangs.

I walked through the cabin, feeling like a stewardess on a redeye flight, what with everyone snoring. So I headed to the cockpit. To hear Reader arguing with someone over the radio.

CHAPTER 20

" . . . I **DON'T CARE.** This situation's escalated out of control." Reader sounded truly upset.

Tim looked back as I came in. "Hey. You want to take the 'com, Commander?"

Oh, it was *that* kind of situation.

Reader nodded emphatically and Tim pulled off his headset and handed it to me. I cleared my throat and tried to flip myself into Major Military Mode. I wasn't very good at it, but I made up for my lack of military-speak skills with a dogged determination to get what I wanted at any cost.

"Hello, this is Commander Katt. Who am I speaking to?"

"This is Karl Smith, head of Canaveral Ops. I'd like you and your team to return to Centaurion Home Base and not get involved, Commander, and I'd like confirmation of your return now."

I looked at Reader and gave him the "WTF?" signal. He rolled his eyes and shrugged, then went back to paying attention to flying.

"I'm sorry, but why, exactly, are you now asking us to go home when you asked us to come out there in the first place?"

"The request was not made by Canaveral Ops." Smith sounded angry. I got the impression Martini, Sr., had broken some sort of protocol by contacting his son. I decided to support the A-C side of the house.

"You know, Mr. Smith, I'd love to just turn around and

go home, but we've already burned all this fuel, and it's a bitch to explain to the guys in accounting."

Dead silence for a moment on the 'com. Tim, however, was snickering up a storm.

"I beg your pardon? Who the hell do you think you are?"

"I think I'm the head of Airborne for Centaurion Division. I also think I'm tightly connected to the P.T.C.U."

"This isn't any of their concern."

"Oh, hell, yes, it is. Whatever's going on there at Kennedy required Centaurion Division's activation. I'm spitballing here, but I'll wager we have a special visitor or two from outer space hanging about the Space Center. Which means both Centaurion and the P.T.C.U. are quite concerned."

Dead silence. Reader nodded his head and shifted his headset. "I wish you'd read the damn files. Yes, shuttle went up, shuttle got hit with something, shuttle landed back at the Space Center, something is in quarantine along with the astronauts."

I thought about this. "Mr. Smith?"

"Yes?" I could tell his teeth were gritted.

"It's pretty unusual for a shuttle to land back at the Center, isn't it?"

"Unheard of."

"But that's what's happened, yes?"

"Yes." The word sounded dragged out of him.

"Karl, may I call you Karl? Karl, has it occurred to you that the only beings on this planet potentially equipped to handle whatever the hell our shuttle brought home are in Centaurion Division?"

"You may not call me Karl."

"Too late, Karl, already did. Now, answer the real question."

He sighed. "Your people are the best equipped, yes." Your people. I wondered if Smith was anti-alien.

"So, why don't you want my people there?"

There was a significant pause. "Go secure."

I looked at Reader. "We're not secure?"

Reader hit a couple of buttons. "Centaurion 'com secured."

Smith spoke, rapidly. "There's more going on than this incident. There have been several attacks on Centaurion personnel in the past few days. Most of them avoided, but we have two A-Cs in critical here. I don't want more of you in danger. We have enough problems—we can't afford to lose Centaurion."

Nice to know he was pro-alien, or at least wanted to appear that way to us. "Look, Karl, every A-C's related to every other A-C. You know that?"

"Yes."

"Then let's be real. They aren't going to stay home if their family's in danger."

"You're human?"

Whoops. "Yes."

"Are you all armed?"

I looked at Reader. He indicated arms might be in our possession. "Somewhat. Why?"

"Good. Look, if you're hell-bent on coming, I can't stop you. Just make sure you've got the means to protect yourselves at all times, don't let your guard down for any reason, and don't trust anyone."

"Including you?"

"For all I know, yeah. It's ugly here right now. You're human, you understand—when things get ugly, good people do bad things."

"Sometimes. Sometimes good people do the right thing and bad people reform."

"I'm talking reality, not a movie."

"So am I."

"We'll do what we can, but that may not be enough. You have to remember, not everyone likes that the A-Cs are here, and some of those people will do anything to get rid of them." I heard something in the background. "Remember what I said, we want you to go back." His voice was back to angry. I could hear voices, faint, but there were at least two other people with him. I could hear Smith talking to them, but his voice was muffled, like his mic was covered.

The voices raised, and I heard some sharp sounds. They were muffled, too, but I looked at Reader, and he made the universal hand gesture for "gun."

"Karl?" No reply. "Karl, are you there? Are you okay?" Silence. "Karl Smith, do you copy, repeat, do you copy?" The 'com went dead.

Reader and I looked at each other. He turned off the 'com. "We're in trouble, girlfriend."

"I think Karl's in worse trouble."

"I think Karl's dead. Tim, see if you can raise anyone at Kennedy."

I gave Tim back his headset, and he started fiddling around. "James, fill me in on everything in the file."

"You have time to get caught up."

"The hell with that. You tell me the pertinent stuff, and I'll skim the damn thing later." I was trying not focus on the fact that if Smith was dead, it was likely because he'd taken the risk to warn us about whatever it was he thought he'd warned us about.

"Fine. The shuttle wasn't actually a shuttle. It was a prototype for long-range space travel, very hush-hush. It only had three astronauts in it. They were heading toward Mars, got hit with something, no one knows what. Whatever it was, it got into the interior without causing a breach."

"Sounds like a parasite."

"Maybe, but none of the astronauts turned into a superbeing."

"Well, that's a blessing."

"One of those astronauts was an A-C, the other two were humans."

Oh? This was indeed news. "Who was the A-C?"

Reader heaved a sigh. "Paul's brother."

CHAPTER 21

"PAUL HAS A BROTHER?" Why this was a shock to me I couldn't say. But in the five months I'd known these guys, they'd never shared this fact.

"Yeah, Paul's the oldest of four. Michael's a couple of years younger. They also have two sisters."

"Why hasn't anyone mentioned this before?"

Reader shrugged. "Not important. All of Paul's family live around and work out of East or Canaveral Base. No one was keeping the info from you, girlfriend, just hasn't been a reason to mention it before now." All of Martini's family did the same, but I knew about them. Then again, I was sleeping with Martini, and Reader was sleeping with Gower, so maybe this lack of information flow was understandable.

"No wonder Richard wanted Paul kept back at Home Base."

"In a way, yeah. No one knows what's going on, but the three astronauts are under the highest-level quarantine, and no one we have access to has been allowed to talk to them."

"We're sure none of them turned superbeing?"

"Not a hundred percent, but seems a good bet so far. I don't think a NASA quarantine chamber could stop a superbeing."

Couldn't have stopped any of the ones I'd ever run

across, but who knew? "How long until we're close to Florida?"

"About an hour," Tim answered.

I looked out the windshield. It looked light. I tried to do the math and gave up. "What time is it there?"

"Right now? About nine," Tim said. "We should land around ten." I opened my mouth, and he put his hand up. "We had to go around some weather, it caused the delay. And, James, I have Alfred on the 'com. He's sending a team to check on Smith."

"Who's Alfred?"

Reader gave me a grin. "Jeff's dad."

"You keep the headsets." Tim and Reader both gave me looks that said I was a chicken. True enough, at least in this case. "Everyone else is fast asleep. Not sure if I should wake them up or not."

"Let them sleep for another few minutes," Reader said. "Jeff in particular needs the regeneration." This I knew to be true. Sex, even great, mind-blowing sex, didn't regenerate him. Sleep did, being in an isolation chamber did it better, and, I'd discovered, watching old TV reruns helped him, too. He insisted that cuddling with me helped as well, but most of our cuddling sessions ended in sexual acrobatics. Then again, we were on an airplane, and I wasn't going to start anything with the others aboard.

"Okay, I'm going back to the cabin. I'll wake them up in a little while."

"Sounds good."

"James, before I go, *do* we have weapons with us?"

"Plenty. We go equipped for war at all times." He was serious. Five months in, this shouldn't have felt like a surprise.

"Good. I guess." I wandered back to my seat. Martini had shifted and looked like a big cat to me, stretched out and ready for a tummy rub. I knew better than to do that, though—too many others about, and besides, he needed the sleep.

He cracked an eye. "C'mere." He pulled me into his lap. "How much more sleep time before you tell me what you're upset about?"

"Thirty minutes or so."

Martini flipped a blanket around me and shifted again, so I was still in his lap but lying down. "Good. Close your eyes, think calm thoughts."

I snuggled my face into his neck and practiced Serenity Time. At least, that's what I called it when I was trying to keep my emotions low and quiet. I wasn't very good at it, even though I practiced every day. Quiet time for me meant "think about all the things I want to do," not "focus on the lotus blossom." My kung fu instructors despaired of my ever getting anywhere in the sport because of it. My track coaches had merely seen it as proof I was a sprinter. Martini felt I was just wired horny. He was probably right.

However, I gave it my best shot with the lotus blossom. Nada. Tried for the Happy Place. Worse . . . now all I could think about was Martini naked. Then again, while it didn't keep me calm, it sure kept me happy.

I spent some time trying to choose my favorite position, naughtiest location, and most mind-blowing orgasm. I gave up on the orgasm—it was like trying to rate different levels of nirvana. Favorite position was "whatever one we're in right now," so while I could enjoy reminiscing over our repertoire, I couldn't come up with a definitive answer.

Naughtiest location, however, was a good one, and that kept me occupied for quite a while. Elevator, the Pontifex's office, top of the Empire State Building, cave off a main trail in the Grand Canyon, and potentially our just left but fondly remembered maintenance closet were vying for positions in the Top 10. Of course, the men's room in Guadalajara and the women's in the Paris Metro were also highlights. The cabana in Cabo wasn't really naughty, but it was still my favorite. The best vacation I'd ever had, one week of pure bliss. We hadn't been able to get away anywhere since then, not even for a weekend.

"My fave, too," Martini murmured. He always knew when I was thinking about Cabo. "You're not clear on how to get to a calm place, are you?"

I shifted in his lap, which caused him to give a low growl. "Not my fault."

"Uh-huh." He lifted me off his lap and deposited me

gently in the seat next to him. He stretched, then kissed me, deeply, for quite a while. He pulled away, eyes half-closed. "I'd love to move this conversation to the back of the plane, but we might as well wake everyone up so you can bring us up to speed."

I nodded. He stood up, belt buckle in my face. I sat on my hands and forced myself to lean back.

Martini grinned at me. "I promise, we'll get a room." He wandered back and shook the others awake while I reined my libido in, albeit unwillingly.

In addition to everything else, the chairs swiveled. Everyone shifted their chairs so we were in a circle, and I brought them up to speed on the little we knew.

"You're sure Smith's dead?" Gower asked.

"Not for sure. Tim said Jeff's dad was sending a team to check on him."

Martini got up and walked to the cockpit. He was back quickly. "Yeah, they found him, shot through the head twice."

"James and I heard two shots. And I know there were at least two people with him." I tried not to let this freak me out. Without much success, if Martini rubbing my neck was any indication.

"Could you identify their voices?" Christopher asked.

"No, they were muffled. Did your father say anything about the attacks?" I asked Martini.

"Nothing. He told me we had a potential unidentified ET at Kennedy. That was bad enough news."

I looked at Kevin. "Any suggestions?"

He nodded. "I want to advise Angela of everything the moment we land. I have the authority to find out what's really going on at Kennedy, but it'll take some time."

"My dad is a cryptologist for NASA's ET Division." This had also been surprising news five months ago since I'd thought he was a history professor at ASU. It seemed I'd been the only one in my family not living a secret life. Now I suspected every relative of being in a covert operation of some kind, though my parents insisted this wasn't the case.

"Good, but that may just mean he's a target," Kevin looked more worried, not less. Wonderful. "I'll mention it to Angela, though I'm sure she's already on it." I knew she was; she'd been protecting my father since they'd met in Tel Aviv. It was a romantic story—just them, anti-Jewish and anti-American terrorists, and a few hundred bullets.

"My parents should be aware, but it never hurts to warn them."

Kevin sighed. "I'm a lot more worried about all of you, though. This team has to be careful—you've already been targeted once. Those lunatics would have been successful if you hadn't figured it out."

"Okay, so no one goes anywhere alone," Christopher said. "We're used to that, we normally work in teams."

"I think you'd better be more than buddied up," Kevin said. "I'd really suggest that there's more safety in numbers. Including when you're sleeping."

I had no intention of bunking with anyone other than Martini. He apparently felt the same way. "We can sleep at East Base if we have to. We have a small base outside of Kennedy, too."

"But are your own people trustworthy?"

It was a good question. As we'd learned the hard way, the answer wasn't always yes.

Martini sighed, and I heard the resignation in his voice. "My parents can house all of us, including you," he nodded to Kevin. "And, though being there might kill me, I'm pretty sure the rest of you will be safe."

CHAPTER 22

"I'M SURE WE DON'T WANT to impose!" I didn't mean for it to come out as a shout, but I wasn't always good with shocks to my system.

Martini closed his eyes but kept rubbing my neck. "They live for impositions. It gives them more reasons to complain about me."

Christopher didn't look any more excited about this than Martini did. "They do live the closest to Kennedy," he said, as if he were admitting to having herpes.

"My parents live in East Base," Gower said. I heard the regret in his voice. "I'm sure we'll have to stay closer to the Space Center than that." East Base was in New York, and since we were apparently not allowed to use gates, there was no way we were staying there, no matter how much most of us were going to want to.

I tried to remind myself that this was going to put a crimp in Reader and Gower's love life, too, not to mention that Tim and Christopher weren't going to have any shot of privacy, either. It didn't make me feel any better. And lord knew how they were going to react to Kevin.

"You sure?" Kevin asked. "I don't want to put your family into danger."

"They're A-Cs. From what little we know, every A-C's in danger." Martini rubbed his forehead. "Besides, our house is secured, and I have five older sisters, none of whom live at home any more. They have a huge house, and they haven't converted any of the bedrooms—other than mine, which is now the grandchildren's playroom."

News to me. I also heard the hurt in his voice, lurking just under the surface of the words. Martini wasn't kidding; this was likely to be a grueling experience.

Tim came on the intercom. "Time to land. I think we want to buckle in, lord knows what kind of welcome we're going to get."

We moved the seats back to their full, upright positions and strapped ourselves in. I held Martini's hand, rather more tightly than usual. Landing had never made me feel comfy when I had no idea how to fly. Now that I did, I knew exactly how many things could go wrong. Reader was our best pilot as well as best driver, but I couldn't keep the nerves at bay.

Martini stroked the back of my hand with his thumb. "It'll be fine, baby," he said quietly.

I leaned my head on his shoulder. "I'm sure. We'll manage at your parents', too. I promise."

He kissed my head. "I hope you're right."

I closed my eyes, took a deep breath, and then we were going down. Landing was smooth as glass, Reader's usual. I kept my eyes closed. Thoughts had managed to enter my brain, and I wanted to hold onto them.

"Jeff, what does your father do at the Space Center?"

"He's the head of their ET Division."

"So, shouldn't that mean he knows my dad?"

"If he does, he's never mentioned it." Martini sounded confused. "But your father's a cryptologist. Mine works on the building of the actual spacecraft."

"So, did he help design the long-range spacecraft that got hit with the unidentified creepy from outer space?"

"Probably. Our people have the most experience with spacecraft, even more than Earth scientists."

"How so? I thought you used gate technology to get here."

"We did, but we'd already explored our entire solar system effectively. There just wasn't time to build a long-enough-range spacecraft to get us here in time to stop the parasitic threat."

More thoughts. And I'd only had one soda since last night's dinner. Amazing. "How many inhabited planets are there in your system?"

"More than half, so ten."

"How many of them have long-range space flight?"

"Not sure. When we were exiled, there were two others. Three of the planets weren't advanced enough and weren't in contact with the rest of us. Two of the planets had no interest in anything outside our solar system, and one had no interest in anything outside their own planet."

"What about the tenth?"

He was quiet for a few long seconds. "They were warlike, more so than the rest of us. More so than Earth."

"So?"

"So, the rest of our planets, at least the ones advanced enough, got together and removed their ability for space travel."

"How could you do that?"

He sighed. "No idea. That's all we were taught in school."

I considered this. "You've never asked for more information?"

"Nope."

"Um, why not?"

Martini shrugged. "Why would our teachers, who are our parents, grandparents, and other relatives, lie to us about things like this?"

I managed not to bite through my tongue. "Oh, I can think of a few reasons." I contemplated how to approach this. "So, doesn't anyone question things when you're all young and learning?"

"Sure. Scientific theory, talent boundaries, control techniques, how to function at human speeds when you don't want to, why we can't be more like humans, things like that."

I reminded myself they had a whole different range of issues than humans did. Didn't make this any less disconcerting. "So, it's an A-C trait not to question your elders?"

"I suppose." He sighed again. "I know where you're going with this. Everyone lied about who Ronald Yates really was, and maybe if we hadn't, we could have found a way to stop Mephistopheles sooner."

"Something like that, yeah. It just seems kind of . . . unusual. That you get into adulthood without a lot of questioning of accepted truths. Or that you're the head of everything, and yet they haven't necessarily told you everything."

"What they did on our home world doesn't matter for how we live here. Besides, if the lie is good enough . . . "

I got his point. I sure hadn't figured out my parents were lying about their entire life histories. I'd cared a lot more about getting to stay out past midnight. "Point taken."

"If it really matters to you, my father might know how that race was contained."

"Think he'll tell me the truth?"

"I think you'll badger it out of him, so probably."

"Does Richard know?" I found the Pontifex rather easy to badger for information these days.

"He might. He'd be as likely to know as my father."

Okay, something to do when we got a moment. Call the Pontifex and demand some answers. While dodging murderous attacks, finding out who killed Smith and why, and making a good impression on Martini's parents. Not a problem, I was great at multitasking.

We taxied into what looked like a humongous hangar and then to what looked like a regular docking bay. It wasn't overly lit inside, and I had a hard time making much out through the windows. It reminded me of every horror movie I'd ever seen. "Where are the weapons stored?" I wanted a gun for some reason.

"In the cache," Christopher said. Martini and Gower pulled up the floor. I was intrigued that until they did it, you couldn't have told there was a storage area under there. Christopher slipped into the hole and started handing up guns and clips.

"Nice," Kevin said under his breath.

"I'm sure they have permits." I doubted it highly, but I had no issues with lying.

Kevin chuckled. "I'm betting they don't, but that's okay. They have their own sovereignty."

"They do?" Geez, what else didn't I know?

"Like the American Indians, only their reservations are a little more spread out."

Interesting—I'd heard the American Indian comparison before, but not the reservation part of the equation. "So, are they considered an ethnic minority?"

"For some governmental purposes, yes, although they're also American citizens, either naturalized or legally born here." Kevin grinned at me. "I only learned this a few months ago myself."

"Yeah, well, some of us get the key information last." Christopher handed me something I was familiar with, a Glock 23. "Awww, my favorite."

"Your mother asked that we have some on hand for you." Christopher shook his head. "Why don't you carry one all the time?"

Because I constantly forgot to set the safety, but I didn't feel like sharing that aloud. "The harpoon takes up a lot of space in my purse."

"That thing could hold an entire department store and probably has," Christopher muttered as he handed more guns out. This was true, but not really the issue at hand.

"How many weapons are we taking with us? I mean, one Glock and a few clips I can carry. I could stuff another set into my luggage, but that's about it." Christopher handed a huge case complete with shoulder strap up to Gower. I took a close look. "A rocket launcher? We carry rocket launchers? On purpose?"

"Yep." Martini took it from Gower as Christopher handed another one up.

"Are you guys insane? We walk out with this stuff, and we'll be filled with bullets faster than you can say 'I'm a sociopath headed to Mickey D's.'"

"Relax," Martini said with a grin. He pushed something on the case and it disappeared. Gower did the same, then grabbed the third launcher case Christopher handed up.

"I think that's good for now," Christopher said as he climbed out.

"You mean there's *more* in there? What is this, the Guns and Ammo Mobile Christmas Catalog? I thought you all were supposedly pacifistic."

Christopher took the third case and turned it invisible. "You worry too much. You need to get her to relax, Jeff."

"Normally I could say that'd happen with a lot of confidence. Considering where we'll be sleeping, maybe we should bring along some grenades."

"We have grenades?" I was hitting a pitch where soon only dogs would be able to hear me.

"Relax, girlfriend. It's all good." Reader sauntered in from the cockpit. "We're supposedly all clear. God alone knows who or what'll be greeting us. I say we have at least handguns ready, though concealed would probably be wisest." Gower handed him two guns and several clips, which Reader put about his person.

Tim came back and got his armaments. Even Kevin took a couple of extra guns. The rest were put into everyone's luggage. I had three Glocks and more clips than I could count shoved into mine. "My clothes are gonna be wrecked."

"Relax," Christopher said. "Your concert shirts are safe." He did know me well, I had to admit. "If you need more standard issue, we can get that easily." The clothes, like the soft drinks and snackage, showed up whenever, wherever, as long as it was an A-C controlled facility. But still, I didn't want to wear Eau de Gunpowder for this entire trip.

"Ready?" Martini asked.

"No."

"Good." He kissed my cheek. "Let's get going and see who wants to kill us at this location."

Martini went first, with Kevin insisting on going right after him. Gower, Reader, and Tim went next. I wanted to be near Martini, but that wasn't allowed. I was, instead, put in the back with Christopher, who had the usual instructions to grab me and run if there was trouble. Where we would run to was a mystery, but then again, perhaps there were several secret exits as well as other weapons caches in this plane. Perhaps we'd leave through the food and drink time tunnel or something.

Martini had started this little "put a lot of bodies between whatever it was and Kitty" pretty much right after Operation Fugly was over. Apparently he hadn't enjoyed seeing me on the front lines at all and wanted to avoid repeat performances as often as possible. Christopher got to be my wrangler because he was just nasty enough that I knew he'd knock me out if he had to. So far he'd never had to, but Martini trusted Christopher's discretion more than mine in these kinds of situations.

We moved out of the jet—so far so good. Down the long tunnel where no airport-type personnel were. I knew we weren't really at an airport, but we'd taxied to a hangar and the ramp had attached to our plane just like at any advanced airport. There should have been someone or something to indicate we weren't enemies entering this area. But there was nothing and no one. So far so very creepy.

"Is it always devoid of personnel? Anybody could waltz in here."

"No," Christopher sounded worried. "Normally there are checkpoints." He had a gun in his pocket and his hand on the gun. His other hand was on his suitcase. "Take my arm," he said quietly.

I did. I could feel his muscles, and they were tensed. "Should I be scared?"

"Do you work better scared?"

"Sadly, yes."

"Then be scared."

I didn't want to think about the fact that Martini was in the lead. Adrenaline wasn't any good for bullet wounds.

Martini turned a corner, then the others did, too. Just as Christopher and I reached it, I heard what sounded like a lot of shouting. And then what sounded like an explosion.

CHAPTER 23

CHRISTOPHER SHOVED ME against the wall and back, the way we'd come. "Stay here."

"Jeff's out front."

Christopher shot patented Glare #5 at me. "And he wants you protected. I'm going to check around the corner. If I get hit or tell you to run, you run."

"I'm not leaving you if you get hurt!"

"Then I can't see if Jeff needs help. You either promise me you'll run if something bad's going on, or I take the assumption we're in trouble and we're out of here together."

"Fine, I promise." I was lying, but they weren't good at telling.

Christopher's eyes narrowed. "I don't believe that for a minute." Damn, he was getting better at it.

We heard more shouts and another explosion. "Okay, fine, just look and be careful." All I wanted to do was run out there and see if Martini was okay or not. None of the others had come back, which scared me to death.

Christopher kept a hold of me and held me against the wall. I didn't have a hope of wrenching out of his grasp. He took a deep breath, ducked down, and looked around the corner. He pulled his head back. "Okay, no idea of what's going on, the room's filled with smoke."

"That's like the opposite of good."

"Your way with words remains unsurpassed."

"Let's go."

"Me, not you. You stay here."

"Why don't I just use you as a shield?"

"Because if I get hit and go down, then you don't have a shield any more." He closed his eyes for a moment. "Kitty . . . I don't want you to get hurt any more than Jeff does." His eyes opened and looked directly into mine. This close up I could see the flecks of blue in them.

Oh, hell, we were back to one of those moments where Christopher and I were at risk of appearing romantically interested again. Or possibly considering being romantically interested again, which was worse. My lusting after Kevin was one thing. Lust toward Christopher was never going to be met with any joy or understanding by Martini.

"Okay, go, I'll stay here."

He nodded and let go of me, a little more slowly than normal. "If I don't come back or call to you, I want you to get out of here, Kitty. You can't help us if you're captured, hurt, or killed."

Great points, all depressing. I nodded, Christopher ducked low, pulled the gun out of his pocket, and moved around the corner. He left his suitcase, but he'd taken the rocket launcher with him.

I did my best to wait patiently, but I didn't hear anything. Okay, I was supposed to run away. But I couldn't. The men I cared about most, other than my father and Chuckie, were all in there, possibly hurt or worse. I doubted my mother would have trotted off and hidden like a rabbit, and I couldn't do that, either.

I got the Glock out, made sure the clip was in, and took the safety off. I hooked my purse over my neck. The suitcases could wait here, but my purse was never leaving my side. I took my shoes off—I could run better without them, and I would make much less noise, as well.

Like Christopher, I ducked low and then turned the corner. The place was filled with smoke, and it was coming toward me. Back to my suitcase and out with my Motley Crue shirt. I wasn't risking an Aerosmith one for this. I wrapped it around the lower half of my face and tied the arms in the back. I undoubtedly looked ridiculous, but it would filter the smoke, and that was all I cared about.

Back to a crouch, back around the corner and through the smoke. No bodies in the rest of the hallway. I reached the doorway, no bodies here, either. So, had they gotten into the room or just been dragged off?

I could hear more shouting. I couldn't tell if the voices were my guys' or not. I also could hear something that sounded like crackling. Well, smoke and fire did go together. But no sprinklers were going off, and neither was a fire alarm. I slid into the room and kept to the back wall, moving against it because the smoke was so thick I couldn't see. I tripped over Tim's body.

My heart stopped, and I knelt down. He was still alive, and from what I could see, appeared unhurt. So he was down from smoke inhalation. I kept on and tripped over Reader a few feet away. Same thing—alive and unconscious.

All the men had been here before. I kept on, hoping that Reader and Tim had been heading for something that would help, like a fire alarm. My shirt was helping, but it wasn't going to be too long before I passed out, too.

A couple more bodies, no one I knew. Couldn't tell if they were A-Cs or not, but they didn't look like the most beautiful things I'd ever seen, so probably human. I moved more quickly. All the humans were heading this way for some reason.

I reached their goal—a fire hose. Great. Only, I had to turn it on and somehow spray it. And I knew without asking that was going to require strength I didn't possess.

However, I also knew that everyone was going to die if I didn't find the means. The three unconscious human males had done most of the work for me—the hose was unrolled and there was a bit of water trickling out, meaning one of them had managed to get the knob started for me. I grabbed the nozzle, turned the water up to full, and braced myself against the wall.

The water came fast, which was a relief. Nothing else was. The hose wanted to move and take me with it. By going into a version of a kung fu horse stance—legs bent, most of my power held in my thighs—to keep my back against the wall, I was able to fight it a bit, but the water pressure ended up sliding me back the way I'd come. This was okay, but I was having a terrible time controlling where the nozzle went, so it was waving wildly through the air.

I was able to jump the humans on the floor I didn't know, but I couldn't keep it up, and I hit Reader and went over. Now on the floor, still holding onto the hose, but I had nothing to brace against or with. I hooked my legs through his and tried to use his body weight as help.

Meanwhile the water was spraying impressively, all over and with no design at all. I sincerely hoped someone, anyone, was still conscious enough to get over to me and give me some help, if that help only covered telling me where to aim the damn thing.

My legs started to slip away from Reader's, and my shifting around to try to hang on meant he got slammed with the water. I moved it fast, now worried I'd drowned him.

I was sliding for real now when I heard coughing, then cursing. "James, are you alive?"

"Girlfriend, are you the reason I'm drenched?"

"Yes. Help me!"

He managed to crawl toward me. Being on the ground meant I had a clearer view, and I could see him catch on to what was happening. Just before I slid away he grabbed the hose and hauled me back.

We stayed on the ground, and Reader pulled me into his lap, locked his legs around my body, and supported my hold on the nozzle. "You know, right now I really wish I was straight. Even though I can't see your face because of whatever it is you're wearing."

"I'm here for you if you ever want to give it a shot. And this is a T-shirt, and it probably saved your life, so I'm not going to apologize for the look. Tim's to our left, and he's out. I have no idea where anyone else we know is, and less idea where the fire's coming from."

"That I can help with." Reader aimed the hose, and then we started laying down a steady stream of water back and forth.

"What happened?" I might was well get the details now.

"Jeff, Kevin, and Paul all made it into this room, then something blew up. I tried to get to the fire hose, but I couldn't. I think whatever exploded had some kind of knockout gas in it."

My fear spiked. "I don't know where Christopher went. But we heard the explosion. Why isn't the fire alarm going or the sprinklers sprinkling?"

"I'm guessing because they want us dead."

Damn, that was my guess, too. "Why didn't I pass out?"

"Maybe your impromptu burka did the trick. Or the gas dissipated due to the smoke. Or something. I'm just grateful for one small favor. And that you never obey anything Jeff or Christopher tell you to do."

"Why change what's been working?" The smoke was starting to clear up, and I could see the flames. We trained the water on them, and they started to die. I could now make out other water, coming from the opposite side of the room.

Out of nowhere, the sprinklers and alarm started at the same time. I didn't know you could be more than drenched, but Reader and I were that much wetter in moments. "There are guys lying facedown," I shouted to Reader.

"I think I can control the hose, you get them turned over."

We disentangled, and while I could tell he was struggling with it, Reader had better control alone than I had. The smoke was lessened enough that I took my shirt off and left it with Reader. Then I moved as fast as I could and got to Tim, moved him into a sitting position and slapped his face. He coughed and came to. "No time, people are lying facedown in water. Get moving!"

He nodded and got to his hands and knees. I helped him up, and he staggered off toward Reader and the men lying that way.

It was undoubtedly wrong of me, but I was looking for my guys, only. I found Kevin first—apparently the humans had been hit faster with whatever it was. I got him turned over—he was still breathing. I was so frightened I didn't even take time to regret there was no need for me to do mouth-to-mouth. I slapped him and, like Tim, he came around.

Same process—got him to his feet and sent him off to

get others out of danger. I tried to figure where my A-Cs would have gone and had to guess straight toward whatever had been blown up. Not that they were idiots, but the hyperspeed would have kicked in, and I knew their first inclination would be to put out the fire.

I found Gower first. He was on his back, but that just meant water was raining down on him. He was breathing, but it was more shallow than the humans' breath had been. I managed to get him sitting up. He was big like Martini, and it was hard to do. His head lolled back against my shoulder. "Paul, come on, wake up." I slapped him. Nothing. I guessed this was really bad, but I knew next to nothing about medicine.

But I knew people who did.

CHAPTER 24

I DUG MY CELL OUT of my purse and made the call.

"Hello?" Lorraine answered on the second ring.

"We're at Code Red. No time, no arguments, no delays. Break necks if you have to. I need you and Claudia at the Kennedy Space Center like ten minutes ago. If there's any way, arrive inside our jet and come in that way." Who knew? Maybe there were minigates installed on the thing. "Bring full medical. I think Paul's dying, and I'm guessing Christopher and Jeff will be worse."

"On it." She hung up, and I waited and prayed.

Lorraine and Claudia were female A-Cs. Like the men, the women were beyond gorgeous, and, to myself, I called them the Dazzlers. Because, young or old, on their worst days they still looked better than I could manage on my best. Lorraine was a buxom blonde a few years younger than me, Claudia was a winsome brunette about my age. I'd tried to hate them but couldn't manage it because they were just so darned nice. They'd become my closest A-C girlfriends during Operation Fugly and were considered a part of my team. They didn't go on a lot of fieldwork, but they were the only female A-Cs authorized to do so, again because of me.

They were dating two of my flyboys, Lieutenant Joe Billings and Captain Randy Muir. Killing big fugly monsters seemed to make for solid romantic relationships.

I was counting in my head. We were at a minute since I'd

called, and Gower's breathing was worse. I wanted to find Martini and Christopher, but I couldn't just leave Gower lying on the ground.

Two minutes, and I heard the sound of running feet. The girls were there, my five pilots with them. All of them had medical cases. A-Cs could move humans at hyperspeed via touch, and we'd learned that as long as the contact was there, one A-C could move several linked humans. Thankfully, the girls had taken the initiative to do so.

Joe and Lorraine took over with Gower, and I raced off, the rest of them with me. Hughes and Walker spotted some folks down to our right. They weren't Christopher or Martini so I didn't care, but those two sheared off to handle them.

We found Christopher next. He was out, facedown. I got him turned over, and he was like Gower—shallow breathing and no response to stimuli. Claudia and Randy started CPR.

"I'm going to find Jeff."

Claudia nodded. "Kitty, more than anything, he'll need the adrenaline."

"Got it." I took off, Jerry with me.

Other people were coming in now, most of them doing what we were, trying to revive the fallen. I couldn't find Martini anywhere, and my panic was going into overdrive.

Jerry grabbed my arm. "There!" He'd spotted some bodies that were very near where the flames had come from.

We ran. I couldn't remember running faster even during a championship race. Martini was facedown, and he was hurt, I could tell. He was on top of another man, also facedown and hurt. It was clear from what I could see of the wreckage that Martini had taken the brunt of the hit in order to protect the other man.

I moved Martini carefully. He was still alive, but barely. Jerry moved the other man. "Jeff's dad works here?"

"Yeah, why?" I looked over. Even hurt, the resemblance was clear. "Oh, God." Of course Martini would head toward and try to protect his father. I couldn't guess which one of them had been the target, might have been both.

"His dad an empath?" Jerry was all business.

"No, standard A-C."

"Doing CPR, then." Jerry started, and I turned back to Martini.

He was the world's most powerful empath, and that meant he could push himself harder and longer than the other empaths. It also meant that when his empathic synapses burned out and emotional blocks wore down, he crashed harder and faster than the other empaths. And when he crashed, if he went too long without isolation or any other kind of regenerative fluids, he had to have adrenaline. Shot directly into his hearts. Or he'd die.

My hands were shaking, but I forced them to stop. You didn't save someone by panicking. That was for later, when things had calmed down. I dug through my purse and found the harpoon case. Ripped his shirt open. Too scared to consider how hot he looked even unconscious and possibly dying. That meant I was beyond terrified.

I heard Jerry's patient start to come around. One small favor.

I filled the harpoon, kissed Martini on the forehead, and said what I always did against his skin. "I love you, Jeff." Then I plunged it straight into his hearts.

His eyes flew open, and he bellowed. I pulled the harpoon out and got it back into the case. This was hard to do because, as always, he was thrashing, and I had to throw my body on top of his to keep him somewhat under control. I had to get the needle put away—there had been an incident early on when he'd grabbed it while thrashing and had unintentionally almost killed me with it.

Harpoon away, I moved so that I was fully on top of him, my arms and legs trying to keep his still. "Jeff, Jeff, baby, try to calm down." He was still bellowing. This was always awful, and it was worse now because I knew he was hurting himself more. "Jeff, it's Kitty. Try to relax. You're hurt, Jeff, I have to get you to medical."

His eyes were wild, and he was stronger than me at any time, even when he was injured. He flipped us, so he was on top of me. This wasn't good, because he was still thrashing, the floor was hard and very wet, and until the adrenaline wore off a little, he was close to out of his mind from pain and the rush, and he could kill me without realizing it.

Someone pulled Martini off me. Two someones, Jerry and the man I had to figure was Martini, Sr. He looked awful, but not as bad as he had. They managed to get Martini onto his back. I was able to get to my knees and move to his head. "Shhh, Jeff, shhh." I stroked his head and face. "Baby, it's okay, please let it pass." He was still thrashing, but it was slowing. "Jeff, you're okay. Come on back, baby, please."

He blinked, and his eyes started to look less wild. His breathing was labored, not a good sign. I was about to start screaming for medical when Lorraine and Joe ran up. She moved Jerry aside and started doing things to Martini, faster than I could see. Joe held his legs, and Jerry moved around to help Martini, Sr., stand.

"Keep him here," Lorraine snapped. "I'll take care of him in a minute." She looked at me. "How's his back?"

"Bloody." I didn't want to add "horribly mutilated" to that statement, because I was hoping I hadn't seen it correctly in the heat of the moment.

She nodded. "We need to turn him, just on his side." I put Martini's head onto my thighs, and then we moved him. He gave a shout of pain. It sucked, but it brought him fully back.

Lorraine sprayed something on him, and Martini made a hissing sound. I stroked his head while she pulled what looked like a huge amount of shrapnel out of his body. "Jeff, hang on."

He reached up and grabbed my hand. "You were supposed to run away." I could tell his teeth were clenched. Lorraine was busy doing things but at the A-C hyperspeed level, so I couldn't really tell what. Not that I wanted to know. I just wanted it to work.

"And miss the opportunity to ruin another suit? C'mon." I stroked his hair. "Our team's still alive." I hoped.

Lorraine nodded. "Paul's okay, Claudia was doing a good job with Christopher. You already got James and Tim going. Jeff's the worst, by far."

"Kevin's okay, too. Human, works for my mother, he

joined us in Pueblo Caliente," I explained for Lorraine's benefit.

"Our Fed's okay? He need mouth-to-mouth?" Martini's teeth were still clenched, but the sarcasm came through anyway.

"You always come out of this like a jerk, so I'm not going to grace that with a reply." I bent down and kissed his head. "No," I whispered. He squeezed my hand.

Lorraine worked on Martini for what seemed like forever but was probably only fifteen minutes. I couldn't tell, I was too busy trying not to think about what his back could end up looking like. A-Cs healed much faster than humans, and I just prayed this applied to regenerating chunks of flesh.

"Okay," Lorraine said as she sprayed something else onto his back—I had no idea what it was, but it wasn't the same can she'd used at first. "Get Jeff out of these clothes. Leave his pants on, he was only hurt from the waist up, which is truly lucky. Alfred, you lie down."

She and Joe focused on Martini, Sr., while Jerry and I got Martini into a sitting position. I considered how to best get him undressed, then figured the clothes were ruined anyway. I ripped what was left of the back off and then took the fabric off each arm. His skin was burned and bloody, but I could see it repairing itself. There were large patches of something sewn onto his back—they dissolved as the flesh repaired. I had to look away, so I checked his chest. Seemed fine. And arousing. Good, I was heading back to normal.

Martini kissed me. "Thanks for saving us, baby."

I stroked his face. "Any time."

I thought I was going to start to lose it when some men came over. They all looked official and human. "What the hell happened?" one of them, a bulldog of a man, barked at us. "What did you people do?" You people. He was actually trying to blame the A-Cs for this attack.

I snapped. I was already in a crouch and I leaped and tackled him to the ground. "You son of a bitch, what do you *think* happened?" I sat on his torso and started hitting him. "You have no freaking security in this damned building, and you have the nerve to act like this is their fault?"

I was landing some great shots. The men with him might have tried to do something to stop me, but Jerry and Joe had guns trained on them. Which was fine with me, because I wanted to kill this guy.

"Stop! Who the hell are you? Stop hitting me!" He was trying to grab my wrists, but I had his body under control, and my adrenaline was pumped so high I could move faster and hit hard.

Someone's arm went around my waist, and I was lifted into the air. "Stop, baby," Martini said softly. The man started to get up, but Martini slammed him back down with his foot. "I feel like crap, and I'm getting seriously pissed. Who the hell are you, and why don't *you* tell *us* what's going on?"

"He's Fred Turco," Martini, Sr., answered. "He's in charge of Security."

"He sucks at it." I'd given up on making a good impression a bomb ago. Martini flipped me around and put me down carefully, keeping a firm hold on me so I couldn't lunge at Turco again.

Turco got to his feet. "Who the hell are you? I'd like to know so I get your name right on the police report."

"She's Katherine Katt." Kevin was with us. "Her mother's name is Angela Katt. You might have heard of her . . . she's the head of the P.T.C.U. And I'm her second-in-command, Kevin Lewis. Let me say that we're all really unimpressed over at the P.T.C.U. Apparently, any kind of terrorist can get into Kennedy, home grown or from outer space." He looked around. "You can shut off the goddamned water now!" He thundered well. Not up to Martini's standards, but no one could bellow like my man.

The water slowed and stopped. Turco was fuming. "She had no right to attack me."

I tried to get out of Martini's hold. "Let's go, you little jerk!"

"She's a bit upset," Kevin said. "And is reflecting our entire team's feelings about this matter. You're the one who should be worried, Mr. Turco. Because unless you have a great explanation for how this attack on Centaurion personnel happened, I'm going to have you taken to Guantanamo for questioning."

"You can't do that," Turco said, but he sounded unsure.

"Try me." Kevin was almost as intimidating as my mother. If I hadn't been impressed before, I would have been now.

"We don't know," Turco said sullenly. "No alarms went off. One of the workers alerted us to trouble."

"The system must have been tampered with," I told Kevin. "The room was filled with smoke and flames when I got in, and there were no alarms or sprinklers going off. They started after James and I had gotten some of the fire under control. Also, there had to be something else in the bomb—everyone was out too fast for smoke inhalation."

He nodded. "I want this place in lockdown, and I want it locked down as of thirty minutes ago, if you get my drift."

"Then I want a personnel check."

"Your mother may be important, little girl, but you're not. I don't take orders from you," Turco snarled.

Before I could try to leap out of Martini's arms to tackle this guy again, Christopher was there and punched him in the face. Turco went down on his butt, holding his nose. "You talk to her with respect, or I just break your neck." Christopher looked at me. "I told you to run away."

"Jeff already complained about being alive. You too?"

"Let's get this place locked down," Kevin said. "Then I'll be happy to let Centaurion Division do the interrogations."

Turco looked nervous. "No. My people will be interrogated by a human."

Martini let me go. "Great." I walked over to Turco. "I'll be glad to play the role of bad cop. And I have seven men with me who will be happy to play the roles of badder to baddest to oh-my-freaking-lord cop. They're all military and A-C trained, and unlike our brothers from another planet, humans know about and love to torture."

Turco swallowed. "You have no authority to do that."

I pulled out the badge Mom had given me. "Wanna bet?"

I looked at the men who'd come with Turco. "This place, locked down, all personnel and visitor records in my hands within fifteen minutes, or I promise you'll be spending the rest of your miserable lives somewhere in Siberia. We have a lovely exchange program, and they're always thrilled when we send some Americans over instead of asking for them back."

The men took a look at the badge, and then they raced off. I turned back to Turco. "You'll get the fun of interrogation first. Jerry, Joe, pick this creep up."

"Where do you want him, Commander?" Jerry asked.

"Let's take him somewhere very private."

"That won't be necessary," Turco said, trying to regain some authority. "I have an office here."

"You lost your chance to play nicely several minutes ago. In the space of a few hours there have been two murderous attacks on my team. That makes me really irritable." I moved right into his face. "And you know how we women get when we're irritable."

He had some gumption. Either that or he was suicidal. "That time of the month?"

The elbow is the hardest bone in the human body, and I'd taken kung fu for many years and, as I'd told Chuckie, I was seriously training again. I did an elbow slam right under his chin. His head went back, and he went out.

"Can we?" Joe asked.

"Be my guest."

They dropped him on the floor.

Jerry grinned. "I love working for you."

CHAPTER 25

I TOOK A DEEP BREATH, did a quick check to make sure my breasts were still in my top and my top was still in my jacket. Intact but pretty much wrecked. Although the Dulce Science Center seemed to have the best dry cleaners on the planet hidden in there somewhere. Of course, it looked as though it was going to be a long time before I got back home.

Unfortunately, I hadn't put my hair in a ponytail. That should mean I resembled a drowned cat right about now. Oh, well, nothing for it. I put my shoulders back and turned around.

Martini was watching me, arms crossed over his chest, a small smile on his face. He looked close to normal if I could avoid staring at the spot in his chest where the needle had gone in—that was red and already bruising. Christopher was next to him, hands on his hips, surveying the scene. He looked okay, too. The others were there as well now. Gower had his arm around Reader's shoulders, but they both looked fine, Tim as well.

"Okay, so all of Alpha Team's accounted for and alive." I looked to Martini, Sr. He was standing near his son, but not as close as Christopher was. Not a surprise from what I'd picked up, but a disappointment. He was a little shorter than his son, but only by an inch or so. I put my hand out. "I'm Katherine Katt, Mr. Martini. Pleased to meet you."

He looked at my hand but didn't offer his. I could see

out of the corner of my eye, and his whole body had gone tense; Christopher had on Martini's shoulder. Martini, Sr., looked at my face. "We don't shake hands with people we care about . . . or who care about us." He walked over and hugged me.

I thought I was going to faint, but I managed to recover and just hug him back. Martini looked beyond relieved.

We pulled apart. "May I call you Kitty?"

"Sure, Mr. Martini, I'd like that."

He smiled, and I saw Martini's grin. Frankly, I saw Martini's everything—hair, eyes, chin, face, body structure—just a few decades older. Genetics, you had to love it. Martini was going to age incredibly well. "I'd be pleased if you'd call me Alfred. Mr. Martini seems a bit formal."

Well, I didn't call anyone but the Sovereign Pontifex "Mr.," and most of the time White asked me to call him Richard. "Okay, Alfred. Thank you." I knew I'd passed some sort of test, but I wasn't sure if it was the final or merely a pop quiz.

"Thank you for saving us. Again, from what I've heard."

No time like the present. "Jeff saved you, I didn't. If he hadn't blocked you, you'd be dead."

Lorraine nodded and then went behind Martini to check on her main patient.

Alfred, as I now forced myself to think of him, gave me a long, penetrating look. "But you saved Jeffrey. And that matters more to me." I could see Martini—he looked shocked, but he put a bland look on his face as his father turned to him. Alfred reached for him, then stopped. "Lorraine, is he—?"

She nodded again. "I'm so good at this. Yeah, he's fine, or pretty much so."

Alfred hugged his son, tightly. I saw Martini's face and got the impression this didn't happen all that often. Christopher's expression confirmed this as a rarity. Alfred pulled him into the embrace now.

"Well done," Gower whispered in my ear. "And thank you, for more than just saving our lives."

I needed someone to hold me all of a sudden, and I didn't want to break up the Martini family reunion. I turned

to Gower, and he put his arm around me and hugged me.
A-Cs were a lot more in tune with things, even the ones
who weren't empathic. Reader put his arm around me, and
we had our own group hug going.

"I'm seriously talking to Paul about that bi option of
yours," Reader whispered to me. I started to crack up.
Thankfully, I managed to keep from moving into hysterics,
but that was due more to Turco's men racing back with a
lot of paper.

Kevin took over. "We're in the Kennedy Space Center and you bring paper printouts? What year is this,
nineteen-sixty-two?"

"She wanted something in her hand," one of them
panted.

"Fine," I said. "We'll take the paper." I finally took a
calm look around. We were in what looked almost like an
auto shop—concrete floor, lots of hoses, what looked like
oil stains—only bigger and without cars up on hydraulic
lifts. There were a lot of Authorized Personnel signs in evidence, but no offices or even desks; however there was a lot
of equipment, most of which I couldn't identify. Whatever
they did here, it seemed to involve big drums with the various warnings plastered on them.

The fire had started among what looked like a group of
five these drums. They were all charred and melted, what
was left of them, anyway, but unlike the other drums and
equipment, they weren't against the far walls. They were
nearest to a door that said Essential Personnel—not right
next to it, about ten paces away. We were lucky the fire
hadn't spread—clearly there were enough drums around
to have created a fireball. But it hadn't.

I looked at Alfred. He was in the standard-issue Armani
suit, so there was no way he worked in this area normally.
He'd undoubtedly come through that Essential Personnel
door. I turned around. There were other doors, marked for
mechanics, maintenance, and deliveries. There were security cameras trained on every, single one of them.

The path we'd come through was marked Air Arrivals, and it had a little stand, under a sign labeled Security
Check, that was clearly where the persons who verified

who was entering were supposed to be. There were security cameras here, too, but there was no one there, and another look around told me the only people in Security uniforms were the ones who'd come in with Turco. They were all dry.

I filed this all away and got back to the matter at hand. "Paul, I want to keep James with me, but can you and Tim take Chip and Matt and go with Kevin to wherever these guys keep their computers? Please make sure whatever terminals they have are safe to use." Gower nodded. "Oh, and take your special case, too." I had no idea where their invisible rocket launchers were, but I was now firmly on the side of our carrying them with us everywhere.

This team went off with Turco's men. Turco himself was coming around. I resisted the impulse to give him a side blade kick to the head. Claudia and Randy had rounded up everyone's luggage, including what Christopher and I had left in the ramp area. Claudia gave me my shoes, and I kept them in my hand—they were the only part of my outfit not wrecked. My Motley Crue shirt I draped over the handle of my rolling bag. It was black and would probably recover.

"I want to change clothes."

"Brushing your hair wouldn't go amiss, either," Reader offered.

"Wow, trying to remember why I wanted you with me."

Reader took the pack of paper out of my hands. "Because I live for the light reading."

I looked at Alfred. "Is there somewhere I can go and change?"

"There is, but the jet is probably the safest place right now."

"Unless someone tries to blow it up while I'm in there."

"I'll go with you," Martini said. "Can I put a shirt back on?" he asked Lorraine.

"Cotton undershirt only," Lorraine said briskly. Martini glared at her. She glared back. He won. "Fine," she said with an exasperated sigh. "Shirt *over* cotton undershirt, only, *no* jacket, no tie, at least not yet." She gave us both a glare and I found myself wondering how closely related to Christopher she was. "No strenuous physical activity for Jeff for hours. Days would be better."

Martini snorted. "Yeah, tell that to the people trying to kill us. Maybe they'll lay off for a while."

I had to give it to the A-C clothing choices, or, as I thought of them, the Armani Fatigues. The clothes were wet but still managed to look good on everyone. My fly-boys were in Navy uniforms, and they looked pretty decent, too. Basically, I was the only one who looked like crap.

Alfred didn't seem to object to our leaving. "I'll take the rest to my offices," he told Martini. He turned to me. "But what do you want to do about Turco?"

"I suppose killing him is out. Kidding!" I said to the shocked looks. Well, sort of kidding. "Let's keep him with us. I don't trust him." I remembered Karl Smith's last words—I didn't trust anyone. Other than Alfred, at the moment, since I had a hard time buying that he'd tried to kill himself along with his son. Unless Martini's mother was that hard to live with.

Jerry nodded. "Joe and I'll run herd on our little friend, Commander, no worries."

The others left us, Reader carrying Martini's invisible case, and the two of us headed back to the jet. "I've never been here before. Does everyone get the exploding tour?"

Martini managed to chuckle. "Only the lucky ones." He wasn't touching me, and I wondered why. "I just want to be away from anyone else and then I'll happily hold you."

"How—?"

"Empath. Try to keep up."

"Humph." We rounded the ramp's corner, and Martini moved in front of me. "Jeff, I don't think anyone snuck in there."

"I don't want to find out you're wrong."

He had a point, and we continued in single file until we reached the jet. His back looked amazingly good considering how awful it had looked just a short while before. Whatever Lorraine had done was indeed good—there were no more patches, and as I watched, the last of the stitches dissolved. I could tell it was still tender, though. His butt, on the other hand, looked spectacular, so I could reassure myself that much, if not all, was well with the world.

Once in the jet, Martini moved to hyperspeed and

checked everything out. "All clear, including the cache." He closed the hatch after me and locked it.

We went into the bedroom. "Do I need to hook you up to anything?"

"Not if Lorraine didn't tell you to. I feel fine."

"You really suck at the lying."

Martini reached out and pulled me into his arms. I buried my face in his chest, while he stroked my back and kissed my head. I was crashing down from the adrenaline rush and wanted to cry but didn't want to take the time or upset him. "Go ahead, baby," he murmured. "It's okay, I'm here, and it's just us."

"No, I just want to get out of these wet clothes."

He helped me out of my clothes. He made some amorous suggestions, but I could tell that while the mind was willing, the body was weak. Martini looked as though he could use a nap of at least twelve hours.

I changed into clean and, most importantly, dry panties, then got him out of his pants. Controlled the impulses and put him into dry underwear as well. "Let's lie down and rest for a couple of minutes."

Martini managed a weak grin. "Only because I'm sure you're tired."

"Absolutely. It's all about me, Jeff, not you."

He nodded. "I think I need to lie on my stomach."

"No problem." I lay down, head on the pillows. He crawled on top of me, nestled his head between my breasts, heaved a sigh, and was out like a light.

I stroked his head and hair and tried not to worry. Normally the adrenaline didn't wear off for hours. But Martini was now snoring softly. I hadn't seen Lorraine give him anything that would put him out, so he was hurting more than he wanted to admit, which wasn't a surprise.

I knew we had to get up, get dressed, and get back into action. But I didn't want to. No matter how I looked at it—either third time being the charm or three strikes and you were out—we'd been lucky twice, and I didn't know if we were on a streak or had used up all the luck we were going to get.

In the middle of action or not, I fell asleep. We probably would have stayed there for hours, or until someone came to get us, but my phone rang. We both jerked awake, and Martini grumbled, sighed, and moved off me. "At least it's not Mr. My Best Friend." He picked up my purse and looked for my phone. Then he gave up. "I don't know how you find anything in here, ever." He handed the purse to me and sat down on the side of the bed.

I pulled the phone out. "I'm a girl." It had stopped ringing, but the number listed on my cell wasn't one I knew. I dialed it back and they answered on the first ring. "Hello? You tried to reach me, I think?"

I didn't recognize the voice, and it was muffled well enough that I couldn't tell if it was male or female. "Get out of Florida and stay out, or we'll kill you and your boyfriend, too."

CHAPTER 26

WE WERE IN ALFRED'S OFFICE. I was in jeans, my Converse, and an Aerosmith T-shirt. Clearly, I needed the support of my boys. My hair was in a ponytail, and I had a Glock in my purse and one shoved into the back of my pants—with the safety on. Purse loaded with clips, re-filled harpoon materials, and everything else I could think of. Ready for anything.

Martini and I had napped long enough that Alfred had had some food brought in for the team. It was almost one in the afternoon, and though I hadn't eaten since dinner the night before, I wasn't really hungry. I was too busy try-ing to figure out what was going to attack us next.

Turco was, I was happy to note, tied to a chair and seemed unconscious. "What happened?"

Jerry grinned. "He was starting to be a pain. So . . . " He shrugged.

Christopher nodded. "We knocked him out."

"It made eating more pleasant," Claudia added.

"I like the gag in his mouth and the tissues shoved into his ears. Nice touch."

"We don't want him listening in," Reader said. "Think we should put a bag over his head?"

"Plastic, for preference."

"No," Martini said as he finished his sandwich, while I tried to ignore the shocked look on Alfred's face. "I'll mon-itor and let you know if he wakes up."

I wasn't sure that Martini was up to using his empathic skills right now but decided not to argue. He was back in the Armani Fatigues, carrying a jacket. For some reason, the A-C males really liked to work in a full-on suit, and I could tell he was uncomfortable being this casual. He looked great, though—white shirt with the sleeves rolled up and the top couple of buttons open, undershirt just showing, black slacks, black jacket hanging over one arm. Shockingly, looking at him made me want to go back to the jet and not rest.

Sadly, that wasn't an option. Alfred had run the number of my mystery caller, and it had originated in the Space Center. However, it was from a general phone in the reception area, and we couldn't find a witness who'd seen anyone near it.

"How did they get my number?"

"No idea," Martini said. "How many people have it?"

I thought about it. I'd gotten a new phone after Operation Fugly—A-C designed, meaning it survived just fine in all forms of weather and trauma. However, I'd kept the same number I always had. It hadn't seemed like a security breach at the time. "Well, pretty much everyone who knows me. But that would mean my stalker is either a Centaurion operative, a family member, one of my friends from school or work, or someone on Mom's team."

"All unlikely," Martini said.

"But, as we've learned, not impossible." Christopher sounded as upset as I felt.

Jerry looked thoughtful. "It could be someone who works here, without too much trouble."

"How so?"

"There are only so many cellular carriers. If I called up with the right government clearance, I could get a listing of all Katts within minutes. How many Katherine Katts could there be?"

"Probably more than just me—my parents can't be the only ones with a sense of humor."

Jerry grinned. "True, but not that many. And probably not too many living in Pueblo Caliente."

"Yeah, just me, I think."

He shrugged. "So, easy. Look for whoever within the Space Center has the clearance level high enough to get this kind of information out of the cellular companies, and we have either our man or our limited number of options."

"Might have had an underling make the call," Alfred mentioned.

Jerry shrugged again. "We'll still find the person with the access."

"Could be someone lower, who faked the authority," Reader said.

"Yeah, but I think Jerry's on the right track." I took a deep breath. "So, at the risk of sounding like I'm cavalier about living, what are they really trying to keep us away from?"

"What do you mean?" Christopher asked.

"Jeff took a call from Alfred. Everyone went into high risk mode. And from that moment on, something and many someones have been trying to keep us from dealing with whatever it was that put us into action in the first place."

"I called because an unknown entity attached to and infiltrated a craft Michael Gower was in," Alfred supplied. "I'm not sure these things are related."

"I am," Reader and I said in unison.

Martini and Christopher both glared. I laughed. "We're human, we think alike."

Reader grinned. "We're both brilliant, too. That helps. But, seriously, the goal was to find out what happened to the *Valiant*. And we still don't know."

"Let's find out now, before we do anything else."

"I'd like to find out who's trying to kill us," Martini said dryly.

"I really think we'll have a better chance of that if we take care of whatever happened on the *Valiant*."

"I'm already having Paul run a cross-check on all personnel against Club 51, Howard Taft, and Leventhal Reid," Reader said. "He'll call if they find anything. Our favorite Fed's alerted your mother to what's going on."

"Good, I hope she's got some helpful suggestions." I turned back to Alfred. "Is Kennedy's security on vacation or lowered alert status or something?"

He looked shocked. I was causing that a lot. Wondered why and if this was one of the many reasons Martini had tried to keep me away from his parents. "Not that I know of. We brought in all our Security team, even those off duty, once the *Valiant* returned. Security's been here twenty-four-seven since then."

"Huh."

"What're you thinking?" Martini asked me.

"There're a lot of security cameras around, but the head of Canaveral Ops was killed while he was talking to us, and no matter what, you'd have thought a security detail would meet us when we docked."

Alfred looked even more shocked. "You mean there was no checkpoint?"

Martini's eyes narrowed. "No, nothing and no one. We got into the room at about the same time you did."

"I didn't notice," Alfred admitted.

"Because of the explosion, I'm sure," Gower said.

"How close was Alfred to the blast?" I asked.

"Close." Martini's voice was clipped. "I saw a spark, that's why I . . . "

"Ran," I finished for him. "Yeah. I'm not really impressed with Turco's team." The questions I wasn't voicing yet were whether Security had been infiltrated, and, if so, had said infiltration been from outside or inside forces. Karl Smith's warning and murder indicated inside, but we didn't have enough yet to be sure.

Alfred shook his head. "Fred has an impeccable record."

"Not anymore."

Alfred shrugged. "I suppose not."

"How long has he been here?"

"Several years. The last five he's been in charge of Security."

"How many issues have you had like this under his tenure?"

"None. As I said, his record has been excellent."

Interesting. And it begged a new question. "What would it take to undo Canaveral Security to the point where we could disembark without checkpoints, and you all could be blown up and almost killed? Especially since

Security's at full and Canaveral Ops, at the least, knew we were coming."

Alfred considered this for a bit but finally shook his head. "I honestly don't know. Ops didn't alert us to anything, but I can't say if they alerted Security or not. We don't interact with Security all that much, really. They're not here to police the employees but to protect them."

"Supposedly, anyway." I decided to refrain from making more comments about Turco's so-called skills, especially since I wasn't sure yet if he had none or had some really good ones he'd hidden for all the time he'd been here.

Martini jerked. "He's waking up." Sure enough, the object of my disdain started to come around.

"So, do you want to question him?" Alfred asked.

"Yes, but I think we should get more up to date on the astronaut situation."

Alfred looked at Martini, who nodded. He headed out, and we all followed, leaving all our suitcases and paraphernalia behind, other than the medical cases Claudia and Lorraine were carrying. Jerry and Joe untied Turco and dragged him along between them. I was pleased and proud to see that they weren't nice about it at all.

Reader walked next to me. "What do you think's going on?"

"Security breach. But who, why, and how is the question. I have no clue at this point. I've never been here before."

"I haven't been here for this kind of situation. Maybe they had all the Security team focused on the *Valiant*." Reader didn't sound as though he thought this was a legitimate possibility.

"Maybe. Maybe my mom will have a suggestion."

"Don't stop to have sex?" he said with a grin.

"Oh, shut up. We were napping. Only." Martini seemed okay, and Lorraine had given him another A-C physical when we'd returned from the jet, so I wasn't feeling overly worried.

I felt a hand on my neck. It pulled me back and up against a body. "Mine, thanks." Martini massaged my neck while Reader chuckled. "So, what were you two whispering about?"

I put my arm around his waist, and I could feel him relax a bit. "Security issues. Mostly. Relax, Jeff. Stress isn't good for you right now."

"Huh." He kept his arm around my shoulders, and I leaned my head against him.

We wandered through the Space Center. It looked very much like what I'd seen in movies, both fictional and documentaries in school. I tried to take it all in, but other than looking for snipers, I couldn't. We were too rushed and in too much danger for me to pay attention to things that weren't trying to kill us.

"Are we going to see Paul's brother?"

"Probably." Martini sighed. "Yeah, I know what you want. James, tell Paul where we're headed and see if he wants to join us."

Reader nodded and closed his cell. "Already taken care of. He's meeting us at the quarantine area." He fell back and walked next to us. "We've got a handful of people with enough authority to have found your cell number. Kevin's got some of the P.T.C.U. team running the cross-checks, and Paul has the gang at Home Base doing the same. We should know something soon."

"Where are our possible suspects?"

"All personnel have been moved to the Mission Control Center. It's the only place big enough to hold everyone where we don't have to leave this main building."

I could get behind that. However, we weren't headed to Mission Control yet. "Who's riding herd on them?"

"Kevin and the rest of that group are. Only Paul's meeting us at quarantine."

"That means Paul will be alone."

"According to the men with them, all personnel are in the Control Center, other than those heading there with Kevin and our pal Turco."

"I don't like it, but okay." I didn't like it. Karl Smith had been very clear right before he died—alone. "Where's Smith's body?"

"Dad," Martini called. "Where's the corpse?"

Alfred stopped and waited for us to reach him. "Near quarantine, why?"

"I was the last person he spoke to before he died. I'd like to see him." Not that I relished the idea of looking at a cadaver, but maybe he had a clue to what was going on somewhere on his person.

Alfred gave me a look that said I was an odd girl. "Okay, we can see the body first, if you want."

"I don't want Paul alone any longer than necessary."

"Tell us where he's at, we'll trot on ahead," Jerry offered. "Me, Joe, Turco here, and Lorraine. That should be enough to keep Paul company."

My humans would have an A-C with them for fast exits, so that sounded like a workable plan. "Okay, be on the phone fast if you run into trouble."

"We will," Lorraine said. "I wish I'd brought some walkies."

"Bringing medical and the boys was more important."

She laughed. "The boys were haunting me and Claudia in case you called. Not bringing them would have been a delay."

"As always, I like how you think."

We continued on down some corridors that started to make me wonder if we'd find a big piece of cheese at the end. Then we hit a T-intersection, and Jerry's team went left while the rest of us went right.

We came to a heavy door. Alfred unlocked it and ushered us inside. The room was dark and very cold. "We use this for the big mainframes," he said. "It's cold enough to keep a human body fresh. We didn't have time to call for an ambulance."

"You had an hour or more."

"We didn't have an answer for the police," Alfred explained. "Security said they'd handle it but wanted the body here until they'd done whatever it is they do in this situation." My impression of Turco went down another notch.

He turned on the lights. I looked around the room. "Lots of big machines, lots of floor space. Strangely enough, no dead body, unless it's hiding inside the big computer boxes."

CHAPTER 27

"WE PUT HIM HERE!" Alfred shouted as he pointed to a table devoid of anything corpselike on it. Nice to see that the bellowing ran in the family. Martini was still better, but perhaps his father wasn't trying all that hard.

"Then either he wasn't dead or someone took him away."

"Thanks for stating the obvious." Christopher's snark was fully on.

"Believe me," Alfred said. "He was dead."

Martini sighed. "Let's search the room."

The four A-Cs moved at hyperspeed. Reader, Randy, and I just stood there. I mean, why bother? We'd get to the table, and they'd have the room done.

Claudia finished, or at least slowed down to human, first. "There are traces of blood on the table, but I think there was more and it was cleaned up." She was examining the slab and the floor underneath it.

"Nothing else." Martini sounded frustrated. I could relate. "Why take the body?"

"Are you sure someone didn't call for an ambulance?"

Reader pulled out his phone and dialed. "Hey Paul, you still alive and unscathed? Great, you know how Kitty worries. No, I'm not calling just because I miss you, get over yourself. I'm actually calling because the Space Center's lost our favorite dead body, and I'm wondering if you can ask the little Napoleon if he authorized the body to be moved or taken away."

Significant pause while Reader looked bored. "He's sure? Uh-huh, yeah, he's a jerk, I wish Jeff had let her beat the crap out of him. Okay, well, tell him we're less impressed with his security team than we were before, if such is possible. See you soon." He hung up. "No one authorized the body being moved. Turco is accusing all the A-Cs of stealing the body and forming a conspiracy to, somehow, blow themselves up."

"I should have let her kill him, you're right," Martini sighed. "Now what?"

"Did you all check the floors?"

"Why?" Christopher sounded annoyed.

"Things drop. In the movies the heroes always find something important when they look under stuff." This was true, I'd seen it a million times.

"How is it you're the head of Airborne?" Christopher asked.

"I was made a Commander after one week. It took you, what, like five or more years? Maybe I should be asking you that question." I loved tossing this one at both Christopher and Martini, it was so fun to see the pretty colors that went across their faces.

"She's right, all the movies agree, search under stuff." Reader grinned. "Not me, mind you, but someone should."

"I'll do it." I was in jeans, after all. I dropped to my hands and knees and started hunting around.

"If my father weren't standing right here, I'd mention that you look really sexy." I didn't have to see Martini's face to know he was grinning.

"You mention these things in front of the Pontifex. I'm sure saying them in front of your dad isn't going to cramp your style."

"You talk like that in front of your Uncle Richard?" Alfred sounded shocked.

"My father's used to it," Christopher said quickly. "He doesn't mind."

"I'll bet he does and just doesn't say anything."

"Yeah, I get written up weekly." Martini had his sarcasm turned up to full.

I got the impression I probably needed to hurry it up. I risked a quick look over my shoulder and revised my opinion. "Actually, Richard doesn't mind. And I don't either. And, if I take the expression on your face where Jeff can't see it to be accurate, Alfred, you don't mind all that much, either. Jeff's thirty years old, and I'm twenty-seven. I think you can stop pretending he's fifteen."

Alfred grinned. "But where's the fun in that?"

I shook my head. "Like father, like son." I went back to my search.

"You know, it's not funny," Martini said quietly.

"You always react, it's hilarious." Alfred was chuckling. "It's so easy to get both you boys going."

"We have enough stress," Christopher muttered.

Claudia was suddenly on the ground next to me. "I don't want to get pulled into the bickering," she whispered. "What are we looking for?"

"Anything that doesn't belong here."

"You know, I think the girls should do a thorough search," Randy drawled. "Take your time, really."

"Randy, not funny," Claudia snapped.

"No, honey, I've never considered you on your hands and knees to be funny." Oh, good, everyone was getting into the act.

"I'm gay and it looks good, so you can't blame the straight guys for enjoying the show." Of course Reader was going to add in; he lived to function as comic relief.

I was determined to find something now. Either that or get everyone else out of the room and let Martini have some fun.

"Oh, love that idea," he called to me. Damn, it was so hard to hide anything from him, particularly lust.

Claudia and I weren't having any luck, but I didn't want to give up. One of the mainframe boxes was a little higher up off the floor than the others. I tried to slide my hand under it and ran into a problem. "Uh, Jeff? A little help?"

"What do you need?" I could tell he was standing over me, but I couldn't look up.

"My arm's stuck."

The snickers started immediately. The only saving grace was that Tim wasn't in the room with us.

Martini managed to lift the thing while laughing. I pulled my arm out. It was covered with blood. Martini stopped laughing immediately. "Don't move. Claudia!"

"It's not my blood."

Christopher grabbed the other side of the computer while Reader helped me up. Claudia washed my arm off. "Kitty's right, Jeff. She's not cut anywhere."

They put the computer back down. "Open it," Alfred said quietly.

"Where?" Christopher ran his hands over it. "There's not a door."

I thought about it, went to the front, and hit it with my fist. It popped open. And a body fell right on me.

I stumbled back, fortunately into Martini. The body was heavy, and it would have taken me to the floor otherwise. The only reason I wasn't screaming was because I'd expected a body to be in there. It just hadn't occurred to me that Martini lifting the thing would have shifted the corpse around.

Aliens were strange. When faced with something incredible or horrible, something that would make the average human start shrieking like a howler monkey, they didn't scream or shout or run around. To a person, they shut up and thought. Randy, Reader, and I, however, were humans. But Reader had been working as an agent for a few years, and Randy was military trained. They were doing what humans who refuse to panic do—making phone calls.

That left me to keep the human side represented. "Jeff? Get this thing off of me!"

"Huh? Oh, sorry, baby." He reached around and pulled it off me, so I was no longer the middle of a Martini and dead body sandwich.

Christopher grabbed it, and they laid it back onto the table.

"You okay?" Alfred asked me.

"I plan to have hysterics and throw up later, but right now isn't good for me, so I'm going to hold off." I checked—no blood on my Aerosmith shirt. Okay, all was well. I took another look at the body. "Is that Karl Smith? Because, somehow, I'd expected him to look different. You know, like he was a man."

CHAPTER 28

READER WAS ON THE PHONE with Gower. "Yes. Yes, we have a dead body, but not 'the' dead body. This one is an older woman who, uh, never went hungry. No, Alfred has no idea of who she is. I think she's maintenance, most likely Cuban. No, not shot. Throat slashed. Yeah, it's gross. We found her because Kitty was crawling around on the floor. Because it's Kitty. Seriously. She was looking for clues. Yes. Right. Yes, clues for where Smith's body went. No, we have no guess on that still."

He looked over to me. "Paul wants to know if you want Kevin and the others to meet up at quarantine."

"No, but make sure they all stay together wherever they're at. And watch their backs. Make sure no one pushes any Mission Control buttons. Oh, and Paul should keep Lorraine in the center over there."

Reader rolled his eyes at me but repeated my instructions. "Um, you know, that's just wrong. Yes, we're a little freaked out. Look, people are dropping like flies around here. Don't let anyone wander alone. Yes, of course I mean you, too. Where the hell would you wander, anyway? You're at the spot we're all heading to. No, I think I speak for everyone here when I say we all hate this trip. Yes. See you shortly."

Randy and Christopher had checked all the other mainframes—they were all real computers.

"So, do we lock up and hope the body snatchers don't come back for her?"

"I don't want to leave anyone alone in here," Martini said.

"Is it always this exciting at Kennedy? I mean, murders, bombs, total chaos?"

"Normally, no," Alfred answered.

A thought tickled. "Um . . . how long have the astronauts been back?"

"A day. I called Jeffrey as soon as we realized we had no idea of what had hit them."

I looked at Martini. "It could be related."

He shrugged. "Or not. But, yeah, let's go find out. We'll lock the doors and see if our latest corpse is here when we get back."

We put this plan into action and then followed Alfred to our next destination. We all stayed close together. Martini kept his arm around me, and I noted Randy doing the same with Claudia. Christopher had Reader right next to him, I assumed in case we had to run at hyperspeed.

"Glad we all like each other."

Martini managed a chuckle. "Yeah. This is getting bizarre."

"I think we left bizarre hours ago. You think the cleaning woman interrupted them when they were stealing Karl's body?"

"Possibly. I'm more concerned with why there's a fake computer down there."

"Maybe they use it a lot."

"Dad, why is there a fake computer in that room?"

"No idea, Jeffrey. I don't spend much time there, ever. Before today, I'd have told you we didn't have homicidal maniacs running around, so my information's not worth much. First time I've had to deal with two dead bodies in a day for a long time."

"Do the A-Cs go to that room a lot?" I was trying to come up with something, but my Agatha Christie didn't appear to be working. I was a lot better with the motivations of parasitic superbeings and psychos, apparently. Then again, it seemed as though we had at least one, maybe many more, psychos running around here, so maybe I'd hit on something soon.

"No. Most of us don't work with the computers, at least not in terms of maintenance."

"Why do you have a key?"

Alfred shot me a look over his shoulder. I saw Martini's "you're annoying but cute so I'll answer" look. I'd been told that Martini looked like his father, but no one had mentioned the similar personalities. "I'm the highest ranking A-C at this facility. I have a key to everything."

Authority ran in the family, and I had to admit this wasn't too much of a surprise—Martini had indicated his father was essentially the head of the scientific stuff. "So you were the target for the bomb."

"I don't think so. It didn't go off until you all arrived."

"No, it didn't go off until Jeff arrived." I clutched Target No. 2's waist. "The bomb was closest to you two." My mystery caller's words rang in my head. "Oh, not again."

"Not again what?" Martini sounded confused.

"We have two freaking plans going at the same damn time again." Why couldn't the homicidal psychopaths and world conquering megalomaniacs take turns?

"Why so?"

"The caller said they'd kill me and my boyfriend unless I left the state. But we've had two attacks that were trying to kill all of us, you and your father specifically in the last one. I wasn't the target, you were." Oh, I hated where this line of reasoning was taking me. "So, for whatever reason, those running Plan A want the Martini men dead."

"Fine, that seems at least a workable hypothesis."

"Why would they want to kill me and Jeffrey?" Alfred sounded far less convinced.

"Maybe they think Jeff can do whatever it is you do here. Or that he will do whatever it is you would do here." This sounded lamer said aloud than in my head.

Strangely enough, my most confusing statements seemed to make the most sense to Alfred. He nodded his head. "Okay, that I could see." Really? I hoped he'd explain it to me, I was confusing myself.

"Great. So, Plan A is to get rid of the Martinis, and I'd

guess that all the others on Alpha Team are targets, too. But Plan B isn't the same thing. Whoever called me wants me to leave, and take Jeff with me, but they aren't in on whatever Plan A is, because they didn't say 'leave or we kill all your friends' or 'leave or we kill all the A-Cs.' "

"Who did you piss off, girlfriend?" Reader asked.

"The list is so long," Christopher said. "Really, do we have all day to go through potential suspects?"

"I'm ignoring you." Besides, I didn't have a suitable comeback. "I think we need to figure out who wants to kill Alpha Team and Alfred, and why." Something niggled. "Alfred? Do you know Leventhal Reid? He's one of the House Representatives from Florida."

He nodded. "Somewhat. He's not a particularly friendly man, but he's been here before, always on House business of some kind."

"What does he look at? What kinds of questions does he ask?"

"He's never here alone." Alfred chuckled. "There are a variety of subcommittees whose work affects or is affected by what we do here. Those committee members come for arranged visits. It's a formal, and standard, process."

"How often?"

Alfred shrugged. "Probably twice a year. Sometimes more, depending on what's going on. Sometimes we have several visits in a row, because different subcommittees are here and they all have different and not always interrelated questions."

"How many people know you're all here?"

"Not as many as it seems."

"It seems like everyone."

Alfred shook his head. "The politicians don't all know that we're . . . different. American Centaurion is considered a U.S. territory, if you will, similar to Puerto Rico. That's how most know us."

"Layers of security and need-to-know," Martini added. "Ranked like all other Military Intelligence. I know you have briefing papers about it. You got them the day you were confirmed as the Head of Airborne."

Reader snorted. "Jeff, you seriously think she ever read

them? I'd bet cash money she didn't even look at them. I'd bet more money she dumped them somewhere, probably in my room with a note saying, 'Give me the high level view.' I'll look when we're finally home."

I shot Reader my most derisive look. He didn't seem fazed. "I've looked at them." Briefly. They were long and boring, from the little I'd skimmed. "And I didn't give them to you, James." I even knew where they were. Bottom right dresser drawer in my bedroom in the Lair. All neatly stacked and waiting for me to have the time, and interest, to send myself to Civics: American Centaurion class. So far, I was missing all the lectures, but I planned to cram and ace the final somehow.

Decided I didn't want Martini fully aware that I hadn't read anything and so was, by A-C standards, asking stupid questions. "So, Alfred, does Reid come every time?"

"Yes. He's involved in many of the subcommittees that have an interest in us. Not all of them, mind you."

"How many years?"

Alfred pursed his lips. "Oh, call it ten or twelve."

"Has Turco been around that long?"

"No. He came on sometime after Representative Reid started visiting. I doubt the Representative is involved. He's not the only politician who's here on a regular basis. We have some Congressmen and -women who are here even more than Representative Reid. And I doubt any of them are trying to harm us or what we're doing here."

I managed to hold the snide comment in. This was Martini's father, after all. Plus, the A-Cs weren't really trained to look at humans as their enemies—even when they were. In the past few months, I'd come to realize the view the majority of A-Cs held was that they were here to protect and defend the Earth from the parasites, and if they could help in other ways, well then they were going to. They felt they owed it to their adopted homeland, even the purists who still hoped to go back to Alpha Centauri one day.

Despite having to deal with Earth governments and all the related bureaus and divisions those dragged with them, the A-Cs seemed remarkably naïve when it came to how low down and dirty humans could be. Maybe it was because they seemed unable to lie that they believed humans were the same way.

But we weren't, and I knew in my gut that whoever was behind Plan A was a human. The question of the moment was whether Turco was in on whatever was going down or if he was being manipulated. It was hard to judge with limited time with him, and I didn't want my personal dislike to cloud my judgment.

Then again, Martini felt my female intuition was normally right, and my mother felt listening to my gut was better in some cases than rational thought. My gut really wanted to kick Turco's face in.

We reached the others outside of quarantine before I could come up with a decision on what Turco's game was. We brought everyone up to speed on the bodies and my current theories. Thankfully, Gower was on my side. "I don't think Plan B's in effect yet," he said. "I'd guess the threat was the start."

"I'll stay alert." The threat to the A-Cs seemed a lot better planned and certainly more focused on effective mayhem. "Let's go see the astronauts."

"We can't all go in there," Alfred said. "They're under quarantine for a reason. You can monitor them from the medical observation lab."

"Can we talk to them from there?"

"Not usually." Alfred looked uncomfortable. "It's for observation. We can listen in from the lab, but they can't hear us. They have terminals they can use to type requests and so forth with."

"What are they saying or requesting?"

"They're saying nothing's wrong and are requesting to leave quarantine."

"Are they sick?" I hoped not; we were talking about Gower's brother.

"Not that we can tell, and they say they feel normal. But we identified a living entity that hit and entered the ship, and we can't find it now."

"We're all trained to kill superbeings." I felt I was stating the obvious, but who knew what Alfred really thought we did all day.

"None of them have manifested." Alfred sounded like I was testing his patience. Well, he wouldn't be the first man, A-C, or Martini I'd done that to.

"Maybe they're lying in wait."

"Maybe you should go to the lab and observe."

"Isn't someone in there, observing right now?"

Alfred sighed. "No. You insisted on everyone being herded into one place. That included the observation team."

Good point. "Everyone other than the astronauts."

He nodded. "Yes, they're still in quarantine. Because we don't know what's going on." Alfred indicated another hallway. "Let's go to the lab."

I looked pointedly at the door in front of us. It said "Quarantine." "Let's go in here instead and observe them in person."

"I don't think that's a good idea," Alfred said sternly. Really, it wasn't intimidating. The Pontifex tried stern on me all the time, so did Martini and Christopher, with limited to no results. The only one who successfully pulled off stern with consequences was my mother. And I knew she'd tell me to go through that door.

"Dad, accept that Kitty's going in there and save us all some pain." Martini had his Commander voice on. "Paul's going too. So are Christopher and I. And, before the protests start, guess what? We're in a Field situation."

Alfred gave Martini a long look. "Pulling rank, son?"

"I don't have to pull it."

Alfred nodded slowly. "True enough." He unlocked the door. "You know you're at risk for whatever they have?"

"We're at risk every damn day." Martini sounded bored. "You want us wearing gas masks?"

"No, I suppose not." Alfred sighed. "We'll monitor you from the observation lab. Just be careful. We really have no idea if anything's wrong or not."

"At this point, we don't know if they're alive, either." I had to say it. "It's a great way to get rid of someone—throw them into quarantine, and then you can kill them while everyone else is running the other way." Everyone stared at me. "What?"

"Why would you think someone wants to kill the astronauts?" Gower asked.

"Why did someone kill Karl Smith? Or the presumed cleaning lady? Or try to blow you all to smithereens? I have no freaking idea. The only answer I have is that the lunatics from Club 51 did their best to ensure we'd blow up before we got here. Otherwise, all we have to go on is Smith's warning, which was that every A-C was in mortal peril and Centaurion Division as a whole was in jeopardy. Since I know we have an A-C in quarantine, I just sort of figure that he's in as much danger as everyone else."

"I hate it when you point out things like this," Martini said.

"Why?"

"Because you're so frequently right."

CHAPTER 29

THE FOUR OF US WALKED down the long corridor Alfred had told us led to the main quarantine area. The men were walking so quickly I almost had to trot to keep up. Not that I could blame them.

The astronauts were in different, but adjacent, cells. Each door had thick glass on the top, presumably so observation would be easy. We got to Michael Gower's first. He was a slightly smaller version of his older brother and looked bored out of his mind when we reached his door.

Gower hit the intercom. "Michael, are you okay?"

Michael looked over and gave Gower a huge smile. "Paul! Man, am I glad to see you." He came over to the door. "Hey, Christopher, Jeff. And . . . who's this?" His voice dropped down a bit and I got a different smile. I got the distinct impression that, unlike his older brother, Michael was not gay in any way.

"Katherine Katt," Gower said. "She goes by Kitty."

Michael's smile got wider and more seductive. "Kitty Katt, huh? Great name."

"She's not a stripper," Martini snapped. He also put his arm around my shoulders.

Michael chuckled. "Staked your claim already, Jeff?"

"Five months ago." Martini sounded really annoyed. And jealous. I tried not to be flattered and failed.

I cleared my throat. "So, Michael, what happened to lock you and your crew up?"

He shook his head. "Damned if we know. Something hit the *Valiant*. We thought it was just space debris. But the sensors showed it as a living thing. Believe me, I was ready to fight off a parasite. But nothing happened. Mission Control had us come back."

"You landed back right where you took off, though."

"Did we?" He looked confused. "I don't remember that." He laughed. "Besides, that's impossible."

"You did it," Gower said flatly. "I saw the video."

"You don't remember?" This was worrying.

"No. It got jumbled there for a bit, once we were hit and then nothing happened."

"Do you remember landing?"

Michael nodded. "Yeah. It was just like we were in a simulator."

I felt a niggling suspicion. "Let's talk to the other astronauts."

"Will we be out of here soon?" Michael sounded bored again. "I'm sick of being in the zoo."

"Who else has come by?" Christopher asked.

Michael shook his head. "Seems like everyone. Been a steady stream of people. No one asked questions, they just came and looked at us through the glass and left. Wouldn't talk to us, either."

We moved to the next room. "Something's really wrong," I said as softly as I could.

"Very." Gower was talking in a low voice, too. "The only people coming through were medical, according to all the security logs."

"Maybe he got hit on the head."

"Maybe." Gower didn't sound convinced, but then, neither was I.

We reached the next cell, to find this astronaut asleep. We knocked on the glass, and he roused up. "Who's there?"

"I'm Michael Gower's brother, Paul."

"I'm Daniel Chee. Nice to have a visitor who'll talk to me."

"Have you seen a lot of people?"

Chee came to the door. "Oh, there're four of you. All talking?"

"Yes," Martini and Christopher said together.

"Nice. And, yeah, lots of people have been by. None of them talked to us. We're all tired of it by now."

We ran through the whole hit by space debris and landed impossibly with Chee. His story was like Michael's, though he didn't have the parasitic superbeing worry. He'd been afraid their hull had been breached.

We went to visit astronaut number three. "This is getting freakier by the minute. Who was here, if the records don't show anyone?"

"That they can't remember the landing worries me more," Gower said.

We reached the third door to find this occupant pacing. I knocked on the glass. "Hi, you okay in there?"

He spun and stared at us. "Kitty?" His eyes opened wide. "Kitty, is that you?"

"Um . . . yes." I had no idea who he was. To my knowledge, I didn't know an astronaut. He was about Christopher's height and build, with straight black hair and bright blue eyes. The thought that he was Black Irish crossed my mind, but I didn't know why. He was cute, not A-C gorgeous, not Reader cover-boy material, but normally cute, a guy all your friends would think was a catch in the looks department.

He came over to the door. "I can't believe it. What are you doing here?"

"Um . . . investigating?" Close up he looked vaguely familiar.

He smiled, and I had to admit it was a good smile. Not up to Martini's standards, but still, attractive. It reminded me of something. "I wasn't expecting to see you for another couple of weeks." I heard Christopher whispering urgently to Martini.

"Um . . . yes. Well. Uh. . . . " I gave up. "I'm really sorry, but, who are you?"

He looked shocked. But it was Christopher who answered. "Brian Dwyer. Your old boyfriend from high school."

CHAPTER 30

CHRISTOPHER WAS THE STRONGEST imageer on the planet. During Operation Fugly, when Christopher was scoping out my place and, as it turned out, me, he'd spent a lot of time with the pictures I'd had on display. One of which was of me and Brian at my sixteenth birthday party, doing a wild version of the tango.

That Christopher was able to recognize Brian after seeing only one picture of him taken eleven years prior and I couldn't recognize the guy I'd lost my virginity to without help said a lot about Christopher's skills as an imageer and Martini's as a sexual impresario.

That Brian recognized my voice after ten years was both impressive and confusing. I didn't have to look at him to know Martini had no love for Brian in his expression. I was willing to bet Christopher didn't, either.

But Brian was only looking at me. "C'mon, Kitty, I don't look that different."

He didn't, but he also didn't look seventeen any more. Or sound it. "Your voice is a lot deeper." I had nothing else, and at least it sounded better than saying I hadn't thought about him for a long while.

Brian grinned. "Yeah, and I'm taller, and, spoken modestly, God love me, more muscular." He was indeed. The rhythms of his speech were starting to come back to me.

"I had no idea you were an astronaut." Totally true. To say that my interest in space and the things related to it had only been piqued about five months ago was an under-statement. I hadn't been ignorant, but I hadn't been overly curious, either.

"You still in marketing?"

Okay, heading into creepy time. "How did you know I was in marketing?" I hadn't had any clear idea of what to major in when we were in high school and had changed my mind three times before I had to declare a major. I finally settled on Business because that's what Chuckie was going for, and that way we'd have a lot of classes together. I'd fallen into marketing as a career, based more on what company had hired me right out of college as opposed to burning desire, so it wasn't as though it had been a lifelong dream.

"I still talk to Sheila." One of my two best girlfriends in high school. Married with three kids and living on the East Coast. We were down to the holiday newsletter on her end and the occasional postcard on mine, along with some semi-regular text messaging that had dribbled down to almost nothing in the past five months—I liked lying to Sheila only a little more than I liked lying to Chuckie. But she'd certainly known what I was doing for a living, at least, six months ago.

"Oh." I had nothing much to add to the conversation, other than shock. "Um, well, before we reminisce, we're here to check on you."

"Why? I mean, why you? I can guess the guys with you are here officially."

I was in jeans and a concert T-shirt. I couldn't have looked less official if I were wearing a tutu. "I'm with them."

"They're here to do a marketing campaign?"

"No, I'm Michael's brother." Thank God, Gower was taking an active part.

"Oh." Brian looked at all of the men again. "You're all . . . from Michael's part of town?"

"Brian? I'm *with* them. As in with-with." I didn't remember him being this dim. Then again, I didn't remember him being smart enough to be an astronaut. I was having trouble coming up with what I did remember.

"Ah. Do you do their marketing or something?" He was really hooked onto the marketing.

"No. Brian, we need to ask you about the flight, okay?"

"Sure. I'm sorry. I'm just . . . well, shocked to see you here. I've been thinking about you a lot recently."

"*If* we could get on with it," Martini snapped.

"Sure, sorry. What did you guys want to know?"

While Gower did the questioning, I ran over what I could manage to remember about Brian. Funny, I couldn't remember a lot. We'd dated for over a year. He'd been a great dancer. Had a wicked sense of humor. Was really proud of being Black Irish. We were on the track team together, though he was a distance runner. That was how we'd met, because I sucked at distance and was always getting left behind in the desert. He stayed with me, every time, so I wouldn't be out there alone.

I'd thought I was in love with him, and I probably was at sixteen. He'd been gentle in bed—getting my virginity hadn't been a conquest for him, it had been an honor. My parents had really liked him. And he hadn't wanted to break up with me.

I couldn't remember why we'd broken up. All I could scrape up was the memory that I'd been the one who made the decision and he hadn't liked it. But we'd remained friendly through graduation. On grad night, he'd told me something, but damned if I could remember what it was.

Brian's answers were the same as the other astronauts, though. Something hit the ship, his worry was mechanical failure, and then they landed. Memory of landing fuzzy at best, a parade of people had come by who hadn't spoken to him or the others.

"Kitty, can you get us out of here? None of us are sick, and we're all tired of being on display."

"I'll do my best." I had no idea if they were all having a mass hallucination or if there was a worse breach in Kennedy security than we'd already discovered.

"You have to get them to let me out in time for the reunion." He grinned. "I actually want to go. It's nice to have accomplished something in ten years."

"You're going to the reunion? Gosh, so are we." Martini put his hand on my shoulder. "See you there." Then he dragged me off.

"Jeff, why did you do that?" I heard Gower making some kind of general promise to try to get them out of quarantine as we passed the other two astronauts, both of whom looked bored and desperate for us to stay.

"Your boyfriend was bugging me."

"Jeff, he's not my boyfriend, you are." I stopped dead. "Oh, wow."

"What?"

I pulled out of his hand and ran back to Brian's cell. "Bri? Do you have an office here?"

"Yeah, sort of. Why?"

"By any chance, do you have a picture of me up in it?"

He looked sheepish. "Yeah, I do." He looked down. "I just haven't. . . . " He looked back at me. "I haven't found anyone I cared about like you. So I keep your picture up, sort of as a reminder of what I'm looking for."

Sweet. On the stalker side of the house, but still sweet. Considering Martini had essentially proposed to me within thirty minutes of knowing me, also not a reason to go "ick." Maybe I just attracted the overly committed, stalker types.

"Have you mentioned the reunion to anyone?"

"A few people, sure. I didn't have the nerve to check to see if you were going, but I was hoping you were. Who is that guy?"

"My boyfriend."

"Oh. Not engaged?"

"No." Not yet. Not ever, if the A-C elders had their way.

"You know he's . . . "

"An alien?" Brian nodded. "Yeah, the double heartbeats gave it away early on. Look, Brian, someone's threatened to kill me if I don't leave Florida. Do you have someone, male or female, who's crushing on you a bit more than would be normal?" I managed not to make a comparison to how Brian was apparently crushing on me, but it took effort.

He seemed to give this some thought. "Not really. I mean, I haven't dated anyone I work with."

"Have you dated anyone in the Space Center?"

"Sure, a few gals. But, they didn't work out."

"Who dumped who?"

He laughed. "Most of them dumped me. I think they didn't like my doing Kitty comparisons."

"Wow, who could see that one coming? Did you dump any of them?"

"Sure, but the ones I did are all in relationships now."

"How about someone you wouldn't think of dating but who might like you?"

"Maybe. I don't know. I just want out of this cell. You're sure someone threatened to kill you?"

"Yeah, me and my boyfriend."

"He looks like he could handle a fight."

"He can. But I don't think they're threatening him. I think they're threatening you."

CHAPTER 31

BRIAN'S JAW DROPPED. "But . . . I'm not your boyfriend. Anymore." I heard the regret but chose to ignore it.

"Right, but, you know, people who threaten other people's lives are not always the most stable Weeble in the playhouse. It's not like there's no precedent for it, either."

"True." He closed his eyes. "I just want to get out of here." He opened his eyes, and I saw them widen. "Look behind you."

I did. Nothing. "Nothing." I looked down the hall—Gower, Christopher, and Martini were still there, all looking various stages of annoyed through to furious.

"They're here again," Brian said in a low voice. "Can't you see all the people?"

I looked around again and tossed what I hoped was an emotional clue to Martini. Considering he was next to me before I could blink, I figured he'd caught it. "What's wrong?" He put his arm around me and pulled me close to him. Brian's eyes narrowed. Great, now wasn't the time for the stag fight.

"Brian sees the people. Can you see if Daniel and Michael do, too?"

Martini looked around. "Sure." He moved off, and I heard him talking to the others. Gower and Christopher joined him.

"There's no one here that we can see," I explained to

Brian. "Maybe whatever hit the capsule is giving you hallucinations."

He shook his head. "They're real. I can see them. Get away from her!" he shouted at something.

Martini was back next to me in an instant. "The other astronauts see them, none of us do. What're you panicking about?" he asked Brian.

"They're trying to get Kitty!" Brian sounded close to hysterical.

It was unlikely to work, and I had no idea if there were any invisible beings there anyway, but since I'd had success using this method with other evil beings from space, I figured what the hell. I dug into my purse, pulled out my hairspray, and sent a stream of it around me and Martini, making sure to not get it in his face.

Martini coughed. "Why?"

"Just in case."

"It worked," Brian said, voice filled with relief. "They backed off."

"Extra hold gets them every time." I flipped the bottle around before I put it back into my purse.

"Nice shootin', Tex," Martini said. "But does that mean we have invisible superbeings or that your boy here's insane and just thinks you scared the ghosts away?"

Another thought niggled. "Brian, do you recognize any of these people?"

He looked intently at what still looked like nothing to me. "Not really . . . but they seem familiar."

Christopher had come over and heard this exchange. He went back to check with the other astronauts. He returned looking thoughtful. "Chee's the oldest of the three of them, and he says he recognizes some people walking by. However, he thinks he's wrong about it."

"Why so?"

"Because everyone who looks familiar to him is dead."

After finding out aliens and superbeings existed, the presence of ghosts seemed normal. "So, does that mean whatever hit the *Valiant* is causing the astronauts to see dead people, or is it really bringing the dead people here?"

"Let's ask Chee." Martini nodded to Brian. "Be right back. Shout if any more ghosts are trying to get my girl."

Brian gave Martini a dirty look. "I'll be sure to."

"Jeff, why are you being such a jerk to him?" I asked as we moved to Chee's holding cell.

He snorted. "Can't imagine."

Chee was at his window. "I recognize at least a dozen people."

"Did you know them?"

He shook his head. "Not personally. But the ones I know were all astronauts who've died."

"In space?"

"No, on the ground, so to speak. Either in a crash, in an accident on the ground or just due to natural causes. Not everyone dies from an exploding rocket, you know."

I let this one pass. "So they're haunting the building?"

"I don't think so." Chee, like Brian, was staring at nothing. "They're really attracted to you." I pulled out my hairspray. "No, wait. I don't think they want to hurt you."

"What do they want?"

"I . . . can't tell."

I sprayed. "Better safe than sorry."

Christopher, Martini, and Gower all coughed. "We're sorry," Christopher said. "Does that count?"

"I want to talk to Michael. Be right back," I said to Chee.

He shrugged. "I'm not going anywhere."

We reached Michael's cell. He seemed agitated. "Why are they out and we're not?"

"What are they doing?"

"Staring at us. At you in particular." He grinned. "Can't blame them."

"Are they all men?"

"No, several women, too." He rubbed his forehead. "Look, all three of us aren't crazy at the same time."

"No, but you could all be affected by something at the same time," Gower said. "None of us can see anything, and Daniel says he recognizes some of the people you're seeing. The ones he recognizes are dead."

"Do you know Karl Smith?"

"Not well, but yeah." Michael looked at the group. "I don't see him here, though."

"How about an older, heavyset Cuban cleaning lady?"

He looked. "Nope."

"This gets weirder by the minute." I closed my eyes. I could feel something kicking in my brain. "Michael, all of you thought something bad had happened to the *Valiant*, but you all thought it was a different thing. And none of you remember doing the landing the way it really happened—you all remember it like it was in a simulator."

"Right. So?"

"So . . . I'm wondering if every person you're seeing was in space at some time. Not just the ones Daniel recognizes, but all of them." I looked at Gower. "Any way we can get some sort of information down here for them to go through, pictures, preferably?"

He shrugged. "Kennedy has pretty good archives, and they have video in these cells." He pulled his phone out and made a call.

While he was talking, I wandered back to Chee. "Daniel, the people you don't recognize, what are the odds they were all in space at one time?"

He studied them again. "It's possible. But . . . people are missing. The *Challenger* crew, for example, they're not here. I didn't know any of them, but I know what they looked like, and I don't see them. So, it's not everyone who was in space." He heaved a sigh. "Something's wrong with us, right?"

"Well, you're seeing dead people and Bruce Willis is nowhere in sight, so I think, yes, Houston, we have a problem."

He rubbed his forehead. "I just want to get out of here."

"All three of you do." It could be natural, or it could be whatever was wrong with them trying to get out. I had a hard time believing it was our run-of-the-mill parasitic superbeing, though, since they looked normal and weren't destroying things. However, there was a sure way to tell.

I went back to Christopher and Martini. "Can either one of you feel Michael through the glass? I mean, the way you did when you discovered Robot Kitty during Operation Fugly?" They'd done a two-man "go team" move on some video footage and determined that the bad guys had created a fake me to take out my mother. My introduction to the A-C crew had been exciting in a lot of really icky ways. I wondered how icky this latest adventure was going to get, then shoved the worry aside. I'd find out soon enough, one way or the other.

Christopher gave me a pained look for the "Operation Fugly" comment and shook his head. "I can't, that's not an image, that's Michael."

"I can. Put your hand to the glass," Martini told him. Michael did as asked, and Martini put his hand opposite. He concentrated, eyes closed, then he pulled away slowly. "No parasite that we're used to is in there."

That we're used to. "What *is* in there, Jeff?"

"I don't know," he said, as he pulled me into his arms. "But it wants out."

CHAPTER 32

I HAD TO FORCE MARTINI to do the same test with Chee and Brian. He confirmed that whatever was in Michael was in the other two as well.

"You need to stay far away from them." He sounded freaked out.

"Why me? I mean, why me more than anyone else?"

"No idea, but I can feel it, and it *wants* you." He was clutching me to him and I got the impression he was ready to hyperspeed us out of not only the quarantine area but the entire Space Center.

"Jeff, it's okay," Christopher said. "She's not going in, and they're not coming out, at least, not right now."

We were standing in front of Chee's cell, and he was paying attention. "If we have some entity within us, we need to get it out."

Martini shook his head. "I don't know what it is. It's . . . odd."

"Odd how?" I could feel his hearts—they were pounding.

"I think they're here to . . . do something. But either I can't tell what it is, or they're confused."

"I can understand something confused gravitating to Kitty," Christopher said.

"The entities must have done the landing, or helped the astronauts to land." I was trying to come up with something that made sense before Martini lost it and decided getting out of Dodge was more important than helping out.

"Yes, we have to assume that now," Gower said. "Jeff, do you get an evil feeling?"

He shook his head. "It's nothing like a superbeing. Only . . . it is, in a way." Martini looked at Christopher. "Put your palm against mine."

Christopher raised his eyebrow, but he did as asked. "Do we say something alienlike now?"

Martini was concentrating. "No. But . . . you feel . . . similar to whatever's inside the others." He did the same with Gower. "You, too."

"So, whatever it is comes from Alpha Centauri?"

Martini shook his head again. "Not . . . quite. Similar, but not the same."

Something knocked in my brain. "Jeff, you said there were a lot of inhabited planets in your system, right?"

He nodded. "And, to guess where you're going with it, there are only a few similarities between planetary species."

"How many are humanoid?"

Gower answered. "Out of the ten planets that had intelligent life when our people came to Earth, only about half were humanoid. The others would, for human understanding, be more avian and reptilian, versus mammalian. Of the humanoids, most were more mammalian than human."

"Hairy gorillas instead of naked ones?"

Martini laughed, which was a relief to hear. "More like walking cats and dogs. The apes were on our planet. And some others, but not all by any means."

"They aren't cats or dogs, like you'd think of them," Christopher added. "And they had no interests in mingling with us."

"No interspecies mating," Gower clarified. "Frankly, we mate normally with humans, but not with the other races in our solar system."

"That's weird." I thought about it. "I wonder how much the Ancients had to do with that."

"Potentially? Possibly a lot. Likely? When your father finishes his latest revision of the Ancients' text, we might know," Gower sighed. "Until then, just speculation."

Operation Fugly had identified a lack in the A-Cs' translations of the texts the original alien visitors, the Ancients, had brought with them. My father had done an initial revision five months ago, but he wasn't happy with it and so was redoing from scratch. The A-Cs saw this as impressive dedication and attention to detail. I saw it as him having a ton of fun.

"So, where are you going with this, Kitty?" Christopher sounded tired.

"I'm wondering if these are entities from your solar system."

Martini considered this. "They could be. But we didn't have any invisible beings."

I had no guesses but was saved from saying so by my phone ringing. I dug it out. "Hello?"

"Leave or you and your boyfriend will both die."

"Oh, you again. Look, he's not my boyfriend."

"Liar!" The caller hung up, but I got the feeling it was a woman, though the voice was still muffled. Interestingly, this call had originated from a different number. I'd see if Kevin could trace it, but after we dealt with the problem at hand.

"My stalker," I said to the look Martini was giving me.

"I'm not your boyfriend?" He sounded pissed, hurt, and suspicious, all in one. I had a feeling his blocks were down, or shorting out, because I was fairly certain I wasn't sending any lustful feelings toward anyone other than Martini, Brian in particular.

"No, *you* are. But I think my stalker is under the impression that Brian and I are an item." I filled them in on my theory about what I was now considering the least of our three main worries.

"I think you're reaching," Martini said.

"I don't," Christopher countered. "I could really see it, especially if he's been mooning about her for weeks."

"Try years," Chee interjected. "I mean, no one can discuss relationships without Brian reminiscing about the girl who got away." He smiled at me. "You're better looking in person."

"Geez, what picture of me does he have up?"

"Pictures, plural." Chee shook his head. "Everything

he's done, according to him, has been to impress you enough that you'd realize you wanted him back."

I could feel Martini start to go into a slow boil. It was silly—there wasn't a human man alive who could hope to match Martini in bed, let alone everything else. I took his hand and gave it a squeeze. "Doesn't that strike anyone else as just way beyond obsessive?"

Chee shrugged. "Sure, but he's a good guy. And he does keep trying to find someone he thinks is as great as you."

"I'm not that great."

"Yes, you are," Martini said. He wasn't saying it as an atta-girl—he was saying it like he was ready to go into the ring and fight Brian for me.

"Jeff, relax. I mean it." I looked back to Chee. "So, any guesses for who's threatening to kill me and my boyfriend if I don't leave? Taking the assumption that this lunatic thinks I'm here for Brian."

Chee considered. "I don't think anyone he's gone out with would want him back."

"Well, the flattery just keeps on coming."

Chee laughed. "I mean that they broke up for a reason. Most of his breakups have been amicable. And I don't think anyone he was with was pining for him back."

"Including me." Poor Brian.

"Someone wants him," Martini snapped. "At least if we take Kitty's theory to be even close to right."

"Jeff, trust me. This one I know in my gut, okay?" I did. There was something about the sheer lunacy of it—it screamed woman on the edge to me. "Daniel, are there some seriously unhinged women who work with or around you guys?"

"Could be a man, you know," Gower said dryly.

I shook my head. "I don't think it is, and not because Brian's straight. Argh. I need to make a call." She was going to be pissed, but oh, well. "Hi, Mom, sorry to bother you."

"That's okay, the President feels what's going on at Kennedy is more important." I wondered if he would agree that this particular issue fell under that "more important" category and decided not to ask.

"Great. Remember Brian Dwyer?"

"Yes, the nice boy you dumped." Yep, she and Dad had loved him.

"Yes, him. Guess what? He's an astronaut and one of the ones in quarantine."

"He still in love with you?"

"Funny you should ask. In a really John Hinckley kind of way, yes."

"Well, I don't know why you're surprised."

"Okay, I *am* surprised. Why aren't *you* surprised?"

Mom sighed. "He told you at grad night he was going to go off and do something that would make you proud of him, and then, when he was successful, rich, famous, whatever, he'd come back and convince you that you two were meant to be."

Oh. Right. I remembered . . . not so much. Okay, it was official—I did attract the really clingy, needy, possessive, stalker types. Then again, if I was going to spend the rest of my life with one, I wanted him to also be so godlike in bed that I didn't care. Ergo, I was Martini's, and Brian was out of luck.

"Okay, well, that might explain some of what's going on."

"You didn't remember that?" Mom sounded shocked.

"Um . . . no. I haven't thought of Brian much in recent years and not at all in the last several months."

"You were in love with him."

"I was sixteen. I was also in love with Steven Tyler and Joe Perry."

"You're still in love with them."

"Okay, bad example. But, I can't believe he's still into me. It's not like we stayed in touch. Though, he stayed in touch with Sheila apparently in order to keep tabs on me."

"How sweet."

"Mom, are you drinking? If this wasn't your dearly beloved Brian, wouldn't you think this was freaking insane behavior?"

She sighed. "Yes, probably. But he's an astronaut."

"He's an astronaut with some outer-space entity inside him, so, sorry if I'm not eager to resume the relationship."

"Fine, fine. Jeff's probably better suited to deal with you anyway."

"What is *that* supposed to mean?"

She barked a laugh. "So cute. So, why did you call, just to tell me you've run into Brian?"

"No." I filled her in on all the various chaos that we were embroiled in. "So, I want to get rid of my stalker so we can concentrate on the things that actually matter, like staying alive and getting whatever creepy thing's inside the astronauts out and neutralized."

"Let me talk to Jeff."

I handed the phone to Martini. "You're up."

He gave me the "what?" look which received the "fake it" gesture from me. He plastered a smile onto his face—I realized if he weren't so good at what he did, he could have quite the career in telemarketing.

"Hi, Angela, sorry we're taking up your time. Uh-huh. Yes. Yes. No. Thanks, it's nice to still be alive. No, I don't think there are entities within the astronauts just because I don't like whatshisname. Right, Brian. Got it. You know, Christopher's still available, too; should I just let the two of them fight it out for her?"

Christopher and I exchanged a look. Yeah, this wasn't going as planned.

"Yes, that was sarcasm. Yes, as I told my own mother only yesterday, I've always been sarcastic, you've just never noticed. No, never about Kitty. Yes, I'd like to find out if her mysterious caller is after Brian because it makes it easier to block whatever murderous move they're going to make against Kitty. Yes, against Kitty. What part of 'leave Florida or we kill you and your boyfriend' isn't coming through clearly?"

Martini shot me a "you'll pay for this" look. "You know, maybe I should talk to Sol about this. No, I don't think he has more experience with stalkers. I just don't think we're making progress here, and I have several hundred A-Cs in, if we take the signs to be accurate, mortal peril. I have three astronauts with something very alien inside them, which is also inordinately interested in Kitty. And we have some lunatic calling at odd times to tell Kitty to get out of town. If we could just go back to Dulce, believe me, I'd go in half a heartbeat."

He was quiet while Mom talked. Martini started looking less upset, so I hoped she was giving him some advice, as opposed to making him more stressed out.

Gower touched my arm. "The visuals are downloaded. I'm going to have all three of them cross-reference who they've seen and are seeing with the archives. Only showing them folks who have been in space and are dead, as a first pass."

"Works for me." Martini was still listening. I put my arm around his waist. His whole body was tensed. I wanted to rub his back but wasn't sure if it would hurt him or not. This couldn't be good for his empathic blocks, though, and I didn't want to have to give him adrenaline again any time soon.

Finally he spoke. "Okay, sounds good. You want to talk to Kitty? Great, talk to you later." He handed me the phone and knocked his head gently against the wall.

"Mom, what did you just harangue Jeff about?"

"Nothing. I just gave him some suggestions and told him to make sure you were safe."

"Nothing my ass."

"I want your ass protected."

"Well, did you give him any help in terms of finding my stalker or did you just spend time telling him how great Brian was when we were in freaking high school?"

She sighed. "I gave him a quick course in how to spot the likely stalker, yes. And I didn't give it to you because it's unlikely the stalker will identify if you're looking at him or her. They're likely to seem friendly to you, in order to lull you into a false sense of security. Or they'll just attack you without warning."

Great news. "Can this get any more fun?"

"Probably." Mom sighed again. "Tell Jeff I'm sorry. The situation in Florida is out of control, and I don't know how much of this is related to all the discussions of what to do with Centaurion Division or not."

"I'd guess a lot. I'm not big on the coinkydinks. I think a

lot of this is interrelated, but I don't think my stalker situation is."

"Wouldn't that then be a coincidence?" I could swear she was snickering.

"Tell Dad I'm calling him next time."

"Yes, Jeff mentioned that, too. Give Christopher my love, and I'll talk to you after your next crisis. Love you, kitten."

"Love you too, Mom."

I leaned against Martini. "There are times when I wonder if she's just pretending to be the head of antiterrorism and is actually giving me advice based on the latest hit soap's storyline."

"Nah, that'd be too easy."

"Jeff, Kitty," Gower was near Michael's cell. "I think we've got a definitive answer."

CHAPTER 33

WE TROTTED OVER TO MICHAEL'S CELL. "Every person the astronauts see has been in space, and every one of them is dead." Gower sounded calmer than I would have expected under the circumstances. He wasn't all that calm, but at least he wasn't screaming. I chose to see this as a positive.

"But not every person who's been in space and has died is in the lineup, right?"

"Right. As Chee told us, the *Challenger* crew isn't here. In fact, no one who's died in an accident or for any other reason while in space is being seen by the astronauts."

"So, what does that tell us?" Christopher asked. "Are we dealing with a haunting of some kind?"

There was something I knew I needed to remember. "That tenth planet you told me about, Jeff . . . the one that you and a couple of the other races felt were a danger. You removed their ability for space travel."

"Right, what about them?"

"And you think the entities within the astronauts are here to do something, but they don't know what?"

"Yes, that's the best I've got. Again, what about it?"

I closed my eyes and tried to figure this out. When we'd met—over a newly formed superbeing I'd killed—Martini had implanted a memory from his aunt, Christopher's mother, Terry, in my mind. But it wasn't only a memory, or a prophecy. There was a little bit of Terry still inside me.

I never discussed it with Martini or Christopher—Terry had programmed Martini when he was a little boy, but he still felt guilty about the implant, even though it had never upset me; and Christopher wouldn't be able to deal properly with the idea that a part of his mother was potentially still alive.

Over the past five months, I'd learned to tap into this little essence of Terry. It was difficult, because it wasn't an active part of her consciousness, but it was helpful when I could achieve a connection, because she was an A-C and therefore knew things intrinsically that I couldn't. It was a melding of my mind and the sum total of her experiences, and the two didn't meet all that often. But I really wanted them to meet now.

I leaned against Martini. Terry had been an empath, and sometimes I thought her essence drew some power from my proximity to the most powerful empath on Earth. He wrapped his arms around me, and I relaxed against him.

"Nap time?" Christopher asked.

"Maybe. Why can't we tell what the entities are?"

"Why are you asking questions that have no relation to each other?" Martini countered. "And, no idea."

"Why don't the entities understand what they're supposed to do?"

"This is fun, Kitty, but not helping." Gower sounded impatient.

"Why do the entities think they have something to do? And why are they and the 'ghosts' more interested in me than in the rest of you?"

"Maybe they think you're cuter," Michael said with a laugh.

My eyes opened. "Maybe they think I'm the only woman available." I looked up at Martini. "The Supreme Fugly wanted me because I was a woman. And you said these things feel similar but not the same."

He nodded. "But I don't see where you're going with this."

I dug my phone out and dialed. "James, everyone okay?"

"Bored to tears, girlfriend. Alfred turned the sound off, so we've been watching the silent movie that's your so-called interrogation of the astronauts."

"Why did Alfred turn off the sound?"

"Security issue, in case the feeds have been tampered with."

"Wise choice, all things considered."

"Yeah. What's taking so long?"

"Long story, catch you up later. What's the most significant thing about the *Valiant*, other than the fact that her astronauts are in quarantine?"

Reader was quiet for a moment. "I'd have to say it's that she's the first viable manned long-range spaceship. I mean, there are other things, but that would be most significant to me."

"I love you."

"Yeah, I know, but Jeff's feeling highly possessive this trip, and I think he can take me, so let's just keep on pretending I'm gay and uninterested."

"If we must." I hung up. "I know what's in the astronauts."

"We're all breathless," Christopher snarked.

"I mean, I think. Michael, how far out were you when you got hit?"

He shrugged. "Pretty far. Past the moon."

"Farther than any manned craft have gone before?"

"Check with Daniel, but yeah, I think so."

We went to Daniel's cell and asked. "Yes. We'd just gone three hundred thousand miles from Earth. I was just about to mention to the guys that we'd officially gone where no man had gone before when we got hit."

"That's it." I spun around. "We keep on thinking that the only risks to Earth from outer space are the parasites. But that's not true. For all we know, your home planet, or one of the others from your system, has decided Earth's likely to be a pain somewhere along the line. I'm betting on your planet—which knows we're all here—as the brains behind this operation."

"Why? And what operation?" Gower sounded confused.

"The *Valiant* passed some outer space fence that was booby-trapped. Daniel just confirmed it—they were farther out, past anything we've done before. Whatever was there, the entities, entered the ship and took it back. I think the confusion is they don't know if it's Miller Time or not, and they also don't know if they can or should phone home."

"More explanation, less Kittyisms," Christopher said.

"I wasn't 'isming'! I'll talk slower. I think it's safe to assume there is at least one planet, maybe more, that doesn't want Earthlings to show up saying, 'Howdy! Can we move in here?' One of those is your home planet. You remember them, the lovely folks who exiled your entire race here because you have different religious views and so you'd lure the parasites to Earth?"

"Rings a bell," Martini said.

"So, let's use them as our working hypothesis."

"Ooooh, she brings out the big words," Christopher said with a laugh.

I rolled my eyes but kept going. "Alpha Centauri doesn't want us to visit or you all to get back home. So, what's the best way to ensure that, short of destroying us? They don't want to destroy us because you're still luring parasites here, so that means parasites are still knocking over on Alpha Centauri's ozone shield there. So, they put up a fence, a barrier, a trip wire of some kind, in whatever radius around Earth they felt was appropriate. We won't see it—if our technology can't see the cloaking you've had here since the nineteen-sixties, I guarantee we can't spot whatever Alpha Centauri's put up since then."

Gower nodded. "It makes sense. Go on."

"The *Valiant* tripped the wire. So, the 'back off' mechanism went into place. Something entered the ship, took over, and took it back—*right* back to where it came from, which, as a human living with A-Cs, strikes me as just your race's kind of efficiency. No human would have or could have done it—a human agency trying to fool someone would have landed the *Valiant* where it should have been, and no sane human would try to land a rocket ship back sitting on its butt. Nor could we have done it without help, alien-type help."

"How do we prove it?" Martini asked.

"We talk to your fathers—they should know what was done to hold that warlike planet at bay. I'm betting it's something like this."

"Fair enough," Gower said, as Martini and Christopher both pulled out phones and started dialing. "But why are the entities still inside the astronauts, and why are they confused about what they're here for?"

"And why are we seeing dead people?" Chee asked.

Martini moved away from me. Both he and Christopher were having animated conversations with their fathers, and both of them looked pissed. I nudged Gower. "I'm right."

He nodded. "Yeah, it makes sense when you explain it like you did."

"The dead people?" Chee asked again.

"The people aren't there. The entities are looking for them. They've seen these people, and they can't find them now."

"There are plenty of living astronauts who aren't on parade here," Chee said.

"I'm sure. The entities are confused. I don't think they're supposed to be destructive—after all, Alpha Centauri needs Earth and needs us populated with humans and A-Cs. I'd imagine that the entities can see us, possibly from much farther off than we could see them. So, they've seen every human and A-C who's ever gone into space. It's lonely out there, isn't it?"

Chee nodded. "It can be."

"They've been sitting there for decades, maybe longer, who knows? Just waiting for someone to trip their wire and give them something to do. So, they took an interest in the space travelers who didn't quite make it to their border. Like . . . like a penguin observer in the wild. You get attached to the penguins, even though the penguins have no idea you're there. You name them, you care about them. And when you come back the next year, you look for 'your' penguins. And maybe you don't find them."

"But how are the entities doing that?" Gower asked.

I looked at Christopher, and the answer radiated out like a beacon.

CHAPTER 34

"**O**NE OF THEM'S AN IMAGEER. Maybe another's an empath or a dream-seer, like you," I said to Gower. "Maybe these entities are a distillation of A-C talents. But somewhere in there is the imageer ability. Christopher drew a picture of his mother in the air for me by rearranging the molecules. It can be done, and I think that's what they're doing."

"So, why are they, and the images, attracted to you?" Gower asked.

"Because a female can neutralize them," Martini growled. He stalked over to us and he was furious. "They knew about this, and it never occurred to them that our former oppressors would do the same thing to Earth." He rubbed his forehead. "You're right, baby, completely. It's the same damn thing they used on that warlike planet. We're surrounded by a net. We cross it, the net tosses us back."

"Humanely, which is an A-C watchword."

"Oh, it's better than that, though." Christopher was also fuming. "If we make enough attempts, and no one's clear on just how many 'enough' is, then they stop tossing back nicely and start killing things *and* making the net smaller."

It was an ugly picture. "America isn't the only country interested in space travel."

"I know." Christopher actually sounded angrier than

Martini, which was saying a lot. "And this isn't going to go over well with the American government, let alone in other countries."

I thought about it. "It's worse. It's going to make Centaurion Division seem less like a positive. And the less positive you seem, the more the pressure there will be to turn you into a military division that's fighting other countries."

"What in God's name are we going to do?" Christopher asked quietly.

"Jeff, what did you mean by a female being able to neutralize the entities?"

"Let's just ask the source," he said. I turned and saw Alfred and the rest of our group joining us. "Sure it's safe to have Kitty, Lorraine, and Claudia all here?" Martini's voice was dripping with both sarcasm and fury.

Alfred shook his head. "We didn't think of it. We were establishing ourselves with the ranking superpower and protecting our new home from a terrible threat. Forgive us for not being as on top of things as your generation."

Oh, the Martini men could both twist the sarcasm knob up to full. "Um, guys? Really, let's focus. What's the right thing to do in this situation, Alfred?"

He shrugged. "I have no idea. It was my grandparents' generation who put up the Physic-Psycho Barrier around Beta Twelve."

"Beta Twelve?"

Alfred chuckled. "We assigned each planet a sequence based on which sun they were closest to and where they were in order. There are eighteen planets in our system, ten are inhabited. The others might be now, but they weren't inhabited when we were exiled."

"But you should only have eight at the most," Chee said. "At least, according to our calculations."

Alfred shrugged. "Your calculations are wrong, and, due to a variety of good reasons, none of us have mentioned that until now. I know, the idea is that the second sun would cause orbital disruptions. But our planets have lemniscate orbits."

"You mean the planets make a figure eight?" This

seemed unreal to me, but then again, so did hyperspeed, and they did it all the time.

"Yes," Alfred nodded. "Exactly. But only some of them. There are specific reasons for it, the metals at our worlds' cores for starters, but really, now is not the time. Alphas One through Three are uninhabited, Alpha Four is our home world, and Alphas Five through Eight are also inhabited. Betas start with Nine, and Nine through Eleven are uninhabited. Twelve through Sixteen are inhabited, Betas Seventeen and Eighteen are not. Beta Twelve is the problem planet."

"And the net thingy?" I couldn't come up with that word again on my own.

"Physic-Psycho Barrier. It's referred to as a PPB."

"What does it mean?"

"Physical and psychological barrier," Alfred explained, only somewhat patiently. "It works like a net."

"Looking for both a physical and a psychological presence?"

"Hence the name." I marveled at how Martini's father could get the exact same amount of frustration into his tone as his son.

I looked up at said son. "Ergo, why our unmanned craft have gotten through—computer brains are not the same as human ones. And the entities are looking for both the physical and mental presences of those they saw before. They're drawing their pictures for the astronauts in the hopes said astronauts will show them where their penguins went."

"Penguins?" Martini looked confused. "How did we get onto flightless waterfowl?"

Oh, right, he'd been on the phone. "You explain it to them," I said to Gower. I went over to Michael's cell. "Have you cross-referenced?"

He nodded. "I've compared every person that came by without speaking to the archives. All had been in space before, and all are dead."

"Do you still see them out there?"

He looked. "No." He looked back at me. "They disappeared as I verified they were dead. But they might come back."

"No, they won't. I'm going to get you out of here soon, Michael, I promise."

"Thanks." He gave me a very seductive smile. "So, have you and Jeff declared for each other yet?"

This was a new one. "No, not that I know of. What does that mean?"

Michael shrugged. "It's how we A-C's begin the commitment process. We declare for each other. It puts both parties off the market—bad form to try to break up a declared couple."

Interesting. Martini had never mentioned this. Ever. "Nice custom."

"And until you've declared, you're open game." He smiled a very wide smile. "Let me know if you want to have dinner some time."

Martini's massive possessiveness started to have a little more clarity. "So, um, in the A-C world, is it against the rules for undeclared couples to play the field?"

"Not really. Until you've declared or accepted someone's declaration, it's pretty common to date other people. We mate for life—you want to be sure you're with the right person."

I'd taken some animal life sciences courses in school, and mating for life was one section I'd done very well in. Interestingly enough, while many creatures mated for life, most of them would still "date" outside of the mated pair. Only one kind of bird actually both mated for life and discouraged any form of philandering. It seemed I was dating a humanoid black vulture. Who'd have guessed it? Not me, obviously.

"It's kind of different for humans."

Michael pointedly looked at my left hand. "I see no ring—marriage, engagement, or promise." He looked back at my face. "Seriously, be sure before you decide." He smiled widely again. "Jeff's not the only one with moves, trust me."

The realization that Gower's younger brother was truly hitting on me with intent to score a grand slam was shocking. I found myself wondering if my perfume really lived up to its hype. I had had an active dating life, both before and after Brian, and I knew I'd dated more than Martini had. But I wasn't used to being the "it" girl of any group. If I hadn't been in love with Martini, this would have been a lot more exciting. Seeing as I was, however, the situation was awkward at best and relationship-threatening at worst.

Martini clearly picked something up because he was next to me now, arm wrapped around me. "What are you two discussing?" he asked in a tone that indicated he already knew the answer.

Michael gave him a grin, and I recognized the look on his face—it was a very male expression. I'd seen athletes give each other looks like this, right before a meet or a game, when they were ready to fight over something they both wanted, like a championship . . . or a girl.

This made me much more nervous than any romantic stress between me, Martini, and Christopher ever had. I took a shot at defusing the situation. "Um, Michael, do you have any special A-C talent? Like, Jeff's the best empath on Earth, and Christopher's the best imageer. Do you have a talent?"

He gave me a slow smile. "Not like that." It was clear what he was insinuating. Martini had insinuated, well flat out said, the same when we'd met. But he'd been funny and charming. Michael was sexual and predatory.

I could feel Martini move from angry and jealous to Raging Bull. "Keep your damned hands off her." His voice was low and he was snarling.

"Up to her, isn't it?" Michael sounded amused and confident. Under some circumstances this could have been flattering and appealing. Under this one, it wasn't. I realized I was huddling closer to Martini—because I was scared. I found myself thanking God there was a sturdy, locked door between the two of them.

"Michael, cut the crap." Reader was there, between Martini and Michael. He sounded mad and also disgusted. "You aren't interested in her, you're interested in screwing with Jeff and Christopher."

Michael's eyes narrowed. "James, you have no idea what I'm interested in."

Reader barked a laugh. "I've watched you for years. You think you're a playa, Mr. Smooth with the ladies. If you ever stopped to think about it, you can't keep a girl because they all get sick of being your latest conquest, being shown off like this week's bowling trophy. You don't give a damn about any of them—if they're hot and especially if someone else cares about them, then you're interested."

Michael looked at me. "Make your own decisions. Just remember, you're not committed, and it's a smart girl who checks out her options before making a final decision."

"I'll keep it in mind." I managed to get this out without my voice shaking.

Reader turned around. "We're all caught up on the penguin theory. Let's figure out how to get the entities out of the astronauts." He looked at Martini. "Let it go, Jeff," he said under his breath. "I can tell she's not interested and I'm not empathic. Don't let him get to you, it's what he wants."

Martini gave Reader a curt nod, spun us around, and dragged me back in front of Chee's cell. Reader came with us. I buried my face in Martini's chest. His hearts were pounding, and I knew I was trembling. "Jeff, how bad are your blocks?"

He sighed. "Going up and down. I'm having trouble . . . "

"Because you're so badly hurt." I tried not to worry and failed. "Michael's sure picking a great time to be an aggressive predator."

Reader put his hand on my shoulder. "True, though predator's the wrong word. He's always been a jerk. It's one of the reasons he and Paul aren't close—it drives Paul crazy the way Michael treats people."

"He seemed nice when we first got here." Martini's arms were around me, and I could feel him starting to pick up how freaked out this had made me because he relaxed somewhat. He stroked my back and my head.

"He can be nice," Reader said. "But he has to know where someone's limit is. Under normal circumstances, anyway."

I moved my head to look at Reader. "What do you mean, normal circumstances?"

He grimaced. "Michael's had a real competition with Jeff and Christopher, all their lives. They're the same age, but he has no A-C talents, so he'd never be in the positions they're in. He's an astronaut, which is pretty impressive, to both A-Cs and humans, but it's not enough. Jeff's in charge of the Field, and that means Jeff's in charge of everything any time it matters. That's a huge responsibility, and one Michael would love to be given but will never have. Christopher, as the head of Imageering, is pretty much Jeff's equal in most situations and is his right-hand man in any others. Again, not a position Michael can ever achieve."

"And his older brother is the Head of Recruitment and the Sovereign Pontifex's right hand."

"Right, again, a position Michael is unlikely to ever achieve. Recruitment requires the ability to see into a person's dreams, for a variety of reasons. So he tries to one-up whenever he can."

"Stealing my girl would certainly be one-upping me," Martini snarled, back to tense.

"Jeff, for God's sake, look at her face if you suddenly can't pick up how she feels about this. Kitty's freaked out, not flattered." I loved Reader, I really did. He gave Martini a close look. "You need to go into isolation."

Martini snorted. "Yeah, like that's an option." He heaved a sigh. "But you're right. And I'll try to calm down."

"Good." I swallowed. "I figure Claudia, Lorraine, and I need to go into the cells with the astronauts."

Reader nodded. "Yeah, according to Alfred, best guess is that the entities need to join with a woman in order to dissipate. We figure one woman per astronaut, just in case."

"Then, let me say right now I'm not going in with Michael, and if he acts like this with either one of the girls, he can keep his entity and stay in solitary for the rest of his life."

Martini's body started to relax. "Who do you want, baby?"

"Want would be the wrong word. I'll go in with Brian. It'll crush him if I don't, and he's already taking a lot of ego beating with my having explained that I'm with you and not looking to make a change in status."

Full Martini body relaxation. "Okay, but I'll be watching."

"I hope so. I have no idea what's going to happen."

"No one does," Reader said. "But I guess we're going to find out.

CHAPTER 35

"SORRY ABOUT MICHAEL," Chee said. He sounded really down all of a sudden. "He gets that way sometimes."

"It's okay, Daniel. Not your fault."

"I suppose." Chee looked despondent.

"Are you okay?"

He shrugged. "I suppose. Guess it doesn't really matter."

This was weird. "Um, okay. Talk to you in a minute." I took Martini's hand, and he and I went to Brian's cell. Reader came along, too.

"What's up with Chee?" Reader asked me.

Before I could answer, Brian saw us. "What the hell are you doing holding his hand?" he shouted at me. "Get away from him! Things are bad enough, you don't need to make them worse!"

"Brian, what's with you? He's my boyfriend, you know that."

Brian started pounding on the door. "Get away from him, from all of them! It's bad enough being all alone, you don't have to rub it in!"

Martini pulled me away from the door. "Okay, you're not going in there."

"Something's really wrong, more wrong than before. Brian wasn't like that, ever. He's not a violent person." I looked at him, then at Chee and Michael, who were looking suicidal and glowering, respectively. My brain kicked. "Oh. Jeff, stay here. I'll be okay."

I let go of his hand and went back to Brian's cell. "Brian, please stop," I said softly. "I understand, I do."

He quieted. "What do you understand?"

I looked into his eyes. "I need to talk to you, whoever you are inside Brian. If I come in there, will you hurt me?"

Brian's eyes seemed foggy all of a sudden, and he shook his head. "Help. Please. So lonely."

"I know, I understand. Are there three of you or just one of you here?"

"Can't answer . . . not like you."

"What are you like? Animals? Insects? Run through Brian's mind and see what sounds familiar."

"Kitty, what are you doing?" Martini hissed.

"Hush, Jeff. Seriously, hush."

Brian's foggy eyes looked at Martini. "Hates me." He sounded angry.

"No, loves *me*. He's afraid you're going to hurt me. He won't let that happen."

"Feel the hate."

"Yes, but it's not directed the way you think. He's jealous. Look in Brian's mind, you'll understand why." Brian's head nodded. I knew it wasn't Brian doing the nodding. "James, can you, only, come here please?"

Reader was next to me quickly. "What're you doing, girlfriend? Jeff's ready to pop a vessel again."

"He needs to calm down. The entities are reacting to the discovery that their penguins are dead, okay? They're upset and reacting based on the person they're inside right now. Get everyone away from the cells, but where the astronauts and entities can see them. Then please come back."

"Okay." He left, and I heard him talking to the others, heard Martini and Christopher both argue with him, heard Gower support Reader.

"Do you understand yet?" I asked softly.

Brian's head nodded. "Males fight for females."

"Sometimes. What are you like, anything I can understand?"

"Bees . . . ants. But like you, too."

"A hive mind? Combined consciousness?"

Brian's head nodded again. "No body."

"You're a combined consciousness of . . . what? A-C talents?"

"Yes. All combined in one, one divided into many, sent here to guard."

Reader joined us again, but he didn't say anything.

"To guard who from what?"

"To guard all of you." Brian's foggy eyes shifted and looked away. Even disembodied A-C entities couldn't lie.

"To guard against us leaving, right?"

"Once." The eyes looked back into mine. "Then saw . . . " He was concentrating and I turned around. To see the only crew of astronauts I could pick out of a lineup.

"The crew of the *Challenger*."

"I don't see anything, girlfriend," Reader said softly.

I turned back to Brian. "How can you show them to me when I couldn't see the others? James can't see them."

"You understand now. He doesn't."

"Did you kill them?"

"NO!" I heard Chee and Michael shout this, too. Apparently all the entities were involved in this conversation. "Too far from us. Couldn't save them." Tears were running down Brian's face. "Took care of them."

"How could you take care of them?"

"Joined with us."

I thought fast. "You joined the crew's consciousness in with yours?"

"Yes. All the others, too."

"You mean any others who died in space?"

"Yes. Ours to protect."

I thought some more. All the thinking was making my head hurt. "Is that why you're unhappy? Because the other penguins—" Reader coughed, loudly. "I mean other astronauts you've seen are dead, and you can't join them with you?"

"Ours to protect!" he wailed.

"James, listen to me. I have to get in there, and Jeff and

Christopher and all the others have to stay out and stay calm. I don't care what you have to do, but get me inside and keep the others calm."

"Oh, no problem, girlfriend. I'll just shoot them or something."

"That would be very bad. I don't want anyone upsetting our protective friends. Tell Jeff they are, right now, more possessive and protective than he could ever hope to be, and we are on the edge of the knife." I knew without asking that the entities were capable of mass destruction, and I also knew they would shoot Martini first and ask questions later.

Reader was back. "Jeff won't let you go in alone. Period."

Figured. "Okay. Then I want Paul. Only."

"Jeff's not my type, so I want to stress that you and Paul need to come out alive."

"Duly noted."

Gower came over after a lot of arguing. "Kitty, what are we doing?"

"The usual, saving the world from all the other things out there trying to destroy it."

"Oh, good. Routine." He unlocked the door. "You're sure we're not releasing the next Mephistopheles?"

"I'm sure if we don't do something, this will escalate to the point where we'll wish Mephistopheles and all his buddies were back and in charge."

"Okay," he sighed. He took my hand, and we moved at hyperspeed into the cell with Brian. The door was locked again by Reader, who was still on the outside.

"Why is he here?" the Brian who wasn't Brian right now asked.

"He can help, I think." I sat down. "I sort of feel sick because we moved so fast." I patted the couch next to me. "Come sit down." Gower did, but Brian remained standing, though he moved right in front of me.

"Why?"

"Why do I feel sick? I'm human, I function differently than A-Cs do."

He looked at Gower. "He is both."

"How can it tell?" Gower asked me quietly.

"Body and brain not like the others." Brian moved closer to Gower. "More like us."

Gower leaned back. "Maybe."

I reached out and took Brian's hand. "He's not ready. Come here."

He knelt before me. "So lonely." He started to cry again.

"I know." I leaned his head into my lap. "James, I want the intercom off."

He sighed. "Okay." I heard something click, and the little white noise that showed the 'com active was gone.

"Paul, you need to listen to me, and this goes no farther than you and I. You can't tell Jeff or Christopher, ever."

"Terry's still in you," Gower said softly.

"Yeah, you knew?"

"I guessed. Once you realized what was going on, I figured part of her was still in there." He put his hands to my temples and concentrated. "It's not a lot of her," he said finally. "Just . . . a trace, really."

"That's what I thought. But it helps me sometimes, and this is one of those times." I stroked Brian's head. "Can you tell me, if you join with someone here, will that mean all the consciousness, what's here and what's still out there in space surrounding us, will all be inside whoever you join with?"

He nodded. "Don't want to hurt you. Here to guard!"

I looked back at Gower. "The entity is a combination of all A-C talents, distilled. They shouldn't have included empathic, but they did. That's what's caused this, which could be good for us. The empathic part got attached to the various astronauts it's seen. And for those who died in space, it pulled their consciousnesses in with it. So there are human minds mingled in. That's why it thinks you're the most like it—you're a human/A-C hybrid."

"How is this good for us?" Gower sounded mildly freaked out.

"The *Challenger* disaster traumatized the entity, just like it traumatized the world. It wanted to save them and couldn't. I'd call that the turning point. It doesn't want to hurt us, it wants to protect us. That's why Jeff picked up its confusion. It wants to help but is supposed to harm."

"Why was it attracted to you?"

"She understands. She thinks . . . right." The tears were still coming; my pants were getting wet.

"Well, there's something out there that believes your mind works the right way," Gower chuckled. "Not sure that's comforting."

I rolled my eyes at him. "Nice. Look, we have to help. And we need your help," I added, as I stroked Brian's head again.

"How?" Brian's eyes were still foggy.

"Why don't you want to stay with Michael?"

"Not right mind. Close, not right. Hurts."

"They need to be with someone who has A-C talent, I think." I took a deep breath. "And I think that means they need to be with you."

CHAPTER 36

"WHY ME?" Gower didn't sound as freaked out as I was prepared for, but he didn't sound completely convinced, either.

"I think they need to be with someone who can interpret dreams. They don't communicate the way we do. This is so hard for them, can't you tell?" He nodded. "But they could communicate with you on a different level, nonverbally."

"Why not Jeff or Christopher or one of the girls?"

"Because they're not hybrids. And because you're on Alpha Team, and that means we put the most powerful consciousness in our solar system into the mind of someone who's already proved he's capable of handling great power and responsibility."

Gower seemed to be considering all of this. Brian spoke, eyes still foggy. "Orders were wrong."

"I know. They didn't understand what they were doing to you, though, I think." I knew they were quite clear on what they were doing to Earth and all who lived on it.

"You forgive them?"

I stroked his head. "They sent people, and you, to protect us. Not for good reasons, but still, that's how it's worked out. All my friends, and the man I love, wouldn't be here but for that. So, yeah, I forgive them."

"This one loves you, too." Brian's eyes closed. "Some others, also."

"I know. But it has to be mutual. That's why Paul has

to agree to let you join him, why you can't just take over a body and make it yours, why Brian and Daniel and Michael are all fighting you. Why you'll have to let Paul take the lead and share with him, not try to make him do what you want."

Brian's eyes opened. Still foggy. "Understand. Agree."

"What if it reneges?" Gower asked.

"Then I pull it out. I can do that, it's why it's attracted to me." Brian nodded. "It's my job, why I'm really on Alpha Team. I'm the one the space entities all wanna hang with."

Gower laughed. "Seems that way." He sighed. "Aside from being kind to a clearly pathologically lonely being, why should I take this risk?"

I looked at him and I knew the smile I was giving him was my mother's. "Because if Centaurion Division controls the PPB net, then Centaurion Division cannot be made to do anything it doesn't want to do."

Gower grinned. "Oh, you are your mother's daughter." He took a deep breath. "What will it do to me, when it joins?"

"No harm," Brian said. "Must protect."

"You won't be able to join all the consciousnesses of the dead any more," I reminded the entity. "That would overload Paul's mind, and you can't afford that."

"Maybe some," Gower amended. "We can decide together, but Kitty's right—I'll have to make the final decision."

Brian nodded. "Agree. Not in charge, here to protect."

"Can you be with someone who *is* in charge? Because Paul has to run many things and make many decisions."

"Will help, decisions must be his."

"Works for me. How about you, Paul?"

He nodded. "Sure." He closed his eyes. "Can I . . . say good-bye to Jamie, just in case?"

"Yes." I stroked Brian's head. "Just don't take too long."

Gower sighed. "I know." He got up and went to the door, Reader unlocked it and then locked it a moment later. Hyperspeed was a wonderful thing.

"He fears."

"I do, too. Don't you?"

"Fear loneliness. Nothing else can hurt."

"Why?"

"No body. Spirit only." We were quiet for a few long moments. "What if he refuses?" I could hear the fear.

"Then I'll find someone else. I won't desert you."

Brian's arms went around me. "I know." He sighed. "So good to touch."

"I know." I leaned my head back against the wall. I wondered if the A-Cs who had created this sentient net had considered how cruel they were being, or if they'd cared one way or the other. I knew it was the empathic portion that was causing the entity's trauma. It was a very loud reminder that Martini felt things more strongly than others. I wanted to hold him and tell him I wasn't going anywhere, but I wasn't sure if he'd pick it up correctly right now.

"He . . . is too close," Brian said. "Loves you so much . . . can't read clearly."

"You mean Jeff can't read my emotions right?"

"When angry, scared, jealous, no." The negative emotions clouded Martini's abilities, at least in regard to me? Interesting.

"How can you tell?"

"Feel it. Out of balance."

"Am I bad for him?"

"No!" Brian looked up at me. "Needs you. But . . . needs to feel . . . safe."

"Safe?"

Before the entity could answer, Gower came back in. "Okay. I'm ready."

"Sit." Brian was still holding me. Gower sat next to me again. "Hold hands."

We did, and I felt something flowing through me, from Brian to Gower. It was strong and lonely and a little bit frightened, but also fascinated and excited. It had seen many things but not much of the things it wanted. It was more powerful than anything I'd ever experienced, like getting electrocuted but not dying from it.

I felt it brush the little wisp of Terry inside my mind, and then it pulled her away from me. I wanted to cry, but it stroked my mind. "Not fair, to her or you. Must be what you are, must let her be what she was. Here, with us, when you need her."

The power flow continued, it felt as if it was a long time, but I couldn't tell for certain. Then, finally, it was over. I felt as if my mind were floating around outside of my body as I watched Brian slide to the floor onto his back. Gower fell against my body, which knocked me down and on top of Brian. I wasn't so out of it that I didn't dread Martini's reaction to this, but I couldn't do anything about it.

"Thank you," the entity's voice was in my disembodied mind. "We will never desert you, either." Something hugged my mind, making me feel loved and protected, and then it let go.

My mind whizzed back into my body and I whizzed right into unconsciousness.

CHAPTER 37

I WOKE UP IN SOMEONE'S ARMS. I felt two hearts pounding, and the arms around me were very familiar. "Jeff?" I wanted to open my eyes, but it was as if there were sandbags on my eyelids.

"It's okay, baby, I'm here."

I could hear other people. "Is Paul awake?"

"Not yet." Martini's voice was tense. "The astronauts are just coming around."

"The entity is inside Paul."

"James told us." Martini didn't sound relaxed or relieved. "Baby, can you open your eyes?"

"I'm trying. I'm so tired." I was. I just wanted to curl up, put my face into his neck, and go to sleep.

Martini shifted me, and my face was right where I'd wanted it. I wrapped one arm around his neck and went to sleep.

My dreams were interesting—I was very aware I was dreaming for starters. I saw things I'd never imagined, things I guessed were from another solar system. I saw a system with three suns—two larger, one very small and red and much farther away. There were a lot of planets. I couldn't count them all, but they moved oddly. There were two sets of three planets that moved around one each of the two bigger suns. The rest moved in odd figure eights around the big suns. I realized I was looking at the Alpha Centauri system. I tried to pick out Martini's home planet as well as Beta Twelve, but I was whisked away before I could.

I flew through space, danced through comets, crossed endless nothing, heading toward a tiny light in the distance that grew into a small, yellow sun, much like the two I'd left. I passed things I recognized as my own solar system's outer planets, circled Saturn and Jupiter, then raced on through the asteroid belt, past Mars, to the blue and green shining jewel that sat out here, so alone. I wrapped myself around it, and then I waited.

The loneliness hit, so hard and all-encompassing that I started to sob. The entity, more than any human on Earth, understood how very alone this planet was. And it was more alone than Earth, because no one on Earth knew it was there.

I woke up still sobbing. Martini was rocking me and kissing my head. "Kitty, wake up, baby. Please, baby, it'll be okay." I clung to him and nodded while he held me tight and kept on kissing me. "Relax baby, I'm here, you're safe."

"Are . . . the others . . . all right?"

"Not so much. They all did what you just did, sort of woke up, then went into a deep sleep."

"Are they crying?"

"Yeah. It's kind of horrible."

I hugged him. "I'm sorry. It's not trying to hurt you. It's just been so alone."

"It isn't hurting me. I think it's blocked this from me. I can't feel anyone's pain, at least not yours, Paul's, or the astronauts'. I can feel James, but not you." I heard the fear lurking in his voice.

"It's just for now, until this passes. It doesn't want you to suffer."

"Watching you cry isn't exactly a fun time."

I forced myself to stop, and then I sat up in his lap. "I know." Martini's expression was so tense, and his eyes were so worried, I couldn't stop myself. I kissed him. He kissed me right back, and the pain washed away.

He ended our kiss slowly. "When will it let me feel your emotions again?" He stroked my face and the back of my neck, and it made me want to purr—and do other things as well. He grinned. "Oh, right now, I see."

"Glad we're back to normal."

Martini's eyes moved away from mine. "Only us."

I turned to where he was looking. Gower was curled up, and Reader was holding him much as Martini had been holding me. Brian was the same, and Claudia had her arms around him. The other astronauts were in the room with us. Chee was being held by Lorraine, and Michael was being held by Alfred. No one looked recovered.

"I have to help them." I slipped off Martini's lap and went to Gower first.

Reader's eyes were wild. "Girlfriend, this isn't really what we were expecting."

"It . . . showed us things. Things we needed to see."

"Why?" Gower sobbed.

I stroked his head. "So we'll never forget. It's us alone out here, and we have to stick together. The entity wants to be with us, but it also wants to be understood. Its pain is ours, only magnified. Are you in there?" I wasn't asking for Gower this time.

He nodded. "Yes, we are." The voice was different, not quite Gower's. "We did not mean to cause so much pain."

"It's okay, we'll recover. People can recover; it's part of how we adapt and survive. Can you help Paul, though?"

"We are . . . trying. He is resisting."

I managed a chuckle. "He's a man. They don't like to accept help unless they have to."

"Am I going to be sleeping with an entire galactic consciousness?" Reader asked me. "Because if so, I think Paul and I are going to need a bigger bed."

"No. We will not intrude. We know how important you are to . . . us?"

"To Paul, and you're now a part of Paul, so that's right." I looked at Reader. "They're going to be confused for a while, I think. Just remember that they're really trying to adapt and not cause problems."

He managed a grin. "I'll do my best."

Gower gave a shuddering sigh. "What's going on, Jamie?" It was his voice again.

"I think we're all making plans to never come to Florida again," Reader said. "But otherwise, you're the new and improved model, and supposedly things will be normal in a while. Oh, and let the entity help you, okay? By the way, girlfriend, we need to give that a name. Calling it 'the entity' is starting to make me expect something to burst out of Paul's chest at any minute."

"Makes sense. What name?"

Gower sat up and kind of twitched. "Oh, this is really odd. Okay, the entity says that it likes the name Kitty."

Reader and I both burst into laughter. "That would be interesting," Reader said with a wicked grin. "But if we're going to do a threesome, I'd rather have the original model."

"So not amused over here," Martini said.

Gower twitched again. "I hope this gets smoother. I feel like I have palsy. I explained that we'd like a name that isn't a duplicate of anyone else's, so that the entity is acknowledged in its own right." Mr. Diplomacy in action. I knew I'd been right about where the entity needed to go.

"What about Bob?"

"Are you kidding? I'm not sharing mind space with 'Bob.'" Gower chuckled. "The entity says it's not wild about Bob, either. No offense meant to the many great Bobs who have come before and will come after intended." It was learning humor already. This was a good sign.

"You want a boy name, a girl name, or a nongender-specific name?"

Gower seemed to be thinking, or having a conversation in his head. He twitched a little, but it was getting more controlled. "Nongender-specific."

"Okay, I'll think about that while I check out the astronauts."

"They don't need checking out," Martini snapped.

"Oh, Jeff, you know what I mean." I got up and went over to Brian and knelt next to him and Claudia. "Hey, big guy, come on, it's okay."

Brian clutched my hand. "This sucks."

"Yeah, it does. Look at it this way—you won't have to live with it every day like Paul will."

Brian shook his head. "I won't be able to ever forget this."

"Yeah, I know you're good with the remembering. That's okay. It shouldn't be forgotten. But, you'll be okay in a little bit. Besides, this is nothing compared to doing hill charges in the monsoons."

"Or stair drills during sandstorms." He managed a smile. "It was good preparation for my career."

"Mine too, at least my second one." Brian looked ready to sit up, and Claudia and I both helped him; he kept hold of my hand. Claudia stroked his head, and Brian leaned back against her. I could see Randy out of the corner of my eye, and he looked no more pleased than Martini did out of the other corner.

"I think it's passing," he said finally.

"Great, let's get you standing up, then."

I started to get to my feet when Martini's arm went around my waist, and he picked me up, conveniently pulling my hand out of Brian's. "I'll help him; you're still recovering, too."

Martini put his hand down to Brian, who took it somewhat reluctantly. Martini moved Brian to his feet rather more quickly than I thought was probably nice or good for Brian under the circumstances.

But Brian just grinned. "Thanks. Still not as bad as reentry." He turned around to help Claudia up, but Randy was already there and pointedly did this himself. Brian looked at me. "I see I'm popular."

"With the ladies." Martini shot me a look that said any more jokes like that wouldn't be taken well. "I'm going to check on Daniel now," I said quickly.

Joe looked far less jealous of Lorraine's holding Chee. This was possibly because Chee was wearing a wedding ring. Lorraine had him sitting up by the time I got to them. "Daniel's going to be okay," she said as she stroked his head.

Like Brian, Chee was leaning back against her. Unlike Brian, he seemed more concerned with everyone else than enjoying his backrest. "How are you? Are the others doing all right?"

"I'm fine, Paul and Brian seem like they'll be okay. I haven't checked Michael out yet." I glanced over. He was still in a ball with Alfred rocking him as though he were a small child. "Not so good over there."

Chee nodded. "I'm not surprised."

"Why so?"

He gave me a weak smile and dropped his voice. "He's the loneliest."

"Not Brian?"

Chee shook his head. "You're here. Even though you're in a relationship with someone else, you two go way back, and you obviously care about him, even if you're not going to become his wife tomorrow. Brian has been so focused on you, or finding someone to equal you, that he's had a lot of long-term relationships. He also has strong friendships, here and in his personal life. Michael . . . not so much."

"The player stands alone."

"Right."

"You've worked with them a long time?"

Chee grinned. "And I have doctoral degrees in psychology and human behavior as well as astrophysics." I thought I detected some drool running down Lorraine's chin. Dazzlers loved brains and brain potential; they weren't so much into looks, though if they could get both, it wasn't considered a bad deal. The younger generation of Dazzlers pretty much only wanted to marry human men, under the notion that they were smarter than A-C males. I didn't agree, but I also felt interspecies mating was something we needed, regardless of the fact I was with Martini, so I didn't put much effort into arguing for A-C male mental gifts.

"What does your wife do?" I figured I needed to give Lorraine, and possibly Claudia, a gentle reminder that this one was unavailable.

"She's a rocket scientist. She helped design the *Valiant*." He sounded extremely proud.

"She sounds great," Lorraine said, with only a trace of envy.

"Maybe you'll meet her; she's here somewhere I'm sure." Chee sounded normal again.

"Jeff, can you help Daniel up?"

He lifted me up first. "Sure, baby. What's your plan for bachelor number three?" he asked as he reached his hand down to Chee. Martini was a lot gentler this time. Joe helped Lorraine up and pulled her next to him. I got the impression he'd picked up the drool moment.

I sighed. "I need to help your father."

"Why you?"

"Because Paul needs to concentrate on adjusting to the soon-to-be-renamed entity, and the next closest relative isn't helping."

"Christopher could give it a try."

"He could, and so could you, but familial rivalries do not a comfort situation make." I looked up at him. "Trust me, I'm not going to let him one-up you, at least not with me."

Martini sighed. "Okay, go for it."

"I don't need any help from any of you," Michael said, between sobs.

Alfred gave me a long-suffering look. "Good luck."

CHAPTER 38

I KNELT DOWN NEXT TO Michael and Alfred. "Yeah, I know, tough guy. You're good all on your own, right?"

"Get away from me," he snarled. At least he tried to snarl. But he was still crying and it didn't come off as intimidating.

I stroked his head. He tried to bat my hand away, but Alfred grabbed it. "Michael, you're not too old to be turned over my knee." He shook his head. "He's normally not this unpleasant."

"Oh, that's open to debate. Plus, he normally hasn't faced his own loneliness and had it thrown back at him a thousandfold."

Michael managed a baleful look in my direction. "Who says I'm lonely?"

"Uh, everyone. And your reactions confirm it." I settled down next to them. "So, any good nongender-specific names you two can come up with?"

"This is supposed to help him?" Alfred asked. He shot Martini a look. "Son, you might want to lend a hand."

Martini shook his head. "Kitty's got it handled. Don't you, baby?"

"In my own way. So, Michael, any name suggestions?"

"For what?" He still seemed angry but he was crying a bit less.

"For the soon-to-be-renamed entity that's now residing within your brother. I suggested Bob, but it was turned down."

"Why is it in Paul?" I heard some resentment. What a surprise.

"Because he can handle it. And you can't."

"Thanks, I feel a lot better." He gave me another nasty look. "I think I may take back the dinner invitation."

I laughed, I couldn't help it. "Michael, you crack me up, you really do." I leaned closer to him and whispered in his ear. "You're extremely handsome, but so is every A-C male. You're not more attractive to me than Jeff, Christopher, Paul, or James. Christopher and I have an understanding, and the understanding is that I'm Jeff's. But if something happened to Jeff, after a long period of mourning, I might be able to face it with my favorite snarkmeister. If James and your brother ever seriously consider going bi, then Jeff might need to worry. Otherwise . . . not so much."

Michael shifted so he could glare at me more easily. Maybe glaring was just an A-C specialty and Christopher was their gold medalist. "What does Jeff have that I don't?"

"Wow, do we have the time? Charm, charisma, killer smile, the greatest body on the planet. Not to mention power and authority, which, as any girl can tell you, are always turn ons. And other qualities best not discussed in front of his father."

"Oh, no, go ahead," Alfred said. "Make me proud."

"He's really so much like you. No one told me."

"They were probably worried I'd steal you away," he said with a grin.

Martini cleared his throat. "Dad? You're heading into therapy territory."

"Always with you it's the trauma." Alfred gave me a wink. "You seem to handle his histrionics well."

"He's worth it." I looked back to Michael. "You, so far, are not. Now, get it together and sit up like a big boy, or at least toss some names out."

Michael glared at me again, but he stretched out and put his hands behind his head. "Paula."

"Nongender-specific, weren't you paying attention?"

He managed a smile. "Just seemed like a good choice."

"Bob was better."

He snorted. "Hardly. How about Leslie?"

"Hate it," Gower called.

We went through a few more, none making any headway in our finding a name, but all getting Michael back to normal. Within a few minutes he was sitting up.

Christopher wandered over. "What about location or something instead of a regular name?"

"Location like what?" Gower asked. "By the way, you want to get off the floor so Uncle Alfred can get up, too?" he asked Michael as he walked over to us.

"I suppose," Michael said reluctantly. Gower reached his hand down. Michael took it slowly. Gower hauled him to his feet. "Thanks."

"Any time, little brother. You want up, Kitty?"

"Oh, my job, thanks," Martini said, as he picked me up and kept his arm around me.

Alfred rolled his eyes. "Thanks for the helping hand, son."

Michael reached his hand down. "Let me." He helped Alfred up and then hugged the older man. "Thanks for taking care of me."

Alfred patted his back. "That's what family's for."

"Think of a name," I said to everyone. "Christopher, any ideas?"

"Dakota?"

"You said you never went to the movies."

"But he reads the trades," Reader said with a snicker.

"It's a collective consciousness from across two solar systems, not a bear," Gower added, sounding peeved.

The rest of the gang got into it. I kept on trying to come up with something that didn't sound silly, having already tossed out Bob. Part of me wanted to suggest the name Terry, but I didn't think Christopher or Martini would be able to deal with it. I leaned my head against Martini's shoulder and let my mind wander.

What had I seen while I was asleep? Alpha Centauri and Earth, though I had no idea which of the many planets cruising around the double stars was the A-C home world.

What did the entity have that made it unique? In a way, it belonged to both Alpha Centauri and Earth. Just like the A-Cs. The A-Cs of Earth.

"Um . . . what about . . . ACE?"

"As in of spades?" Christopher asked, sounding unimpressed.

"No, as in Alpha Centauri and Earth. All capital letters, sort of thing, A-C-E."

"That'll sound like he's got a great pilot in there," Joe said, sounding uncertain.

"Or a card sharp," Reader added.

"A tennis pro," Randy suggested.

"There aren't a lot of negatives associated with it," I reminded them. "Most people would take being called the ace as a compliment."

"You just like it because you thought it up," Christopher said. This was true, but I still thought it was good.

"We like it," the voice that wasn't quite Gower's said.

Gower twitched and nodded. "I'm fine with ACE."

Reader's phone rang. "Hello. Uh-huh. Yeah, we've solved the astronaut problem. No, nothing on the other two. Oh, yeah? Great, we'll be there shortly." He hung up. "Glad we have that whole naming issue taken care of, because that was Kevin. He thinks he's found Kitty's stalker."

CHAPTER 39

WE FILED OUT, astronauts in tow. Martini sent Christopher, Reader, and Gower to verify if the dead cleaning woman's body was still in the computer room. It was, which was something of a relief.

We wandered more halls and walked through areas that, if we weren't in the middle of all the life and world threatening situations, would have been fascinating. I could hear Chee pointing out some things to Lorraine and Claudia, both of whom were flanking him, with their guys hanging on tight. It occurred to me that bringing the girls here was like taking them to their version of Disneyland and Chippendale's combined.

Jerry was still riding herd on Turco, assisted by Gower, Reader, and Alfred, all of whom were discussing how they were looking forward to ensuring Turco never did security at so much as a Taco Bell. I'd almost have felt sorry for him, but he was still busy insinuating that the A-Cs were responsible for all the world's problems, up to and including global warming.

Christopher and Michael were behind us, but close enough to hear our conversation easily. Martini had a firm hold on my hand, in part because Brian was walking next to me. "So, you really think someone's out to get you because of me?" Brian asked, sounding a little weirded out and a lot flattered.

"I know, hard to believe, isn't it?" Martini snapped.

I squeezed his hand. "Jeff, stop. Yeah, Bri, I really do think we've got someone who loves you just a little too much."

He sighed. "I hope whoever it is doesn't have a gun."

"Yeah, me too." We had no idea if Kevin had the suspected stalker in custody or if he had merely narrowed the potential suspects down to one.

"So, what're your parents up to?"

Wow. I had no idea of how to answer that—on the one hand, everyone I hung with on a daily basis knew exactly who and what my parents were and did. But Brian fell into the gray area of someone who might be safe to tell but also might not be. I went for the classic. "They're great. Mom was thrilled to hear we'd run into each other."

"Really? That's so nice. Your parents were always the best."

"Yeah," Christopher said from behind us. "They like me a lot, too." Martini was starting to growl under his breath. "Jeff . . . not as much."

I didn't have to look behind me to know Christopher was grinning and having some fun at his cousin's expense. Brian, of course, had no knowledge of their relationship, or mine with Christopher. "Oh, did you date Kitty, too?" Brian asked, innocently as far as I could tell.

Martini was walking faster, and I could feel anger radiating off of him. Gower, or ACE, more likely, must have felt it, too, because he fell back. "Jeff, we need to chat, just for a second."

Martini didn't want to, I knew. "Jeff, I'll just wait a couple of feet away, okay?" He let my hand go, so I took that for a yes. The other three went with me, and we waited at a corner. Chee was still leading the others off; we were going to lose them in a second or two. "Michael, you know how to get to Mission Control, right?"

"Gosh, I hope so. I only work here."

"Sarcasm is such an ugly trait in an A-C."

"You seem enamored of it." Michael jerked his head toward Martini.

"He makes it look good."

Brian cleared his throat. "I know how to get there, too, Kitty."

Now I felt bad. Oh, well, story of my life, chronic foot-in-mouth disease. Martini assured me there was no cure but claimed to find it an endearing trait. "Sorry, Bri. I'm just having a hard time thinking of you as an astronaut."

"What did you think I was going to become?" he asked, sounding somewhat huffy.

I didn't have the heart to tell him I hadn't given his career choices a lot of thought once we'd graduated from high school. "I don't know. Maybe a lawyer."

He shook his head. "I don't know why. I could see you in marketing—you were always creative."

"No I wasn't. I was good at bullshit. It's considered a great gift in marketing. But I wasn't an artist or a writer, Bri. I was a marketing manager. It means I told some people what to do and took orders from other people."

"As opposed to now," Christopher said, "where she gives everyone orders and ignores the orders from people she's supposed to listen to."

"You're not over me not letting you guys die yet, are you?"

"You really didn't see me becoming successful, did you?" Brian asked.

I wanted a subject change, but more I was wondering what Gower and Martini were talking about, because while it wasn't an animated conversation, it was taking a little long for the "cool down" talk I'd thought Gower was giving him. So I didn't really think about what came out of my mouth. "Why did we break up?"

"What, you want me to recite the reasons you gave me in front of your ex-boyfriend? Why don't we wait so I can tell your current one your reasons, too." Ah, this sounded more familiar. I really attracted the jealous types. Or else I really found them attractive, because I'd had a few others in between Brian and Martini. Only, as I thought about it, I hadn't been in love with any of them.

"Brian, Christopher is not my 'ex' anything." Unless one counted a few minutes of pawing each other like crazed wolverines in an elevator until my sanity came back as being an "item." And I didn't, in part because I'd almost lost Martini right then, before I'd even realized I never wanted to lose him. Christopher and I both had the real excuse that the Supreme Fugly was affecting our emotions, his in particular, but that excuse only worked because we'd stopped and Martini had finally realized I didn't want Christopher over him. I didn't want anyone over him, but some days he still didn't believe it.

This line of thought always did two things—made me feel guilty and incredibly horny at the same time. I wanted to go somewhere, anywhere, and make love to Martini for the next several hours and let everyone else deal with the crap. Only we couldn't, and I knew it.

"Then why do you want me to talk about why we broke up?" Brian wasn't going to let it go, even though we were with Christopher and Michael.

Interestingly, Michael was the one who answered that question. "Because she doesn't remember." Brian started to argue, but Michael shook his head. "Bri, I've got more of a chance with her than you do, and she was pretty clear that I have no chance at all. She didn't recognize you, okay? Accept it. You're still in love with her, but she moved on, as near as I can tell, about ten years ago."

Brian looked at me, and his expression was hurt. "Is he right? You didn't remember me? You don't remember why we broke up, or anything else?"

I sighed. "Brian, I have your picture up, still. It's one of the few that really matters to me, the one of us dancing at my sweet sixteen." An oxymoron in and of itself, if you bought the tagline of "never been kissed." I'd already been kissed a lot by then. "You'll always be someone very important to me, for a variety of reasons." I heard Christopher snort and made sure I didn't look at him—I was certain he knew my full relationship with Brian from that one picture, perhaps more than I did.

"But, I haven't spent the last decade wondering where you were, other than the occasional thought that I hoped you were doing well. You're trying to pick up a relationship over ten years after it ended, and you're trying to do it without understanding that I spent the time actually living, not staying a static memory."

"You don't know her any more," Christopher said gently. "You think you do, but you don't. You've both changed in ten years, more than either one of you realize. Even if she weren't in love with my cousin, you'd have to rebuild, learn if you liked each other as you are *now*, not however you were a decade ago."

Brian nodded slowly. "I guess that makes sense." He gave me a grin I remembered. "You're not engaged or married. That gives me a shot."

This wasn't the line of thought I was hoping Brian was going to go for. "Um, I suppose. But, Brian—I'm really happy with Jeff."

He shrugged. "Maybe you only think you are."

"Brian? Do you perhaps remember any of the posters and books in my room?"

"Yeah, and sorry. As an independent woman, you know your own mind." He sounded like he'd memorized this and still found it annoying.

This rang a bell. "Did I use that as a reason we were breaking up?"

Brian nodded. "That and I was possessive, jealous, overly protective, somewhat smothering, needy, clingy, and overcommitted to commitment. I was a good kisser and, from your limited experience, good in bed, you did throw me those bones."

"Erm . . ." Wow, he'd just described Martini in, pretty much, a nutshell. Only, fabulous kisser and out of this or any other world in the sex department in my much less limited experience.

Christopher was laughing, so hard he had to lean on Michael to stay upright. "Glad to see your tastes have changed *so* much."

Surprisingly, this comment didn't make Brian angry. He grinned at me. "So, I do have a shot. Good to know."

Michael patted my shoulder. "I know you think I'm a jerk, but if you want to try someone who isn't anything like just described, I'm your man."

"I'll keep it mind." For want of anything better to do, I looked around the corner. The others were long gone. Martini and Gower were still in deep discussion.

My phone chose this moment to ring again. I wasn't disappointed. I dug it out and saw the number, however, and my relief quickly faded. "Hi, again, odd stalker person. For the official record, Brian's not my boyfriend."

"You're both going to die now!" The voice wasn't muffled any more. It was a woman, and she was screaming at the top of her lungs. I had to hold the phone away from my ear in order to retain hearing. She was so loud the others could hear her easily.

"Why? He's not with me. We're not together. We are not a couple. Can I explain that any other ways you might comprehend?"

"I can see you, and he's right next to you, that two-timing bastard!"

"Yes, we're walking somewhere together. But that doesn't mean we're an item. Why don't you calm down, and maybe you can explain to Brian why he should be in love with you."

"It's too late for that. You had your chance, but you refused to leave. You want him for yourself? Fine! Prepare to die, you man-eating bitch!"

CHAPTER 40

A-C REFLEXES MIGHT MEAN THEY couldn't drive cars or fly planes safely, but they sure came in handy during a crisis situation. Christopher grabbed me, Michael grabbed Brian, and then we were all running at hyperspeed back the way we'd come. Martini and Gower were also with us.

The bomb went off as we rounded one of the many corners. Fortunately A-Cs were also much stronger than humans, because the shock waves knocked me down, and I would have gone flying if Christopher hadn't managed to wrap his arms around me.

We stopped. "MOVE!" Martini bellowed. I saw a fireball headed toward us. Whoever was "in love" with Brian had some serious skills with explosives.

We all ran again at hyperspeed. Christopher still had my hand, but Martini was on my other side. He didn't touch me, not because he was in a snit but because doubling the hyperspeed effect was more than hard on humans.

I had no idea where we were going, but Michael was in the lead, dragging Brian along, and the rest of us followed them. We weren't headed back to quarantine, that I was sure of.

We came to a stop what seemed like far away in the maze of hallways from where we'd been. Brian and I both dropped to our hands and knees and started retching.

"This sucks worse than being possessed," Brian gasped out between gags.

"Better than blowing up," I managed to reply. I'd kept a hold of my phone somehow. It was still open, and I put it up to my ear. "Are you still on, psycho stalker person?"

She was. Lucky me. "How did you survive that, you bitch?"

I hit the speaker option so I could keep on retching while chatting with my favorite unknown loony. "Look, babe, I have no idea who you are or why you think committing felonies is the way to any man's heart, let alone Brian's, but I think I now speak for both of us in saying you are one truly whacked-out piece of work, and when we find you, we're going to enjoy locking you up somewhere for good." I was no longer amused, felt anything like pity for her, or considered this the lowest-level threat we had.

"You'll both pay for this." She was crying. "How could you escape the bomb? You're the devil, aren't you? That's why you've enticed him all these years!"

"You religious at all, babe?"

"Very, and I can spot a she-devil."

"Then, let me just say I'm gonna go all kinds of Old Testament on your ass whenever we finally meet up. That is, if you're not too freaking scared of me to stop trying to blow me up and just settle this like women have through the ages."

"How's that?" She actually sounded interested. I was so good with the psychopaths. What a fab skill.

"Girl fight. You pick the spot, I'll be there. Whoever wins gets to keep Brian."

She was quiet for a few moments, and I got to my feet with an assist from Martini. Michael helped Brian up as well, while Christopher carefully handed me the phone.

"Fine," she said finally. "The Lighthouse."

Michael shook his head violently.

"It's not close by and not in this building," Martini whispered in my ear.

"I was thinking somewhere closer and a whole lot sooner."

"I'll be there, at dawn."

"What time, exactly, is dawn around here?"

"I can't believe he's interested in someone so stupid. Dawn will be at five-forty-seven."

"Great." I loathed mornings. "See you at o-dark-thirty. Looking forward to kicking your pseudoreligious ass to Kingdom Come."

"Come alone, or I'll just kill you," she added.

"Oh, come on. I thought you'd at least want Brian along so he can see the action."

Another significant pause while all the men with me looked at me like I was crazy. "Fine, but only him."

"No worries, who else would want to see this?"

"Tomorrow, dawn, the Lighthouse. You don't come, I kill you both."

"Yeah, yeah, yeah, heard it before. See you then." We both hung up, and I made sure my phone was really off.

"Bri, Michael, do you recognize her voice?"

They both shook their heads. "I think it was disguised, even though she was screaming," Michael said.

"The technology for that is pretty easy to come by," Brian added.

"Figures. I cannot freaking believe I have to fight this chick at freaking dawn."

"I can't believe you think you're going to, and alone at that," Martini snapped.

"I can't believe you want me to go with you to watch," Brian said. "I don't want you to go, I want a SWAT team to go."

"How can she meet you anyway?" Michael asked. "You said everyone's in lockdown."

I couldn't help it, my eyes rolled. "Freak chick's not in the building." They all stared at me. "Dudes, how could she be? She's not even aware the place is in lockdown, is she? She's got some sort of visual going on, because she sure as hell knew where we were standing. Unless Turco's so bad she just rigged every single part of the entire Space Center."

"No security is that bad," Christopher said. "Besides, the entire place didn't go up, just where we were standing."

"How could she do that if she wasn't in the building?" Martini asked.

I shrugged. "How would I know? I don't make these plans up, I just have to foil them."

"How did she know you were here in the first place?" Michael asked. "I mean, my own brother showed up and I had no idea he was coming."

"You were in quarantine," Gower reminded him.

"But . . . that's a really good question. I mean, she called me after the first bomb went off, the one trying to kill Jeff and his father." My brain whirred, and my stomach mentioned it was now devoid of anything and food was going to become a necessity very, very soon. "So, how did she know I was here? How, in point of fact, did anyone know I was here, other than Alfred? The only other person who had a chance of knowing I, personally, was coming was Karl Smith, and he was dead before he could mention it to anyone."

Something was tickling my brain. I dialed the phone. "James, you guys okay?"

"Yeah, but we heard a huge explosion. Another attempt on Jeff's life?"

"No, mine and Brian's. Stalker chick has some skills."

"Great."

"Who does Kevin think is stalking me? Does he have the person in custody?"

Reader sighed. "Yeah, but I think he's wrong. It's an older woman who everyone says sort of mothers Brian. She's mild-mannered and really doesn't seem like a lunatic. But she's the administrative assistant to one of the highest-ranking people here, and we've identified her as the one who found your cell phone number."

"Has she had access to a phone or a bomb trigger in the last few minutes?"

"No, she's been with Tim and Kevin the whole time since Kevin called us when we were at quarantine."

I caught Reader up on what had happened, including my upcoming Rage in the Cage. He was quiet for a few moments. "You think she's protecting someone?"

"Yes, because she's not the one who called or the one who tried to turn us into crispy critters. Is she human or A-C?"

"Human. Why would you even think she could be an A-C?"

My brain kicked. "Is she pro or con A-Cs?"

He sighed. "I'll ask Alfred." I could hear him talking in the background. "Michael, how many A-Cs work here?"

"A few hundred."

"How many women?"

"Most, really. Kennedy has the second highest female A-C population after Dulce."

"Baby, what are you thinking?" Martini sounded suspicious and worried. He was a lot smarter than the Dazzlers wanted to give him credit for.

"Brian? Do you think it's okay to date an A-C?" He was silent and looked embarrassed. "Bri, I don't care about the answer. I won't hate you for the answer and neither will anyone else standing here."

"I hate him already, so, yeah, won't change my opinion," Martini said, almost cheerfully.

Brian grimaced. "I like all our A-C personnel. They're good people. But, I just don't think it's . . . right . . . to cross-pollinate, if you will."

I nodded. "Not a surprise." After all, the first thing he'd asked when I told him I was dating Martini was if I knew Martini was an alien. "Have you dated any A-C women?"

"No. I wouldn't ask someone out I didn't want to pursue in a meaningful way."

"So, you're the anti-Michael."

"Dying with laughter," Michael said. But he didn't look all that insulted. He looked as if he knew where I was going.

Reader came back on. "Alfred says that, as far as he's ever been able to tell, the admin pool is very positive toward A-Cs. Some of them are jealous of how the women look, but most of them get along so well with the human women that they're pretty popular." That made sense to me—I'd wanted to hate them, too, but couldn't. Because they were so nice. I wanted Claudia and Lorraine to be able to marry Randy and Joe because it would make them so happy.

"James? Ask her, gently, which A-C woman she's protecting."

I could hear him talking to someone. "She won't tell me. She's crying, by the way, so you're right. Again. Don't know how you did it without me, either, girlfriend."

"I didn't, that's why I called you."

"Oh, good point. But we're not closer to who it is."

"Or how she knew I was coming." My brain kicked, hard. "Oh. Duh. James, ask Alfred if his admin is an A-C. And also if she happens to be in the office today."

"Oh, God. You really think?" He was talking to someone urgently. "Hell. Yeah, she's an A-C, and she was here, but she left before we arrived, said she was feeling sick, so before the bomb went off that put us all into lockdown. And our main suspect is looking very guilty when this gal's name is mentioned, too."

"What's her name and is she scientifically minded?"

"Already asked. Her name is Serene, and she's quite good with the sciences. You'll love this—her specialties are explosives and miniaturization."

"I'll bet she's good with long-range spying and related talents, too. Why is she working as Alfred's admin?"

"She took the position because she said she wanted a break, and Alfred needed the help because his human admin went on maternity leave."

"Okay, tell Kevin that the very inaccurately named A-C is our bomb chick, and I'm going to need to get out of the building before dawn."

"I don't want to know, do I, girlfriend?"

"Probably not. I don't know how long it'll take us to get back to you—she tossed a huge fireball bomb at us. It's really a good thing the place is in lockdown, because she'd have killed someone with that if it weren't."

"I'll mention it to Alfred and Kevin. Anything else?"

"Yeah, see if Kevin can trace her phone number." I gave it to him. "Probably a cell phone, but maybe we can GPS it or something."

"Maybe. If she's got the skills, though, and it looks as if she does, she could make it untraceable."

"Figures. Well, try."

"Will do. Paul's okay, right?"

"And you claim you don't care. Yes, we're all fine. Tired, hungry, and nauseated, but that might only be me."

"Maybe you're pregnant." He snickered.

"Anything's possible. But I get the feeling Jeff would know before I did."

"Probably. Well, we'll see you when you get here. Call if you have any more problems I can help with."

"Still love you best."

"I know, same here. Working on turning straight, I swear."

"Promises, promises."

CHAPTER 41

READER AND I HUNG UP, and I turned back to Martini. "Okay, so your dad's admin is loco. Brian, you know anyone named Serene?"

"Sure. Like you said, she's Alfred's admin right now."

"You get along with her?"

He shrugged. "I do my best to get along with everyone. Yeah, I like her, she's funny and like all the A-C women, she's brilliant."

"She's also completely unhinged. Because she's our stalker."

"I can't believe that. She goes to church with me and some of the others here. She's really religious, I can't see her doing something like this. Besides, she's not interested in me that way."

"Wait, she goes to Catholic church with you? Every week?"

"Yeah." He shrugged. "She's taking catechism classes."

I put my head in my hands. "A-Cs have their own religion, Brian. If she's taking an interest in yours, what does that tell you?"

"That she's open-minded."

"That she's in love with you," Martini said flatly. "We aren't really fascinated, as a whole, with Earth religions. Ours is similar enough that there seems to be no need."

"Plus we were exiled because of our religion, so we're all kind of attached to it," Christopher added.

"Serene's younger than us," Michael added. "And she doesn't want to marry an A-C. She's almost militant about it."

"You ever go out with her?"

Michael laughed. "No. She isn't interested in male A-Cs. She wants a human. She prefers their minds." Just like all the other A-C females of the generation born on Earth.

"So, she's in love with Brian, because he's smart enough to be an astronaut, as well as a nice, cute guy everybody likes. And he's looking for a mate, a perfect mate, and she wants to be said perfect mate, to the point where she's willing to turn her back on her own religion and, clearly, kill off the perceived competition." I turned to him. "See, Bri? You *are* desired."

"By someone who's insane," Christopher added.

"She's never said anything," Brian protested. "None of the other girls have hinted about it, either, and they usually do."

"Bri, I haven't seen you in a decade, but I could pick up that you weren't comfortable with the idea of dating an alien. I'm sure the others know that. She was probably trying to bring you around gradually. Might have worked if I weren't part of Alpha Team." The pity was back. I couldn't help it. It was too easy to understand why she'd lost it. It didn't forgive the crimes, but I could think about forgiving the criminal. If we survived unscathed, of course, which wasn't exactly a given.

"So, you're still planning to go to the Lighthouse?" Gower asked. "Because I think it's a really bad idea, compounded by the fact you're not going to be dealing with a dangerous human but rather a dangerous A-C."

"I've taken on crazy A-C psychos before, if anyone would care to recall." One with a Louisville Slugger, but then, I was testy about evil people trying to hurt my men.

"I try not to think about it too often," Martini said, as he pulled me next to him. He was tense, not a surprise. I leaned into him and felt him relax a bit.

"No ball and bat with us, either," Christopher added. It was nice to see he was feeling nostalgic about Operation Fugly, too. "I'm with Jeff. You sure you can pull this off and stay alive?"

"Of course I'm sure." I wasn't, but there was no way I was going to admit it. "We should try to rejoin the others, and, along the way, maybe figure out how she's seeing us while we're inside the building and she's not. I think it's an easy bet that the older woman who got my cell number is the one who let Serene know I was here. She probably made the first call, also. The last two were from a different number."

"Why didn't you ask Kevin to trace her number earlier?" Christopher asked, sounding peeved. Michael headed off, and the rest of us followed. I gave up trying to determine where we were.

"Because we were sort of busy when call number two came in. Besides, I figured the stalker was moving around in the building. I don't know the prefixes out here, so it's not like I can recognize a Space Center number." I saw Brian's mouth open. "Nor do I care." It snapped shut.

"So, now what?" Gower asked.

"Now we try to take care of whoever actually tried to kill Jeff and Alfred, not to mention the rest of you. Serene's not in Club 51, at least I truly hope not."

"Club 51?" Brian asked. "I've heard of that. But why?" He was quiet while we walked along. Michael seemed to be taking us through maintenance alleyways. and I found myself again feeling as if I were going to get a big piece of cheddar when we finally reached our destination. I wanted the cheddar by now, with a side of steak and potatoes. I was starving.

"I shouldn't have passed on the sandwiches your dad brought in."

Martini hugged me. "I'll find some food for you."

"When and where?"

"I have my ways."

"Good, put them into action fast. I'm ready to faint."

"I can tell. Don't worry, I'll catch you."

"It is your specialty."

"Oh," Brian said quietly.

"What?"

"Specialty, that's what it was. I was invited to a Club 51 Specialty a few months ago."

"By whom? And did you go?"

"I didn't go. They didn't seem like my kind of people"

"Why not?"

He shrugged. "They were saying some nasty things about some of the A-Cs. I just don't want to associate with people who aren't tolerant. I mean, marriage is a little different from friendship," he added quickly.

"True enough. And no worries, Bri, everyone here's aware that you're not a bigot." He looked relieved.

"You didn't answer Kitty's question about who invited you," Christopher said.

"Oh, right. It was someone I don't know really well, one of the guys in Security."

I stopped walking. So did everyone else. "Come again?"

"Security. One of the guys in Security invited me to their thing. It sounded like a lecture, though he said it was more like a convention. He tried to make it sound fun, but it just seemed like a rally, and I wasn't interested."

"What was his name?"

"Frank Taft. He's still here, works closely with Mr. Turco."

All the security breaches suddenly seemed explained. I looked at Martini. "They're near your dad, and everyone else in our group . . . and the only one being covered is Turco."

Martini grabbed my hand, Michael grabbed Brian, and then we were all going at the fastest hyperspeed I'd experienced yet.

If humans go too fast, they black out. My tolerance had improved over the past five months, but it was being tested now. I saw Brian collapse; Michael tossed him over his shoulder and kept going.

I was heading for a blackout. "Jeff, don't barge in. . . . " I couldn't talk any more, and my vision went to a pinpoint of light. I felt Martini lift me into his arms, but I couldn't hold on, and it all went black.

CHAPTER 42

I WOKE UP WITH SOMEONE'S hand covering my mouth while another hand massaged my neck. I was able to figure out the hands belonged to the same person in a few seconds. I could tell the person was Martini in a few more.

Gower was doing the same for Brian, while Michael and Christopher seemed to be watching something. We were all on the ground, the conscious men crouched low.

"We didn't barge in, thanks for the warning," Martini said softly. "Let me know when you can sit up without gagging—we can't afford the noise."

I nodded—slowly. Head felt reasonably okay. I nodded again, and Martini helped me get to a sitting position. My lower back hurt, and I reached around—amazingly, the Glock I'd shoved into the back of my pants was still there. I'd forgotten about it. I wondered if this meant my butt was too big.

"No, it's perfect, we've just been busy." Martini grinned at my expression. "Some of your emotions are like reading a bulletin." I raised an eyebrow. "You reached behind you and felt surprised, then insecure," he explained, grin still on full.

"Nice. So, what's our situation?"

"We're going to wish you had more guns in your purse," Christopher said, his voice low and tense. "Take a look, but be careful."

I realized we were under a set of windows. I moved up

onto my knees, Martini supporting me, to see an interesting sight. The room was big, and it looked just like in the movies, so I knew we were at Mission Control. There were two groups of people, one on each side of the room. Well, three groups—but I didn't count the guys in the middle who were holding a lot of guns trained on the other groups.

I spotted our team with the smaller group of people. A good many of these were female, and all of them were really great looking. The other group had what were clearly humans in it.

"Remember dear Maureen from Saguaro International, and her big scene?"

"Yes," Martini said. Christopher and Gower nodded.

"Well, this is exactly what she was claiming. They've separated the A-Cs and overt A-C supporters away from the regular humans."

"That's beyond bad," Brian said. He was looking at the scene like the rest of us. "Some of your guys look the worse for wear."

Kevin, Reader, Tim, and my five pilots were all bound, and the Security team had done some soccer practice on them. Chee was also bound, as were a couple of other human males I didn't know but had to assume were A-C friendlies.

"Well, at least most of our weapons are in your dad's office."

"Think we have time to get them?" Christopher asked.

"I don't think we can use them," Martini said, and he sounded as he always did in these kinds of situations—pissed off and totally in charge. "Too many civilians, too much risk."

"I could try creating a diversion." It was interesting to hear the word 'No!' hissed by five different men. I felt as though I were in a room full of big, angry cats. A weird idea hit me. "Um, Jeff? Are you strong enough to wrestle an alligator and win?"

Dead silence filled our little area. Christopher broke it. "Did I actually hear that right?"

"Yes. Can any of you wrestle an alligator and have a hope of winning?"

"Probably," Martini allowed. "But why?"

Brian chuckled. "Same old Kitty. There are alligators here; we're kind of proud of them. And we have some big ones, too."

"How nice. A zoo trip. Perhaps after we save everyone." Martini had the sarcasm knob up to full again.

"No, a distraction. I don't care how safe a gun makes you feel, it doesn't compare to a big-ass alligator heading for you with intent to snack."

Gower was twitching. "Paul, are you okay?" Michael asked.

Gower sort of nodded. "ACE is having trouble understanding what's going on." He looked at me. "Can you give it a go?"

"Sure. ACE, there are people who aren't as nice as others. People who would have been happy if you'd killed Michael instead of getting him home safely."

"Why?" Gower asked in the voice that I was recognizing as signifying ACE was in control of their brain.

"Lots of reasons. But the main one is that he's an A-C. The men in there with the guns, they don't care that they're threatening helpless people. They want to get rid of the A-Cs, and they don't care how they do it."

"But A-Cs here have nowhere else to go. Exiled. Must live with Earth. They help Earth, every day."

"I know. But those people with the guns don't care."

"ACE is from A-C, too. Would they hate ACE, even though here to protect?"

"Yes, they would. They would fear you, like they fear the A-Cs."

"But why?"

Brian answered. "Because, in so many ways, they're better than we are."

"Explain. Please."

Brian shrugged. "They're stronger, faster, more resilient. Smarter. Much better looking. More honest and normally more decent. Other than Michael here," he added with a grin. Michael cuffed Brian's head gently.

"But Brian likes them, Brian and Kitty both."

"Sure. I've never had an A-C treat me with anything but

respect and affection. They're professionals and fun to be
with. I spend more time with the A-C women, but I don't
have anything against the men—they don't normally make
me feel inadequate, at least not intentionally." He shot a
look at Martini but then looked back at Gower. "But even
if I didn't like them, they don't deserve to be herded into a
group and slaughtered."

Gower looked at me. "Slaughter? They will kill them?"

"Yes. They tried to kill us already, twice before we . . .
met you."

"How can ACE help?" Gower's body was shaking.

"I need to speak to Paul, ACE, okay? Let him filter to
you now."

Gower nodded and then he twitched again. "So much
for losing the palsy."

"Paul, I don't think ACE can kill someone, right?"

"Oh, it can. But I think you mean is it willing to? And
the answer is no. At least, I'm not willing to have ACE
go insane on me. I think requiring it to kill anyone would
cause a major malfunction."

"Yeah, that's what I meant. But can ACE put some kind
of shield around the hostages?"

Gower had the expression I was coming to know as him
having a chat with ACE in his head. "Yes," he said finally.
"But ACE isn't sure how well it will work, since this will be
the first time we're trying this together."

"We'll have to chance it." I looked at Martini. "Really, I
mean it. Can you, Michael, and Christopher go wrangle up
some alligators?"

"Why not a couple of grizzlies while we're at it?" he
snapped.

"If there were any here, I'd ask for them by name, but
we have to work with what we've got."

"You're insane," Christopher said. "I know I say that a
lot, but it's true."

"Boys, the longer you wait to get my requested prehis-
toric attack dogs, the more chance we have of people we
care about getting hurt, more hurt, or killed. Oh, and don't
hurt the alligators—they're a protected species."

"Unlike the three of us," Martini grumbled. He shook

his head. "I can't believe I'm actually going to put this latest plan of yours into action." He heaved a sigh. "But I am. Michael, you'll have to lead us out, and we're going to have to get through the lockdown somehow."

"Piece of cake, we'll just break out a wall." Michael seemed serious. I decided not to question.

"Be careful."

"Now she suggests that, after we're committed to 'gator capture. Unreal." Christopher glared at me and then at Gower. "You get to stay. Why?"

"I've got ACE. That's a big responsibility." He was grinning. "Besides, someone needs to ride herd on Kitty while you're off having fun."

"Fun. Right." Martini gave me a long-suffering look.

I grabbed his shirt, pulled him to me, and kissed him. "I really do mean it, Jeff . . . be careful."

He nuzzled my ear. "Always. I wouldn't miss the opportunity to make you pay for this later for anything." He pulled away from me, stroked my cheek, and then the three of them headed off. One second there, the next, gone.

Gower sighed. "What are we going to do while we wait for them to round up some alligators?"

"Figure out what we're going to do if our Club 51 friends start up with the mayhem before the others get back."

"Oh, good. Back to routine."

CHAPTER 43

"SO, WHILE WE'RE WAITING AND PRAYING,** what is Club 51, exactly?" Brian asked.

"Remember Chuckie?"

"Oh, yeah, Conspiracy Chuck. Vividly. I never understood why you got along so well with him."

"Because he was smart and funny, and we both liked comics."

"Right, my girlfriend, the comics geek. I remember."

"Funny. Anyway, Chuckie was really into all the UFO stuff, and that didn't wane when we got to college. He knew every theory, rumor, or supposition, basically." And, as my life proved every day, he'd been right, too. "He told me about these guys, and he didn't like them. They're anti-alien, militant about it, too."

"Like skinheads?"

"Worse."

"Wonderful." Brian looked away from the window and at me. "You have a spare gun?"

"Yeah." I dug the extra Glock out of my purse and handed it to him. "How well do you shoot?"

"Better than you."

"Hardly." I'd been practicing a lot.

"Well, we're probably going to find out." He looked at Gower. "Do you have a weapon, Paul?"

Gower opened his jacket—he had on a shoulder holster.

"Since when do you pack heat like that, Paul?"

He laughed. "Since your mother insisted on it."

"She didn't make Jeff or Christopher wear a holster."

"No, they told her they were wearing them and then didn't."

Figured. "So, is James carrying concealed?"

"Yes, so's Tim, but I'm sure they were searched already."

I took another look. Couldn't tell if the guns the creeps were holding were ours or theirs. But there weren't any extra guns lying about. "I wish we could hear what's going on."

Gower twitched. "ACE says we can." He reached out and touched the backs of my and Brian's necks.

It was like watching a movie. "You're going to learn why working with these . . . things . . . was a bad idea." This was Turco.

"My father knows what to do with things like you," another man said to the A-C side of the room. He was big and looked like a stupid thug.

"Frank Taft," Brian said.

"Not a surprise. Bri, are the guys with guns the entire Security force here?"

"No, just about half of them."

"Where are the others, then?"

He scanned the room. "Not in there."

"Hope they're not dead like Karl Smith and the cleaning lady."

"Why are you doing this?" Alfred asked. His voice was calm. I noted all the humans had an AC next to them. It occurred to me that Security was, as always in my short experience here, lax.

"Brian, before today, did you know an A-C could run at hyperspeed?"

"Not really. I knew they were faster than us, just like they're stronger, but not what all they could really do."

"You think they don't know our abilities, Kitty?" Gower asked me.

"I'm confident. The loons in Arizona thought we could read minds, but hyperspeed was never discussed, and they don't know about empathic abilities since they didn't guard against it."

"Turco was with us when we were in quarantine." Brian sounded worried. "Did we say anything that would give us away?"

"No idea. The three of us were rather deeply involved with ACE, and so was Michael."

"I promise you Jeff and Christopher were paying more attention to what was going on with Kitty than anything else," Gower added.

"So was James, not that we can talk to him." My brain kicked. I dug my phone out from my purse.

I could hear Reader's phone ringing. "You wanna let me answer that?" he asked. He was so cool, he didn't sound worried at all.

"Why should we?" Taft asked.

"There are some of them missing," Turco replied. "Let's round them up." He reached into Reader's inner jacket pocket and pulled out his phone, opening it just in time. He put it to Reader's mouth, and a gun to Reader's head. The way the phone was held I knew Turco and Taft were able to hear whatever was going to be said.

"Hello?"

"Jamie, baby, how goes it, lover?" Reader jerked, grinned, then pulled it together, all in the space of about two seconds.

"Hey, um, pretty great. I miss you a lot, babe." Turco nudged him. "Can't wait to get together. Have you ditched the jerk yet?"

"Working on it, hon, working on it. Trying to get him distracted, but you know how he never lets me do anything. I had to sneak into the bathroom to call you. So, where're you at, babycakes?"

"Tell your girlfriend we want them to meet you at Security," Turco whispered.

"I'm at Security, honey. Very secured and all."

"Oooh, alone?"

"No, I wish."

"Bummer. I was hoping to tie you up, in a chair, with your hands behind your back and then do *terrible* things to you." This wasn't so much true as an exact description of what I was seeing.

Taft made a gagging sound. Reader grinned. "Look, great as that sounds, and, believe me, it sounds like something I could get used to immediately, I think I need you, Jack, Peter, and Carlton to come here. Need some help with some, uh, prisoners."

"Where's Security?" I watched to see if anyone was moving toward us, but they all seemed stationary.

Reader looked up at Turco and shrugged. "Tell them you'll have someone meet them wherever they're at," Turco whispered.

"I don't really know, kind of lost and confused. You know I've never been here before. I'll send someone to fetch you. Where're you at?"

I looked at Gower. He gave me the universal "fake it" sign. Brian shook his head. "Tell him you're at the break room."

"We're in the break room. I was parched. The water here is like glass, it's delicious. And you know, they have lots of things you can't find at home. I'm so hungry I could eat a raw chicken whole."

"Um, oh, yeah?" I could tell by his voice that this clue wasn't giving Reader anything to work with. "Well, when we can get out of here, I'll take you to dinner."

"You're so much more in tune with me than Jack the Jerk. By the way, I want to go to dinner someplace where they sell regional specialties, like jerked chicken, fried alligator, and hush puppies. You know how I love fried foods."

"Oh! Yeah? Yeah, but, uh, I don't know how you think we're going to get out of here any time soon, babe."

"Well, if we can't get out, maybe we can find someone who can bring it in. Soon, since I'm really starving. And, if not, I'll have Peter and Carlton put their mind spell onto whoever tries to stop us. I'm ready to take over, aren't you?"

"So ready." Turco shoved the gun into Reader's head. "Babe, I'm sending those guys for you now. Sit tight, okay? Like you always do when I ask."

"You know I can't help but follow your orders to the letter, babycakes."

"It's why I love you, sugartits." Scary situation or not, I almost lost it and laughed.

"See you soon, my walrus-boy." We hung up, and I saw Turco motion to a couple of the Security creeps. They were going out the side opposite where we were.

"Sugartits?" Gower asked me. "Walrus-boy?"

"Don't. I can barely control the inner hyena right now."

"I get sugartits," Gower admitted. "But walrus-boy?"

Brian blushed. "Rumor has it the walrus has the second largest . . . you know . . . of all mammals."

Gower looked at me and started to grin. "Don't start, Paul, or we'll all lose it." Despite the situation, I was close to losing it anyway. The only saving grace was that Martini wasn't here.

Turco was talking to Reader again. "You and your girlfriend are sick and twisted, 'walrus-boy.' Typical alien scum."

"He thinks James is an alien?" Gower asked.

"He's good-looking enough, so I don't doubt it."

Reader shrugged. "So, what's your boyfriend call *you*, Turco?"

"I'm not gay, you sick son of an alien bitch," Turco snarled.

"They seem gay to *me*," Tim said, from behind Reader. He was tied up in the same way. "I think this one's the groom," he jerked his head at Taft.

"We have to stop those Security guys." They were out of the room, and I couldn't see them any more.

"I'll do it," Brian said.

"Not alone." Gower seemed torn. "Look, we'll be there and back fast. Kitty, will you be okay here alone?"

"Sure, even though I won't be able to hear what's going on. Get going. The faster you take them out, the faster you're back."

Gower nodded, grabbed Brian's hand, and then they disappeared. I looked back inside. Tim and Reader were getting a couple of nice hits to the stomach. I saw my five pilots' mouths moving, and they started getting hit, too. I assumed they were all following Reader's lead with the gay-baiting.

I wasn't destined to have to watch this too much longer. I heard something, then smelled something, and saw Christopher carrying a reasonably small alligator, maybe only six feet long. It was clearly pissed and struggling. He was having some trouble with it, particularly since he was crouched down.

"Kitty," he gasped. "Open the damn door!"

CHAPTER 44

THE ONLY ISSUE WITH OPENING the door and releasing the alligator was that I didn't have hyperspeed, and Gower wasn't here to have ACE do crowd protection. On the other hand, it was clear Christopher wasn't going to hang on too much longer.

I compromised. I reached up, flung the door open, and screamed, "ALLIGATOR IN THE HOUSE!" as loud as I possibly could.

Christopher shoved it in and slammed the door. We both dropped to the floor. I could hear screams and gunfire. "I hope that's working like we wanted it to."

"It's a plan of yours, Kitty. I'm sure it's going to go haywire somewhere."

"Thanks for the vote of confidence. By the way, not clear on the idea of a big 'gator, were you?"

"I was, but that was the biggest I could handle alone. My clothes look like yours normally do."

"They smell much worse than mine ever do."

"So we let you believe."

I was about to say something scathing, when I saw Martini and Michael heading toward us, carrying the largest alligator in, I guessed, existence. It was much more pissed than the other one had been and was struggling with clear intent to at least maim, if not kill. Even in a crouch, though, they had it fairly well under control.

"The door," Martini hissed. "Like now!" Okay, maybe not all that much under control.

I flung it open again. "BIGGER ALLIGATOR IN THE HOUSE!" They flung Gigantagator in, and Christopher slammed the door again.

"I just want to say that I hate your plans." Martini leaned against the wall. "And as they go, this one was both the grossest and the most dangerous to life and limb, and, yes, I'm including when we took down Mephistopheles and all the others."

"Not to mention the wonderful odor we're now all carrying," Michael said.

"Hopefully there's something in the medical kits for it," Martini said. "I don't want to smell like swamp for the next day and a half."

"Oh, stop whining." I risked a look up. "Oh, wow. You guys have to see this."

I had no idea where Gower was, but ACE was on the case. All the hostages were floating up near the ceiling in what looked like two big, protective bubbles. This left those with the guns and the alligators alone on the floor.

Hitting a moving target is not as easy as it looks in the movies, and hitting a moving target when you're running for your life is even harder. I looked more closely and could see small, protective bubbles around the alligators. How sweet, ACE had heeded my "don't harm the 'gators" directive.

"Anyone have any hyperjuice left? Or should we just stun the creeps with your aromas and fashion-forward outfits?"

"I do," Gower said, as he appeared next to us. "My God, what's that smell?"

"Hilarious." Martini glared at him. "Where the hell were you?"

"We've got the two they sent to capture us knocked out and tied up in the break room, and Brian's guarding them, Glock at the ready."

"Good. ACE is doing an awesome job with the hostages. But I want to get the guns away from the creeps, just in case."

Gower nodded. "Happy to." The door opened and closed so fast I only saw it because I was looking for it. I was alone in the hall, however, just me and some puddles of stinky swamp water. No Glock in my hand anymore, either, meaning one of the men, Martini most likely, had taken it, probably to keep me out of the action. Well, the heck with that.

I could see guns flying through the air and landing in someone's hands. When I didn't see any more guns in human creep hands, I opened the door.

To see the smaller alligator right there, mouth open, sharing its displeasure with me. It was through the door before I could slam it, and I decided that I'd run track for years for a reason.

I leaped back, so its jaws just missed me, and then I spun and ran. It was after me, and I remembered that these puppies could move when they wanted to. And this one wanted to. "Alien hater!" I shouted at it as I skidded around a corner.

It kept on coming, and I kept on running. I'd never been great with distance, but it's amazing how much stamina pissed-off nature on the hoof snapping at your heels can give you. I didn't have just an alligator after me, I had the Flash of 'gators after me.

I rounded more corners, and Alliflash kept up with me. When did these things get tired? Ever? I kept on running, but I had no idea where I was in the maze. I just prayed I didn't hit a dead end.

No sooner prayed for than denied. I rounded a corner and there was nothing but a door at the end. I tried to open it, but it was locked.

I heard voices. "Hey! Let us out!"

"Hey, let me IN!"

No use, door was locked from the outside, apparently, and I didn't have a key. I turned around. Alliflash was approaching, slowly now, and it looked really pleased. Okay, I'd been a hurdler. I could do this. And I had to do it right away, or I wouldn't have enough room to get my speed up.

I took a deep breath and then ran right toward it. I was

the rare hurdler who had a perfect four-step, which meant I'd learned to lead with either leg. So it wouldn't matter where I pushed off from, as long as no part of my body was in Alliflash's jaws. On the other hand, I wasn't a tall girl, so if I jumped too soon, I'd land somewhere on the 'gator's body, and I knew instinctively this would not be good.

Got to where I could see its beady eyes, and then I sailed over the scariest hurdle of my life.

Landed on the end of its tail and managed to keep going without falling or twisting an ankle. Sadly, this meant that Alliflash was aware of where I was, but at least I wasn't cornered any more.

I tried to head back the way I'd come, but I hadn't been paying a lot of attention to landmarks. I risked a look behind me—damn thing was still right there, relentlessly coming after me and simultaneously going for the land speed record.

Rounded more corners that I hoped looked familiar. Found myself wondering how badly it hurt to be eaten alive by an alligator. Decided it had to be pretty bad and found the will to keep on running at top speed.

I thought I was close to Mission Control but, shockingly, discovered another dead end. This one had three doors. All locked, but no one behind them, or if there were people locked inside, they were shy. These doors had the long bar handles and they were set up in a "U" shape. I didn't have a lot of options.

If necessity is the mother of invention, then terror is the father of ability. Additionally, five months of wild sex with Martini had toned a lot of my muscles. I put my back to one of the corners, put my hands on the unmoving sides of the door handles next to me, and pushed up and jumped at the same time. It took three attempts, but I managed to get my feet onto the metal.

This was great in that I wasn't on the floor. However, Alliflash didn't have too far to go to be able to grab me. I needed a weapon. Of course, I'd had one, but it had been taken away to keep me safe. I'd ponder the irony later, if I got a later. Then again, even if I'd still had my Glock, not only were the alligators officially protected, they were ACE protected, too. I didn't figure I'd have had a chance of hurting it with a bullet anyway, and having my hands free was probably in my best interests.

As Alliflash again started coming toward me in a slow and menacing way, I rummaged in my purse—carefully. My balance was precarious at best, and I had a feeling I wasn't going to be able to jump it again. My legs were shaking, and I was sprinted out.

Things I'd used in the past as weapons of sorts came into my hand. But I couldn't fathom how music would calm this particular savage beast, no pen in the world was going to penetrate that hide and I had no prayer of hitting an eye, and I just couldn't see hairspray, not even Ever-Hold, managing to do anything other than piss Alliflash off even more.

My hand hit some papers and I pulled them out. I didn't remember carrying any papers with me. Took a fast gander—briefing stuff. Okay, Reader must have slipped this in my purse when I wasn't looking in the hopes I'd read it myself. I had nothing else worth trying.

I balled a piece of paper up and threw it over Alliflash's head. It snapped at it, then turned back to me. Fine. If it was willing to play, I was willing to keep it distracted. Balled up another piece and tossed again. It snapped again. Cool, it liked to play fetch, or in this case, snap.

This was great in that Alliflash wasn't trying to eat me. Yet. But I was going to run out of briefing papers soon. Within a couple of minutes, I was down to the last piece of paper. I looked at it. It had two pictures on it. Two men, one big and older, who looked mildly familiar. The other well coiffed and reasonably attractive, but with a lean, mean look to him. I checked the names—the first was Howard Taft, the second Leventhal Reid. I realized Taft's son resembled him, which was why he'd looked familiar. I stared at their images for a few long moments. Then I balled my last page up and tossed it.

It didn't go far and landed on Alliflash's back. It snapped at it, turning around to try to catch the paper. Good, anything to focus its attention on something other than me.

The paper rolled off, and the alligator stomped on it. That was going to be me in just a few seconds. For sure, since Alliflash turned back to me now, jaws open, beady eyes twinkling as it contemplated its dinner of Kitty on the Hoof.

I decided I'd tried everything else. I screamed.

CHAPTER 45

ALLIFLASH WAS RIGHT UNDER ME. We were staring into each other's eyes, and I could feel its breath. Interestingly, it didn't smell nearly as bad as the guys who'd been in the swamp had, but I didn't think I was going to live to share this with anyone. I was still screaming but thought about stopping, because what was the point? I'd be shrieking in pain in just a few moments anyway.

It lunged toward me, and my scream went up. But before its jaws closed on me, it whipped away. I followed the movement to see Martini swing the 'gator by its tail and fling it down the hall.

"Get it out of here!" he thundered at someone.

"You couldn't knock it out?" Christopher's voice shouted back.

"Jump!" Michael's voice. "Shit! Jump, jump, jump!"

"Stay there," Martini said to me. He disappeared. I stayed put.

I heard some loud bickering, then it got quiet again. I stayed put. I didn't want to discover Alliflash had outrun an A-C. Because part of me figured it could.

Martini was in front of me again. He was still a mess, but he had a jacket on and didn't smell anymore. I assumed one of the girls had something that got rid of swamp gas or else he'd stopped to shower fully clothed.

"Why the *hell* did you open the door, where the *hell* did you go, and what the *hell* did you think you were doing?"

he shouted. At least it wasn't a bellow. "Paper balls? You were throwing balled up paper at an *alligator*?"

I couldn't help it; my lower lip started quivering, and tears came into my eyes. I tried to talk but realized I'd burst into tears if I did, so I shut my mouth.

Martini's expression softened. "Oh, baby, I'm sorry." He reached for me, and the tears came. He pulled me into his arms, and I buried my face in his neck and let the hysterics come. My legs were tired, but I couldn't be sure that an alligator wasn't coming by, so I wrapped them around his waist. I didn't care about the ick on his clothes, I just wanted to be safe, and I knew I was safe if he was holding me.

He turned around so he could see down the hall, and he rocked me. "Kitty, baby, why'd you open the door?" He stroked my back.

"I wanted to help you." This came out like a wail.

"Why didn't you scream when you first saw the alligator? I could have gotten to you a whole lot sooner if I'd realized you were in danger."

"You couldn't feel how scared I was?" I felt hurt and a little bit betrayed. He was the super empath and he didn't notice?

He kissed the side of my head. "Baby, you were scared already, everyone else was radiating some form of fear or terror, and my blocks are going haywire, so my filtering isn't working well. We had to secure the room, Lorraine went ballistic and sprayed me down while giving me the big lecture about overdoing it, I had to convince ACE to put the hostages down, things were hectic. By the time I felt your fear move up to terror, you were nowhere in sight. I tried to follow you, but you were moving so much that it was an erratic trail." His arms tightened around me. "It had you cornered twice, didn't it?"

I nodded, my face still buried in his neck. "I hurdled it the first time." Memory tickled. "There are some people locked in a room wherever I was cornered first."

"We found them. You left a strong signature there."

"You make it sound like I lifted my leg against the wall."

He laughed. "No. Emotions leave a trail like scent does.

Normally it's fairly easy to hone in on terror, but you were moving so much and so fast, it was confusing the trail."

"I'm sorry." My tears were slowing down, but I was still a long way from calm.

"Screaming was a good idea. Wish you'd done it sooner."

"I'm sorry."

Martini sighed. "Baby, stop apologizing. You were just . . . being you." He moved me so I was looking at his face. "I love you, Kitty, and I don't want anything to hurt or frighten you."

"Is everyone okay?"

He smiled. "Yeah, baby, everyone's fine. Our human guys are a little beaten up, but they're okay. Oh, by the way . . . sugartits?" I was still crying but I started to giggle. Martini shook his head. "And, walrus-boy? What the hell were you doing calling James walrus-boy?" He gave me a beady look. "You're not really interested in his walrus, are you?"

I burst into laughter. "No, Jeff, only yours."

He grinned. "Good to know." He bent and kissed me, and my body started to relax.

Our kiss lasted a good long time, and he ended it slowly. I leaned my head against his collarbone. "I'm still hungry."

"I know. You ready to go back with the others?"

"Maybe. Where're the alligators?"

"Being wrangled. Not sure if they're still in the building or not."

"I can stay right here."

He laughed and put me down. I didn't want to be down, and I tried to crawl back up. Martini tried to get me onto the ground, but I wasn't having any of it. He wrapped his arms around me but I kept on attempting to get back up. He kissed me as, I was sure, a distraction, but even this didn't make me stop. Alliflash wanted to eat *me*.

Somehow, his hands stopped trying to get me to stay on the ground, and instead one was wrapped in my hair and the other was pushing my pelvis into his. My hands imitated his, one running through his hair and the other clutching his back. He removed my purse and dropped it on the ground, then moved us into a corner, his body grinding against mine. My tears were gone, wiped away by his mouth and body.

Surviving death was a major turn on. Making out with the man who'd saved me from being alligator bait was more of one. Martini moved his mouth to my neck, and I moaned as my legs tightened around him.

He jerked, just a little, and it wasn't a sexual kind of movement.

Even though we were in a hallway, we were both ready to go for it. But there were alligators on the loose, not to mention a lot of people. And Martini was still hurt. That jerk had been from pain, and I knew it, even if I also knew he wasn't going to admit it.

I let my legs drop. "Jeff, we shouldn't. Someone could come by any time."

He sighed. "You're probably right." He set me down, and this time I didn't protest because that had been too easy and I was too worried about him.

"How do you feel? Did Lorraine give you something?"

"I'm okay, and you mean other than a tongue-lashing? Yeah. I got another shot. In my arm, not adrenaline," he added quickly due to, I assumed, the look of horror on my face. "She said I could take some aspirin if I needed it."

"I have some in my purse if you want it."

"You have everything in there." He pulled away from me and grinned. "Anything you don't carry in the magic suitcase?"

"It's not quite that big." I stroked him. "Not nearly as big as this."

He gave a low growl and kissed me, strongly. "Have I mentioned I'm glad you're such a bad girl?" He knelt down and rummaged in my purse.

"Once or twice. Have I mentioned I like how you punish me for it?"

"Once or twice." He sighed. "I can never find anything in here. I don't feel that bad, baby. I can probably wait."

I gave him a once over. Okay, a twice over. I never got tired of looking at him. "Well, you look terrible, but if you think you can make it, we could wait and get aspirin from Lorraine."

"Wow, you say the nicest things." Martini looked up at

me, and his expression changed. It was the same as he'd had in the maintenance closet at Saguaro International—he looked like he wanted to tell me or ask me something important. My mouth went dry, and my chest felt tight all of a sudden. "Kitty . . . I—"

"What in the world's been taking the two of you so long?" Alfred's voice came from down the hall.

Just as in the maintenance closet, Martini's eyes closed, and his expression changed. Disappointment washed over his face; then he looked back down at my purse—whatever moment we were about to have was gone again. I tried to keep the disappointment from washing over me. For all I knew, he wasn't really trying to do what I sort of thought he was. Maybe he was just planning to tell me he wanted me to change deodorants or something.

"Just trying to get Kitty calmed down, Dad," Martini said, still rummaging in my purse. "Thought someone else might be able to handle the situation now that the danger was past."

Alfred was nearer to us. I saw his eyes go back and forth between me and Martini. He gave me a gentle smile. "How are you doing? I heard one of the alligators tried to get you."

"Okay. Better due to Jeff saving me from being Alliflash-food."

"Alliflash?" Alfred sounded confused.

Martini looked over his shoulder. "Trust me, Dad. She named it." He looked up at me. "What'd you call the other one?"

I felt my cheeks get hot. "Gigantagator."

He grinned at me. "I love you." He said it softly, but I didn't mind. I didn't want any more of this particular moment ruined than had already been.

Alfred looked shocked for a moment, then he burst into laughter. "It *was* pretty huge. Might have been our biggest one out there."

"Have been?" Guilt flitted through me. The alligators were protected. Sure, one had tried to chow down on me, but I'd been the one who'd insisted on bringing them inside in the first place.

"Oh, they're both fine. Both seriously angry, but fine. Doing a great job of anti-alien menacing."

"They're still in the building?" I resisted the urge to leap onto Martini's shoulders.

He stood up and handed my purse to me. "I won't let them hurt you." He said it quietly again. I didn't care that his father was there. I flung myself into Martini's arms and buried my face in his chest. He stroked my head and back. "It's okay, baby. I'm here." He kissed the top of my head. "We have to swing back into action, baby."

I heaved a sigh. "Okay." I looked up at him. "But I don't want to."

"I don't either. We don't get the luxury."

"I know." He shifted me to his side. I kept my arm around his waist, and he kept his around my shoulders. "Oh, before I forget, I want my Glock back." Might as well have it, even if I couldn't shoot the alligators.

"No argument. I wish I'd let you keep it." Martini pulled it out from the back of his pants. I dropped it into my purse.

"It's okay. You saved me, so it all worked out."

"So, what've we got?" Martini asked as we joined Alfred, back to all business.

"The men locked up were the rest of the Security team, the ones who aren't anti-alien. We confiscated all cell phones, pagers, and other handheld electronics. Christopher and Paul are going through them right now, to see what we've got."

"What about Brian and the Security guys he was covering?"

"Brian's fine, his charges are with the others." Alfred chuckled. "I have to admit, I love the way you think. Alligators. They fired at them but missed every time, and you should have seen their expressions. Priceless."

"Any hostages hurt?"

"Not by the alligators, no. ACE did a great job." Alfred shook his head. "I'm amazed, and I don't know how you did it, but it may be the single most important thing that's happened for our race since we got here."

I didn't know what to say to that. "No problem" was far too flippant and also inaccurate. "Happy to" didn't seem to cover it. "I'm awesome that way" seemed a bit conceited, particularly if I was saying it to Martini's father. "I'm glad, but I still would have rather spent the time being ravaged by your son" was by far the most accurate, but was definitely a no-no. And, "Will this make your wife like me?" was probably not a great response, either.

"I'm just here to help."

"You did."

"She always does." Martini hugged me. "Dad, I need to get some food into Kitty. She's close to fainting." This was true, but I was trying to play it cool.

"No problem, son. Your mother will have dinner ready for everyone in our group."

CHAPTER 46

MARTINI STOPPED DEAD. "What do you mean? I thought the big family dinner would be after we finished up here."

"We *are* finished." Alfred chuckled. "That federal agent friend of yours, Kevin, he's efficient. Smart boy." He looked at me and winked. "You could do worse."

"He's married, happily. And I'm already doing better." Martini's body was so tense I wondered if he was going to need adrenaline. I squeezed his waist.

Alfred shrugged. "Maybe he has a brother. Anyway, Kevin called in his antiterrorism team. They're taking the conspirators into custody. Paul and Christopher altered human perception of what happened. And Christopher altered the images of what the astronauts did. I think we're good to go."

"I have to be back here at dawn."

"Why?"

"I have a catfight planned." This was true, after all.

"The stalker," Martini said, through clenched teeth. "The one who wants to kill Kitty over Brian."

"Now, there's a nice boy," Alfred said. "You two used to be an item, too, didn't you?" My head was near enough to Martini's chest—his hearts were pounding so loudly I could hear them. He was going to lose it, any moment now.

"Key phrase is 'used to be.' No strong interest on my side to renew." I gave Alfred a close look. Yep, there was definitely a twinkle in his eyes that was familiar. "Alfred, Jeff's not really up to the kidding right now. Can you please stop?"

"What are you talking about?" Alfred asked. I could see he was trying not to grin.

I sighed. "Look, the ribbing, it's hilarious. But it's hurting him. He doesn't get that you're kidding. He thinks you want me to run off with some human. Maybe you do, at that, but Jeff doesn't really need you pointing out options to his girlfriend in front of him."

Alfred shook his head. "The super empath and he can't pick up when I'm joking." He gave Martini an amused look. "You'd think you could spot it by now."

I thought about what ACE had told me. "He can't. He's too close to you." I managed not to add that Martini had said he had some major blocks up against his parents. I doubted he wanted to admit it, but the reactions he and Christopher had around Alfred told me both of them felt like the redheaded stepchildren.

Alfred took a closer look at Martini. "I'm sorry, son." He reached over and patted Martini's cheek. "I was teasing. You could use a sense of humor."

Martini's father didn't think he had a sense of humor? Oh, this was illuminating. And dread-worthy, since it was likely the entire Martini clan didn't think he had a sense of humor. Meaning he was so miserable around them he was in his Commander-mode at all times. Or worse.

"Whatever," Martini muttered. We all started walking again. "I don't think tonight is a good idea. We have more operatives here now."

"Claudia and Lorraine should go back to Dulce," Alfred said sternly.

"Oh, so sorry, but they report to me. And I don't want them going back." Unlike Martini and Christopher, who were used to doing it, I loved to pull rank.

"What do you mean, they report to you?" Alfred looked shocked.

"Head of Airborne, remember? All five pilots, Tim, and the girls report in to my unit. And, considering how much activity we've had, the fact that all my humans are the worse for wear, and the fact I have to deal with Psycho Chick at dawn, I want my medical team and my flyboys here."

"Seven additional members," Martini added.

"Oh, and I want Michael, Brian, and Daniel with us, too, because I think we need to keep the astronauts under observation for a while. No idea if Daniel and his wife have kids, but that's at least four more people. Now, if Daniel insists, I'd be okay with some A-Cs going home with him to keep him under observation, but they would be A-Cs not directly reporting to me."

"So, way too many for dinner, let alone sleeping arrangements," Martini said, trying to sound businesslike and not panicked. "We'll settle into a hotel nearby or go up to East Base."

"How many rooms do you think you'll need?"

"Over twenty," Martini said quickly.

Alfred gave him a long look. "I'm sure some can bunk together."

"Yes, and I'll be happy to tell you who'll be bunking up." Alfred looked at me with his eyebrow raised. "Lorraine and Claudia will be with Joe and Randy. I'll be sleeping with Jeff, James will be with Paul. Tim, Jerry, Matt, and Chip can bunk together in one room for four or two rooms for two. Michael and Brian, same thing, and Kevin can bunk with Christopher." I sort of figured this was letting him have it with both barrels, but, oh, well. "So, eight rooms, give or take. However, we're all fine with going to a hotel somewhere. None of us want to put your family out for this."

"No, it'll be fine." Alfred pulled out his cell phone and dialed. "Hello, dear. Yes, all's well. Several close calls. Yes, we should be home in a short while. We have more operatives than originally estimated, though. Oh? You plan so well. Yes, the guesthouse needs to be ready, too. We'll need every available room." He was quiet for a bit. "Yes, they do plan that. I'll ask." He looked at me. "My wife would like to request that the, ah, couples sleep separately."

I gave him a very nice smile. "We'll be at a local hotel." I started walking again, dragging Martini with me.

Alfred caught up. "You'll be safer at our house." He still had the phone open. I had a feeling Martini's mother was listening in.

I kept on walking. "We're all adults. The youngest person who's in a couple situation is Lorraine, and she's twenty-four. We just saved your asses at least three times over, we've had multiple attempts on our lives, I had to outrun the fastest alligator on the planet, we're hurt, tired, cranky, and *starving*."

I stopped and looked right at him. "If we were going to my parent's house, they wouldn't argue the sleeping arrangements. They're clear that every person sleeping romantically with every other person is in a committed relationship and that we're all adults. Now, if you can't manage to grasp or accept that, that's fine. No arguments or complaints on our side. We'll just go to a hotel and eat and sleep there." I leaned up so my voice would be clear in the phone as well. "We don't want to be a problem, but we're also not going to be treated like children. We happen to be grown up and *in charge*, whether you like it or not."

I backed away and started walking again. I found myself wishing my parents were here, because while they liked to pretend to Martini that they didn't think he was quite good enough, in truth they'd be angrier about this than I was.

"I wish they were here, too," Martini said quietly to me.

"How do you do that?"

"You broadcast your emotions."

"So you say. I still don't understand it."

He sighed. "You started longing for your parents. It's a clear emotion for an empath. It's almost impossible to explain to a nonempath. But I could tell you wanted them here. We could call them in," he added, sounding as though he wanted to but didn't think we should.

"Mom's with the President. I doubt Kevin wants to call her in to help clean up."

"I'm sure he doesn't." Martini looked over his shoulder and stopped walking. "My father's arguing with my mother." He sounded beyond depressed.

"Jeff, no matter what, you're the baby of the family. They probably still think of you and Christopher as little boys. It took Operation Fugly for my parents to realize I was a full grown-up. It's probably something similar."

"Maybe."

We were in sight of Mission Control. "Let's get assembled and figure out what we're doing, as a group."

"Yes, Commander Katt." He grinned at me. "I love it when you give orders."

"Mmmm, same here." I wasn't disappointed to go to a hotel. I wanted to have Martini give me a lot of orders, for hours on end.

He chuckled. "I love how you think. Lust," he added with another grin. "Yours is clear and has a lot of different levels. I like all of them."

Alfred caught up to us. "Okay, I've made arrangements. There's a secured hotel between Kennedy and our house. You're all booked there. However, dinner will be with us."

"Why?" Martini asked. "So Mom can harangue me?"

"That's fine," I said quickly. "How soon can we eat?"

Alfred looked relieved. "Soon. Everything's ready, just waiting for all of us to arrive."

Claudia and Lorraine had spotted us and came over. "What's the plan?" Lorraine asked. "We're all exhausted and hungry."

"Our house for dinner," Alfred replied. "Lucinda's made meat loaf."

Both girls squealed. "Oh, that's so great!" Claudia said. "I'll get everyone rounded up!" She ran off.

"It's that good?" I asked Lorraine.

"Better than that good." Lorraine sighed. "One day, she might pass on the recipe, too."

"Not too likely," Alfred chuckled.

"No loss," Martini muttered.

"I want to have Daniel and his wife under protection," I told Lorraine, to avoid getting into the meat loaf argument I was sure we were going to end up having no matter what.

She nodded. "James said you would. They have kids, so Kevin assigned a couple of P.T.C.U. operatives to go with them, and Christopher called in a team of A-Cs from East Base. They're all headed home already."

"Great. Are we ready to go, then?"

"Yes, we are," Kevin came up behind Lorraine. "All under control. I want to get Alpha Team out of here," he added. "We searched all personnel for Club 51 cards. Only a couple of non-Security humans had the cards. They've been detained."

"What about my stalker's assistant?"

"Also detained. Held pending full investigation."

"Can any of these people get out on bail?"

Kevin gave me a smile that looked remarkably like my mother's most intimidating one. She must have trained her whole team to do it. It was still massively impressive, made more so by Kevin having such great teeth. "Suspected terrorists don't get bail. Suspected terrorists who tried to kill the daughter of the head of the P.T.C.U. and destroy Centaurion Division don't get anything but a nice trip to a very nasty place."

"No Geneva Convention?"

"Who's Geneva?" he asked with a wicked grin.

"Fair enough." It was amazing how my perspectives had changed in less than six months. Scary things and people constantly trying to kill me and the people I loved the most on a regular basis did that to a girl. "Where are the alligators?"

"Your pets are being taken back to the swamp by Animal Control." Kevin laughed. "You should have seen the looks on Turco and Taft's faces when those came in. The first one was bad enough, but then when the giant one arrived . . . man, it was great."

"Sorry I missed it." Very sorry. I was still a little out of breath.

"So, can we use a gate to get out of here, or are we still trying to impress people who want us dead that we're just regular folks?" Martini's voice dripped sarcasm.

"Gate," Kevin replied. "I'm with you—the hell with playing nicely with others. I think this whole brouhaha about Centaurion's long-term purpose was started to get your key personnel into precarious positions. I represent Angela here; she outranks the rest, and I'm saying we're going into our own version of lockdown."

"I like how you think," Martini said with a grin.

"Start of a beautiful friendship and all that," Kevin said with a laugh. "Now, let's get going. I heard something about the best meat loaf in the known universe being served somewhere."

CHAPTER 47

OF COURSE, we couldn't race off as fast as anyone wanted. We had to secure the jet, gather our belongings that were now scattered all over the Space Center, assign some teams to figure out how badly Kennedy's Security had been infiltrated, assign a different team to get said Security back up and running, handle a couple of other issues, and make sure someone dealt with the body of the cleaning woman. One thing was missing, though, and it was troubling.

"Why can't anyone find Karl Smith's body?" I asked Martini and Kevin as we finally headed to a gate.

"Does it matter?" Kevin asked. "I mean, to what's going on?"

I thought about it. "I don't know. It's just . . . he was right. He knew Centaurion was in danger. He knew *we* were in danger. He told me not to trust anyone and not to let any of my team go anywhere alone." He'd died trying to protect Centaurion Division personnel, and that made it important to know what had happened his body. Memory tickled. "I slipped and he caught on that I was human. He stressed to me that people weren't good." I looked up at Martini. "He must have tried to warn the A-Cs, and they wouldn't believe him."

"Dad, did Karl Smith try to warn you about anything?" Martini called to Alfred, who was ahead of us, ushering personnel through the gates. There were two, and one was marked "Secured Parking." The humans and most of the A-Cs were going through this one. All the people I knew were going through the other.

Alfred gave it some thought. "No, not that I can recall."

"Do all the human personnel know they're working with aliens?"

"All the ones in our division, yes," Alfred answered. "You've only seen a portion of Kennedy and only some of the personnel."

"How do you keep them from telling everyone?"

He shrugged. "There are ways."

"Mind control ways?"

"Sometimes. Usually not. We screen everyone carefully before they move over to any job involving Centaurion personnel."

I managed not to mention that they didn't screen so carefully that Club 51 hadn't infiltrated, more than one person had been murdered, and a stalker had gotten her own little gang going. Plenty of time for that tomorrow.

"High security clearances, like for all forms of military intelligence," Kevin added.

Couldn't help myself. "Then how did Turco and Taft get on board?"

"Leventhal Reid," Reader said, without missing a beat. "Trust me, all the strings are going to lead back to him."

I didn't argue. Between the two of us, Reader and I had rarely proved to be wrong. And I'd seen Reid's picture—he looked like someone I'd want to stay far away from.

Alfred nodded. "Turco had all the right clearances. All the security measures for this area are his."

"Well, that explains how security was so easily disrupted. He set it up." The thought that this had to have taken some serious long-term planning occurred to me. I didn't know Turco or Taft at all, but neither one of them had struck me as having the ability to plan something this devious. Which meant, unsurprisingly, that they were probably following orders. I didn't have to think long or hard about whose.

"Let's deal with it after dinner," Martini said. "I want some food. I'm actually hungry enough to eat the meat loaf."

"It's your mother's specialty," Alfred chided.

"And I've never liked it. I hate meat loaf. Not just hers, anybody's."

"You'd like Kitty's if she made it for you," Alfred suggested.

Christopher was at the gate and Reader was still next to us. It was a toss-up between which one of them was laughing harder. "I'd pay money to see Kitty's meat loaf," Christopher managed to get out between snorts of laughter.

"As long as I wouldn't have to eat it," Reader added.

Alfred looked shocked. "Boys, that's very rude."

"I don't really cook. I can, I just don't like to. I live at the Science Center—we have the greatest commissary on the planet. I'm good with it."

"But, sometimes, a man wants a home-cooked meal," Alfred protested.

"My man can cook. Better than me, I might add."

"You cook?" Alfred asked Martini, clearly shocked.

"I can dress myself, too. And sometimes I can handle all Field operations for the entire Centaurion Division. Amazing, isn't it?"

"We also both like going to restaurants on those rare occasions when we can. I'll wager we could gate it over to East Base and find a restaurant in New York open and ready to serve. If you catch my drift. I'm ready to eat people, including people I know and like. Food, now, please. Or else I'm going to go ballistic."

"Leaving now," Christopher said, as he stepped through the gate.

"Everyone else ahead of me," Martini said, as Alfred appeared to be waiting for us to go first. Kevin and then Reader stepped through.

"My facility," Alfred said.

"My responsibility," Martini replied. They looked ready to stare each other down for dominance for, potentially, hours.

"My stomach is growling."

Alfred gave in first. "Fine. Can't keep our heroine waiting." He gave me a fond smile, but I could see worry in his eyes. "Don't dawdle." Everyone always told me and Martini not to waste time when we were at a gate. We'd only made out once in this kind of situation. Well, maybe twice. Okay, maybe a lot. But it had never been an issue.

"No worries. Food is supposedly waiting for us."

"Indeed." Alfred stepped through.

Martini did a couple of calibrations. "What're you doing?"

"Setting it up so I can carry you through." He looked at me. "Unless you want to step through alone."

"Never do," I said cheerfully. "Take your time."

He reached out with his free hand and stroked the back of my neck. "I wish."

"Jeff, it'll be okay. I'll do my best not to screw things up with your mother."

"Baby, there's nothing you can do. It's not you, it's them and me."

"Your father loves you, I can tell. He's just *like* you, and he likes to tease. Just like you do. You tease me all the time."

"But I mean it with love."

"So does he."

"Maybe."

"And your mother probably doesn't think anyone's good enough for her baby boy."

Martini snorted. "Right."

"I've dated a lot more guys than you have. It's pretty common. Most mothers don't think any girl's good enough for their son. Just the way most fathers don't like any guy who's interested in their daughter. Like, you know, my dad."

"Your dad came around."

"See? Your parents probably will, too."

"My father likes you. I can tell."

"I like him, too. I'll probably like your mother, and I'll bet she'll like me, too. You know, once we get to know each other."

"Anything's possible. Unlikely, but possible." He finished the calibrations and then swept me up into his arms. He shifted me to his hip and I wrapped my legs around him. Martini grabbed both our rolling bags in one hand, kissed me, and then we stepped through.

I leaned against his shoulder and kept my eyes closed. I hated going through gates even more than hyperspeed, and the farther away my face was from the safety of Martini's neck, the worse the experience. I discovered it was much worse when I was in starvation mode—the nausea was intense.

But, as always, it didn't take too long. We were through, and I looked around. Large room, not overly furnished. Christopher was the only person there. "Where are we?"

"Basement of my parent's house." Martini put me down, and I took my bag from him. "Welcome to hell."

"It's worse," Christopher said. "All your sisters are here, and their husbands, and their kids."

"Oh, God." Martini sounded ready to die.

"And," Christopher added, "they're all upset with us for being so late."

"Are you kidding me? How did they expect us to get here on time, whatever that was? We were busy. What time is it, anyway?"

"Around eight," Christopher sighed. "The family usually eats at six."

"I suppose eating without us and doing the family dinner, say, tomorrow wasn't an option?"

"It never is," Martini said, in a voice of doom. "Seriously, if we break up after this, I'm prepared. Sort of."

"Jeff, I'm not breaking up with you over your family's oddities."

"She says that now." Christopher sighed. "Kitty, just trust us—it's going to be grueling, and they're going to piss you off."

"Oh, good." My stomach growled. Loudly enough to be heard.

"Food, first," Martini said briskly. "Torture for dessert."

He took my hand, and we headed upstairs, but not at hyperspeed, more as if we were heading to the gallows. Neither one of them wanted to join everyone else. I thought about what Christopher had said. "How many people are upstairs?"

"An unreal number. Something like forty, maybe more.

I lost count." Christopher sounded serious. Martini just groaned.

"Jeff, do you have blocks up?"

"Not as many as I'll need."

I shot a worried look at Christopher. He gave me a weak smile in return. "You have Jeff's adrenaline, right? And Claudia and Lorraine have medical kits. We'll be okay." His voice said he was a terrible liar, but I knew that already.

"How are you both feeling, physically?"

"Okay," Christopher said.

"I'll live." Martini sighed. "I may not want to, though."

We crested the stairs, and I was greeted by the sight of . . . not too much. Long hallway, basically. We walked down it; I kept hearing a dirge in my mind. Rounded a corner and finally saw what looked like a room. A huge room, as we got into it. "What room is this?"

"Entryway. Both the gate room and the front door lead here."

"Um, how big is your family's place?"

"About twelve thousand square feet," Martini said, as if this was no big deal.

"Come again?"

"Twelve thousand square feet, give or take," Christopher confirmed.

"So, your family lives in a mansion?" We could pretty much put five of my parents' houses inside Martini's one. For some reason, this made me feel a little uncomfortable.

"There were six of us kids, seven when Christopher was here," Martini said, again, as if this were no biggie.

"Your dad said there was a guesthouse."

"Out on the grounds, yeah. It's smaller, though." The grounds. He said it as though, again, it was no big deal.

"Your family's loaded."

"I guess." He looked down at me. "Does it matter?"

"No." I hoped not. I had a horrible, sinking feeling in my stomach, though. But maybe A-Cs didn't go in for class and money prejudices, just as they ignored skin color and sexual preferences as issues. Then again, Martini's mother didn't approve of me—maybe she knew I didn't have a clear idea of which fork to use, ever.

The rest of our team's luggage was here, so we dropped ours off and kept on going.

I could hear children now, shrieks and cries and so forth. We finished the trek through the entry room and got into what I assumed was the family room. Either that, or it was where they performed Shakespeare. Huge, but very filled with people, most of whom were male or under the age of twelve. I saw the majority of our team in here.

A voice screamed, at the top of its lungs. "Uncle Jeff!"

CHAPTER 48

I COULDN'T DETERMINE THE AGE or gender of the child who'd spotted Martini initially, but it hardly mattered. We were dog piled in moments.

Or he was. Christopher managed to drag me aside just in time. Martini was being overrun by children—they were climbing on him, hugging him, clamoring for his attention. And he was delivering. Children were being tossed and caught, flipped around, put onto his back, swung through his legs, hugged, kissed, and generally loved on.

I couldn't count heads, they were moving around too much, but there were well over a dozen children, from little ones just walking to teenagers a tad too old to be mauling their uncle. But it wasn't stopping them, they were in line for attention, too.

I heard another shriek. "Uncle Christopher's here, too!" I knew enough by now to leap out of the way. Christopher was grabbed by two of the older kids and dragged into the family pile. I risked a quick look around. Gower looked as though this was a normal occurrence, and so did Reader. There were some men I didn't recognize—all drop-dead gorgeous, so I assumed these were Jeff's brothers-in-law. Most of them were talking to Gower.

One of the older teenagers extracted herself from the riot and came over to me. She gave me a very obvious once over. "Are you Uncle Jeff's girlfriend?"

I saw no reason to deny it. "Yes."

She nodded. "You know you can't marry him."

Oh, my God. Martini hadn't been kidding. "Well, that's sort of up to your Uncle Jeff and me."

She shook her head. "No, it isn't. Great-Uncle Richard says you can't, so you can't. My mother says so."

"What's your name? And how old are you?"

"I'm Stephanie, and I'm fifteen."

"I'm Kitty, and I'm twenty-seven." I leaned close to her. "You know what *my* mother says?" She shook her head. "*My* mother says I can do anything I damn well please. And, trust me, my mother can take your mother." My mother could take anyone.

"Whoa, Kitty, come and meet the guys!" Reader grabbed my hand and dragged me away from Stephanie. No matter, she was headed off, presumably to where the women were, to report back. I was doomed.

"A little late on the save there, James."

"This is sucking more than normal," he said in a low voice. "We've already had Kevin's authority to make any decisions questioned. It's not a pretty place for a regular human right now."

"Why not?"

Reader shot a look over his shoulder. "Want my honest opinion?"

"Always."

"They're all jealous as hell of Jeff and Christopher. We work with them, so they're taking out what they can on us."

We reached the others now, and I was introduced. I knew I looked like crap—most of us did, Alfred included. But the looks I got from the men weren't what I was expecting. To a man they checked me out, and I didn't get the "you're not good enough for our boy" reactions—I got a lot of wide, friendly smiles.

I couldn't keep any of their names straight—and I stopped trying after a bit. Somewhere along I'd learn them if I had to. Otherwise, I just wanted to get to the table and eat something, anything.

Alfred extracted me. "Come and meet the girls," he said, as if this were going to be fun for me. I said my regretful good-byes to the males, shot a desperate look at Martini and Christopher, but they were both too occupied to notice I was leaving the room. On my own. I got that gallows feeling again.

We went through a huge hallway into the largest kitchen I'd ever seen outside of a restaurant. There were fewer people in here, but all of them were women. A-Cs were very traditional, and apparently they'd happily taken on prior-day Earth standards. All the women looked perfectly put together and were, naturally, gorgeous. Claudia and Lorraine were bustling about, helping out, and chattering away to women I assumed were Martini's sisters.

There was an older woman who seemed to be running everything, and it didn't take genius to figure she was Martini's mother. She looked like a slender, smaller, female version of Richard White, which made sense since she was his sister. She had streaks of gray in her hair, but they just made her look exotic.

Alfred cleared his throat, and all the female heads turned. "Everyone, this is Kitty Katt, Jeffrey's girlfriend. Kitty, my wife, Lucinda."

"Nice to meet you, Mrs. Martini."

"Is she a stripper?" I heard one of the women hiss to Claudia.

"No!" Claudia hissed back. "She's the head of Airborne!"

I let it pass and waved. "Nice to meet you all." I was human, I could actually lie well.

Unlike their male counterparts, none of these women looked happy to see me, other than Claudia and Lorraine. Martini's mother plastered a smile onto her face. "How nice to finally get to meet you. I'd hoped Jeffrey would bring you by sooner, and not because of work."

"Well, he's wanted to," I lied, keeping a happy smile on my face. "But you know, we've been so busy, one national and international emergency after another. Hard to find the time."

"Clearly. Hard to be on time, either."

I let it pass. "Evil doesn't keep nine to five hours."

"Quaint. These are my daughters—Sylvia, Elizabeth, Constance, Lauren, and Marianne."

"Nice to meet you all." I assumed she'd called them out

in age order. They all looked like their mother. They all gave me forced smiles. Okay, Martini's women really didn't like me.

There were a couple of other women in here who didn't look like family. A mother-daughter team, if I had to guess. "And this is Barbara and her daughter, Doreen." The older one glared at me, the younger one looked at her hands.

"Nice to meet you, too. Are you cousins?"

"No," Barbara said icily. "Doreen is Jeffrey's intended."

CHAPTER 49

"**B**EG PARDON?" I could have sworn she said something that didn't compute.

"Doreen is Jeffrey's intended," Barbara repeated again. "They are betrothed. Supposed to marry. Do you need another definition?"

"No, got it." I looked around. Claudia and Lorraine looked both shocked and freaked in that bad, "we should have seen this coming" way. All the other women looked triumphant. Other than Marianne, the youngest sister. She looked resigned and a bit unhappy. "Interesting. So, has Jeff agreed to this?"

"It's not his to agree any more," his mother said.

"Oh, really? Why is that?"

"We have traditions, we have rules. Jeffrey is thirty years old, and it's time for him to declare for someone." Ah, that declaration thing Michael had mentioned.

"What about Christopher? Is he required to declare, too?"

Eye shifting. I loved A-Cs—even their women couldn't lie. "No," Lucinda said.

"Really? Why not? He's the same age as Jeff." Not that I wanted them to drag Christopher off into an arranged marriage, either, but I had to keep talking or lose it totally.

No one answered. I looked at Doreen. She didn't seem thrilled . . . or jealous. She seemed uncomfortable. "So, Doreen, you're all happy to be marrying Jeff?"

"Um, yeah," she said looking down.

"You're about, what, Lorraine's age?"

"Yeah." Eyes still downcast, whole body cringing. Barbara nudged her. "Twenty-three."

"Wow. Seven years younger than Jeff. Not that age is an issue."

"No." Doreen moved away from her mother and closer to Lorraine, who looked straight at me and gave me a very tiny nod. I loved my girls.

"So, Doreen—your parents really hate the fact you're dating a human, don't they?"

Immediate reactions. Other than Lorraine and Claudia, who were giving me "go girl" signs, every single woman looked at me with their mouths open and eyes wide. Except Doreen, who burst into tears. "I don't want to marry Jeff! He barely knows me, and I don't want to live in the desert! And I don't want to leave Irving! He's the nicest man in the world!"

Irving? No argument from me. My dad's name was Solomon, after all. "No worries, Doreen."

She looked at me, tears streaming down. "They won't let us get married! Irving's done everything he was supposed to—he even converted to our religion. But they say he's not right for me."

"Yeah, they *really* hate me." I looked at Lucinda and Barbara. "You chicks are real pieces of work, you know that? What year do you think this is, eighteen-fifty? And what country, Russia? My great-grandparents had arranged marriages, but they're all dead now. My grandparents had it suggested to them. They said, 'No, thank you.'"

I looked at Alfred, who contrived to look shocked. "You know, crap like this makes Jeff sick, literally. It affects him physically, mentally, emotionally." I looked back at Lucinda. "No wonder he doesn't think you care about him or Christopher. The worst thing ever to happen to them was Terry dying, in more ways than one."

I spun around and left the kitchen, hoping I was headed back to the family room. I wasn't halfway there when someone was next to me. Doreen, of all people. She grabbed my arm. "Help me, please help me."

Lorraine and Claudia were with us now. "That's it," Claudia said, and she was furious. "I've had it. If they think they can do this to Jeff, then they think they can do this to all of us."

"Will the rest of your generation really do what the older A-Cs tell you?"

"We have to. We all swore to obey the Pontifex's rules." Claudia was shaking, she was so angry. "They made us promise before we realized it meant we'd have to marry whoever they said."

"Why don't you break those promises? Why doesn't anyone rebel?" I mean, it *wasn't* the olden days.

They all looked at me with a sort of horror in their expressions. Okay, this was a biggie. "We promised," Lorraine said slowly. "We . . . can't just break those promises."

Claudia and Doreen both nodded. "We'd be excommunicated," Doreen said. She sounded as though this was the worst thing in the world. Okay, for the A-Cs, it *was* the olden days. "We also have nowhere to go." She swallowed. "But I don't care anymore."

"We have to find a way out," Lorraine agreed. "All of us."

I thought about what my mother had warned me about and the biggest reason I wasn't pushing for Martini to leave—medical. "Can enough of your generation do medical work?"

Lorraine nodded. "Almost all of us, women, anyway. And we can train anyone who can't."

"How many are at the point Doreen is, where they just don't care about breaking that promise any more?"

Lorraine and Claudia looked at each other. "Probably everyone," Lorraine said finally, though she didn't sound confident. "There's been a lot of . . . talk about what you just said, Kitty. That we should maybe think about breaking a promise that we gave before we understood all the ramifications."

"If I could get the Pontifex to say that no one would be excommunicated, would that change things?"

"Absolutely," Claudia said. The others nodded. "If you can get that confirmed, everyone would break that stupid 'only marry within the A-C race' promise, or at least everyone who wants to marry a human would."

"Good. Then we get out. It's called total rebellion. We find someplace where we can all live, like Dulce, only ours, and we go there. With our mates, whatever race they may be. And, if we have A-Cs who want to support this even if they don't want to do it themselves, them, too."

"We do," Lorraine said firmly.

"And we do it now."

"I'm in," Claudia and Lorraine said in unison.

"Me, too," Doreen said. "And all my friends are in, too."

"It'll be better for both races, in the long and short run. Are you sure you can detach from your parents, though?"

"I can't wait to get away from them," Doreen spat out. "They don't care about what I feel or what I want. It's all 'good of the race' and 'you have to.' Never any thought about what might be good for *me*."

I'd known the younger A-Cs were angry, but I hadn't realized they were already past furious and living in Rage Central. Fury was useful, but I didn't want the A-C community fighting itself. There were too many other factions trying to wipe them out.

Before I could say anything, Lucinda and Alfred joined us. "I'm not marrying Jeff!" Doreen shouted, loudly enough to be heard in the family room, I was pretty sure. She moved behind me. I realized she was afraid they were going to try to drag her off somewhere.

"This is ridiculous." I took a deep breath. "Kevin!"

The men must have been listening in, not that it would have been hard to miss. Kevin ran to me. "What's up?"

"Kevin, please contact the head of the Presidential Terrorism Control Unit. Ask her to advise the President that we have political refugees. I'm not sure how many, could be hundreds, might be thousands. They're asking for protection from the United States Government due to religious persecution."

Kevin pulled his phone out. "On it."

"Stop." Lucinda's voice was quiet. Kevin didn't stop dialing. "No, don't do this."

I got right up into her face. "You want to go head-to-head with me? No problem. I stared down your murderous father and his fugly alter ego. And I helped kill them. Without a moment's remorse. I killed that bitch Beverly who was torturing and attempting to murder Jeff. And I have more remorse about using her head as a softball—and I have *no* remorse for that—than I do about pissing you the hell off. You pose no terrors for me. You currently also represent the kind of bigotry and repression my family's spent their entire lives trying to stop."

I took another deep breath. "Christopher!"

"Yeah, Kitty." He was next to Kevin.

"Call your father. Tell him that unless he puts a stop to any form of forced arranged marriage and excommunicating anyone who goes against that edict, I'm going to become a worse threat than Club 51 and all the Super Fuglies combined."

"You got it." Christopher started dialing.

"Christopher! How can you do this?" Barbara had joined the party. At this rate, the hallway was going to be a total fire hazard.

He shrugged. "I know who's next on the forced-marriage rolls."

Kevin put his hand over the phone. "Kitty, your mother wants to know if she needs to provide military guard to get the refugees out, or if you'd rather just have Caliente Base annexed as their refugee station and send them there."

"Kitty," Christopher said before I could answer, "my father says he has no knowledge of any kind of forced marriages in any part of our community. The Pontifex's office officially does not authorize or sanction this kind of behavior. If, however, you feel the U.S. military needs to be involved for the safety of some or all of our people, he gives you full authorization, and there will be no excommunication of anyone for any reason related to this." He looked over at Lucinda. "Oh, yes, he also said you're acting far too much like your father, and you need to cut it out right now."

Lucinda had the grace to look embarrassed. Barbara, however, seemed dead set on making what I assumed was considered a great marriage for her daughter. "Nonsense. These are our traditions. Tell the Pontifex that we have made and accepted declarations on behalf of Jeffrey and Doreen."

"Barbie, babe? You really have a lot of chutzpah, I'll give you that. However, it's sadly misplaced. You say one more thing I don't like, and I'll put every threat I've made and all the ones I haven't in action. Trust me—you can't take me, and you sure as hell can't take my mother."

Barbara's eyes narrowed. "You have no right to speak to me, in any manner, let alone this one."

"Sure she does." Martini's voice came from behind me. I turned to see him at the back of the group, leaning up against the wall. He looked amused. "See, the hilarious thing is, Kitty outranks every single person in this house, hell, in our community, other than me and Christopher. So, what you're doing is called insubordination. As I recall, our traditions have a lot to say about that, all of it nasty."

"That's by declaration and decision of the Pontifex," Christopher added. "My dad's waiting, Kitty. What do you want to do?"

I looked at Kevin. "Annex Caliente Base."

CHAPTER 50

THE BEDLAM STARTED. I was surprised. I'd gotten
used to A-Cs thinking with their mouths shut. Then I
realized none of them were thinking so much as freaking.

"SHUT UP!" Martini bellowed, and the windows shook.
No one could bellow like he could. The room went still.
"Gee, thanks. Now . . . I think we can all handle this nicely.
Barbara, I'll marry your daughter when hell freezes over,
no offense meant to you, Doreen."

"None taken," she said. She was still hiding behind me.
I hadn't realized I presented such a protective figure. Then
again, maybe they had guns and she was merely using me
as a body shield.

"Now, Mom, while this has just been the most fun home-
coming *ever*, I'll give you a choice. You can apologize to
Kitty—and by apologize I mean generally abase yourself
and grovel, beg, and plead for her to forgive you—and we
can all eat that meat loaf I still don't want, or you can continue this ridiculous gambit, and we can all leave. Oh, and
if we leave? I'm never, ever coming back. You can be at
death's door, and you'll never see me again. For all I know,
that's what you want. In which case, happy to be going now."

Christopher went and stood next to Martini. "Not that it
matters, but that goes for me, too."

I looked at Lucinda; she looked like she was going to
lose it. Alfred had his arm around her. "Boys, that's a bit
extreme."

"No, it's not. You don't get it, do you? They're *all* leaving. All of them. All your children, and I promise you, all their children, too. You want to see how it'll play out? Take a look at some history books and see what the American Immigrant experience was like. Those who came over held onto the old ways, but their children, and especially their children's children, rebelled and took on American ways."

"But we're different," Lucinda said quietly.

"No, actually, you're not. Not in the ways that matter." I looked around for Gower. He was near Martini. "Paul, what does ACE think?"

Gower shook his head. "I'll let him answer." He twitched. "ACE is confused why anyone would not want Kitty. Kitty saved world, saved ACE, saved everyone at the Space Center. Jeff loves Kitty, why is that wrong?"

"I'm a human and they're A-Cs, ACE."

Gower's head shook. "Not so different. Come from same origins." There were gasps in the room.

I looked at Martini. "I knew it. ACE, our common ancestors, were they the Ancients?"

Gower shook his head again. "No. But helped. Helped evolutions."

"Yeah. We can breed pretty true, so there has to be something back there. Basic genetic theory." I turned back to Martini's parents. "So, it's a simple decision. Are we in or out? Because I'm freaking starving, and either I get some goddamned meat loaf or at least a roll, or I start eating small children, of which, thankfully, you have a large supply."

I felt a tug at my leg. One of the littler kids was standing there. "You're funny," she said with a giggle. "Are you really gonna eat one of us?"

"Yep." I picked her up and made loud eating sounds near her neck. She squealed with laughter. I looked at Lucinda. "Seriously. Make a decision. She's awful tender."

Barbara snarled. "I say, get out."

Lucinda looked at her. "I beg your pardon? This is *my* house, and you are a guest in it. As such, you don't tell my son or any other guests what to do."

"I'm his future mother-in-law," Barbara argued.

"Bet me."

I saw it coming. Barbara lost it and lunged for me. I had a kid in my arms, but kung fu trained you for many things, and I already had her on my hip. I shoved Doreen to the side, leaped out of the way, and gave the back of Barbara's neck a really vicious chop with the side of my hand. She went facedown on the floor and stayed there.

"That was fun, can we do it again?" the little girl asked.

"What's your name?"

"I'm Kimberly and I'm three."

"Nice to meet you Kimberly, I'm Kitty."

"Are you gonna marry my Uncle Jeff?"

"That's the issue of the day, there, Kimmie."

"Kimberly," Lucinda corrected.

I looked at Lucinda. "Which do you prefer, Kimberly, Kim, Kimmie?"

"I like Kimmie!"

"Then Kimmie it is. Lucinda—if you don't want me calling you Luci and giving every single person in this house not one, not two, but at least three nicknames each, don't correct me. Ever again." I looked back at Kimmie. "And, really, what we are or aren't going to do is no one's business but mine and your Uncle Jeff's."

"Okay. Will you sit by me at dinner?"

"If we ever see dinner before midnight, sure." I looked back at Lucinda. "Seriously. Make a choice. I'm gonna eat the kid raw." Kimmie giggled.

"Dinner will be on the table in five minutes," she said quietly. Then she turned and went into the kitchen. The other women, other than Claudia, Lorraine, and Doreen, went with her.

Barbara started to come around. "Someone keep her away from me, or I'm going to pretend she's Beverly and go to town."

One of the men I hadn't been introduced to wandered in, looked down, and sighed. "She gets like this."

"Daddy," Doreen said, "I'm marrying Irving!"

"Fine, fine. I heard the proclamations." He looked at me. "You're going to destroy our race, you know."

"No, actually, I'm going to save it. But I don't expect you

to understand. Closed minds, brilliant or not, can't comprehend new ideas."

He picked Barbara up and left. I hoped they were leaving for real, but who knew? I figured I'd better be prepared for Barbara to come up behind me with a butcher knife.

"So, we staying?" Martini asked me. "She didn't apologize."

I shrugged. "I don't care. Food is here."

He nodded. "Fine." Martini looked at his father. "Thanks for the head's up."

Alfred shook his head. "I had no idea they were really going to try to go through with it. Been a little distracted the last day or so." He sighed. "I'm sorry, Kitty. I apologize on behalf of our entire family."

"I don't care. The person you should be apologizing to is Jeff." I stalked out of the hallway, still carrying Kimmie. "Where's the dining room?"

She pointed through the kitchen. I walked around the various women and did my best to ignore them completely. "Mommy, I'm going to sit with Kitty!" Kimmie said to Marianne.

"Good," she said quietly. "I'll just help you two get settled."

We walked into the massive dining room. Clearly the Martinis were used to feeding small armies. "Nice place to grow up."

"It was fine. I'm sorry about my mother and Barbara. Despite how it looks, my mother doesn't hate you."

"She's faking it really well."

"She's afraid for you."

I looked at her. "Come again?"

Marianne shook her head. "Empathic children are the most difficult." She led me to a spot somewhere in the middle of one of the two big tables in the room. "The closest comparison I can come up with is autism. Only it's worse with an empathic." She sighed. "I can remember how much my parents wanted a boy and how happy they were when Jeff arrived. And then . . ."

"Then he was a little work?" I tried not to sound huffy and failed.

"No. You don't understand. Babies can't filter anything. Most empathic talent shows up later, but Jeff was empathic at birth. And Jeff was so powerful—if our mother was tired, or cross with us, or angry with our father, he could feel it all. It was horrible. If Aunt Terry hadn't been able to take him, we'd have had to institutionalize him, for his mental safety."

"But there's nothing wrong with him."

"Now. Oh, unless you count someone having to shoot adrenaline into his hearts to keep him alive." She was trying not to cry. "He's my baby brother—we all wanted him so much. And then we couldn't be around him, couldn't even hold him, because we couldn't keep all emotions from him. And we could see it was killing him."

"Okay, so it's difficult. But isolation chambers, medical, learning how to get to the Happy Place. You all have a lot of empaths, not just Jeff, and I know some of them show their talent earlier than puberty or adulthood Surely you have techniques."

"It's rare to get an empath of Jeff's power in a nontalented family, but, yes, there are things to do. Things that are easier for an A-C to do than a human."

"Jeff's pretty good at all this stuff," I said dryly. "I'd imagine he'll be able to do what Terry did."

"If he's alive."

"What do you mean?"

Marianne shook her head. "We know what kind of jobs you do. Jeff almost died how many times today?"

"Three or four." I'd lost count.

"One day, he won't be lucky. The bullets will hit him, the superbeing will be too much for him, the adrenaline won't get to him in time. And that will leave you with a child or children you can't hope to take care of. That's what our mother's trying to protect you from."

"By alienating her son?"

"By driving you away."

"I don't roll like that, sorry. I'm really stubborn. If I'm told 'you can't,' then that's exactly what I'm going to do. Oh, and that includes taking care, proper care, of any children I might have." I was clutching Kimmie to me, I realized.

The little girl patted my back. "It's okay, Kitty. You don't have to be upset. Everyone likes you, even though they were pretending not to. Well, other than that mean lady. But she doesn't like anyone, not even Grandma, though she pretends to. I don't like her. I'm glad you hit her, she wanted to hurt you."

Marianne's eyes widened. "Kimberly. . . . "

"It's okay, Mommy. You don't have to be so scared."

"That's right." Martini said from behind me. He took Kimmie out of my arms. "We took care of all that, didn't we?"

Kimmie hugged him. "Yes. I do what you taught me every day."

He kissed her. "Good girl." Martini looked at Marianne. "She's empathic. Not as strong as me, but pretty close."

"But, Jeff, how . . . ?" Marianne sounded close to fainting.

He shrugged. "I was there when you delivered her. I handled it then."

"Handled what?"

"I implanted what she'd need to survive until she was old enough to protect herself. Just as I've done for all the other kids in our family who are empathic." He gave her a small smile. "Mom and Uncle Richard might not have talent, but no one's stopped to realize that dear unlamented Granddad was incredibly powerful. It skipped their generation, but not ours, and not hers," he nodded to Kimmie. He looked at me. "Aunt Terry taught me."

"I figured." As fascinating as this was, I was wondering what the holdup on the food was.

"They had to make more food, reheat other food, figure out how in the world to apologize to you without sounding like the most interfering bunch of biddies the world has ever known," Martini said, rather cheerfully. "You know, routine."

"Food?"

He bent and kissed my cheek. "Coming. Nice move on Barbara."

"I'm making a decision to hate all A-C women whose names start with B."

"Could be a sound policy." Martini put Kimmie into a

chair and pulled out the one next to it for me. "I understand one seat next to you is already taken."

I sat down, and he pushed my chair in. I felt a moment's panic until he sat next to me. Marianne sat next to Kimmie. She looked pale. "Jeff . . . how many of the kids are empaths?"

"Half. The others are all imageers. Don't worry, Christopher's taken care of them."

On cue Christopher came in and sat down across from me. "Thought we weren't going to tell anyone."

"I like to break the rules."

"Every day in my memory. Kitty, you okay?"

"Hanging in. About to faint, but great otherwise."

Martini was up and then back in seconds. He had a bowl of rolls. "Here. Go to town."

I grabbed two and started wolfing them down. "V'ry good. Th'nks."

"Can't have you fainting on me unless I cause it."

"Mmmm huh." I was on rolls three and four.

"Jeez, you ever feed your woman?" Reader pulled up next to Christopher. "Paul and ACE are having fascinating discussions with the elders. I don't think ACE is clear on the whole 'body needs fuel to survive' concept. Oh, girl-friend? Toss me some rolls."

I did, reluctantly. I gave one to Christopher and Martini, too. And Kimmie. Marianne said she could wait. Only one roll left.

I ate it and shoved the bowl back at Martini.

He grinned. "Yes, master."

CHAPTER 51

DINNER WAS FINALLY ON THE TABLE, and everyone was seated. I was never so happy in my life to have them pass on the blessing. I managed to ignore the "due to our guests' overwhelming hunger" gibe and just dig in.

True to its hype, Lucinda's meat loaf was to die for. The rest of the meal was pretty great, too. I had a few more rolls, two helpings of mashed potatoes and gravy, a good portion of corn, some odd jello-type salad that tasted nothing like it looked but was still food, and a variety of other side dishes I ate too fast to contemplate.

In the middle of my third helping of meat loaf I realized Martini hadn't eaten much. I thought about it—he didn't make food like this whenever he cooked, and he didn't order food like this when we went out.

I got up without fuss, told Martini I'd be right back, and went into the kitchen. It was huge, but I figured I could spot a refrigerator without too much trouble. Did, and it was fully stocked. Grabbed six eggs and then looked for where they hid the spices here. Found them near the pots and pans, which hung decoratively from a ceiling rack. My other best girlfriend in high school, Amy, had come from a wealthy family. I recognized the way the kitchen was set up—Amy's mom had hers done similarly. The rich all thought alike, which made it easier for the middle class to make their man an omelet.

This was the one dish I made with reasonable frequency,

and only because Martini genuinely liked them and loved that I made them for him. True, I usually served these to him in bed, but I knew everyone on our team had been starving, and he hadn't eaten enough to stay healthy. Besides, I had no clear idea of how to quickly make anything else that he liked.

Found the right pan, got to work. Decided to see if there were additional ingredients he liked about. Mushrooms, check. Cheese, check. Several varieties, double-check. Chicken livers, not a check and not a surprise, either. Same with lox. He liked those, but he had only been introduced to them by me and my family. Well, couldn't have everything.

I was good at this, didn't burn the pan or anything. Found a plate, slid my pretty good-looking omelet onto it. Turned off the stove, moved the pan to cool. Miraculous. No fire alarms had gone off, the pan wasn't burned, no kitchen tools had been harmed. It was a cheerful cooking moment.

I got back to the dining room in time to hear Lucinda ask Martini why he wasn't finishing his food. He was playing with it, just staring at the plate. I walked over, kissed his head, took his old plate, put his new plate down, and went back into the kitchen. I ate his meat loaf in there, then came back out. I mean, it was really delicious and I wasn't sure when I'd see another meal again on this trip.

Returned to the dining room and sat down. The omelet was almost done. "You want another one?"

He grinned at me. "No, this is great."

I looked over at Lucinda. "He really hates meat loaf. Not just yours, everyone's. And, if I made it, which I don't, he'd hate mine, too. He hates my mother's. The thing is . . . my mother, having made it once and discovering Jeff hates it, has never made it again when he's been over. If, for some reason, there is a meat loaf on our table, she has something else for Jeff as well."

"That's catering to whims," one of the older men said. He was sitting with Sylvia, but I couldn't remember his name.

"Yeah. What's your point?"

Sylvia rolled her eyes. "As if I don't cater to you."

"Maybe I was raised wrong. My mother caters to my

father. He caters to her, too. It's part of how they show they love each other." I wasn't sure if this was a great line in front of Martini's entire family, but it didn't get the outrage it might have had an hour earlier.

"It's everyone else's favorite," Lucinda said.

"Yes, I can see why. It's great. Caviar is great, too. So's sushi. But not everyone likes them. He's thirty, not three. He's not *going* to like it, ever." I looked down at Kimmie. "Just remember, you should always try things, but if you don't like them, for real, then you shouldn't have to eat them when you get bigger."

"I hate potatoes," she said.

"Well, sometimes your tastes change. It's worth it to try things again, every once in a while, just in case." Me, I loved potatoes, but I was also of the "more for me" mind-set.

The other children took this as an opportunity. "I hate peas." "I hate mangos." "I hate beets." Soon the room was ringing with food hatred. I snagged another roll.

"You like these rolls?" I asked Martini.

"Yeah."

"Can you make them?"

"Yep."

"Good. Plan on it. My parents will think you're a culinary god. No one makes decent rolls in our family, and these are to die for."

Martini put his arm around the back of my chair. "This is possibly the best family dinner I've ever had." The listing of hated foods had gotten the adults caught up. Everyone was sharing what they didn't like to eat. I even caught a couple mentions of "meat loaf" in there.

I was feeling full, finally, but still took another roll, just in case. I was ready to suggest going to the hotel, wherever it was, when my phone rang.

Dug it out, but not a number I recognized, again. "Hello?"

"You've started something you can't win." It was a man's voice, muffled, but menacing all the same. "You're going to end up with bullets in your brain, just like your friend."

"Did you kill Karl Smith?"

"Stay out of my business, or you'll find out." The phone went dead.

All our team were sitting near me, or near enough. They'd all stopped talking and were looking at me. "Kitty, who was that?" Christopher asked quietly.

"Someone in charge of things."

"How do you know?" Martini asked, his voice taut.

"He said 'my business.' " I looked at Reader. "Ten to one I just got a call from Howard Taft or Leventhal Reid."

"Give me the phone," Kevin said. I passed it down the table to him. "Not a Kennedy number." He pulled his phone out and called someone. "I need a trace on a number, stat."

"I'd really hoped to nap before we had to roll again," I told Martini.

"You have your little stalker friend to deal with, too."

"I think she should just pass on that one," Reader said. "Seems like the least of our worries."

"No, Psycho Chick's got skills. She could cause problems or kill us. I mean, she almost did already."

"Nothing much on the number," Kevin said. He sounded frustrated as my phone moved back to me. "More than we got on Serene's cell phone, but only just. It's a payphone in Miami."

"Not exactly next door."

"Not that far, in reality." Reader said. "Few hours' drive or a quick flight to get from Cape Canaveral to Miami."

"Or Orlando," Kevin offered. "Could have gone in and out of there, too."

"Fabulous."

I felt a tug on my arm. Oh, hell, I'd forgotten Kimmie was right there. "Will you bring Uncle Jeff back soon?"

"What?"

"I know you're all leaving. Will you bring him and Uncle Christopher back soon?" She seemed preternaturally calm.

"I implanted blocks," Martini whispered. "She can't feel anything but top layer emotions and even those are muted."

"I'll do my best," I told her.

Kimmie nodded. "Good. We miss them. Grandma cries about it a lot."

Oh, really? I shot a look at Lucinda; she was trying to pretend she hadn't heard this exchange. Maybe she hadn't, but like all small children, Kimmie wasn't clear on the concept of Inside Voice. I had to figure most of the room had heard her.

Families were weird. It seemed logical to me that if Lucinda wanted her son and nephew around, she'd make them feel they were wanted. I'd only been in their house a short while, but it was pretty clear Martini hadn't exaggerated anything.

"Well, they miss you, too." I figured this wasn't a lie. Martini and Christopher probably did miss the kids.

"We have to go," Martini said, in his Commander voice, happily moving the conversation off uncomfortable family things. "Alpha and Airborne, move out. Michael, Brian, we need you, too."

Everyone got up, said thanks, and we headed to the entry room. "Where are we going?"

"The hotel's secured, so we'll go there. If we're lucky, we can sleep at least a couple of hours." Martini gave me a wide smile. "Or at least relax."

"I like how you think."

CHAPTER 52

SECURED HOTEL MEANT HOTEL WITH a gate in alien-speak. This was a relief—the last thing I wanted to do was put more time between me and a bed or Martini and a shower. Or, preferably, me and Martini in a shower and then in the bed.

Alfred had taken care of everything, so we just walked to the front desk, got room keys, and headed off. We were all on the top floor, but the hotel was only four stories, so we weren't looking to have much of a view.

Rooms were nice, all suites, so we had a living room/ office/kitchenette, large bathroom, and private bedroom. Martini did a quick security check, pronounced the room bug-free in all ways, and we raced to see who could get out of our pretty much awful clothing fastest. Stuffed the clothes in the plastic laundry bag provided and got into the shower.

He insisted he felt fine after having had a meal, and I checked him out carefully. He looked healed and better than fine. We were finally alone, and my sex drive said "what the hell."

Martini was a pro at mind-blowing sex in any kind of location, and we were both pros by now at doing it in the shower. In deference to the alligators and the swamp, we cleaned off first, then Martini proceeded to remind me why it was great to be his woman.

We were in the middle of my third orgasm when we both

heard my phone ringing. "You think we should get that?" He paused to make sure I heard him. I was impressed we could hear the phone over my howls, but I chose not to mention it.

"If it's important, they'll leave a message." I tightened my legs around him to give him the none-too-subtle hint that I wasn't happy about the pause.

"Your phone's been kind of emergency central."

"Jeff, do I look like I care right now?" I was still squeezing and thrusting.

He grinned. "No. You look totally sexy." He kissed me and continued doing what I wanted. He made up for the interruption in fine form.

Finally out of the shower and dried off, we both fell into bed. My phone was beeping to let me know I'd missed a call. I checked the number. "So glad we didn't interrupt for this." No voicemail message, so I called back.

"Hello?"

"Serene! How goes it for my favorite romantically obsessed lunatic?" I rolled and draped myself onto Martini. He stroked my hair and back while I nuzzled his chest.

"What have you done with Helen?" She sounded mad and freaked, but she wasn't screaming.

"Who's Helen?" I looked at Martini. He shrugged and shook his head. "Not ringing a bell."

"She's my friend. What did you do to her?"

I was tired, but great sex really did a lot for my mental abilities. "Oh, you mean the gal who found my cell number so we could be pals? The one who made the first phone call to me? Her?" I kissed Martini's chest, quietly.

"Yes. Where is she?"

"As far as I know, she's under arrest for suspected terrorism, conspiracy to commit murder, being an accomplice in the destruction of government property, illegal information search, and probably a variety of other things." My free hand began roaming Martini's body. He started the low growl that always sounded like a big cat purring to me. I loved that sound, and I liked to do things to make it happen and keep it going.

"Why did you do that?"

"Babe, *you* did that. The minute you decided to go Freak of the Year on me over Brian? You did that, and you pulled her into it. By the way, there's a warrant out for your arrest, for most of the same charges, only yours are at a higher level." My mouth felt compelled to follow my hand, so I went with it.

"What are you doing with him?" Her voice was taut.

"You mean, what am I doing right now? I'm with my actual boyfriend right now. I have no idea what Brian's doing at the exact moment, but I'm pretty sure he's not having the same level of fun we are. By the way, sick as it sounds, he was sort of flattered over your lunacy. Not to the point where he wants to cuddle, but, hey, maybe he'll be willing to wait for you." I trailed my tongue down Martini's chest and stomach, following what my friends and I had always called the Happy Trail. It certainly always made Martini happy.

"Wait for me for what?"

"To get out of prison." I was nuzzling my favorite thing in the world and really didn't want to talk much longer. "Serene, is this a 'leave town or else' call, an 'I'm going to try to kill you again for no sane reason' call, or a 'remember we meet at dawn' call? Kind of busy, so let's cut to the chase." My tongue really enjoyed tormenting Martini. At least, I always told him it was my tongue's fault. His purr was on full and heading toward the point where I was going to make him moan the way he normally made me.

"I don't want you to hurt Helen. She hasn't done anything wrong."

I found myself wishing Serene talked in longer sentences. "Mmmm . . . actually, she has. You might have thought this through a little better, but you didn't, and she's going down for it." So was I.

"Where is she? Where's Helen?"

Martini's hands were clutching the bed, and I really wasn't interested in talking. But I forced myself to pause again. I did have a hand free, after all. "I have no idea. The Feds took her away. Guantanamo, maybe. No clue. Oh, and should you manage to kill me, Brian, or anyone else with us, not to mention some innocent person along the way?

You'll never see Helen again. You have nowhere to go. The entire A-C community is looking for you—things are really tense right now, and you've made them worse. You can try hiding with humans, but you know, you're going to run into problems there somewhere."

The positive thing about having to talk to Serene while my hand was around Martini was that she really threw off my calm, and my hand was clenched and moving furiously. He enjoyed it, if his thrusts and groans were any indication, but I preferred to be a more active participant.

"I didn't mean for this to get so out of hand." Serene's voice was low, and for the first time, she sounded sane.

"Look, hold that thought, keep the sanity right there in front of you, and stay up. I'll call you back, promise." I hung up and put my mouth to far better use than talking to the poster girl for the stalkerazzi.

Martini's head was back, his body thrusts wild, while he groaned and panted and gasped my name. I loved doing this to him—normally I was the one helplessly begging for more. It was nice to turn the tables on him occasionally. And this kind of revenge was incredibly sweet.

I contemplated holding him on the edge for a long while, but I did have a crazy person to call back, and who knew how long she'd stay on the Good Ship Sanity? On the other hand, this was so much more fun and enjoyable. And he wasn't begging yet. I stopped worrying about anything else and just concentrated on enjoying what I could do to him and how much he loved it.

"Please . . . baby, please . . . oh, God, Kitty . . . baby, *please. . . .* "

Okay, so he was begging now. But was it enough? Should I take pity? Martini groaned loudly, and I knew he was so close, I might as well be kind. I moved a little differently, in a way I knew from experience sent him screaming over the edge. Still worked perfectly.

Enjoyed my reward for a job well done, then lapped my way back up the Happy Trail so I could toy with his chest some more while his body slowly stopped shuddering.

"You're such a bad girl," he purred at me when I was finally up to his pecs and he was able to talk again.

I laughed against his skin. "Good girls go to Heaven. Bad girls go down."

"C'mere, you." He wrapped his arms around me, pulled me up and kissed me, his tongue deep inside my mouth as it twined around mine. This, of course, caused me to start grinding against his leg. Which caused him to pull me on top of him. Which caused me to grind against him with more emphasis. A-Cs had wonderful regenerative abilities, a fact I'd learned early and appreciated beyond almost any other trait.

After the last day, making love naked and in bed seemed exotic. He was back in control—and he ensured I loved every second of it.

I was collapsed on top of him, kissing his neck while he stroked my back when I remembered I had to call Stalker Chick back. I reached around on the bed until my hand hit the phone, looked away from Martini's neck long enough to dial, and then went back to important things.

"Hello?"

"Yo, Serene, how's the sanity holding on?"

"You took a long time to call me back."

"Yeah, I was occupied. So, are we still sane, or are you about to start shrieking and flinging bombs again?"

"I don't want Helen to get into any trouble."

"Too late. You want to get her out of it? Turn yourself in."

Long pause. Martini shifted us so we were on our sides, then flipped me, gently, so my back was up against his chest. He slid one arm under my neck, wrapped himself around me, and hugged me against him with the other arm. I yawned. This felt nice.

"I can't turn myself in," Serene said finally. Good thing, I was almost asleep.

"Look, you still want to fight at dawn? I'll be there. Otherwise, it's been a busy day, and I'd love the opportunity to sleep in."

Martini nuzzled my head.

"Does Brian know who you're with?"

"Yes, he's clear on the 'I have a boyfriend and it's not you' concept."

"So he's not jealous?"

"No idea. Don't care. I haven't talked to him or heard from him for ten years. You know more about him as he is now than I do. He doesn't know me at all, he just thinks he does. Why?"

I could tell she was crying. "I just wanted him to love me the way Alfred's son loves you."

Something was wrong with this sentence. I knew because I was wide awake now, just from hearing it. I nudged Martini and turned the speakerphone on. "If you knew I was with Alfred's son, why did you try to kill me?" Alfred's son? No one I worked with referred to Martini this way; to pretty much everyone who knew him, he was in *charge*.

"I couldn't tell until tonight." She was sobbing.

"How could you tell tonight?"

"Seeing the two of you together. I wanted that with Brian. Why doesn't he want me?"

My body went cold. "Serene? Are you watching Brian right now?" She didn't answer, but she was still there, because I could hear her crying. "I know you're watching me and Jeff."

"Y-yes. Brian's asleep. Everyone in your hotel is asleep."

"Serene? This is going to sound like a really prying, personal question, but since you just got to watch the two of us perform for you like a live porno show, I think you owe us an answer. How are you doing it, how can you see us no matter where we are?"

She sniffled. "I've always been able to."

Martini moved his head so his lips were near my ear that was against his arm. "We don't have those kinds of talents."

"Serene . . . are you a hybrid? A cross between A-C and human?"

"Yes." And yet no one had mentioned this fact. Why not?

"Um . . . Serene . . . which parent was the A-C?"

"My mother. I . . . I don't know my father, just that he was a human."

"No one else knows, do they? Your mother didn't tell anyone."

"No. She died when I was little. I was raised by my cousins."

"How old are you?"

"Twenty-two." Interesting . . . I'd thought she was older for some reason. Helen's attachment and bizarre attempts to help made a little more sense now.

"Okay, so you can see us? How?"

"I just think about the person I want to know about. If they're close enough to me, I can see them."

"What's your range?"

"About fifty miles." She gave a shuddering sigh. "I'm in real trouble, aren't I?"

"You think? You're using a heretofore unknown and hidden talent to cause destruction and mayhem. I don't think that goes over well with A-Cs *or* humans."

"What am I going to do?" Why was she asking me? Did I have savior printed on my forehead or something?

Martini cleared his throat. "Serene, if you come in now, we can work to get charges reduced."

"I can't. I just can't." She sounded panicked.

"That's okay," I said quickly. "I understand. Listen . . . this will sound out of left field, but can you find a dead body?"

CHAPTER 53

"WHAT?" Serene sounded shocked. As if, somehow, spying on people with her second sight talents and trying to kill them was normal, but searching for a dead body wasn't?

"Someone murdered Karl Smith today while he was at Kennedy. But we can't find his body. There's a huge anti-alien plot going on, people are trying to kill every A-C and those of us who work with them, and they almost succeeded multiple times today. Smith was trying to warn me when he was shot."

"Sorry, but I can't. If he were alive and in range, I could. But I can't see anyone once they're dead. I've tried before."

"Worth asking." Dammit.

"You're sure he's dead?" she asked slowly.

"Positive. I heard it happen, and Alfred and a team found his body. It was stolen from where they'd left it."

"Well, there are ways around here to get rid of a body." Serene sounded a bit ill. "I'm looking at some right now."

I figured she was at the Lighthouse. Where else? She'd suggested it, and I had to figure it was because she was there. Maybe the height gave her talents a boost. So, what would she be seeing from the vantage point? Oh, duh. "You think they fed his body to the alligators?"

"Yeah, I do." Amazing. We sounded like we were working together.

Martini nodded and mouthed, "Makes sense." I hated the people who were responsible even more now.

"So, sorry, but this is just an idle curiosity question. How *can* you see us? I mean, how does it work?"

"I've never talked about it to anyone."

"I can understand why, but you're going to have to, sooner or later. Practice on me. Oh, and how did you send the bomb at me and Brian? I mean, I know you weren't in the Space Center." I hated to admit it, but I was honestly interested in the answer, for a variety of reasons. I heard the phrase "next step in our evolution" ringing in my head. This was what I was expecting out of a lot of A-C/human pairings, but discovering that the first real protomutant was dangerously unhinged was sort of taking the wind out of the high side.

"I need to have met the person, or at least have seen them before. I . . . know who they are from looking at them."

"Imageering talent," Martini said. He rolled out of bed. "Serene, I'm going to get Christopher White in here with us, okay?"

"Why?"

"Because he's the best imageer you have, and he's Jeff's cousin."

Martini pulled out a clean pair of pants and looked at me. "Get dressed."

I sighed and did as he told me. Martini left the room. "So, while we wait, why Brian?"

"He's sweet. And smart." Ah, the old smart thing . . . apparently it was *the* Dazzler weakness.

Another thought occurred. "Serene, have you ever seen a picture of either Howard Taft, the father of Frank Taft from Security, or Leventhal Reid, who I think is a senator or representative from this state?"

"I think I have . . . yes. I've been in Frank's cubby a couple of times. He's a big man, kind of looks like a walrus?"

"That'd be him."

She was quiet. "He's not in range."

"Do me a favor, and this is between us. Check for him

periodically, and when you can spot him and where he is, call me immediately."

"Okay." She sounded confused. "Are you not mad at me?"

"Um, how can I put this? For trying to kill me, Jeff, Brian, and everyone we were standing near earlier today? Yeah, I'm pretty pissed. But you seem to be on the normal side of the seesaw right now, and your talent is pretty damned awesome. The best thing you could do for yourself is be helpful, because anything you can do to help us stop the anti-alien conspiracy is going to go a long way toward making the rest of us go, 'Oh, young girls get fanciful ideas' and push for a really light sentence. For you *and* Helen."

"She's like my mother." Serene was crying again. "I can't believe I got her into so much trouble."

"Help me, and I'll help you get her out of it. Deal?"

She was quiet again, but when she spoke she sounded both sane and determined. "Deal."

Just in time—I was dressed, and Serene was now acting as my personal spy, as Martini came back with Christopher in tow. Christopher had also chosen to put on only pants. This was unfair to me, in a lot of ways.

Looking at both of them standing there half-naked, with rumpled bed hair, was enough to make me start drooling. Martini was big, broad, and ripped, with a perfect six-pack, awesome pecs and biceps, and just generally looked like the hard-body poster boy. Christopher was lean and wiry, muscular but a little less ripped, smooth-chested, but carrying the family rock hard abs. Not an ounce of fat on either one of them. Take the pants off and pose them, they'd make awesome Greco-Roman statues. My only saving grace was that they weren't wet or oiled.

The last thing I wanted Martini to catch me doing, ever, was lusting after Christopher. "So, Serene!" I said brightly, as I turned to stare intently at my phone. "Jeff's back and Christopher's here, too. Tell us about your talent. How do you do what you do?"

Martini came around behind me, slipped his arm around my waist, lifted and carried me to the bed. He sat down at the edge and put me on his lap. Christopher pulled up a chair. We were all staring at the phone, nestled near a pillow.

"I need to see someone," Serene said haltingly. "In person or a picture."

"Right," I said, hoping I sounded encouraging. She was either scared again or so busy staring at Christopher and Martini in her mind's eye that she couldn't talk. Me, I voted for option B. I was staring at my phone as though it were the most fascinating thing in the world. "Go on."

"If I concentrate, I can see them, in my mind. What they're doing and where they are, I mean."

"Fifty-mile range," Martini added.

Christopher whistled. "Damn. Go on, Serene. Is that how you knew Kitty was coming?"

"Not so much. I mean, I didn't know she was coming, but when your plane was landing, I saw her."

"Why?" This seemed odd to me.

"Brian's been talking about your reunion. I . . . I've been thinking about you a lot."

I managed not to say, "No kidding," but it took effort. "Okay, so we came within range and, what? My face appeared?"

"Yes. I couldn't see who you were with at first. But I've seen pictures of Alfred's son and nephew."

"You can call us Jeff and Christopher," Martini said dryly.

"Where have you seen their pictures?"

"In Alfred's office. He has a book with pictures of them from when they were babies up until now."

I looked over my shoulder. Martini looked stunned. Risked a glance to my left. Christopher was the same. "Who else could you see with us?"

"Their cousin and his boyfriend. Alfred has some pictures of them, too."

"Did he show them to you?"

"Oh, yes, I didn't sneak in to look or anything. But I'm filling in as his admin, and he showed them to me. He has pictures of all his family, but he has the most of, um, Jeff and Christopher." She said their names like she was both afraid and a little thrilled. Maybe I was jaded—I didn't find either one of them imposing, but then again, I didn't find the Sovereign Pontifex imposing, either.

"Why?" I figured one of us should ask.

She was quiet for a few moments. "Because he says he almost never sees them, so he has his pictures to look at. He looks at them every day. Even more than the ones of his grandchildren, and he looks at their pictures a lot."

I didn't look at either one of them. "Okay, so you could identify Jeff, Christopher, Paul, and James. Could you see anyone else with us?" I was driving the conversation instead of Christopher, but I had to figure he and Martini were still dealing with the news that Alfred, at the least, loved and missed them far more than he'd ever told them.

"No. I can only see the person I've seen before. I can't hear, only see. So I could tell by the way you were all moving and looking that there were other people with you, but I couldn't see them."

"Now, this will be an uncomfortable question, but we do expect an answer. When you tossed that bomb at me and Brian, you could see every person with us, couldn't you?"

"Yes." Her voice was low. "I didn't know it would be so big."

"What would be?" Christopher asked. His voice was strained.

"The explosion. I created a floater."

"A floater?" Martini sounded confused. Not good.

"A bomb, small, invisible. I control it using simple transistors, like for those motorized toy cars. I didn't think it would be so powerful."

"You use cloaking technology to make it invisible?" Christopher's voice was taut.

"Yes."

"Who knows about this, other than you? That you've created it, I mean?" Martini asked. His voice was very soothing, but I could feel that he was tensed.

"I don't think anyone. I worked on it at night."

"At home?"

"No, at the Center."

I thought about it and got a bad feeling in my stomach. "Serene, you're a typical A-C woman, right?"

"I guess so."

"I mean, by human standards, you're drop-freaking-dead gorgeous, right?"

"I suppose." She sounded embarrassed.

"So, a pretty girl's staying late working on a special project. I just can't believe all of those many *male* security guards waltzed on home and told her to lock up and not let the alligators bite on the way out."

"Oh. No. Mr. Turco would stay late with me. Or Frank."

"Frank Taft, right?"

"Right. I, um, think he maybe wanted to ask me out." She now sounded really embarrassed. "But, uh. . . . "

"He's too damned stupid to interest you?"

"Yeah."

"Thank God." Truly. I could see how this was unfolding, and it was horrible scary. "Okay, Serene, you need to listen to me, and you have to, and I mean *have to*, trust me. Can you do that?" I looked at Christopher and Martini—they'd made the same assumptions, I could tell, by their expressions.

"I . . . I don't know."

CHAPTER 54

"SERENE, what do you think we're going to do to you?" Martini asked, voice very gentle.

"I don't know. Arrest me?" She sounded scared, and I could tell she was crying again. "I didn't mean to try to kill you, I just wanted to scare you and make you go away."

"Listen to me. We have to get you. The hell with your little Unrequited Love from Hell routine. You are marked for death or worse, and not by us. Frank's father is the head of Club 51."

"Oh, right. He invited me to go to a rally of theirs, but Brian said it didn't sound like any fun, so I said no."

It was worse. "Did he ask you after he'd stayed late helping you?"

"Yes, that's when I got to know him. He said he didn't like most A-Cs but he liked me."

Much, much worse. "Serene, honey, Club 51 is a huge anti-alien conspiracy organization. They believe that aliens are here, and, yes, I know, true, but you're hiding in plain sight, normal humans don't believe, blah, blah, blah. The humans who do believe are crazy."

"But Frank works with us. Of course he believes."

"Yes, and so does his father. That makes them dangerous. To all the A-Cs and to you personally." I knew where she was, where she had to be. But others might as well.

Martini moved me off his lap. "Serene, they tried to kill

Alfred today, and me. And they used one of your bombs to do it."

She gasped. "There's no way! I have them set to a specific frequency. And I only set off the one."

"Great, but we all almost died," Christopher snapped.

"Do any of them have something in them, something like a gas, that would knock out a human faster than an A-C?"

"No, but we have that gas already." She was so matter-of-fact. It was so easy to see why Reid and people like him wanted to turn Centaurion into the War Division—they were halfway there all by themselves and without realizing it.

"What was it created for?" Martini asked.

"Experimental. For dangerous situations—we were hoping to put human astronauts into suspended animation while leaving the A-Cs alone. We're also working on one that does the opposite, but it's not perfected yet."

It had gone from worse to "Oh My God" in seconds. "Okay, look, I can't think of a way to get through to you other than this. You're in the most extreme danger there is, and if we don't get to you, someone else will. Then I can promise you'll never see Brian again because they'll kill you or, worse, they'll kill him to make you do what they want."

She was quiet again. "He's asleep. He's fine."

"Serene . . . look for Turco and Taft."

"They're not nearby."

One small thing—they were presumably still under lock and key and far away. But that just meant people she didn't know were close by. "Serene, do you have hyperspeed?"

"Yes, but I can only run five miles."

"We're fifty away," Martini said softly. "If she's where we all think she is."

"Okay . . . we're coming to you. Me, Jeff, Christopher, and Brian, at least. Maybe more, maybe our whole team."

"But, you don't know where I am."

"Lighthouse." The three of us said it in unison.

"Oh. Yeah."

I looked at Christopher. "Get the others awake and

dressed, pronto." He disappeared. "Jeff, put on a shirt and shoes. Serene, are you at the top?" I pulled on socks and my Converse. They were still gross, but I had a feeling they were going to get grosser soon.

"Yes, so I can see better, both ways."

"Okay . . . is anyone there with you?"

"No." She sounded uncertain. "Well, I did hear something while I was waiting for you to call back. But I didn't pay a lot of attention." Because she was watching me and Martini do triple-X porn, but that was beside the point. "There might be someone at the base, but I can't tell."

"Serene, I'm the head of all Field operations." Martini's Commander voice was activated. "This is now officially a Field situation, and I'm giving you a direct order. Do you understand?"

"Yes." She sounded scared. First sane thing she'd done all night.

"You are not, I repeat not, to go with anyone other than those in Alpha or Airborne teams. If you don't know them, don't believe them. If you haven't seen them with us, don't trust them. Run, fight, scream, be very afraid if someone comes near you. You will come with us when we get there, but until then, your orders are to remain alive and unkidnapped."

"Yes, sir." There was no irony in her voice.

"Kitty, keep her on the phone and talking. Serene, I want you talking about Brian. No more discussions of your powers or the bombs. Start now."

"Okay . . . um . . . I really like Brian."

"No kidding. I'm taking you off speaker, it's just going to be you and me."

"Okay. Am I in trouble?"

"Girl, I'm scared to death for you, and you tried to kill me all day. You do the math."

"Oh, God."

"Prattle, okay? Talk to me as if I were Helen, like you're telling me why you adore him, okay? Jeff wants you faking it in case they're close to you. Don't get so wrapped up that you stop paying attention."

"Okay." She took a deep breath and started a litany of

Brian's virtues. I listened with one ear. The other was busy listening to Martini and Christopher move everyone out. Our whole team was going—we had no idea if we were safe or not, and we didn't want our human operatives in danger. But we were going in shifts.

Martini, Christopher, Brian, and I were going at top speed. Brian had both insisted, and it was logical—she would come to him, that was a given. A part of me wondered if we were rescuing a girl or a spooked Labrador; then I thought about it, and figured, in one sense, she was a combo. Gower, Michael, and the girls would bring everyone else. The girls had their med kits, the boys had some guns, I had my purse. Everyone was set.

Martini grabbed my hand, Christopher grabbed Brian, and we were off, but at a speed Brian and I could handle. It was hard to hear Serene going this fast, but I could tell she was still relatively okay, because we were on to Brian's advanced degrees and good-Catholic-boy nature.

It was dark and I'd never been here before, so I had no idea what we were flashing past. Fifty miles for Martini and Christopher was nothing, but I was more on Serene's level—five miles if it was a good day. Of course, if the situation called for quick bursts of speed or leaping over obstacles in the path, I was your girl.

I kept my eyes closed in the hope that it would keep me from passing out. It allowed me to concentrate more on Serene.

"So, um, I was wondering if you think Brian might ever like me. Or if, you know, I should go for a guy like Frank. Or even an older guy like Frank's father." Her voice was more urgent.

"Oh, hell. Jeff, Howard Taft's there!" We sped up to A-C warp speed.

"Not right yet. But soon." Serene sounded terrified. "Kitty, help me!"

Pity we were going so fast I was starting to black out. I shoved the phone at Martini. He grabbed it and me and kept on going. I knew without looking that Brian was already over Christopher's shoulder. And as I passed out, I knew that it still might not be enough.

CHAPTER 55

I WOKE UP ON GRASS, with someone massaging my neck. After the few seconds of reorientation, I realized the hands massaging me didn't belong to Martini. They weren't doing nearly as effective a job.

"Jeff and Christopher have gone in," Brian said, his voice taut. "I woke up first." I realized I could see him pretty clearly and looked up. Full moon. Made the crazies even crazier, as my parents had always told me.

Martini was back. "She's gone. The phone went dead, too." He sounded frustrated and worried.

"Track on terror."

"I'm trying, but . . ."

"But she's looking at Brian because she's scared, and so she's concentrating on him, on her power, not on what you need to track." I sat up. "Bri, kiss me."

"WHAT?" Three male voices shouted that in unison.

"Brian, kiss me. Jeff, track on total unhinged rage." I grabbed Brian and planted a wet one on him.

His arms went right around me, and we were making out, just like when we were teenagers. I could remember what kissing him was like now. It was good, but not Christopher good and nowhere close to Martini, who was the Mount Olympus of kissers as far as I was concerned.

"Got her." Martini grabbed me and wrenched me out of Brian's arms. We raced off again. "Do I believe that was for the greater good?"

"Jeff, seriously, they're going to kill her, or, worse, they're going to turn her into their Little Miss Weapon of Mass Destruction, and you know it."

"Yeah. He didn't seem to mind."

"Can we discuss this after I wake up again?" My vision was starting to go to pinpoint.

He swung me up into his arms again. "Hang on, baby." He slowed down. "Christopher, is Brian still conscious?"

"Yeah, just barely."

Martini cursed. "I can't believe I have to suggest this. Brian, you and Kitty stay here and make out." He put me down. "Just try not to enjoy it, okay?"

"Um, okay. Be careful."

"Always." Martini and Christopher were gone again.

I looked at Brian. "Let's go." I put my arms around him, and he started kissing me again. "Um, Bri? A little less real enthusiasm, okay?"

He squeezed my butt. "You sure?"

"Yes. We are faking it, 'cause she can't hear us or pick up our emotions." I nuzzled him. "Pretend you're a spy or something."

"I'd rather pretend you wanted to do this." His hands were moving.

"Brian, if you touch my boobs, I'll knee you so hard you'll wish you were dead."

He sighed. "Fine." He kissed me again, still with a great deal of enthusiasm. I wasn't returning it. This surprised me a bit. When Christopher and I had lost it in the elevator, I'd responded like Queen of the Sluts. But being with Brian like this didn't feel illicit—it felt like work.

He pulled away. "There is absolutely no spark, is there?"

"Not on my side, no. And I just heard the list of your many accomplishments and strengths." I cuddled up, lest Serene realize we were doing this to save her life. "I realize she's several comics short of a complete collection, but are you really that blind? Or that xenophobic?"

"I'm not xenophobic!"

"Um, they're aliens, and you don't want to date her because she's an alien. I can't think of a better definition of xenophobia."

"I can. Besides, I didn't know she liked me."

"Yes, you did. Or you would have if you hadn't spent the last decade mooning over me. It's so nice to be someone's perfect woman. Only, I'm not perfect, so whatever you're mooning over isn't me, just what you've chosen to imagine as me."

He was running his hands over my back and in my hair, squeezing my butt, even thrusting against me. But I could tell he was acting now.

"Yeah, I guess." He sighed. "I had this fantasy of how I'd win you back."

"I'm sure. Don't tell it to me, I don't want to know."

"Well, I didn't think it would be anything like this. I can't believe you're working with Centaurion Division, let alone one of the ones in charge." He sounded amused.

"Um, why not?" Tried not to be insulted. Failed.

"I don't know. Just didn't seem like your thing."

"What did seem like my thing?" Tried not to get pissed off. Failed.

"I'm not trying to insult you. But, like Conspiracy Chuck. I mean, what could that guy be doing other than still living in his parents' house and haunting UFO sites? Maybe working at a Circle-K."

"Chuckie worked at Circle-K in college." Tried not to anticipate my next statements with joy. Failed.

"See?"

"He went into their management program in our freshman year, left it in junior year, and started his own local convenience store as his upper-level class project. This turned into a state-wide chain before graduation. Got bought out by Circle-K five years ago for undisclosed multimillions. He lives half the year in Australia and half the year in D.C. He sends me nice presents from Europe and Australia all the time. He's also taken me to Vegas, skiing in Aspen and Vail, and to New York. Because, in addition to the first multimillions, he made another whopping set of millions in the stock market. He's not Bill Gates level . . . yet . . . but if you want to know who should win 'Most Successful' at the reunion, it's him."

Maybe I should have married Chuckie, now that I

thought of it. Sure, he'd been joking when he'd suggested it, but we did have a lot in common, his parents adored me and mine adored him, and no one would ever think he was a geek these days. Ah, well, another opportunity gone.

"You're kidding!"

"No, I'm not. You saw a geek. I saw a cool guy with similar interests." Tried not to anticipate his next question. Failed.

"Did you date him?" Brian sounded horrified.

"No." Thank God he hadn't asked if I'd slept with him. Dating and a wild fling in Vegas for a week were *not* the same things. I tried to remember why we hadn't flung more. Couldn't. Oh well. Sex with Martini had pretty much wiped out my clear memories of the men who'd come before him. Though, if I tried, it wasn't all that hard to remember the fling—before Martini, Chuckie had been the gold standard. Still the best human male I'd ever been intimate with. Which would have begged the "why didn't we do it more" question if we weren't in a life-and-death situation.

"Well, good."

I noted another difference between Martini and Brian—Martini absolutely would have asked if I'd slept with Chuckie. Because he knew me better than Brian. Chuckie knew me better than Brian, too. Chuckie might know me better than Martini, but, again, not the right time to ponder that. Frankly, it was easier to come up with those who didn't know me better than Brian than those who did.

The rest of our team arrived. "Um, girlfriend? What the hell are you doing?" Reader sounded mildly freaked.

"Making Serene go psycho so Jeff can track her. She's been kidnapped by the Club 51 Goon Squad."

"She's not enjoying it," Brian added, sounding disappointed and somewhat insulted.

"Jeff going to believe that?" Reader asked.

"Sure," Michael chimed in. "She's making out with Bri, not me. Now, if she were making out with me, Jeff'd have a reason to worry."

"Everyone's a comedian. You think we can stop now? Could she really continue to buy that we're in a love clinch with the rest of you around?"

"Kitty, she's a psycho," Jerry said. "I think she could believe it if you were in the middle of O'Hare."

Probably true. Brian and I continued to cuddle. I found myself bored. Maybe it was just that he was a human, and I was already aware of the benefits of A-C stamina. More likely, of course, was the fact that I wasn't remotely interested, let alone in love with him.

My phone rang. Martini must have put it back into my purse when I was unconscious. Dug through, happily, it was him. "Jeff, are you okay?"

"Yeah, baby, we're fine. We have Serene, but her kidnappers got away." He sounded pissed. "You can stop fondling Brian now."

"Gladly." I pulled away and went over to Reader. "How's her mental state?"

"Oh, beyond great." His sarcasm was on high. "Just this side of frothing at the mouth."

"How are you handling her?"

"Roughly, because we've had no choice. Christopher said to tell you that she's not quite as bad as the alligator, though."

"Can you get back to us?"

"Not using hyperspeed. We got to her just in time. A couple more miles and she'd have been too far for us to catch her on foot."

"Where are you, we'll come get you."

"Find a vehicle. Seriously." He sounded tired, and I could hear him panting a bit, though he was trying to hide it.

"Jeff, do you need adrenaline?" I tried to keep my voice from rising, but I failed if Reader putting his arm around me was any indication.

"Probably not any time soon." He couldn't even lie on the phone.

"Okay, look where are you? How do we find you?" I was moving to hysterical, I could feel it.

Gower took the phone out of my hand. "Where are you, exactly? Uh-huh, right. Okay, Kitty and I'll be there." He hung up, handed me my phone, Reader let go of me, Gower grabbed me, and we were off.

Not at full speed, I assumed because Gower didn't want

me to pass out. We whizzed around more things that were completely unfamiliar. I wasn't even trying to look. I was trying to stay calm.

We stopped in an area that looked like wetlands. The others were a few feet away from us. "Make it fast," Gower said. "I'm pretty sure we have alligators about."

"Fabulous."

Martini was on his knees, hands on his thighs, looking as though he'd run a marathon. Christopher was struggling with Serene—there was nothing he could do to help because she was nuts. "Serene, cut the crap, you moron," I snapped as I ran to Martini. "You really think I want Brian when I have Jeff? We were doing it because you're just stupid enough to fall for it, and that way Jeff and Christopher could save your life."

"You lied to me!" she screamed. "You tricked me!"

"ACE! I need help here! I don't know what you can or can't do, but she's super powerful and she's totally nuts. She's a threat, but most of it's not her fault. Is there anything you can do?"

"Yes, Kitty," Gower said in his ACE-voice. "Will help Christopher."

I laid Martini on the ground. "Baby, this is gonna suck." I ripped his shirt open.

"Just tell me . . . you didn't like it with him." He was gasping.

I dug out the harpoon and filled it. "Didn't like it. Didn't dislike it. It was work, part of the job. It wasn't fun, it wasn't titillating. It was boring." I did what I always did, leaned down, kissed his forehead. "I love you, Jeff."

Then I plunged the harpoon into his hearts, and he bellowed in agony.

CHAPTER 56

JUST AS AT THE SPACE CENTER, I had to fling myself on top of him to try to keep him somewhat still. I managed to get the harpoon put away and put my whole body on him. I was crying, I couldn't help it. He was out of his mind again, and I'd had to stab him twice in less than twenty-four hours. This was dangerous for him and horrible for me. And Christopher and Gower had to deal with Serene, so I had no help at all.

Martini was thrashing wildly, worse than when he'd been injured. He flipped us, and my head slammed into the ground. He reared back, and I managed to roll out of the way of his fist. His eyes were wild.

"Jeff . . . Jeff, it's me, it's Kitty. Stop."

He grabbed me, and I could tell he didn't know who I was. He was roaring, and he started to shake me. He could kill me like this—he was strong enough to do it normally, and the adrenaline made him even stronger. I tried to fight him, but I couldn't do it. I was still crying, but now it was from fear.

"Jeff . . . *please.*" I heard something, something not human. Gower had said there were alligators nearby. "Jeff, something's going to kill us. There's a 'gator coming!" I was freaked and terrified, and I couldn't get free from him.

An image appeared, close to my head. It was floating, but it looked sort of like a warped devil. Martini spotted it and let go of me to try to grab it. He rolled off, still thrashing and bellowing, now hitting air.

I managed to drag myself to my hands and knees. Christopher and Gower seemed to have Serene under control. But there was something out there, and Martini was fighting a figment of, I had to guess, Christopher's making. I staggered to my feet and went to him. I could feel the animal watching us, and all I wanted to do was run.

Martini was still going strong. I waited until he was on his stomach, then I dropped onto his back and wrapped an arm around his neck. He flipped again, but I had my head tucked this time. He was heavy, but I wrapped my legs around him and squeezed. I'd learned how to ground fight, and I'd also been taught that I wanted my opponent unconscious. My arm tightened on his throat.

"Jeff, please, *please* come back." He was struggling still, but maybe a little less. I didn't relax my legs or my armlock around his neck. "Baby, please come back. I'm so scared."

His thrashing was slowing. "K-Kitty?" He sounded borderline out of it still.

"Yes, it's me." I was still crying.

"Why are you strangling me?" He was confused and hurt, and it took time for him to remember what had happened.

"You're trying to kill her," Christopher snarled. "She's a little upset, therefore. Jeff, get it together. We're surrounded by hostiles."

I could feel him force himself to calm down. "Who's around us?"

"Alligators." I tried not to let my voice shake, but I couldn't. I also didn't let go.

"Kitty, you can stop now."

His hearts were still pounding like mad. "I don't think so."

He looked around. "Well, yeah, hold on, but stop strangling me." He flipped to his hands and knees and stood up, all in about the blink of an eye. "Stay on my back."

"I need my purse."

Martini managed a strangled laugh. "Right." He bent,

grabbed it, and handed it to me. "You're right, they're all around us."

"I want to go home."

"Me too, baby." He edged to Christopher and the others. "Thanks. How's Serene?"

"ACE knocked her out humanely. I was just going to punch her." Christopher sounded pissed. "You almost killed Kitty, Jeff. Twice."

"Thanks, I need a guilt trip right now. Paul, you out of juice?"

"Yeah, so's Christopher."

"Jeff, you can't go to hyperspeed now. It'll kill you. I can't give you more adrenaline so soon." My voice was heading to the dog-only register.

"Okay, baby, it's okay."

I was still crying. "No, it's not. They're going to eat us." I'd stopped strangling him, but my arms were still wrapped around his neck.

He took my hands in one of his. "I won't let them hurt you."

"Hope you have some ideas," Christopher snapped. "Unless I'm hallucinating, I think those things closing in on us have other ideas."

"ACE? Can you put a shield around us?"

"Yes, Kitty."

I saw a shimmer, and we all started to float. "Okay, Paul, apparently we need to have a sit-down so I can explain that, since you now share mental floor space with the most powerful consciousness in the galaxy, it's probably okay to personally ask for an assist now and then."

The 'gators saw their tasty treats start to get away, and they rushed us.

"Kitty, stop screaming."

"I always scream in terror when things are trying to kill me, Christopher, it's my thing." One snapped at Martini's feet, and I shrieked. Its snout hit the shield and it bounced away.

"Baby, I need the eardrums. It's a shield that stopped bullets when it was activated before. I think ACE can stop a couple of 'gators." There were at least a dozen of them. I chose not to point this out.

"How long can ACE keep us protected?"

"How long do we need?" Gower asked. He sounded strained.

"Paul, is ACE drawing on your power to do this?"

"I think so, at least somewhat." He was definitely gasping, just a little, but much more than he'd been before ACE had started shielding us.

"So, not much more time." I dug into my purse, pulled out my phone and dialed, thanking God the A-Cs put massive extended-life batteries in these things.

Reader answered on the second ring. "Where the hell are you, girlfriend?"

"Up to our asses in alligators. I know that's considered a folksy little saying, but I mean it literally right now."

"Not a great help."

"I've never been here before! Wetlands. Alligators. Scary. It's all I've got for you."

"Tell James to follow the main road that leads into the wetlands," Martini said. "The gate's open, we're past the parking area, but not too far off it. A car should be able to drive off-road in this area."

I repeated Martini's directions. "Please tell me you have a vehicle."

"Um . . . yeah. We do." Reader sounded underwhelmed.

"What's wrong with it? It's not some horse cart is it?"

"No . . . not like that."

"James, we're in trouble. What the hell are you in?"

"A nineteen-seventy-five Volkswagen Super Beetle."

I let that one settle into my mind for a moment. "All of you?"

"No, of course not."

"Who besides you?"

"Lorraine, so we'd have medical."

"That should leave room for . . . Jeff, only, in the back." Good lord, we were going to die.

"No, it's a convertible. And in mint condition. Plus, we

can shove Serene into the hood, since the engine's in the back."

"Oh, well, that makes all the difference." I looked at the others. "We're going to die. Just thought I'd share."

"We'll be fine," Martini said reassuringly.

No sooner were the words out of his mouth than I saw two snouts, one in particular, I recognized. "Oh, really? 'Cause I would swear that Gigantagator and Alliflash have spotted that some of the people they hate most in the world are here, just waiting to give them a second chance at a feeding frenzy."

No sooner were these words out of my mouth than the shield disappeared. Martini and Christopher each managed to grab Gower, who wasn't unconscious but was pretty close.

I went back to the phone. "James? I just want to say that it's been a pleasure, and I really hope you find more friends and a new boyfriend soon. Try not to mourn us past five years."

Then Alliflash ran toward us, and I was too busy screaming to chat any more.

CHAPTER 57

I'D EXPERIENCED SOME SHOCKING THINGS in my life, most of which had happened in the last five months. Aliens being real, totally gorgeous, and God's gift to sex. Lots of life on other planets out there, much of it unfriendly. Parasitic superbeings that wanted to kill people. My mother being the head of antiterrorism and a former member of the Mossad. My father being a cryptologist for NASA's ET Division. Every single event of the past twenty-four hours. But nothing had prepared me for what happened next.

Alliflash was in front of us, one snap away from making Martini have to dress up as a pirate every Halloween, when it spun around and started hissing at the other alligators.

Gigantagator did the same thing: got right up to where it was in position to have a Christopher-snack, then spun and did the same, only louder.

"Back up, slowly," Gower said.

We all did, Martini and Christopher still holding Gower up. Alliflash and Gigantagator were snapping, but not at us. Alliflash started to trot around us in a circle—it moved as we did, hissing and snapping at the 'gators surrounding us. Gigantagator rushed some of them and drove them back, moved nearer to us, and did the same thing in another direction.

"What's going on?" I asked in a stage whisper.

"No idea," Martini said in the same voice. "Just don't mess up whatever it is, and we'll be fine."

I realized I still had my phone in my hand and hadn't hung up. I could hear Reader yelling. "Yes? Sorry, what?"

"Are you all still alive?"

"Amazingly, yes. I don't know how, but we are. Not sure for how long."

"I think we're close. Let me know if you see headlights."

I forced myself to look over my shoulder. Got to see Gigantagator chase off all the alligators that were behind us. Also spotted a couple of pinpoints of light. "Yeah, I see something that could be an ancient VW without enough room for all of us in the distance."

"Did I hear that right?" Martini asked.

"Yes, you did."

"Girlfriend, stop complaining. At least it's motorized."

"James, we're going to draw lots for who gets to be 'gator chow. I'm not seeing the upside yet." I was, instead, seeing Alliflash racing around hissing and snapping, ensuring that the few alligators behind us that Gigantagator hadn't spooked would take the serious hint. The lights were getting brighter.

In a minute or so I could hear the car. It sounded like it was going all out. Its all out didn't sound like much over forty miles per hour. I knew Alliflash was faster, and I suspected Gigantagator was as well. Not to mention all their friends and relations.

"Is that our ride?" Christopher asked, sounding mildly horrified.

"Yes, I think so."

"He's really in a VW? That wasn't a joke?" Christopher sounded more horrified.

"It's apparently vintage, in mint condition, and a convertible. It's also a Beetle, so, um, I want to say I think I have the most to live for. Ability to bear children and all that."

"We'll be fine." Martini seemed to have attached to this phrase. It dawned on me that he was as scared as I was, but he was both male and the highest-ranking individual here, and so he was doing what he was trained to—pretend to be calm, cool, and collected. I felt a rush of possessive pride. He really was the most awesome man I'd ever known, even beyond my dad and my Uncle Mort.

The screech of slow-moving tires hit our ears, and we all turned to look. Sure enough, a convertible Beetle skidded to a less than impressive sideways stop just outside Alliflash's circle.

"Oh, look. 'Herbie the Love Bug' is here to save us." I hung up the phone and dropped it back into my purse.

"Hilarious," Reader shouted. "Get in!"

"Where?" Martini and Christopher asked in unison.

"Toss Serene into the trunk in front."

"You're kidding." Christopher sounded appalled. "I mean, I wanted to punch her, but that's kind of carrying it too far."

"She's small enough, she can fit, and she's unconscious. Or we can drop her here. Your choice."

"Everyone move toward the car together," Martini said. "See if we lose the alligator perimeter or not."

The men inched over and the 'gators inched with us.

"A little faster would be good," Reader shouted. "There's a bunch of them on the other side of the car."

No sooner out of his mouth than Alliflash expanded its circle, and Gigantagator did a rush where I couldn't see it. We moved faster. Reader popped the hood, and Christopher dumped Serene in and carefully closed it.

"I can't believe she fits and we're doing this," he snapped.

"Oh, shut up. We need to get Paul into the car. Not to mention the rest of us."

"How?" Martini asked. "I mean, really, how? There's no room. Tell you what, you get in, James gets you out of here, the three of us manage. Somehow."

"The hell with that." I studied the car. The advantage I had over all of them, Reader included, was that I'd actually hung with people who owned cars smaller than this one. "Okay, Lorraine, sort of climb onto James for a minute."

"Okay." She did, with a lot of cursing on both their parts.

"Put Paul in the passenger seat, then Lorraine, you sit on his lap."

Done, with more cursing, though Gower was able to move a bit better.

"Jeff, put me down."

"No. Not just no, *hell* no."

Couldn't imagine why he said that. "Okay, put me on the hood."

"Why?"

"Just do it!" He backed to the car, and I dropped down. I grabbed the windshield, just in case. "Great." I looked at him and Christopher. "Jeez, guys, get into the back!" You wouldn't have thought I'd need to tell them.

"We can't fit," Christopher said.

"Sit on the convertible part and put your legs on the seat."

"You're kidding." Martini sounded as though he was going to argue more.

"No. Do it, and hang onto the convertible stuff so you don't fall out."

They clambered in, with much grousing. "We're in, if you can call it that," Christopher snarked.

"Great." I was going to get off the hood and climb into the back, too. But wisdom and experience had me hook my purse over my neck first.

"Kitty, ACE has to let the animals go or Paul will not be well."

I knew it was too good to last. "James?"

"Yes, girlfriend?"

"Floor it."

"WHAT?" Martini was bellowing, but fortunately Christopher had a hold of him as we took off. To use the phrase loosely.

"Jeff, just stay there! I've done this before."

"You have?" Lorraine asked me. She reached over and grabbed my arm. "Why?"

"College broadens your horizons and all that." I looked behind me. The alligators seemed confused. "Christopher, make a copy of me and toss it into the 'gators!"

As I watched, I saw a reasonable facsimile of myself appear in the middle of the alligators. They weren't fooled by the lack of scent, but some of them were curious enough to try a bite, just in case. So that was what a feeding frenzy would look like. I looked back at the other occupants. It was night, but the moon was full, and I could see the horror in everyone's expressions.

"James? Can we get more speed out of this thing?" Martini's voice was very calm, very controlled.

"Trying. It's kind of overloaded." Reader downshifted.

"Why are you doing that?" Christopher asked, sounding only a little less calm than Martini.

"He's going into a lower gear to get more power. It burns out the engine faster, but I think I speak for all of us in saying I don't care." I looked around the side of the car. Most of the alligators had lost interest. One hadn't. "Oh, crap. James? Burn this puppy out. Alliflash is no longer on the side of right."

CHAPTER 58

WE RACED ALONG. "This is only slightly faster than those luggage carts we had to use against Mephistopheles at JFK," I shouted to Reader.

"You know, if you want to get out and run, girlfriend, feel free."

We hit a bump, and I started to slide off. Lots of people shouted my name. Lorraine managed to keep me on the hood. Reader had to swerve around a log and I slid toward the driver's side. Another swerve, another slide. This was so fun.

The car went over a big bump, and I lost my hold. I managed to grab the windshield wipers. They extended, and I slid forward. Kicked up my feet so they weren't dragging on the ground. Considered my options. Looked around, to see Alliflash still after us.

"It's like freaking *Jurassic Park*!" I shouted to them. "It's still coming! James, get some speed out of this. Make the hamsters in the engines do some damn work."

Reader cursed. "Okay, hang on." He spun the car, and hanging on became questionable. The car stopped, and I felt someone pounding on the hood.

"James, what are you doing?" Martini sounded ready to lose it.

"Most powerful gear is reverse," Reader snapped. I heard the gears shift.

"Pop the hood." I jumped off, he popped it, I jumped

in on top of Serene. "Go, go, go!" Alliflash was really close and gaining.

We took off again. I couldn't see what the others were doing, but that was fine. I had a great show watching Alliflash prove it was NASCAR material.

"What's going on?" Serene shouted. "Why did you lie to me?" She started to hit me.

I grabbed her jaw and turned her head, hard. "Look at that, you idiot. Alligator, trying to kill us. You piss me off any more, and I'll throw you to him so the rest of us escape, got it?"

This got through to her somehow. Maybe it was because Alliflash was clearly in the headlights. I looked behind it.

"Is that another one coming, too?" Serene asked.

"Yes, I think so." Gigantagator was backing its buddy. "Now, you want to live or be 'gator chow?"

"Live." We both leaned back.

"Hold onto something. It's been a real bumpy ride so far." On cue, we went over something.

"Hold onto what?" she asked frantically. Reader was driving erratically, which considering he was driving backward, wasn't too much of a shock.

"Side of car, hood, whatever." I had hopes the alligators were tiring. There was a burning smell coming from the car.

She clutched the hood and my arm. Oh, well. "Why did you kiss Brian?"

"To save your life. You didn't do what Jeff told you, you didn't get scared."

"I *was* scared."

"You concentrated on Brian."

"Yeah. How'd you know?"

"Serene? There's a saying I've found to be true. I just applied it to you and went with what popped into mind."

"What's that?"

"Bitches be crazy. You're one freaked out chick, you know that?"

"Yeah, I guess so. I wasn't always like this."

"When did the crazy start?" I was expecting something like when she started menstruating, when her mother died, when she first met Brian.

"In the last year or so. When I started at Kennedy."

I was so shocked that I looked at her. She was serious. "You weren't a psycho before then?"

"No. I . . . I know I'm not acting right any more. Not all the time, but so much of the time. It's getting worse and worse." She started to cry. "Brian's never going to like me, is he? I'm going to go to jail and be alone with no one to love me."

My brain kicked. "You go through some sort of psycho-analysis to work at Kennedy, right?"

"Yes, everyone gets tested for aptitude, mental stability, things like that."

I considered Chuckie again. He'd been the conspiracy king and still was, much as I hated that nickname he'd gotten stuck with. He always said most things that happened were an elaborate ruse to gain either money or power. He felt there were far more active conspiracies at any given time than there were straightforward power bids. He didn't believe in coincidence—which was a reason I didn't as well, years of his association—it was all part of the grand scheme of those who wanted more money and/or power. I used to consider this funny, with possibly a kernel of truth thrown in.

But Chuckie had firmly believed aliens were here, and he'd been right. So what if he was right about the whole elaborate ruse thing? Or that the conspiracies were alive, well, and active?

I couldn't risk calling him or sending a text right now, so I tried to look at this situation as Chuckie would. He had a simple rule—find the person with the most to gain, and, as unlikely as he or she may be, that's the head of the conspiracy.

I didn't have to look long or hard. Leventhal Reid was a politician, he knew the A-Cs were here, he was leading efforts to turn Centaurion Division into a military unit. Plus, he had Club 51 clearly in his pocket, and the son of the head of Club 51 working at Kennedy.

I extracted my arm from Serene's grasp and put it around her shoulders. "I have a feeling I'm going to be able to help. If, you know, we survive rescuing you."

No sooner said than I heard an exploding sound and a lot of male cursing. "Out of the car," Reader shouted. "It's dead."

Serene and I scrambled out, so did the others. "Lorraine, any speed available?"

"No, I used it up getting to the stupid lighthouse."

Figured. "Serene, you have any hyperjuice left?"

"Yes, but I can only do five miles."

"Good enough. Everyone, link arms, now!" I hooked with Serene, Lorraine with me, Gower, Reader, Christopher, and Martini. "Run, Serene, now."

She took off, and our terrified daisy chain went along with her. I looked back to see Alliflash just miss Martini's foot. Then we were stopped, far away. Everyone collapsed. I dug out my phone and dialed. "Jerry?"

"Where are you guys?"

"I have no idea. On a paved road. The car is about five miles farther back, probably being eaten by alligators. Do something, anything, and pick us up."

"No problem. I contacted East Base, and we are now in an extended Hummer heading toward you. At least, I hope we're heading toward you."

I looked down the road. "I see big headlights. Don't go too fast—none of us can get out of the way right now." The headlights didn't slow. "Um, Jerry? Seriously, slow down."

"Uh, Kitty? Tim's driving, and neither one of us sees any people yet."

Oh, hell. "Everyone up! Move, move, move! We have hostiles coming!" I got up, dragged Serene to her feet, ran to Martini and did the same to him. "Christopher, keep hold of Serene. They're after her, trust me."

We took off, Lorraine and Reader both holding onto Gower. We were moving, but I realized I was actually the only one with any speed. My brain casually mentioned I was carrying something I could now use without any remorse.

I pulled out of Martini's grip, dug through my purse, and pulled out the Glock. "What are you doing?" he shouted at me.

"Preparing to shoot. You all have guns. Now is really the time to use them."

"Actually, I don't," Martini said.

"Me either," Christopher admitted.

"Then get behind me. That would be an order, by the way. And get ready to have to move, because if this goes right, the car's going to be out of control."

Gower and Reader moved up next to me, guns out. "You know the problem with pistols is that they have to be really close for us to hit them." Reader sounded very calm.

"Who's the more accurate of the two of you?"

"Me," Reader said.

"Shoot out the tires. Paul, shoot the windshield."

"What are you aiming for, Kitty?" Gower asked.

"The driver."

The car barreled toward us. Only, it wasn't a car. It was a monster truck, with huge tires. Good and bad. "Changed my mind, take out the tires, everyone."

It got close enough, and we started firing. Reader and I were concentrating on the right front, Gower on the left. The right blew first, and the truck started to go wild. It skidded and flipped.

I felt lucky, until I realized it wasn't the only vehicle. There were two more, both sedans. They were side by side and coming right for us. We started firing again. Out of ammo, new clips in. Gower and Reader a bit faster than me since I had to find another clip in my purse.

Got a tire on one car and the windshields on both. Out of ammo again before I could hit anyone. The car that had lost a tire slammed into the other one. Sadly, they both kept on coming toward us.

As deaths went, this was potentially better than being eaten alive by alligators, but it was still not up there with death by orgasm. However, I didn't see how any of us could get out of the way in time.

Just before I screamed good-bye to everyone, the air shimmered, and Gower was on his knees. I dropped and held him. Reader did the same and held us both. We all cringed as the cars headed right toward us. I looked back to see the others in the same kind of crouch, Martini shielding Lorraine while Christopher shielded Serene. Martini looked up at me, mouthed, "I love you," then winced. I knew the cars were about to hit.

But before they reached the shield, the cars exploded. I looked forward to see flaming parts flying through the air. The wreckage sailed toward us, hit the shield, and blew over. There was another explosion, and the monster truck blew up.

I looked through the flames to see Claudia standing in the middle of the road, holding a rocket launcher. There were headlights in the distance behind her. I hoped it was our ride, but I figured she was ready in case it wasn't.

The car parts stopped flying, and the shield went down. "Stay with Paul," I told Reader as I extracted myself and ran to Claudia. She was shaking. "You were awesome."

"No one kills my team while I'm around," she said. "You know what? I *like* fieldwork. I don't want to stay in the lab all day, I want to do this, all the time." Another adrenaline junkie added to the corps.

"Did anyone get out of the truck, that you saw?"

She shook her head. "No idea. I got here just in time."

"Totally in the nick of time, which is perfect hero stuff." I took the opportunity to put a fresh clip into my Glock. "Those our boys in the distance?"

"Yeah, I didn't pass anyone else on the way here." We started walking back to the others, but stopped dead.

There was a big man who resembled a walrus standing there, next to Martini who was on his knees with his hands behind his head. Martini's shirt was still open, and this scene was far too reminiscent for comfort. The man was holding a gun to Martini's temple with one hand and Serene's throat with the other. She wasn't struggling, but I could see she was conscious. The rest of the team were facedown on the ground.

"Move and I kill him."

CHAPTER 59

CLAUDIA AND I DIDN'T MOVE.
   "Put the weapons down," Taft said.

Claudia slowly put the rocket launcher down. I didn't move.

"You want me to kill this alien piece of shit? Happy to," Taft snarled. "I said to drop the gun, bitch."

My mother had spent some time with me at the shooting range since I'd discovered she was the Annie Oakley of antiterrorism. She'd had a lot of advice for situations like this. Drop your weapon was not one of them.

I was in a good enough stance for shooting because of how I'd stopped, legs about shoulder length apart, well balanced. Distance wasn't an issue, plenty close enough. The issue was, could I aim, fire, and hit Taft before he pulled the trigger and blew Martini's brains out?

I made eye contact with Martini and did my best to send some sort of emotional signal that I wasn't backing down and he should do something to help me. He closed and opened his eyes slowly—I had no idea if he'd gotten my clue or was saying good-bye.

"So, Howard Taft, right?"

"That's right. Drop your gun."

"Why? So you can slaughter all of us more easily?" Keep 'em talking, that was my modus operandi, and it tended to work in my favor.

"I'll let you all live if you cooperate. I have what I want."
He shook Serene. I heard her whimper.

"Yeah, you've done a nice piece of work on her. So, before you go, how'd you get the crazy juice into her?"

He gave me an evil smile. "You figured it out? You're smarter than you look."

I resisted the urge to give a sarcastic reply. "Wow, thanks. So? How? I'm not smart enough to figure it out." I heard a car stop behind us, but no doors opened. I hoped this was our guys and they were clear on what was going on.

"These aliens are so trusting. Especially if they have abandonment issues and just want another mommy."

I got a sick feeling in my stomach. "Helen is one of you?"

"Oh, yeah." Serene sobbed and he grinned. "We identified this one as the right stuff for what we wanted. Give her home-baked goodies laced with drugs that make her a little bit psychotic. Focus her onto a jerk who happens to be enamored of someone we know is connected to Centaurion Division. Encourage, drug, encourage. Have to say, her bombs were an added plus. She's a keeper, and we'll be keeping her nice and safe."

"You people really are the scum of the Earth, aren't you?"

"This is *our* world. They don't belong here. If they're going to stay, then they're going to do what they should."

"Be your weapons?"

"Be our slaves."

He meant it. This wasn't just a bid for power, this was Hitler all over again. I had to hand it to the little goosestepper—he'd tapped into what appeared to be a universal goal of megalomaniacs everywhere: purity of the race and death or enslavement of any not considered good enough.

"So, Leventhal Reid—he happy with the job you've done?"

"He's a friend. He supports our cause." So, Taft was the puppet, which was more of a confirmation than a surprise. "Oh, and you boys who think you're getting out of the car so quietly? Move and I shoot."

Taft was looking at them. I wasn't going to get a better chance.

It was as if everything were in slow motion. Moved in the fast but relaxed way Mom had taught me. Aimed for the head due to hostage placement. Saw Martini fling himself away and Serene yank at Taft's arm. Fired and kept on firing. Saw Taft's head explode like a pumpkin while bullets from his gun hit the ground. Serene pulled away and staggered back. Kept on firing, into Taft's body now.

Someone was behind me, arms around mine. "Stop now, Kitty," Kevin said soothingly as Taft's body fell back and hit the ground. "It's done, he's dead." He slid his hands down my arms to my hands. "Don't want to hit the team with stray bullets." His hands closed over mine, and then he yanked upward and pulled the gun out of my hand.

Kevin spun me around and held me as I started to shake. "It's okay. You did it right. Just like your mother." He was rocking me. "Jeff's okay, I can see him getting up. Everyone's alive, they don't look hurt."

I nodded, kept my face buried in his chest, and kept on shaking. Other hands were on me now and Kevin's arm released. Martini turned me toward him and picked me up. I wrapped my arms around him, buried my face in his neck.

"It's okay, baby," Martini murmured to me. He moved us off, I wasn't sure where. But I could hear people running around us, and then it was quiet. "We're away from the others. Can still see them, but they can't hear us." He kissed my head. "It's okay, you know."

"What is?"

"To not feel remorse for killing him."

"Mom says so, too."

"So, why are you so upset?"

I pulled my head out of his neck and looked at him. "I don't want to become like them, someone who doesn't care what they do."

Martini leaned my head back against his shoulder and rocked me. "You're not like them, Kitty. You never will be. He was going to shoot me the moment you dropped your gun. And he was going to kill everyone else, too, starting with you. I could feel it. He *wanted* to kill us. You wanted to protect us. That's the difference, why you'll never be like him, or Beverly, or any of the other people we have to fight against."

I took a deep breath and tried to get it together. "Okay."

He laughed softly. "Not yet, but you will be." He kissed my head and sighed. "I wish I could be the one to kill these people instead of you."

"Why?"

"So I could protect you from moments like this."

I tightened my arms and legs around him. "As long as you're still with me during moments like this, it's okay."

"Well, that's good to hear. So, Serene isn't crazy all on her own?"

"No. Poor thing."

"Might be working out for her in the long run." He sounded amused.

"How so?" I pulled my head out again and looked where he was. Serene was sitting with her arms wrapped around her knees, crying and rocking herself. No one was paying any attention to her, and I couldn't figure out how Martini thought this was good for her.

As I watched, Brian went to her with a blanket. He knelt down, wrapped it around her, and lifted her up. He cradled her in his arms the way Martini did with me and then walked to the Hummer limo they'd arrived in.

I looked up at Martini. "He just being nice, or has the reality of the situation finally hit him?"

He grinned. "Well, hearing that Serene isn't naturally psychotic was probably a big argument in her favor."

"Staring xenophobia in the face might have helped, too."

"Probably."

"Plus a bird in the hand is worth two Kitty's who want nothing to do with you in the bush."

"So to speak." He looked at me. "So, you really didn't enjoy it?"

"With Brian? Um, no."

"I've heard from Christopher that I'm just like your old flame."

"Hardly."

"Possessive, jealous, overcommitted . . . I could go on."

"You are. I don't care." Well, not all that much, I added for virtue's sake.

"Why not?"

I thought about it. Great sex was certainly a reason. Fabulous kissing, too. Being the most gorgeous thing on two legs was also a factor. But they weren't why, just added benefits. "Because you treat me like an equal. You think I'm funny and smart, and you listen to me, even when no one else will. You run toward danger to save me, even if you're mad at me." He chuckled. "And I love you."

He kissed me. "And here all along I thought it was the great sex."

"Well, not *only* the great sex."

"Works for me. I was willing to be happy with great sex as the answer."

"I'm willing to have more great sex if it'll make you feel more secure."

"I love how you think."

CHAPTER 60

WE LOADED EVERYONE INTO THE Hummer limo.
Why the A-Cs even had such a beast was beyond me,
but I couldn't argue. It was huge, but even so, we all just
made it inside.

Tim was driving, and Hughes and Walker both rode
shotgun. Lorraine had done some major medical on Gower
and Martini, and she wanted them quiet. So Reader and I
were holding them, and we were all lying down in the back,
on a thick foam pad, complete with pillows. I found myself
wondering why this was in this vehicle and chose to believe
it was because it functioned as a rescue van as opposed to
the A-C cruisin' love machine.

Randy and Claudia were in the middle section nearest
to us with Lorraine and Joe. Lorraine was still working on
Serene, and Brian was right by her side. Lorraine and Claudia both were far more jazzed about this experience than
Joe or Randy. The guys were trying to be cool, but I could
tell they were freaked out.

Kevin, Jerry, and Christopher were in the middle portion of the car closest to the front. Kevin was making a lot
of phone calls, and so was Christopher. Jerry was functioning as adjunct and passing information back and forth to
and from the rest of us as needed.

I had Martini cuddled into my breasts, and Reader had
Gower in pretty much the same position. We were prone

but not so much that I couldn't see over the seats. "So, what now, girlfriend?"

"I want to go home."

"I want to never come to Florida again." Reader sighed. "But we have to rest before we fly home. I'm not leaving the jet, and Tim and I, as well as the others, are too tired to fly safely."

Martini fumbled in his pocket and pulled out his cell. "Dad, sorry to wake you. Oh? Really. Sorry they called and worried you. No, we're okay. No, really. Well, yeah, okay, not perfect, but alive and functioning. All exhausted, yes. You're sure? No separate sleeping quarters when we show up, no arranged marriages waiting to be performed? Yeah, then every room, including the guesthouse."

He was quiet for a minute or so. "Yeah, sounds good. But figure lunch, at the earliest. Okay." Another long pause. "I love you, too." He hung up. "Going to my parents'." Martini turned his face back into my breasts and promptly went to sleep.

Reader and I looked at each other. He gave me a wink. "Nicely done."

I passed our destination on to Claudia, who sent it on up to Tim. I was still tense, and I could feel the rest of the car's occupants were, too. I wasn't sure if Martini had any blocks left or if he was completely burned out, and I just wanted something to help us all relax.

Tim seemed to read my mind. I heard the Wallflowers' "Three Marlenas" start up. No one grumbled or complained, and the tension seemed to be dissipating somewhat.

"So, James, where did you find that Beetle?"

"It was parked at the Lighthouse." He shrugged. "I didn't argue."

I decided not to question. "Did we pay for it?" I looked toward the middle of the car. Claudia was asleep, leaning on Randy. I thought he was snoozing, too. Lorraine finished with Serene, sat back, snuggled next to Joe, and was out like a light. He'd been waiting for her, clearly, because as soon as his arm was around her, he leaned his head against the window. The Wallflowers' remake of David Bowie's "Heroes" came on.

"No." There was something about the way he said that word that made me look back at him.

"Why not?"

"I think it was the caretaker's." Reader's voice was low. "He was dead when I found him."

"Where?"

"Near the car. He must have seen something and tried to escape."

I looked to the middle of the car again. Serene seemed better, but she was shivering. Brian gently pulled her next to him and covered her with the blanket. She gave a shuddering sigh, and he hugged her. I looked back at Reader. "Who did it?"

"I'm guessing one of the Club 51 Goon Squad. Wasn't Jeff or Christopher, and I don't think Serene would have done it, either." He made the throat-slitting gesture.

"Ugh."

"Got that right. Kevin called someone; the body should be taken care of soon."

We drove on through the night, my Wallflowers mix continuing to do its good work. I checked, and as far as I could see, the guys in the front part of the car were all awake, with the exception of Christopher, who I was pretty sure I saw slumped in his typical napping-in-the-vehicle position.

Reader shifted and lay fully down. Gower made a grunting sound, wrapped his arm around him, and snuggled closer. Reader's eyes closed, and his breathing went rhythmic.

Martini snoozed while I stroked his hair. Most of any car's occupants sleeping meant I was awake. For whatever reason, my tiredness would disappear if the majority were out of it. No idea why, but I guessed it had to do with feeling that someone had to be ready.

Quiet time never meant contemplation or relaxation for me. It meant my mind wandered. We'd cut off the head of the Club 51 snake, but that didn't mean the rest of the little serpent's nests would go away. The one picture I'd seen of Leventhal Reid swam in front of me. This was our head fugly, only he was a human and a normally attractive man, not a parasitic superbeing. We were all better equipped to fight threats from outer space than threats from human beings. Humans were so much more devious and tremendously nastier.

I thought about killing Taft. I killed superbeings regularly now, but even the first one I'd killed didn't make me feel remorse. But I could admit I hadn't liked killing anything, not the superbeings, not Taft, not even Beverly. It had just had to be done. Them or me. Them or others, really. Maybe that's what Martini and my mother meant—some evil has to be killed, but you don't have to enjoy doing it.

My mind wandered to ACE. So powerful and so innocent at the same time. I'd known without asking that if we'd shot at the alligators, ACE would have gone haywire. I wondered if my killing Taft had affected ACE in a negative way.

No, I heard in my mind. ACE is clear why Kitty had to kill. Alligators were not evil, just being alligators.

How are you talking to me?

Still everywhere while also all inside Paul. Paul is a good person, Kitty chose well for ACE.

Thank you for saving us. We wouldn't be alive if you hadn't shielded us when we needed it.

ACE would like to do more. . . . Its voice trailed off in my mind. I thought about why it wouldn't or couldn't.

You shouldn't. You could solve all the problems for us. But that would make us dependent on you, to the point where we couldn't do anything for ourselves. And it would make you so powerful that you would risk becoming something I know you don't want to be. Though my viewpoint was a lot different when those cars were headed toward us.

But Kitty did not ask ACE for protection, and neither did Paul.

You did that on your own? Thank you even more.

Kitty is welcome. ACE is learning when to step in and when to stay quiet. Just like always, watching and protecting.

Like God.

No. God is much greater than ACE.

There is a God?

Why do you ask, when ACE can see you already know?

Confirmation, I guess. Sometimes it doesn't seem as though He's paying much attention.

God is vast. Many galaxies, many worlds, many beings. Free will exists so God does not have to do everything.

I wanted to continue this discussion, but the car stopped. I realized we were on what looked like a residential street, waiting at a big double gate attached to high walls. I could hear Tim talking to someone, but I couldn't make out any of the words. The gates opened, and we drove in.

At first I thought we were in a private, gated community. After we drove along a winding drive for a minute or so, I saw a house that looked at least double my parents'. For a moment I thought we were going there, but Tim kept on driving. A minute or so later we reached another house, larger than the first. Didn't stop there either. Another couple of minutes and we arrived at the White House. Well, it wasn't, but it looked that big to me.

I nudged Martini. "Jeff, are we at your parents' house?" It was that or the Alpha Centaurion Embassy. I was kind of hoping for Embassy.

"Mmmm?" He nuzzled into my breasts. "Nice here." He went back to sleep.

It was a circular drive, and Tim brought the car to a stop in front of what I assumed was the front door. My class intimidation meter was set to high. I couldn't imagine telling my father about this place—the lecture on how money needed to be spread to the less privileged would last for weeks.

I shook Martini. "Jeff, I think we're at your house."

He blinked and yawned. "Good. Let's go back to sleep." He wrapped both arms around me, snuggled right back into his personal pillows, and started snoring.

I looked over the seat. Lorraine was waking up. "Lorraine, what did you give Jeff? I can't get him to really wake up."

"Good. He needs the sleep."

"But I can't exactly carry him out of the car."

She looked over. "I'll have someone bring out a gurney."

"Uh, I don't think he needs a gurney." I hoped.

"He needs sleep more than anything else right now."

"I guess we can stay in the car."

Doors were opening, and the team was climbing out. I realized all our things were at the hotel still. Oh, well, nothing we could do about it now. Reader woke up and shook Gower awake. Gower seemed fuzzy, but at least he was able to sit up.

The back hatch opened, and several male A-Cs I'd never seen before were there. They helped Gower out, though Reader waved them away. "You need help with Jeff, girlfriend?"

"Lorraine gave him something—I can't get him to wake up for more than a second."

Reader looked out. "Need a gurney."

"He doesn't need a gurney!"

"Yeah, he does." Reader grimaced. "He should go into isolation, too."

"You're telling me they have the entire acreage of Rhode Island in this compound and no isolation chamber?"

"No, I'm telling you he should go into the isolation chamber they have for him here." He said it a bit louder.

"I don't want to," Martini said, sounding annoyed. "I just want to sleep, if any of you would let me."

"Jeff, we're at your parents' humongous estate. Do you want to walk in on your own steam or take the gurney ride?"

He growled and grumbled, but he moved into a sitting position. "I'll walk." The A-C assistants tried to help him, but he waved them away. They continued to try. "I'm getting seriously pissed. Back off, I can walk."

He climbed out, slowly but on his own steam. Reached in, put his hands on my waist and lifted me out, easily as far as I could tell. I wrapped my arm around his waist, and he put his around my shoulders. Martini heaved a sigh. "I really hope this visit goes better than the one we had a few hours ago."

CHAPTER 61

THE HOUSE WAS EVEN MORE massive seen from the outside than I'd felt it was when we'd been inside before. Earlier it had seemed huge. Now I felt as though I were about to enter Tara and wondered if Rhett and Scarlet were to greet us. They had steps leading up to the front door as well as a winding ramp. I assumed they'd seen the wisdom of rolling gurneys as opposed to carrying them.

I steered Martini to the ramp, assuming it was easier to walk than stairs. He didn't argue. The A-Cs I didn't know were following us, rather closely. I got the impression they were ready to catch Martini if he collapsed. This was both comforting and unsettling at the same time.

"Our stuff's still at the hotel." I said this to avoid asking if Martini's parents were actually drug dealers. They were living palatially enough.

"Someone'll get it."

"Sir, we already retrieved all the team's belongings," one of the assistant A-Cs said. His tone was extremely respectful. "They're in the room assignments Commander Katt gave to Mr. Martini."

I had? Oh, well, what seemed like weeks but was only hours ago I had. But we had an additional member along. "We need to have a guard around Serene."

"Yes, ma'am, Commander." One of the other A-Cs zoomed off.

I looked up at Martini. "What's going on?"

"Routine." He grinned. "I'll explain it when we're alone."

"If you can stay awake long enough, you mean."

"Give me a reason."

I wanted to, but I had a feeling Lorraine would kill me if I actually did.

We reached the front door finally. I recognized the humongous entryway from our last visit. It looked bigger coming in through the front door than it had coming up from the basement. Either my perspective was different or it had been designed to instantly create feelings of inferiority for those entering the "normal" way. I looked down the hallway I knew we'd come from last visit—it just looked big and long. I gave up trying to figure out if M.C. Escher had done the architectural design and focused on getting Martini resting as soon as possible.

The A-C assistants ushered us all into the family room and faded back against the walls, just like the Secret Service. There were four doorways in this room—one we'd just come through, the one I knew led to the kitchen, and two others. Alfred came in from one of the others. He looked worried and upset but also relieved, as any father does when his errant children are finally home safely.

Christopher was closer to him than we were, and Alfred grabbed him and hugged him tightly. I could see Christopher's expression—he was shocked but in a good way.

That embrace finished, Alfred headed toward us. I disengaged from Martini just in time. Alfred grabbed him just as he had Christopher. Martini looked shocked, too, while he hugged his father back tightly.

They disengaged and Alfred turned to me. "And you."

"Huh?" I wasn't sure what that meant.

He grabbed me and hugged me. It was reminiscent of the bear hugs my mother had given me during Operation Fugly. I wondered if he'd let me breathe soon. "Thank you," Alfred whispered to me. "Thank you for saving my boys."

I hugged him back while I tried to get air. "Dad, she can't breathe."

"Oh? Oh!" Alfred released me and I gulped air. "Sorry about that."

"No problem. You Martini men aren't aware of your own strength sometimes."

Martini got a funny look on his face. "Yeah. Let's get everyone settled. We need sleep in the worst way." His voice sounded funny, too, as though he was upset, but quietly. I didn't think Alfred picked it up.

Alfred nodded. "As soon as I greet the rest of the family." He went over to Gower and Reader. They got the bear hug treatment, too. He moved to Michael next and then the girls.

I went back beside Martini. "Jeff, what's wrong?"

"Nothing." He wasn't looking at me.

I thought about it. "Baby, I know you don't know what you're doing after I harpoon you."

"I almost killed you twice." His voice was low and he was staring at the ground.

"Christopher created a distraction, and I got you under control. It's okay."

"What's it like when we're alone? When there's no one to distract me?" He looked straight into my eyes. "How many times have I almost killed you?"

I put my arms around his waist and leaned my head against his chest. "Many fewer than you've saved me or protected me." He clutched at me, and I decided Lorraine was right. Martini needed to sleep. "Let's get into a room and go to bed, okay?"

"Sounds good." He was still upset, I could tell, but I didn't want to discuss this in public any more.

"Who's sleeping where?" I asked Alfred as we walked over to him.

"We figured the bachelors could take the guesthouse."

"That sounds like a good plan, but where are we going to put Serene?" I didn't want her sleeping with Brian tonight. Not that I suddenly wanted him for myself, but she was too fragile and still drugged, so we had no way of knowing what she would or wouldn't do.

"Lorraine told me what was done to her," he said softly. "I think it will be best to keep her with me and Lucinda."

"Um, in the bedroom with you?" This sounded beyond freaky.

Alfred grinned. "Not quite. We had to install a . . . special annex in our bedroom."

"When I was born," Martini said, voice clipped. His body was tense again.

Alfred nodded and looked straight at him. "Yes. We didn't mind. We minded that you were suffering, not that we had to find ways to deal with it."

"So, why put Serene there?" I asked before this turned nasty or weepy, neither one of which I thought Martini was up to right now.

"It's something of an isolation chamber, but it also monitors other functions, including brain waves. Under the circumstances, until we can identify the nature of the drugs given to her and what effect they've had, I want to keep her under observation. However, I don't think she can emotionally handle being separated from your group."

"No, I'm sure she can't. I don't want to just dump her off somewhere. She's been treated badly enough."

Alfred gave me a long look. "She tried to kill you. More than once."

I shrugged. "It wasn't her fault. I'm sure she would have resented me under normal circumstances, but her becoming poster girl for the unhinged was due to what Taft's people did to her."

He nodded. "Yes, I agree." Alfred walked off to have the A-C attendants get the guys over to the guesthouse.

"Which one of the other two houses is the guesthouse?"

"The one nearest our house. The other one's the servants' quarters." He said it so casually, as though it was nothing. I managed to keep my mouth shut. Of course, Martini picked up what I was feeling. "Why does it bother you?"

"I had no idea your family was loaded. No one acts like it."

"We don't care about it all that much. Money's a useful thing, the more of it you have, the more you can take care of your people."

Well, I knew my father would be pleased with that sentiment. "How is it your family lives like this?" Most of the A-Cs I knew lived in the Dulce Science Center, with a few at Area 51 and Caliente Base. As I'd understood it, the entire A-C population lived in or around each of the bases worldwide. But while this was close to Canaveral Base, it resembled standard A-C housing like a Ferrari resembled a Yugo.

"My father holds some patents—he's one of the few male A-Cs with scientific aptitude. Not a birth-talent, just skill and ability. Several of our female scientists do as well. It helped that they came here with more advanced scientific knowledge than Earth had."

"So, why the huge estate?"

Martini shrugged. "Humans are impressed by wealth and the show of wealth. So we make sure we have a few showcases, just in case." He looked at me. "Most of our human operatives get over it quickly. Why aren't you?"

"I've known for less than a day." Another thought occurred. "The allowance you give me—where does that come from?"

"We call those wages, and it comes from the fund that pays people." He grinned. "You worried you're stealing from my trust fund?"

"Actually, yeah."

He laughed. "You're not. You're being paid for services rendered to the United States Government, Centaurion Division, and the World Safety Organization."

That last one was a new one to me. "World Safety Organization?"

"The name we use when we have to work outside the U.S. You've heard me use it, in Paris for sure."

Paris. The main things I remembered from that trip were great sex in the women's bathroom in the Metro and Martini catching me when a superbeing knocked me off the side of the Eiffel Tower. It had been a short, excitement-filled trip. "Uh, right."

"You need to pay attention more."

"It's Kitty, why expect her to pay attention to what we think is important?" Christopher was next to us. "I'm heading over to the guesthouse. Make sure you get some rest—this isn't over yet, just paused." He gave me a sidelong look. "That's probably up to you. The isolation chamber is in the basement, should you need it."

"Like I could find it."

Christopher shrugged. "We lived in the Embassy when we were little. It's bigger than this."

"There really is an A-C Embassy?"

"In D.C., yeah." He sighed. "I miss it there, sometimes."

"Me, too." Martini sighed as well. "Okay, well, get some rest yourself. See you somewhere in the daylight hours."

I'd never seen them do this kind of farewell just because they were going to bed. They seemed uncomfortable being separated here. I grabbed Christopher's arm as he turned away. "You know, you don't have to go to the guesthouse if you don't want to."

"Uh, what?" He looked slightly freaked.

Martini chuckled. "She's picked up we don't like to be apart when we're here." He hugged me. "But we're big boys now and can handle it."

"You sure?"

Christopher nodded. "Yeah. We're in charge, now." He leaned down and gave me a kiss on the cheek. "Thanks for the offer, though." He clapped Martini on the shoulder, then wandered off.

That left the eight of us who were couples and Serene. Gower and Reader seemed at ease, as did Claudia and Lorraine. Randy and Joe looked as uncomfortable as I felt. Which somehow made me feel better.

Serene seemed like a scared rabbit, but I couldn't blame her. It was clear from how she'd talked to and about Martini and Christopher that she was in awe of their status, and I had the feeling she hadn't been over to Martini Manor before now.

I heard a woman's voice, talking to Christopher, but out of sight. The words weren't clear, but it didn't sound unpleasant. That conversation over, I was somewhat unsurprised to see Lucinda come the way Christopher had gone.

She hugged Gower and Reader, then came over to us. I tried to move away from Martini again so they'd have free hugging room, but he clearly didn't want me to, because his hold on my shoulders didn't release. He was tensed up again.

Lucinda noticed, but she didn't get upset. She just came

and hugged us both. Martini's body relaxed, and he hugged his mother back. I just sort of got squished, but I managed not to take it personally.

"Do you need to go into isolation?" she asked as the group hug ended.

"No, just to bed."

She nodded. "Can you take the others up? I want to get Serene tucked away."

"Yep." Martini moved us off. I looked over my shoulder—Lucinda had her arm around Serene and was leading her off in a different direction.

"How close to your parents' bedroom will we be?"

"Different wing. We move fast enough that the rooms don't have to be close for a parent to get to a child." He grinned. "The room monitors turn off easily, too. And the rooms are pretty well soundproofed."

"Good. Not that this will be a worry tonight," I said as sternly as I could manage.

Martini chuckled. "That's what waking up's for."

CHAPTER 62

OUR THINGS WERE IN A ROOM, it had a bed, we got undressed, crawled into said bed, cuddled up, and both fell asleep immediately.

I woke up to see daylight streaming in the window. It was a shock. Dulce living floors were all underground, and I'd become accustomed to the pseudo-daylight the master-computer-controlled lighting provided. Real sunlight was a rarity these days.

I was alone in the bed, which caused me a lot of worry. "In the bathroom," Martini called. "Nice to know you care." I heard the shower turn on.

Rolled out of bed and joined him. Tried for quiet sex. Failed. Decided not to care.

Whoever ran the laundry services at Dulce had the contract for Martini Manor as well. All our clothes were back, cleaned and pressed. My Converse had been snatched in the night and cleaned off as well. I chose not to wonder how—time spent thinking about that was not time well spent for me.

It was midafternoon before we got out of the room, and not because we'd spent that much time in the shower, but because we'd slept in so late. Martini seemed better, at least his back looked perfectly fine, but I wasn't so sure. No isolation likely meant not enough regeneration.

Everyone gathered in the dining hall, where another great meal was served. This one seemed designed to cover all the bases—sandwiches, fruit, vegetables, fried chicken, hamburgers, hot dogs. I had some of everything, Martini stuck with sandwiches, fruit, and veggies. He was a much healthier eater than I was. He avoided the cookies, brownies, and cupcakes. I took one of each and snagged some for the road, too.

This meal was much more relaxed as well. Lucinda and Alfred seemed happy to have us there, as opposed to trying to run half of us out of town. I wondered if Marianne had told me the truth and decided she might have. I also assumed she'd told her mother that pushing me away wasn't going to work.

Kevin had been up the earliest, making phone calls and arrangements. Sadly, no one had been able to connect anything definitively to Leventhal Reid, so he was still out and about, doing his nasty work. With Howard Taft dead, that avenue was closed. Kevin had people working on Frank Taft, Turco, Helen, and the rest of those we'd taken into custody, but so far, nothing.

Daniel Chee and his family appeared safe, but Kevin didn't relax the guard on them—just in case. They were going to have A-C and P.T.C.U. guards until we knew if Reid had been stopped or was in custody. I liked how Kevin thought.

Michael and Brian got word that they had to get back to Kennedy and report in, so they were going to stay with the Martinis another night and go with Alfred the next day. The Martinis were also keeping Serene—she was still in their antechamber, having the drugs flushed out of her system.

That left the rest of us who all wanted to get back to Dulce. Only, there was a small wrinkle. "You all have to go to Caliente Base," Kevin reminded us. "It's annexed. And, from what Angela's said, there are a lot of the younger A-Cs there already."

"Our stuff's in Dulce."

"Probably moved over," Martini said. He didn't seem concerned. "We'll deal with it when we're back."

Good-byes were said, and then we all trooped to the gate room. "You sure it's safe to go to the jet?"

Martini shrugged. "Fifty percent chance."

"Oh, *great* odds."

"I don't want to leave the jet," Reader said.

"Are we arriving inside the jet?" How did the gates do this? And why did I never know?

"Yes." Martini looked at me out of the corner of his eye. "One day, I'll tell you how."

"Humph."

Just like before, Martini insisted on going first and tried to make me wait to go last with Christopher. I threw a mild fuss and got moved up ahead of the girls and my pilots, but still right behind Christopher. Oh, well, it wasn't at the end of the chain.

We moved through rapidly, about two seconds between entries. I closed my eyes and walked through. Still sucked. Opened them when my foot hit something solid. Thankfully, it was the floor of the jet.

Everyone filed in, and Reader and Tim went to the cockpit. I followed. "Guys, what if they put a bomb on the plane?"

"Scanning now, girlfriend." Reader looked up at me. "Sometimes we're ahead of you."

"You sure it'll pick up things like Serene's invisible floating bombs?"

"Yep."

"Okay." I wasn't sure if I should relax but decided to have some faith.

The plane deemed safe, everyone settled in and we took off. Martini still seemed tired, and as soon as we were airborne, Lorraine insisted he use the bed. I went with him, though with a full plane, the last thing I wanted was to garner Mile High Miles.

Lorraine hooked Martini up to a variety of equipment, as well as an IV with some kind of regenerative saline drip. They both insisted this was routine for empaths who weren't able to go into full isolation, so I stopped worrying. Sort of.

Of course, as isolation chambers went, the jet bedroom was a huge improvement. The real ones looked like Frankenstein's lab mixed with a creepy Egyptian tomb theme and some science fiction horror elements added in just for fun. Isolation chambers didn't have beds so much as they had padded, super-duper hospital gurneys that rotated like the Tilt-A-Whirl. They also slept one, to use the term loosely. Individual models, particularly those for the younger empaths, resembled futuristic sarcophagi crossed with an Iron Maiden, not, sadly, the band. I figured even Eddie would hate having to go into any form of A-C isolation.

Normally Martini had tubes and wires going in everywhere, including his head, so sitting on a king-sized bed with an IV drip into his arm and a couple of sensors attached to his chest and temples seemed tame and almost cozy. I didn't have the impulse to rip everything out of him and run away hysterically, which was a bonus, too. The medical teams and empaths claimed isolation was harder for the empath's loved ones than for the empath, but I still didn't believe it.

Right after Lorraine left, Martini tried to ask me something, but whatever he was hooked up to knocked him out before he could get more than a couple of words out. I laid us both down, but I didn't sleep. I lay there, held him, and wondered why we were being allowed to leave so easily. There was something we were all missing. The threat wasn't over.

Kevin had gotten a lot of Club 51 people rounded up. Most of these were harmless crackpots, but a few had been dangerous enough to take into custody. But Kevin felt there were hundreds, potentially thousands, we didn't have tabs on yet, and I knew he was right.

Leventhal Reid had an airtight alibi, since he'd been with my mother, the President, or a variety of other politicians the entire time we'd been on this mission. Which meant the threatening phone call I'd gotten during dinner at Martini Manor had come from Taft.

I tried to think like Chuckie again. Power plays like this were chess matches. You sacrificed whatever piece you had to in order to win. Reid was the king. Taft wasn't a pawn, he was at least a bishop on Reid's board. So, who were his other pieces? Serene had been an unwitting one, more powerful than a pawn, call her the queen they thought they were controlling. The others at Kennedy were pawns, rooks, maybe knights, but no one got rid of all their pieces. You could still win if you had a pawn or one power piece, even if your opponent seemed to have the upper hand.

So who was left? Were all the pieces taken so Reid would have to regroup and find new ones? Or were we overlooking a power piece or a pawn standing on the edge of the board?

I worried about this the entire way home, while Martini slept like the dead. In fact, the only way I knew he was alive was that he would occasionally nuzzle his face more into my breasts or hug me closer. Otherwise, he was more out than I'd ever seen. Whatever Lorraine was giving him was heavy duty.

The flight was uneventful. We landed at Area 51 and were greeted by the Pontifex. Hugs all around. White seemed relieved we were all back. "I'm sorry for what happened," he said to me as we went into Headquarters. He'd ensured we were walking behind the others, and that Martini and Christopher were far ahead.

"It's okay, we're kind of used to things trying to kill us."

He laughed. "I meant what my sister tried to pull."

"Oh, that. Yeah, that was interesting." I took a deep breath. "So, is Caliente Base really annexed?"

"Oh, yes. We were fully cooperative. The U.S. military were thrilled to be escorting so many young ladies to safety."

I winced. "Sorry."

"Don't be." White shook his head. "You've made it easier."

"What easier?"

"Lifting the interspecies marriage ban."

"Seriously?" I tried not to think about Martini's reaction. I wasn't sure if he'd be thrilled or not. A part of me still sometimes wondered if he was with me because I was exotic and forbidden.

"Yes. It will require more negotiations and a huge show of resistance on the part of my Office, but I expect things to be approved in the reasonably near future."

"You don't seem upset."

"I'm not. Your arguments in favor have been more compelling than you realize. However, I have an entire race of people who have to be moved to a mind-set that, for many, is incompatible with our traditions."

"Yeah, I got a load of those firsthand."

White chuckled. "No one had accepted on behalf of their children on Alpha Centauri for at least three decades before we came to Earth. Barbara and Lucinda just figured it was worth a try."

"So, does your sister actually hate me?"

"We had a long chat. No, she's afraid being married to Jeffrey will be more than you can deal with and that you'll leave him, either before or definitely after you have children."

"I got the word on empathic children from one of Jeff's sisters."

White shrugged. "My wife dealt with Jeffrey very well. And Christopher. Imageers are not always the easiest babies, either, at least those whose talents manifest early." He chuckled. "Imageers are much harder to deal with as children and teenagers than empaths, in some key ways."

"You don't seem worried."

He laughed again. "In the five-plus months I've known you, you've proved to be many things, but a quitter isn't one of them. Nor are you a coward. I feel confident that if Jeffrey ever does declare for you, and you accept, that you will manage to successfully deal with his many quirks."

I didn't really think of Martini as quirky. "That would be my plan, yes."

"Good." He sighed. "Well, another mission over, and completed quickly."

"I suppose." I stopped walking. "Richard, do you really think it's over?"

"In the grand scheme of things, no. But it appears you've crippled a huge anti-alien conspiracy as well as saved our personnel at Kennedy. While creating freedom for our young people at the same time."

"Right. Do we really have to go to Caliente Base?"

"Yes, but no worries. Your belongings have already been moved there, and while it's smaller than Dulce, there should be sufficient space. And I don't expect it to remain separate from the rest of us all that long. As soon as I can gracefully acquiesce to your demands, we'll return to normal, with a few differences. And, of course, we hope that Alpha Team will continue to straddle the lines between old and new. So come by any time," he added with a grin.

I didn't argue with him, but I was still worried. We filed some reports, White took each member of Alpha Team aside to tell them what he'd told me, and then we gated to Caliente Base. I insisted on taking my car, and Martini stayed with me while the others went ahead.

"Jeff, do you think it's over?" I asked while we waited to get flagged through the vehicle gate.

He was quiet. "Why would you ask me that?" His voice was strained.

I looked at him; the color had drained from his face. "What's wrong? Are you okay?" I put one hand to his forehead and grabbed his wrist to check his pulse.

"You're asking me if we're over." He sounded ill.

"Oh! No, Jeff, I wasn't. I meant the thing with Leventhal Reid." I stroked his face. "Why would you think I was asking if we were over?" My stomach tightened.

"I don't know." He sounded tired.

"Baby, are you sick?" I checked his heartbeats. Like his pulse, a little fast, but not out of the ordinary for him being upset. His skin felt a bit clammy.

"I'm fine. As for Reid, I don't know." He looked at me and gave me a weak smile. "You don't think it's over, do you?"

"No, I don't." Time to drive through. I looked at Martini. He still looked as though he wasn't feeling well. I shifted into first, then held his hand. It seemed to help him. Got through the gate, drove to the motor pool area.

Caliente Base was the smallest base I'd ever been in. Meaning that it only went ten stories into the ground and didn't house a huge scientific research facility or well over ten thousand people. It was housing several thousand, though. Caliente Base was busier than I'd ever seen it before.

I saw a variety of people, including Doreen. She was hanging on the arm of a guy who looked as though he'd won every Science Fair from kindergarten through graduate school. He had a dazed, "how did I get this lucky?" expression every time he looked at her. I predicted a happy marriage.

Due to space limitations, couples were pretty much required to share quarters. Other than soundproofing issues, this presented no challenges since we didn't have anyone with refugee status younger than twenty, which was considered the A-C age of consent.

Martini and I found our room. As Commanders, we got bigger digs than most. All of Alpha and Airborne were on the same floor. In addition to this pointing out how much power our refugee status was going to have within the A-C community, I really prayed for soundproofing. I didn't want to deal with the jokes from Tim and Reader if they heard me yowling.

I said as much jokingly to Martini and had to spend an hour calming him down. I went from somewhat concerned to really worried. He picked it up, and we almost got into another fight, but thankfully our sex drives solved the problem.

The sex was great, but when we were done, he was out again, head cuddled on my breasts. This wasn't totally unusual for us, but normally he'd hold me. I tried to tell myself nothing was wrong, he'd just gotten used to it on the jaunt to Florida.

I stroked his hair and knew I was a liar.

CHAPTER 63

THE NEXT TWO WEEKS WERE remarkably uneventful, to the point of dullness. Oh, sure, we had the random superbeing manifestations, but none of them required Alpha or Airborne.

Club 51 seemed silent, and Leventhal Reid had backed down on his demands to turn Centaurion into a military unit. Some of this was assumed to be because of ACE, though only a handful of high-ranking humans knew about what had happened. We'd have preferred that no one else know, but Kevin had to brief my mom, Mom had to brief the President, and the President pretty much could and did tell whoever he thought needed to know, so we weren't in a position to keep anything hushed up. Most of the team, Martini included, moved to the opinion the operation was over.

Some of the time was spent determining which human households were getting gates installed. After this, no one wanted anyone involved with Centaurion driving or flying if they didn't need to.

I personally spent some time being evasive with Chuckie and texting with Caroline. I was well-practiced with Chuckie, so that went as well as could be expected, meaning I lied, he got frustrated, and I spent a lot of time feeling guilty. This set even less well with Martini than it usually did, and we spent a lot of time snapping at each other.

It was even harder with Caroline. I didn't want to talk to her because I didn't know how much she might know, and I didn't want to have to play verbal gymnastics, but I wanted to see if she had any info on Reid and related issues. So I had to really word my texts well, and that took some work.

All I got for my efforts was that the situation in Paraguay had quieted down and the government was taking a wait-and-see attitude. She was able to confirm that her senator didn't like Reid, but she was slim on the whys and wheres-fores. She promised to let me know if she heard anything new about Paraguay or Reid, and that was pretty much all I could hope for from my lone Washington "insider."

Most of the time was spent discussing Caliente Base's status. My parents ostensibly came to help, though they spent most of their time just hanging out. My mother had assigned Kevin to Caliente Base, so he was around a lot.

I was thankful he was, because he was the only person besides me who was still on edge. Even my parents felt it was over, at least for a good while.

Kevin and I were having coffee in the commissary. Caliente's commissary wasn't as good as Dulce's, but it was still better than most five-star restaurants. "I don't like it," he said for the fifth time in fifteen minutes.

"I don't either. And everyone else thinks we're crazy."

"Yeah. Even Angela thinks we're spooked or overreacting." He sighed. "Maybe we are."

"We're not. I know it in my gut, and so do you." I took a deep breath and tried to articulate what was bothering me. "Something's missing. Like in *Star Wars*, when the *Millennium Falcon* gets away from the Death Star, and Princess Leia says the bad guys let them go, because their escape was too easy?"

"And she's right, yeah." He cocked his head at me. "I don't know that I'd call our escape easy."

"You sound like you're auditioning to be Han Solo." I had to admit Kevin could do it, but Martini would carry the role off better. "It's the jet."

"What about it? No bomb was attached. It was scanned before we left and once we were back, too."

"It was also sitting at Kennedy, unguarded, for two days."

"But there's nothing wrong with it."

I closed my eyes. It was there, the answer, just tickling me at the back of my brain. I wondered if ACE had left that little bit of Terry inside me if I'd know what it was, be able to see what was wrong. Maybe, since I couldn't get it.

I felt a hand on the back of my neck and jumped. "Hey, why are you so nervous?" Martini asked.

"You startled me. I was trying to think." I tried to arch into his hand, but he took it away.

"Sorry, I'll let you two be alone." He stalked off.

Kevin raised his eyebrow. "Something going on with you and Jeff?"

"I don't know. He's been . . . different since we got back from Florida."

Kevin's eyes narrowed. "Different how?"

"Moody, suspicious, overtired. He's taking anything I say to mean I don't want to be with him." My stomach was in knots.

"Maybe you two should get away for a few days."

"We go to my ten-year high school reunion tonight." I wasn't packed, but that was because I was stalling.

"That should be fun."

"I'm dreading it. But Jeff really wants to go." I looked around. He wasn't in the commissary anywhere.

"Go after him. I'll handle the worrying about what we're missing for both of us for a while." He grinned and his smile made me feel a little better.

As I headed to our room, I realized that part of why Kevin's smile was comforting was because I hadn't seen Martini's too often since we'd been back. Riding in an elevator without him tended to make me horny. Today it made me want to cry. My real fear about our relationship—that I was attractive to him because I was forbidden fruit—stampeded up and waved at me. He'd started acting differently as soon as we'd gotten back and White had confirmed that sanctified and approved interspecies marriages were on the horizon.

By the time I reached our room, I was almost in tears. Martini was in there, sitting on the couch, looking upset. "So, you and Kevin having a thing?"

I closed the door and forced myself not to cry. If he was going to do this to me, I wasn't going to let him know how much it hurt. "Jeff, what's wrong? Are you sick or just out of it?"

"You seemed into it with him."

"He's happily married!"

"He never goes home!"

I pressed my lips together, counted to ten. Went to twenty. Could talk at thirty. "He goes home at night. We go to bed, he goes home. If you'd care to recall, we installed a gate in his house, just like at my parents', since he's now the official P.T.C.U. Liaison to Centaurion Division."

"And I see that means he's assigned to spend every waking moment with you." Martini glared at me. Still wasn't up to Christopher's standards, but he was working at it.

I forced myself to go sit on the couch next to him. He shifted away from me. I folded my hands and looked at them. Maybe I could keep it together if I didn't think about what was slipping away. "Why are you doing this?" I kept my voice low.

"Doing what? Catching you cheating on me?"

"Jeff, I'm not cheating on you. Not with Kevin, not with Christopher, not with anyone." I took a deep breath. "Why don't you just tell me the truth?"

"What would that be?"

"That you want to break up with me."

The sentence hung on the air. My eyes filled with tears, but I refused to let them fall. I batted my lashes until I got the tears to go back. He still hadn't said anything. I thought about all the times he'd said he loved me—apparently he was a *great* liar, I just hadn't wanted to see it. I was clenching my hands together so tightly my knuckles were white.

He still hadn't spoken. I didn't look at him, I just got up and went into the bedroom. My rolling suitcase was there, and I packed for the reunion. The temptation to not wear the dresses he'd wanted me to was high, but he had great taste, and I might as well look good since I was now going stag.

I finished packing, but he hadn't come into the room. Went back to the little living room, and he was still on the couch. I risked a look at him in case he was passed out or something, but, no, he was still breathing and still glaring. At nothing, as far as I could see.

"I'm going to go to the resort."

"Why?" Oh, so he was still able to speak.

"Because you registered us for my reunion and I'm going to go."

"Thought you didn't want to go."

"I didn't. I still don't. But clearly I can't sleep here any more, and I just don't want to explain this to my parents . . . since I don't understand it."

He looked at me, and his eyes were cold. Even when he'd been furious with me for my time in the elevator with Christopher—and he'd looked cold and angry then—it was nothing compared to now. I backed away. "You understand exactly what you've done." He was snarling at me.

"No, Jeff, I don't. I don't know what's happened since we got back from Florida. But I do have a guess."

"What's that?"

"You've had a lot of fun being with a human, a good time complaining about the system, but that was because you didn't believe Richard would ever condone interspecies marriage. Now that it looks like it's coming, you feel trapped, and you don't love me, so you're being a total asshole to drive me away."

I turned around and went to the door. "It's worked. I'll get the rest of my things sometime after the reunion weekend's over. I'll make sure you're not here."

"Kitty." I froze, hoping for a miracle. "The reservation's under both our names. The hotel's already paid for. Consider it a . . . paid vacation."

"Thanks so much."

I got out of the room and into the hall. I couldn't see, my vision was blurred with tears. I didn't want anyone I didn't know well to see me, I couldn't handle trying to explain what I didn't want to believe. I went down the hall and bumped into someone.

"Kitty, are you okay?" Christopher grabbed my upper arms to keep me from falling down. I was still trying not to cry, so that meant I couldn't talk. "What's wrong? What's happened?" I shook my head. "Let's get you back to your room."

"No." One word, but the floodgates opened. I started sobbing, and Christopher pulled me into his arms.

"Kitty, what happened? Where's Jeff?"

"We broke up."

"*What*?" He moved me to look at my face. "Did I hear that right? You and Jeff broke up?" I nodded, tears still running down my face. "Why?"

"He doesn't love me. He just wanted to play around, and he's angry and accusing me of having an affair with Kevin."

"With Kevin?" Christopher looked confused. "I know you think he's hot, but hell, you think the entire A-C population's hot, too." He looked more closely at me. "You sure it's not me?"

"Positive. Your name didn't come up. Oh, but, you know, if he sees us together, I'm sure he'll decide I'm cheating with you, too. Probably James and Paul and Tim, as well. Probably your dad. I mean, why not?"

Christopher looked down. "Where are you going?"

"We were supposed to go to my reunion tonight. I'm going. It'll give me three days to figure out how to explain this to my parents. And I can't be around him. He doesn't love me—I don't think he ever did."

"Kitty, that's not true. He loves you so much."

"Oh. yeah? Well, you go talk to him about it and see how much he loves me." I took a deep breath and forced myself to stop crying. "I'm not sure if I can stay with Centaurion."

"We need you." Christopher sounded panicked. "I don't know what's wrong with Jeff, but we'll fix it."

"Good luck. Figure if I do come back I'm going to base anywhere Jeff isn't, okay?"

"Don't make any decisions until the weekend's over, okay? Promise me that. Something's wrong, let me try to fix it first."

"I should have stayed with you." I'd been thinking it, but I hadn't meant to say it out loud.

Christopher stroked my face and then pulled me into his arms again. "I told you if he ever hurt you I'd kill him. I meant it. But before I kill him, I want to find out why he's lost his mind. Okay?"

"Okay. You don't have to kill him. Just don't let him know that I care, okay?"

He let me go and nodded. "I'll call you, if only to check on how you're doing."

"Thanks."

He let me go, and I ran for the elevator. Made it to the motor pool area without anyone noticing how awful I looked. Flung my luggage in the trunk, myself into the driver's seat, and got the hell out of Caliente Base.

CHAPTER 64

THE PRINCESS WAS A BEAUTIFUL resort. I managed to remind myself of that as I drove up to the valet. Plastered a happy look on my face, and managed to keep it all the way through the registration process. When asked where the other party was, I just said he was running late and would check in when he arrived.

The room was beautiful, a huge suite. There were a dozen red roses in a crystal vase. At first I thought they were standard, but I spotted a card in them. I pulled it out.

"Kitty, you're more beautiful than any rose could ever be, all my love, Jeff"

I managed to make it to the bed before I collapsed in tears. I couldn't believe someone who could think of something like this ahead of time would be so cold when it was time to say good-bye over nothing. Now that I wasn't near him, I found it hard to believe it had happened. From the moment we'd met, Martini had been charming, protective, loving. The man I'd fallen in love with was nothing like the man I'd spent the last two weeks with.

I wanted that part of Terry back more than ever. I knew she'd know what had happened, what I'd done to bring this out in him, how to fix it.

My phone rang. My purse had come to the bed with me, so I managed to answer on the fourth ring. "Girlfriend, what the hell's going on?"

"Oh, James. . . . " I couldn't talk and started to bawl again.

"Kevin said Jeff was acting like a massive jerk, Christopher told me you two broke up, Jeff got into a fight with Paul—"

This shocked me out of tears. "A fight with *Paul*? Why?"

"Hell if I know. Paul won't talk about it, but he's furious. I think he managed to knock Jeff out, though."

"Jeff got into a *fistfight* with Paul?"

"Something's wrong, really wrong."

"Well, I'm here crying my eyes out, so tell me something I didn't already know."

"Babe, I don't think it's you."

"Gee, thanks."

"No, I mean something's wrong with Jeff. Not that you did anything. He's lost it."

"Yeah, well, he seemed fine with me leaving."

"That's what I mean. The man lives for you."

"No, the man lies well."

"They can't lie. You've seen that for almost six months. They literally can't."

"He did. Really well, too. I assume he's had a lot of practice at it." And I'd fallen for it, so very willingly.

"Kitty, he wasn't lying. I've known him for several years. Jeff's not a womanizer. At all."

"Right. Well, I know he dated about ten human women, and more than ten A-C girls."

Reader burst into laughter. "Did he tell you that?"

I pulled it up from memory. "He said that he'd dated fewer than ten humans and more than ten A-Cs."

"Truthful, yet a lie at the same time, I'll give you that. As we both know, the only way they can manage it. If he was counting the girls from school that Christopher's told me about, and Lissa, then we do get to all of eleven A-Cs. Keep in mind that seven of them he dated when he was between twelve and twenty. In terms of the humans, if we count you, he's dated exactly one."

"One other?"

"No, one. As in you, only."

"So, I *was* his exotic event." My heart ached and I couldn't even cry.

"No, he's in love with you. He's been in love with you since you two met."

"He doesn't love me any more, if he ever did. Feel free to ask him about it. I'm sure he'll suggest you and I have been cheating on him the entire time."

Reader sighed. "No idea. Look, do you need me to come and be your date?"

"I love you, James. No, but I can't tell you what the offer means."

"I love you too, you know that. Look, just hold it together, okay? We'll figure out what's going on."

"I'll do my best."

We hung up, and I looked at the clock. Plenty of time before the first event, which was a dinner-dance. Wonderful. Made worse by the fact that I knew my girlfriends weren't coming. I'd seen Amy when we'd been in Paris—she was living there and said since she'd met Jeff, she didn't need to come out. I wondered if she could get here anyway. She could afford it. But I couldn't bring myself to call her and ask.

Sheila and I had texted about it, and I knew she wasn't coming due to finances and the same reasons I hadn't wanted to come—she didn't really care about anyone she wasn't still in contact with. I was currently willing to pay to fly her out, too, but again, couldn't bring myself to even suggest it.

Both of them would come, both wouldn't care that I needed them because my heart was broken—that's what friends were for. But it was too new, too raw, and I couldn't imagine telling them about it and not being known for the next decade as the chick who had a meltdown at the Princess.

I'd forgotten to let Chuckie know I was coming, so he was out, and it wasn't fair for me ask him to come save me anyway. He would, if I called him, not only because he was that kind of friend but because I couldn't lie to him at all, and he'd know how upset I was, and then nothing would stop him from coming. But having that meltdown with Chuckie would be no better than having it with Amy and Sheila. I'd still be the Class Loser for eternity.

I took a shower and forced myself to not notice that it would be an awesome place to have sex. I was never doing that again. Not sex—at least I hoped I wasn't going to end up celibate—but doing it in the shower. I'd never be able to have sex in a shower and not think of Martini.

Of course, as I toweled off, the issue was that there were far too many places where sex was going to remind me of him. Like, everywhere. I forced myself to think about who might be there tonight.

As I got dressed, I realized that probably no one I liked was going to be there. Brian was a maybe now, and that meant I was not only going to this thing alone, but I was going into enemy territory alone. I'd had a lot more friends in high school than Chuckie had, but we'd both agreed that college was a hell of a lot better.

I went through my purse. I'd brought a small handbag for the evening events—they were formal after all. Put the room key, my cell phone, driver's license, and some cash in. Contemplated my iPod and decided that was admitting defeat too early. Looked at the Glock. Realized why people killed themselves in hotel rooms. Put the Glock back into my purse.

I took a look in the mirror. I was in a long, slinky, sleeveless black dress that cut low in the front and back. It was tight around the hips and had a slit up the right side to the knee. I was in high black sling-back stilettos. I looked good. Unless you saw my expression, and then I looked like crap.

I played around and decided to put my hair up. I rarely did this, but I had so much time to kill. My experience over the last few months told me that if Martini were here with me, there would be no time wasted, and we'd be late because we'd be so busy doing the deed in every part of the room.

That line of thought was agonizing, so I went back to my hair. Managed to get it up and have tendrils hanging down. Looked good. I'd do it more often, but I rarely had ninety minutes to kill on hair prep.

All ready to be first in line to sit down. How fun. I considered a wrap, but it was still pretty warm in early October in Pueblo Caliente, and, miraculously, the hotel didn't seem over air-conditioned. My mind mentioned that if Martini were with me I'd just wear his suit jacket if I got cold. He loved to put it on me the few times we were out—it let him take care of me and mark me as his at the same time.

Only, he didn't care about that anymore. I tried to come up with lines of thought that didn't lead right back to Martini. Failed, utterly. I wanted to take my purse but grabbed my handbag instead. See? I was a big girl, I could mix it up and handle change. I hung the Do Not Disturb sign on the door, as much to repel robbers as to pretend something fun was happening in there.

Mercifully alone in the elevator. Stared at my reflection the whole way down and practiced smiling. Normally not an issue. Today, not doing so well.

Elevator opened up right in front of the lounge. I didn't drink any more because A-Cs were deadly allergic to alcohol, and I'd never wanted to risk getting alcohol into Martini's system through kissing me. Considered the benefits of getting stinking drunk but just couldn't do it.

Wandered through and found the room. Signed in and had to explain that my significant other was late due to a delayed plane and so probably wouldn't make it tonight. It was a good lie, and I was going to use it throughout the weekend. Damn those airlines. My mind tickled again—I thought about the jet but came up with nothing.

The women checking me in looked vaguely familiar, and I realized they'd been in Student Government when we were in school. Couldn't come up with their names, didn't bother to try hard.

I didn't choose a table. I wandered the room instead. There were huge blowups of pictures I vaguely remembered as being from our Senior Yearbook. I found the track team. There I was, right next to Brian. We both looked really young and reasonably happy. I couldn't remember if I'd broken up with him before or after this picture had been taken, but he had his arm around me and I didn't appear to mind.

Looked at all the pictures, studied them, really. They represented things that I might not remember all that clearly or think about too often, but these years had helped shape me into who I was now.

I got to the Chess Club picture. I was the only girl in it. I hadn't wanted to join, but Chuckie had begged me to, so I'd given in. I was standing next to him in the picture—it was one of the few pictures of him he'd ever allowed to be taken during these years, and only because I'd insisted on it since he'd been the Chess Club President for our entire four years of high school.

He was shorter than me, wearing thick glasses and ravaged by acne. I laughed to myself. His acne had cleared up pretty much right after this picture was taken, he'd spurted a foot and a half in our freshman year of college, and he'd gotten contacts. He'd also matured into a pretty hot-looking adult.

Someone was behind me, I could feel it. Close to six months of killing superbeings had honed a lot of my senses. I prepared for some kind of attack.

"Boy, we look young." It was a man's voice, and extremely familiar.

I turned around and looked up into the face of a tall, pretty handsome guy you'd never suspect had dealt with bad acne as a teenager. "Chuckie?"

He smiled, and it was a nice smile—gentle, confident, and affectionate. "You look beautiful, Kitty." I felt my cheeks get hot. Chuckie was making me blush? Since when?

"I didn't know you were going to be here." It was lame, but better than standing there with my mouth hanging open or asking him why he'd decided to come to a reunion we'd both told each other we were going to avoid.

"I asked your mother not to let you know I was coming. I wanted to surprise you."

"I'm surprised."

"Good. Then step one of my master plan is achieved."

CHAPTER 65

"YOU HERE WITH ANYBODY?"

Wow, what a question. I was proud that I didn't burst into tears. "I was supposed to be, but . . . I'm not."

"His loss." He smiled and took my arm. "Love the dress."

"Thanks. Is that an Armani suit?"

"You're good. You always could tell the designers."

"Never wore them."

"Before. Because that's an Armani dress."

"Yeah." I was confused. Chuckie was acting far smoother and much more confident than I remembered. True, I hadn't actually seen him for over a year, due to his schedule and my new secret life. But I just didn't remember him as being suave. "Chuckie, I thought you were in D.C."

He chuckled. "You know, you're the only person who still calls me Chuckie."

My cheeks were hot again. "Sorry."

"No, I don't mind. From anyone else I would, but from you it's like . . . a pet name."

He led me to a table near the dance floor. "You sure you want to sit here?" We'd always hung in the back if we'd gone places together, even comics conventions. Even when we'd taken trips together as young adults, he'd kept us in the back of the room.

"I'm not seventeen any more, so, yeah." He smiled. "Yes, I still like the back of the room under normal circumstances. The reunion isn't one of them." He pulled my chair out and slid it in, then seated himself next to me. "You look great. No engagement or wedding ring, I see."

"No." Managed to get that one syllable out without losing it.

"Good."

Good? I checked his hand. No ring. Not that I'd expect him to get married to someone and not tell me. We told each other everything. Well, we had up until I'd met the boys from A-C. Guilt tried to join my emotional party, but Heartbreak was still in control, and Confusion insisted that it had shotgun right now. Guilt slunk to the background, hovering around, waiting for its opportunity to make me more depressed.

Chuckie looked around and hailed a waiter. "What do you want to drink? Alcohol or Coke?"

"Um, Coke."

"One Coke, light ice, and a straw. And one beer, imported if you have it." I thanked God he wasn't ordering a martini. I also realized he remembered how I took my soft drinks. True, he'd heard me order this for years, but it registered that he'd paid attention to it, to something very small that still mattered to me. He turned from the waiter back to me. "So, how long ago did you two break up?"

"Beg pardon?"

Chuckie shook his head. "I know the look. You're trying to hold it together. You looked like this when you broke up with Brian. And, well, all the others."

"I did?"

"Yeah. The endings were always really hard on you."

"Endings usually are."

"Ours wasn't." The drinks arrived and he paid the waiter, leaving a generous tip.

"We didn't date."

He grinned. "I suppose calling Vegas a date would be stretching the term, yeah."

"I think of it as a fling."

"I think of it as the best week of my life." He said it so casually, as if he were commenting on the weather. I almost spilled my Coke.

"Um, what?"

"I hear Brian's an astronaut." Everyone was on top of things other than me.

"Yes. He's doing well. I just saw him a couple of weeks ago, in fact."

"He's coming tonight?"

"Not sure. He was planning on it, but work might not let him make it."

"He ask you to marry him yet?"

I gave Chuckie a long look. "Um, in a way, yeah."

"And you said no."

"Right again. How did you know?"

"I always paid attention. That's why I did well with the convenience stores. And with my investments. And everything else." He gave me a small smile. "I've missed you these past few months." Guilt crowed triumphantly and leaped into the fray.

He was sitting with one arm leaning on the table and his other hand resting on the back of my chair. It was a position that said he was only interested in looking at me, especially since his eyes weren't wandering.

"I know. I've been . . . busy." I was the Queen of Lame Responses tonight. "What are you doing now?" I managed to ask. "I mean to keep busy. Besides investing."

"I work for the government in its Extraterrestrial Division."

I managed not to react. "Right."

"Not the same one as you," he added. "What's it like, dating an A-C?"

I felt cold all of a sudden. "Why are you asking me that?"

He shook his head. "I'm going to assume you're reacting like this because you just broke up with him." He leaned closer to me. "I'm not here to scare you, Kitty. I just know what you do, and I thought it would be nice to let you know I'm in a similar field."

"What is it you think I do?"

Chuckie grinned. "I think you're the recently appointed head of Airborne for Centaurion Division. You're doing a great job, too. My people are very impressed."

"Do your people report to Leventhal Reid?"

His eyes flashed. "That asshole? No, we don't. Why, do

you think I've become anti-alien or joined Club 51 after all this time?"

"No. I don't know. No one knows what I do." I felt panicked for reasons I couldn't name.

He stroked my arm. "Stop. I'm not here to hurt you or threaten you. I'm happy to recruit you, if I can, but I didn't come for that, either."

"Why did you come then?"

He slid his hand up my arm, over my shoulder, up my neck, along my jaw to my chin. He drew my face to his and kissed me.

It wasn't a kiss like Martini's, but it wasn't bad, either. Honestly, it wasn't bad at all, bordering on pretty darned great. And unlike Brian's, Chuckie's kiss made me respond. He drew away from me slowly. "I came for you."

Rebound relationships are never wise. Rebounding from one guy to another within the space of the same day not only wasn't wise but put a girl high up in the running for Slut of the Decade. I knew this, and yet I found myself okay with the fact that Chuckie had just kissed me. As long as I didn't allow myself to think about kissing Martini, I was fine with it.

"This seems sort of sudden."

"No. I've been in love with you since ninth grade." Again, said so calmly.

"You never said."

"I needed your friendship more. If I'd told you, I'd have lost you." He stroked my neck. I tried not to react and failed. He gave me a half-smile. "This still make you sing?"

Vegas was coming back to me in full force. It had been pretty great, and my brain raced through the quick comparisons and confirmed what I'd registered in Florida—there hadn't been a human male of my experience who'd been as good in bed as Chuckie. My brain also shared that part of why I'd been single and available when I'd met Martini was that I'd been waiting for someone to actually *be* better than Chuckie before I made a real commitment.

I forced myself not to make the comparison. No human could win against Martini, so why compare them to him?

Besides, Chuckie was right on a spot that turned me into a puddle. "No," I lied.

He gave me a slow smile and bent toward me. I wanted to move away but didn't. His tongue stroked where his fingers had been, just for a few moments, while I gasped, and I just sat there, staring at nothing as his mouth moved up my neck. "Jeff, not here—"

Chuckie pulled away from me. "Jeff, huh? So I'm competing with Jeff Martini. Interesting." He took a drink of his beer. I got the impression he was confirming what he knew or suspected, as opposed to discovering.

"Why would you think that's who I meant?" My voice was stilted.

He grinned. "You're a Commander. Who would you be dating, one of the grunts? I've seen Martini and White. They're both your type." He took another drink. "Why'd you pick Martini? I'd have put my money on White."

I did not want to have this conversation, to the point where I unfroze and stood up. "Great seeing you." I knocked my chair over, but managed to get away from the table without any other damage. The room was filling up, but I didn't particularly care.

I got out to the hallway when a man's hand grabbed my arm. Chuckie spun me and pulled me into his arms. "Stop running."

"This is a really bad time for this, okay? Yes, we just broke up. Not exactly the perfect timing, sorry."

"Better than having to fight him for you. I probably couldn't win." He had his arms around me, but he wasn't holding me so hard that it was frightening. But I was scared anyway.

"Chuckie, why are you doing this? This isn't like you. You're not acting like I'm used to." Wow, I'd had a similar conversation with Martini only hours before. Today officially sucked beyond all other rotten days.

Before he could answer, my phone rang. I pulled out of his arms and got it out. "Hello?" Silence. "Hello." Nothing. The caller hung up. I looked—not a number I recognized, but certainly local.

"Who was that?" Chuckie asked me.

"Wrong number, I guess. Look, can we just agree that you're not going to be amorous right now? I can't take it."

"That bad?"

"No, honestly, pretty good. But your timing is the worst ever. I can't handle this."

He sighed and rubbed his forehead. "Look. I'm rich. I'm successful. I'm reasonably good-looking, and before you walked on the alien side of life, we were pretty compatible in bed. I'm working in a similar field, so you'd never have to lie to me. I didn't come here to terrorize or upset you. I came to ask you to marry me."

My jaw dropped. He reached out and closed it gently. Then he reached into his jacket pocket, pulled out a small jewelry box, and handed it to me.

"Open it. Please."

I did. I was too stunned not to. Inside was a beautiful diamond solitaire, not too big. I didn't like large stones because I thought they looked like paste on my hands. This was exactly the size I would have picked for myself. I didn't know that much about precious stones, but I could tell the diamond was of exceptional quality.

"I know you're not recovered. But I also know that once you say it's over, it's over. So, I don't need an answer today, this week, not even this month. I just want you to at least consider the fact that I love you and want to marry you.

"Where was all this popularity when I was in school?" Whoops, again, not something I'd intended to say out loud. I managed not to ask why he'd waited until now to propose—it wasn't as if we hadn't seen each other over the past few years. Of course, I'd been essentially avoiding him for the past five or six months, so it's not as though he'd had any opportunity.

Chuckie laughed. "It was there, you just didn't notice all the time." He stroked my face. "You never noticed, did you? That I was in love with you?"

I was still staring at the ring. I tried to ignore the fact that I'd thought Martini was close to proposing, officially, really proposing, a few times recently. I'd wanted that, so much. For him to do something romantic instead of just saying "marry me" while we were at breakfast or killing a fugly. He'd said "marry me" thirty minutes after we'd known each other. Of course, he'd said "I love you" a lot, too. And Chuckie never had until tonight.

"No. You never said anything, and it never occurred to me." Not even in Vegas.

"I couldn't risk losing you." I looked up at him. He gave me a half-smile and shrugged. "I wasn't kidding—I couldn't have survived high school without your friendship, and college wouldn't have been all that great without you, either."

A small thought waved at me. "Is that why you went to A.S.U. instead of Cal Tech or MIT?"

He grinned. "Well, that and the fact that I'd already figured out that I was going to be happier in business than I was locked in a science lab." He stroked my face again. "But, truthfully, if you'd wanted to go to an all girl's school, I'd have found a loophole somehow that would have let me go there with you."

I'd never considered Chuckie in the stalker-boyfriend category, but clearly, even the laid-back guys who liked me were at least slightly obsessive. I'd have complained, but I'd been overjoyed he'd gone to college with me.

I felt beyond dense and emotionally battered. I closed the box and handed it back to him. "I'm not saying no. I'm not saying yes. I'm saying I can't keep this unless or until I say yes."

"Fair enough." He put the box back into his pocket. "So, ready for dinner?"

"Not really."

"Well, fake it. Pretend you're having fun. I won't be overly amorous unless someone we hated is nearby and then we'll be totally into each other. You need to eat, and you might as well dance. I know you've always thought I was kidding about this, too, but I've taken ballroom dance for years. You'll love my tango."

I started to laugh. "Okay, I think I can handle it, even the tango."

CHAPTER 66

DINNER WAS RELATIVELY OKAY. We ended up with people neither one of us had known well at our table and so got away with not having to talk to them too much.

I managed to choke a little food down, mostly because Chuckie coaxed me into it. It all tasted like wood chips to me, but my stomach hurt a little less.

He kept me filled up with Cokes. The waiter was extremely attentive, I presumed because Chuckie tipped well. There was something vaguely familiar about him, but it was dark, and I had other things on my mind than checking out some little guy in an ill-fitting tux. I had a big guy in a perfectly fitted Armani tux to deal with.

True to his own hype, Chuckie was a great dancer now. Why he hadn't shown this to me over the past several years I didn't know, but he could have made at least the finals of *So You Think You Can Dance*. Martini had taken me dancing a few times, and I'd relearned how to follow a man's lead. It was actually fun to be dancing, and I only pretended Chuckie was Martini half the time.

He was muscular under the suit, but more like Christopher, lean and wiry. He'd bulked up since Vegas, though, that was for sure, which was, as I thought about it, the last time I'd seen him naked. Not that he'd been scrawny then, just less obviously muscular.

I was having to reassess everything I'd ever thought about him, and my brain wasn't cooperating all that much.

The awkward kid I'd befriended in ninth grade had already turned into someone successful before we'd gone to Vegas together to celebrate his buy-out. But he'd still been a little shy and unsure then.

Though, as cheerful memory reminded me, not so shy that he hadn't put the moves on me before the plane was up in the air at the start of that trip. Come to think of it, there was still one place I could have sex that wouldn't remind me of Martini. Of course, now that my memory had been jogged, it sure would remind me of Chuckie.

Chuckie was the opposite of awkward, shy, or unsure now. He was smooth, suave, debonair, and, frankly, appealing in a way I'd been unprepared for. I wondered if he'd been this way for the last few years and, like everything else, I just hadn't noticed. I had a horrible feeling he had been. The realization that I'd put Chuckie into a box in my mind and had never let him out of it, even after having wild sex with him for a week, would have been enough to reduce me to tears if I hadn't already had enough to cry about.

And yet, here he was, not berating me for being a moron but instead patiently asking me to finally take the lid off that box and look at him the way he'd always looked at me. In that sense, he was the same Chuckie he'd always been. We still had all the things in common we'd used to, but now we had much more.

The musical choices were odd. We'd graduated in the late nineties, but the deejay seemed intent on an eighties revival with current hits thrown in. I was reasonably okay with this—I liked music from all eras and genres, after all—until he spun John Mayer's "Dreaming With a Broken Heart." It was a slow song, and we were dancing close together. But the lyrics cut through me like a knife, and the tears came. Not too many, but enough to make me glad I hadn't worn makeup.

Chuckie noticed, but all he did was wipe them away with his fingertips. Then he leaned my head against his chest, and we kept on dancing.

We did tango, more than once. It was fun, but it was also sexual and romantic. I was glad I had to concentrate on not tripping, because if I'd been comfortable with all the dance moves, I would have felt worse than I already did. And I felt pretty bad, because a part of me was wondering if it was right to enjoy being like this with Chuckie while I still wanted to be with Martini. The short time in the elevator with Christopher I could put down to lustful insanity and fugly interference. Having the dance equivalent of hot and heavy sex with Chuckie seemed much more . . . intentional. I started working on my acceptance speech for Class Super Slut and went back to concentrating on not stepping on Chuckie's feet.

The evening's entertainment ended, and we wandered outside to one of the pools. There was no moon out, but there were enough lights from the hotel to be able to see decently. I heard a beeping and realized I must have missed some calls. Only one, as it turned out. I dialed. "Hello, I think you called me?"

"Kitty, it's Brian. Glad you called me back." He sounded tense.

"What's up?"

"You're at the reunion?"

"Yes. You're not."

"We were coming. Got delayed."

"We?"

"Me and Serene. Don't say it, yes, I was an idiot, yes, she's a great girl now that she's not being drugged, yes, I was acting xenophobic."

"Good, good. So, why are you calling?"

"Serene needs to talk to you." I could tell the phone was passing from him to her. "Kitty?"

"Hi, how're you feeling?"

"Better. Why aren't you with Jeff?" Well, apparently she was always blunt, drugged or not.

"We . . . we broke up."

"Why?" She sounded strained.

"I really don't know. Um, Serene, this is a horrible time for me to be talking about it."

"No, we have to talk right now. I can see you—you look really nice, by the way—but I can't see who you're with."

"Okay, not a shock. I'm with someone I went to school with. Tell Brian it's Chuck."

She relayed the news, I could hear Brian making a snide comment in the background. "Look, something's wrong with Jeff." Serene sounded worried.

"Yes, so everyone seems to think. I do, too."

"When did it start and what did he do?" Serene still sounded freaked, but I could hear the Dazzler scientific mind back there, too.

"It started when we got back from Florida. He got more and more distant. Everything I said was a reason to break up. Every man I spoke to I was cheating on him with. He got belligerent, angry, cold. I could go on. It got worse every day, ending with this afternoon when he just didn't care that I was leaving and seemed to want me to go."

Chuckie was listening to this, and his eyes were narrowed. I figured asking for privacy now was stupid.

"Kitty, did anyone give Jeff something?"

"What do you mean?"

"A shot, something odd to eat, anything like that?"

"Why do you ask?" My brain started whirring.

"He sounds like me, only much, much faster. The drug they gave me works on the id; it focuses on your negative emotions, like jealousy and rage, and it enhances them. We studied it these last couple of weeks, and it's self-replicating. The more you get, the more it creates inside you."

"That seems impossible."

"It's A-C technology, okay? We've been working on ways to put humans and A-Cs into suspended animation."

"How much would you think he'd have to have taken to be this bad in two weeks?"

"A lot. Not just one shot. It took months for me to get as . . . deranged as Jeff seems to be right now."

I thought about it and my mind went right back to the jet. "Hang on." I looked at Chuckie. "I need help with a conspiracy theory."

"I'm your man."

I brought him up to speed very quickly on what had happened in Florida. "My question is, what's the overall goal? I already know who's behind it."

"Leventhal Reid." I nodded. "Okay, so ultimate goal?" He pursed his lips. "Destroy Alpha Team. Take away Centaurion Division's leaders, leave their Pontifex exposed and unprotected. Chaos enhances the ability to make bad decisions."

"How do you figure?" I decided I'd ask how he knew all this later.

He shrugged. "Every attack was centered around Alpha Team, and around its leader in particular. Martini's apparently out of his mind. You're here, without him, without any of them, so without any form of backup. What are the others doing? Fighting with Martini or trying to figure out what the hell's going on with him."

Serene spoke. "Brian just showed me a picture of your date."

"We're not on a date." Chuckie raised his eyebrow. "Well, not a planned date."

"I can see him now. He's cute."

"Thanks." This was getting surreal. "How'd Brian have a picture?"

"He brought his yearbook." Amazing. I didn't know where mine was, Brian schlepped his from Florida to Arizona. "Chuck looks a lot better now."

"I agree." I found myself wondering if all the drugs were really washed out of Serene's system. "So how did the drugs get into Jeff's system?"

"I don't know. Did he eat anything at the Space Center?"

"Nothing other than what Alfred brought in—we were too busy dodging attacks. Besides, that was days prior to when Jeff started acting weird. Did Taft hit him with something, right before I killed him?"

"No, nothing. When did he start, before you left Florida or when you got back?"

"Once we were back. He was tired and worn out. We didn't have time for him to go into isolation . . ." My voice trailed off. There were standard things the A-Cs did for empaths who needed regeneration. Isolation, adrenaline, regenerative injections. Or, in the case of our flight home, an IV drip. That was sitting in an unprotected jet for two days. And it wouldn't need a power chess piece to contaminate the drugs—a pawn would be better, more likely to be ignored or seem innocuous. "Serene, get to James, right away.

Tell him whatever's in Jeff's system is in the medical bay of the jet we used in Florida. He took in five hours' worth of the stuff."

"Oh, my God. That would explain it. And it's replicating inside him." She sounded out of breath.

"What are you doing?"

"Running at hyperspeed."

"Good plan. I'm going to get back to the Base."

"Okay, meet you there, somewhere."

We hung up, and I put my phone away as I turned back to Chuckie. So I didn't see the gun he was holding at waist height until I looked up. "Interesting wrinkle." I didn't know what else to say.

He wasn't smiling and he looked deadly. "Kitty, it's time."

CHAPTER 67

"TIME FOR WHAT?" I was too close to have a hope of getting out of the way if Chuckie pulled the trigger.

He moved faster than I'd remembered him having the ability to do, grabbed me with his free hand, and flung me behind him as he fired. "Time to get out of here." He spun and started running, dragging me along.

I looked behind us. "Is that our waiter?"

"Yes. He's not looking for a better tip." This was true. He was carrying a gun and firing back. Chuckie flung me around the side of a building, used it as a shield and fired again. "Do you have a car here?"

"Yes. But my keys and valet stub are in my room."

He cursed. "Okay, Plan B."

"You don't have a car?"

"I assume my car's rigged by now."

"You know, they could be after me."

"They *are* after you! But I'm not stupid enough to assume they're not after me, too."

"Oh." I ducked down and risked a look at our would-be killer. He was running toward us, and as he went under a lamppost, I gasped and flung myself back. "That's Shannon the Toothless Weasel!"

"Who?" Chuckie stopped firing, dropped the clip, put in another, fired once more, then grabbed me and started running again.

"He's a nobody in Club 51. One of the guys who was trying to blow us up when we were leaving from Saguaro International. But he was arrested by the Feds. I don't know how he got out."

"I do. Reid." We ran around another building and he cursed. "That wrong number you got earlier? I'll bet it was one of them, confirming where you were and that you were with your phone."

"Come again?"

"Satellite technology, you can track via cell phones." He looked at me. "A-C technology at the core." We were headed to the valet area. There was a convertible Porsche in front of us. "Get in." He shoved me toward the passenger's seat. "No, dammit, don't. It's a stick."

"*You* get in," I said, as I slid over the hood. "Unlike you, I'm a real driver." Keys were in the ignition, great. I started it as he leaped in, and we peeled out, valets and Shannon running after us. "Okay, I'm now in for grand theft auto. What's going on?"

"You tell me. They're after you."

"Why are you here?"

Chuckie made a sound similar to the one Martini always did when I frustrated him. "I told you. I came to propose. I thought it would be romantic."

"It was. Seven months ago would have been better timing." Bullets whizzed by, and I looked in the rearview mirror. "Oh, great. They have a humongous Escalade, and it seems to have something extra under the hood." More bullets flew past, one of which hit the left side-view mirror. "We took a convertible why?"

"It was there and it's a damn sports car. I should think you could outrun an SUV in this."

"I can. It's the several police cars I'm having a hard time with. Turn on the radio."

Chuckie cursed impressively. "You don't have any identification on you, do you? I mean that lists you as a federal officer?"

"Yes, in my purse." He opened it. "That's my handbag, however. Turn on the radio. Classic rock, KSLX or something."

"Well, we have cash for bribes. If they're really cheap cops. The radio why?"

"You want to survive? I need tunes." He cursed again but turned it on. The owner was a kindred spirit, or God did love me. The deejay announced a twelve-song block, and Aerosmith's "Dude (Looks Like a Lady)" came on. "Turn it up." He did.

I downshifted. In for a dime, in for a dollar, right? "They aren't going to be a problem." I floored it, ran a red light, and skidded us onto the 101 Freeway. This was one of Pueblo Caliente's newer freeways, and the joke was that the speed limit was the same as the name. I intended to break that limit.

It wasn't my car, but it was pretty good. We screamed down the highway, Screamin' Steven Tyler and the rest of my boys providing our soundtrack, swerving in and out of traffic. It was eleven on a Friday night—there were still plenty of cars out. We outdistanced the police cars, but the Escalade was still with us, albeit farther back. My hair was out of luck, I could feel it streaming out behind me. Oh, well, the windblown look was in, right?

There was nothing like scary people trying to kill me to put things right into perspective. Stay alive, worry about relationships later. "I Stole Your Love" by Kiss was on now. Appropriate—I was sure whoever owned this car loved it.

I wanted to get to a men's room at Saguaro International. We needed a gate, and we needed one that didn't have to be calibrated. All bathroom gates recalibrated automatically after any use to the Crash Site Dome, the main gate hub. I couldn't see a gate to calibrate it, but I knew where one gate was far too well.

However, I wanted to lose our company, too. There were a few ways to do it, but I was feeling reckless for some reason, so I took the option that was both crazy and would be hard for any big car to manage. I waited until we were by an appropriate on-ramp that had few cars merging onto the freeway. "Hold on." I spun the wheel and headed down, dodging some cars coming toward us.

Close to the airport, excellent. Worked my way there off the main streets as much as possible. Went into the airport via the freight entrance. No one was following us anymore, so I slowed down to merely fast.

"I never want to drive with you again," Chuckie said.

"Why not? We lost them, and we're still alive."

"I think I had a heart attack."

"Keeps you on your toes." I drove into the airport proper sedately—not only did the airport have cops, but there wasn't anyplace much to go to escape said cops. Pulled into the Terminal Three parking garage, found a spot, and parked. Took the keys, just in case.

We got out and ran for the terminal. We passed the maintenance closet I remembered well. Tried not to look at it. Failed, but kept on moving.

We hit security, and the problems started. I wasn't used to going through it anymore. With an A-C, you just went to hyperspeed, and no one was the wiser. But Chuckie wasn't an A-C.

He pulled me aside, and we stared at the arrivals screens. "We don't have boarding passes. This isn't going to work."

I pulled out my cell and dialed. "Girlfriend, where the hell are you?" Reader was shouting.

"Saguaro International. In a lot of trouble with no time. We can't get through Security. I need a gate—where's the closest one in Terminal Three that's in the general areas?"

He cursed. "The only one like that's in the old terminal, Two." He described where it was.

"We're doomed. Okay, hopefully you'll see us soon." I jerked my head, and Chuckie and I started off. We were probably better off on foot because we could get back inside if we had to.

"Who the hell is 'us'?" Reader asked as Chuckie and I trotted.

"Chuck Reynolds."

There was a pause. "Do you mean Charles Reynolds, the head of the government's ET Division?" Chuckie was the head of the division? I considered his track record. Of course he was the head of it. Probably had been hired in the mailroom and worked up to top guy in about six months to a year. Freaked or not, being chased by deadly, horrible people or not, I was still proud of him. I'd spent a lot of years being proud of him, after all, and he'd never given me reason to stop.

"Yes, pretty sure, yes."

"What are you doing with him?"

"Remember my friend, the one who was into UFO stuff, the one I checked with about Club 51 when we were heading to beautiful, deadly Florida?"

"Conspiracy Chuck? Oh, hell no!"

"I know everyone. So, anyway, Chuckie's here, thankfully, since Shannon the Toothless Weasel is out and already tried to kill us. Tell Kevin. Whoever released him is working for Leventhal Reid."

"Chuckie?"

Why was Reader asking? He'd heard me talk about Chuckie a lot over the past few months; if nothing else, he'd heard Martini whine about my still having a special ringtone for Chuckie and given me a pseudo-lecture about it. I decided I wasn't the only one freaked out and let it pass. "It's what I call him. Sort of like a pet name." Why not? Chuckie snorted a laugh, grabbed my free hand, and kept us moving.

Another pause. "Don't tell me, let me guess. He asked you to marry him."

"You're good."

"You're hot."

"Why aren't you straight?"

"It would make things too easy. Look, Jeff's a mess, but I think Serene's got everyone on the right track. Lorraine's freaked out, since she gave him the bad juice."

"She didn't know. Tell her I can't afford for her to lose it, she may have to come save our lives shortly."

"Why don't we come to you?"

"Because one member of Alpha out in danger's enough." I filled him in on Chuckie's theory. By the time I was done, we were at the end of Terminal Three. We went outside and now had to get across traffic. Chuckie doubled us back, and we waited for the airport bus. I couldn't speak for him, but I felt naked and exposed.

"Stay on the phone with me," Reader said. "That's an order from Christopher."

"I'll do my best." I remembered that I hadn't plugged it in to recharge since we'd gotten back from Florida—

worry over what we were missing and Martini's personality switch had been all-consuming. Oh, well, the batteries had that A-C extended life thing going for them, I probably had hours worth of phone life left.

The bus arrived, we boarded, sat in the back. Chuckie put his arm around me, and I tried not to pull away or enjoy it. I also tried not to give in to the desire to bury my face in his chest and pretend none of this was going on. Gave up, leaned against him, and let him hug me. Felt a little better. "So, we'll get to the Dome and get back to where, Caliente or Home Base?"

"Caliente. I don't think we can move Jeff." There was something funny in Reader's voice.

"Is Jeff alive?"

"Yes." There was something about how he said that one syllable—something was wrong. More wrong than everything that was already wrong, that is.

"What aren't you telling me?" Reader didn't answer. "James, kind of stressed here, being pursued in evening dress by evil, horrible, ugly men who want to kill us. No time to be holding the horror back, okay?"

He sighed. "We don't actually know where he is."

"*What*?"

"Calm down! He's here somewhere. We think."

"How could you lose him? He's kind of big."

"We had him strapped into an isolation chamber. Claudia and Tim went to check on him, he was gone. Straps were broken."

My turn to be silent. "You haven't gotten the drug out of him, have you?"

"Takes a while to flush. We thought we'd gotten some of it. But if it's affecting the brain and emotion areas Serene said, then. . . . "

"Then he's totally nuts, and stronger than normal." I felt scared and guilty. I should have realized something was wrong and taken care of him. He was sick and I'd been with him two weeks and hadn't figured it out.

"It's not your fault. No one else figured it out either." Reader's voice sounded faint.

We got off the bus and ran into Terminal Two. I checked

my phone. "James, I'm almost out of battery." It figured. I didn't even bother to curse my luck, I was so used to it working like this by now.

"Does your latest paramour have a phone?"

"We're at the bathroom, hopefully it won't matter." Hopefully it wouldn't, because my phone died. I dumped it back in my handbag which I hooked over my neck. Why let a good habit lie fallow?

We got into the men's room, only one stall occupied. Of course the stall we needed. Chuckie banged on the door. "Open up!"

"It's taken," a man's grumpy voice answered. "There's plenty free."

"We need this one," Chuckie said.

"We? What do you mean, we?"

"Get off and get out," I said.

"What, you two couldn't get a room?"

I looked at Chuckie. "This is my life. I'm always in gross men's bathrooms trying to get in or out of a stall."

"Maybe you shouldn't have become a crack whore," the man's voice suggested.

"She's not a crack whore," Chuckie snarled.

"Sorry. Meth addict."

"I'm not on drugs, you horrible man. I'm a federal agent." I had a badge back in my hotel suite to prove it, too.

"Yeah, yeah, and I'm Tom Cruise, I just fly cheap because I'm thrifty." The toilet finally flushed.

The stall door opened to expose a heavyset middle-aged man who looked both unimpressed to see us and rather disgusted. Chuckie grabbed the man and tossed him out of the stall. He ended up behind me. Chuckie grabbed my arm, but a man cleared his throat and Chuckie froze. "Oh, Mr. Reynolds, please don't try anything."

We both turned toward the door as this man walked closer to us. He was about six feet, slender, sort of attractive in a reptilian way. He was familiar—and he was holding a gun.

"What an interesting sight. So rare to see Centaurion teamed up with your group, Mr. Reynolds."

I shrugged. "We have an exchange program, Mr. Reid."

Leventhal Reid gave me a slow smile. "I'm looking forward to learning all about it, Miss Katt."

"Look, I have nothing to do with these people," the man behind me said. Reid moved the gun and shot him.

I would have screamed, but I was too busy body slamming Chuckie into the stall. Only one could go through at a time and he was closer. "Help them, help me, help Jeff." I shoved again and he flew through and disappeared, shouting my name. For once, the bad guy wouldn't have a man I cared about to use as a hostage.

Of course, the alternative was that Reid had me as a hostage. "Let's go, please," he said pleasantly. "I'm sure you don't want to have to explain that man's body to the police."

"I'd love to see the police right about now." Particularly the trigger-happy rookie from the first part of this adventure from hell. Sadly, he didn't appear to be around.

Reid grabbed my upper arm, made sure it hurt, and then dragged me out. He slid the gun into his jacket pocket and took his hand out.

I spotted a Mazda3 sport wagon right in front of the sliding glass doors. Its driver was out of the car and the car was running. Stilettos are the greatest shoes in the world if you want to cause someone pain, and I did. I faked a stumble, slammed my heel into the tender part of Reid's foot, and leaned all my weight on it. According to the research, since my stilettos were reinforced with metal rods and the heels transmitted such a large amount of force into a tiny area, this was the equivalent of an elephant jumping onto his foot.

He screamed, I wrenched my shoe out of his foot and my arm out of his grasp, and ran like hell for that car. Pulled out the Porsche keys and tossed them to the Mazda's owner. "Federal agent, you're trading up, Terminal Three, third floor!"

I leaped in, slammed and locked the door, and floored it. Reid was doing that running-hopping thing you do when one foot is hurt. He fired at me, but I was out of range.

Raced through the airport like a bat out of hell. The car had a full tank and handled almost as well as my Lexus. It also had Sirius. I turned on the radio, found the hard rock station, and tried to think.

My first reaction was to get to Caliente Base. But I had to figure Reid knew where it was by now. There was probably a tracking device on something in the jet, maybe even in our luggage. He was here, in Pueblo Caliente, so he had to know we were, too.

The police could easily be in his pocket. Not all, but it wouldn't take many for me to be dead fast. I didn't have a gun or even hairspray. I had a hundred dollars, a room key, my driver's license, a dead cell phone, and a stolen car.

No way I was going to my parents'. Chuckie was hopefully safe in the Dome, but that was a state away, and I needed a gate to get there. I could try going back for my car, but the Princess was a one way in and out place, and getting trapped there would be too easy.

Bon Jovi's "Lost Highway" came on. Well, why not? I had a full tank and Tucson had an airport.

CHAPTER 68

IGOT ONTO INTERSTATE 10 and put the pedal down. Easy enough drive, and I'd done it a lot. When I'd been a marketing manager, two of my big accounts had been in Tucson. Sometimes I drove, sometimes I flew. I knew the highway and the airport. I was good.

Had plenty of time to think, and a ton to think about. I wanted to focus on staying alive, but what I ended up coming back to was Martini. And now Chuckie. Brian hadn't been a romantic issue. Even if I'd been interested in him, Martini and I had been a couple all of two weeks ago. Not being with him had seemed like an impossibility.

But something Serene had said about the way the drugs worked was gnawing at me. They enhanced feelings already there. So Martini suspected me of being unfaithful, and he was pretty angry about it. He had some reason, but there were only so many times I could apologize for the brief moment of lustful insanity between me and Christopher before it became a cancer. Maybe it already was.

Sped around the remainder of Pueblo Caliente's late night drivers and mercifully hit an empty stretch of highway. I was still in shock from seeing Chuckie here and now, let alone from his proposal. In love with me since ninth grade. I'd had no clue. My mother's comments about my density rang through my mind. The week we'd spent in Vegas had been great. Really, the best vacation I'd ever had, and not just because of the killer sex. At least, until Martini took me to Cabo.

Fortunately, I was on that empty stretch, was a good enough driver, and knew the road well so I could drive with tears running down my face. I wanted to ask the cosmos why Chuckie hadn't come to get me seven months earlier. Of course, he couldn't have told me the truth then about what he was really doing to pass the time between making more money appear like magic and traveling the world. And, just as he knew when I was lying, dense or not, I'd have known he was hiding something. Something that, seven months ago, he couldn't have told me about. And that way lay badness.

And, maybe he hadn't come these past few months because he'd known I was with Martini. So, did that mean he knew we'd broken up? Or was it more that he'd chosen this time to give it one last shot? He'd called my mother, and she loved him, so I had to vote for her having told him I was involved and helping him go for the last ditch effort. After all, he'd checked to see if I had a ring on, and reality said that if I was engaged, he'd be one of the first to know—and if he'd thought proposing at the reunion was romantic, perhaps he'd thought Martini would feel the same. But all that took at least some planning, so maybe it had just timed out right. If I could call the current situation "right" in any way, shape, or form.

Maybe he was supposed to show up right now, right when it was over with Martini, to say, "Here I am, the right guy for you." I considered the idea. Hard to do, but I forced myself to think about it—it was so much better than crying or thinking about what was going to happen if Reid caught me before I could get to a gate. And I wasn't alone on the highway here, so thinking while getting around the various diesel trucks on this patch of road was going to be much wiser than sobbing.

I went for logical—assessment of pros and cons. It wasn't too hard to run through my limited options here. Aside from Martini, of all the men I knew, the two I felt I'd be happiest with long-term were the two men who were my best friends—Reader and Chuckie. Reader being gay and apparently not going bi any time soon let him out of the realistic running, no matter how often we joked otherwise.

Chuckie wasn't gay, and he also wasn't an alien. There were no complications. No one would fight anything if we got married. Our families would be thrilled, religion wouldn't be an issue, and neither would the internal makeup of our children. No worries about empaths or imageers or anything else. The only worry would be if we weren't smart enough to keep up with our offspring. Somehow, Chuckie's parents had managed, so I figured we would, too.

Honesty compelled me to look at my dating prior to Martini. I'd dated a lot. But the longest relationship had been Brian. Particularly after the Vegas trip with Chuckie. After that, no one had seemed right, and I hadn't stuck around.

Which begged the obvious question—had I been waiting for Chuckie, without even realizing it? I had to admit I was dense enough that it was possible. I certainly judged other men against him and always had.

So, did this mean this had all happened so I'd realize Chuckie *was* the right guy? Or was it all just down to lucky timing? And, if so, would all this fall under divine plan or coincidence? Chuckie didn't believe in coincidence, and, according to ACE, the divine plan was to let us handle it ourselves.

As I hit another stretch of open road, my mind shared that, waiting for Chuckie or not, judging others against him or not, the man I'd actually fallen deeply in love with was Martini. Who was God knew where, doing God knew what, though I had a suspicion that hating me was involved along the way there somewhere.

Someone at the radio station certainly hated me—the hard rock channel spun Mayer's "Dreaming With a Broken Heart." It had been bad enough hearing it before. It was worse when I was all alone, driving toward nothing.

I cried through the whole song and then forced myself to think again. Thankfully, Social Distortion's "Prison Bound" was the next song. I probably was, but at least it didn't make me want to kill myself.

Something was wrong with my theory—the one about

how Reid was tracking me, not the one about Chuckie, which I was now fairly sure was accurate. The jet was at Area 51, so if there was a tracking device on it, the most likely place for one to be, then Reid should be in Nevada.

Helen had gotten my cell phone number, so that would explain why he could call me. Martini had registered us weeks ago, so it would have been easy to know where we were supposed to be this weekend, which explained Shannon's presence at the reunion dinner, and probably Chuckie's as well, with or without Mom's assistance. But how had Reid found us at Terminal Two? We'd parked the Porsche at Three, and it seemed overly lucky to assume he'd spotted us in the terminal bus by chance.

Chuckie's comment about satellite technology came back to me. They were tracking me via my phone. That meant the headlights way in the distance behind me were a good bet to be hostile. I dug the phone out of my purse. It was dead and now my personal albatross.

I resisted the urge to toss it out the window. Do that, they'd know I'd figured it out. I was coming up on Casa Grande, not the biggest burg in existence, but like the rest of the area, it was growing. Pulled off the freeway and into a gas station. Dumped the phone in a trash can, got back on the road. Two minutes used, max.

Decided to go for the high-level risk and turned the headlights off, though I could keep the instrument panel lit in this car. Now I'd only show up if they had radar or I had to brake. Additionally, no moon meant no reflection on a lot of the road. The highway was empty again, and I was the fastest thing on it as far as I could tell.

I drove on through the night, watching the headlights get closer. They faded at what I was pretty sure was Casa Grande. Fifty percent chance they'd assume I'd headed back to Pueblo Caliente. Of course, that was the same chance Martini had given for the jet being okay. I assumed they'd be after me shortly.

I came up on a group of cars and had to turn the headlights back on while moving through them. There were a lot of trucks in this portion of the road, and they were unintentionally impeding my ability to get around them. Within minutes we were down to a crawl. I saw signs—roadwork ahead.

The people after me had no compunction about murdering innocents. Karl Smith, the cleaning lady, the caretaker, the man in the bathroom, lord alone knew who else. I couldn't stay on the highway—they'd just blow through the truckers and the families around me.

The train tracks were to the left of the freeway, and soon I wouldn't have a chance to get off due to the construction I could see ahead. I waited for the next highway patrol turnout, drove across the dirt divider, floored it across the oncoming traffic. The Mazda was low to the ground, but it was a worker. I bumped over things I wasn't supposed to be driving on and reached the tracks. A huge train was there, but that was fine. I could go faster for certain. If I was lucky, I could get ahead of the train and cross the tracks, thereby hiding myself from my pursuers. I didn't expect luck, but I was going for it anyway.

The 69 Eyes' "Perfect Skin" was growling at me. I loved this song. I put the pedal down and started gaining on the train's engine. Reached the head before the song was halfway done. Risked a look in the rearview. A large SUV that looked a lot like an Escalade was crossing the highway. And SUVs were far more equipped to handle off-road driving than sporty little Mazdas.

"Come on," I said to the car. "Prove you're girl enough to run with the big dogs." The car and I decided we were. I had the accelerator to the floor. Top speed was supposedly 140, and we were almost there. I could see an area up ahead where I might have a chance of crossing the tracks without flipping or being rammed by the train.

Time to see what the skills really were. The needle hit 140, and we passed the engine as if it were standing still. Reached the might-be-a-crossing and turned. It worked great if I didn't mind being airborne. No Jerry to tell me how to land this one.

I was a child of pop culture. The Duke Boys had never had an issue flying in the General Lee, and I didn't plan to have one either. I kept the wheel under control just as if I were on the road but took my foot off the accelerator a bit.

Landed hard but on all four wheels. Bounced a lot and hit my head on the roof since I'd been too busy staying alive to put the seat belt on. I was whooping just like the Dukes when I finally got the car under control. I headed toward the mountains in the distance. I had nowhere else to go.

"Emergency Assistance," a well-modulated female voice said. "Are you injured?"

"Ah, no, not really. Hit my head."

"I heard screams. Have you had a collision?" It dawned on me that I'd turned on a live service when I'd bounced. And a live person meant I might be able to get a message through to someone.

"No, but I need your help."

"I show this vehicle as being stolen." Damn, the Mazda's owner must not have been able to drive a stick. "Suggest you pull over and wait for the police."

"Ma'am? If the police can get to me, that would be beyond wonderful. I'm a federal agent, and I'm being pursued by people who are trying to kill me."

"What is your badge number?"

Oh, hell. No idea, but I could bet Mom and Kevin could rattle theirs off without missing a beat. "Shit!" Had to swerve around a huge saguaro and just managed to avoid running over a lot of prickly pear. Poor car.

"I beg your pardon." She sounded offended.

"Sorry, sorry, my bad. Look, what's your name?" Silence. "I'm Kitty, and I'm pretty sure I'm going to die soon, so, since you're likely to be the last person I speak to, I'd like to know your name."

"Gloria."

"Nice to meet you, Gloria. It's a long story, but I don't have my badge with me, and I'm new enough that I don't have the number memorized. I work for a government agency you've never heard of and am affiliated with two others you've never heard of. And there are some really scary men after me and my boyfriend and I just broke up." Whoops, my mouth was not doing a good job with censorship.

"Ah," she said, sounding like this wasn't a new one. "Another woman?"

"No, he thinks I'm cheating on him."

"Are you?"

"No! And I have options," I felt compelled to add. "An old boyfriend asked me to marry him two weeks ago and my best guy friend who wasn't really ever a boyfriend but was a fling asked me to marry him tonight."

"You rich or just gorgeous?"

"Neither. I'm not barking or anything, but I'm not the most gorgeous girl in the room." Especially if that room was filled with A-C women. "And if they're hoping for a trust fund, I'll inherit four dogs, three cats, and a lot of allergy meds, and that's about it."

"So, anyone else after you that your boyfriend would be jealous of?"

"His cousin likes me. And one of our friends, but he's gay, but if he weren't I'd marry him because he never, ever makes me cry." Like I was right now. "But he thought I was having an affair with a different friend, who's great looking and has bags of charisma, but he's happily married and besides, I love Jeff."

"Jeff's your boyfriend?"

"He was. We broke up this afternoon." Looked in the rearview. There were headlights coming after me. "And it was my ten-year high school reunion, and he's the one who wanted to go, but I ended up having to go alone, and then Chuckie was there, and he proposed, but I can't even think about it because these horrible warmongers are after me, and I'm going to die. And my hair's a mess."

"Why'd you two break up? You and Jeff, I mean?"

"I don't know. I think he's sick or got drugged by someone."

"Is that why you stole the car, to support his habit?"

"He's not a drug addict! He doesn't even drink, but they want to kill him, too. He doesn't take anything. Well, other than adrenaline, but he has to or he'll die."

"That's what all addicts think."

"Look, he's not, okay? And I didn't steal the cars to pay for his habits. I stole them to stay alive."

"You stole more than one car?"

"Chuckie and I had to steal the Porsche because Shannon the Toothless Weasel was trying to shoot us. I gave the owner of the Mazda the keys as a trade. I had to steal this car because Reid had me."

"Reid another one in love with you?"

"No, he's the guy trying to kill me. Leventhal Reid. He's a Representative from Florida."

"What's his connection to the weasel?"

"I think the weasel works for him. Shannon's a part of Club 51."

"That like Price Club?"

"No, it's like UFO whackos who want to kill all the aliens."

"So, there are aliens, too?"

"I'm not saying."

"How hard did you hit your head, honey?"

"Not that hard. Look, can you please call someone for me? They're in an SUV, and they're gaining."

CHAPTER 69

THE ESCALADE WAS CLOSE ENOUGH for me to see the grillwork. "Gloria, can you please call Solomon and Angela Katt of Pueblo Caliente and let them know that I said I love them?"

"Those your parents?"

"Yes."

There was a pause. "Your name is Kitty Katt?"

"Katherine, but they call me Kitty. Everyone calls me Kitty, though James calls me girlfriend and Jeff used to call me baby." I sobbed on the last word but kept it sort of together, to use the term loosely.

"James is which one?"

"The gay guy I'd marry if he was straight."

"Right. We have another agent putting in a call to your parents."

"Thanks."

"No problem. It's a slow night."

I got a sneaking suspicion. "Um, are the other folks over there listening in?"

"Yes. You have seven who think we should send a helicopter, five who think you're crazy, and two marriage proposals, sight unseen."

"Gee. Thanks, I'm flattered. Bad timing, let me get back to them. And, just out of curiosity, what *are* you doing?"

"We've contacted state and local authorities."

I felt a bump. "Tell them to look for a smoking heap of

twisted metal. The Escalade's on top of me." I floored it again, cacti be damned.

"Any message for, let's see, Jeff, the old boyfriend who proposed two weeks ago, Chuckie the best friend who proposed tonight, Jeff's cousin, James the gay guy, or the married guy with charisma?"

"Why didn't anyone but Kevin listen to me?"

"Who's Kevin?"

"The married guy with charisma."

"He listens to you?"

"Yes. Jeff used to."

"But he doesn't any more?"

"He doesn't love me any more." Swerved around a saguaro the Escalade barreled over. "I am not the one who just destroyed the saguaro! I want that on record. They are our state tree, or whatever, and I respect the cactus. The Escalade ran over the saguaro, not me."

"Noted. I'm sure it'll lighten your sentence."

"Gloria, I'm not going to live long enough to be arrested, let alone tried and sentenced. I left my purse in the hotel room, so I don't have my gun, I don't have my iPod, I don't have my hairspray, nothing. And my cell died and I had to throw it away because they were tracking me with it."

"Seems like they found you anyway."

"Yeah. I liked that phone, too." The Escalade was trying something new. It was alongside me now. It swerved at me, and I spun the wheel to the right.

"Why are you screaming? What's happened?" Gloria was shouting.

"Always scream when I'm terrified, Gloria, it's my way of sharing the fun. I'm spinning out." Car settled a bit, it wasn't facing the Escalade, I hit the gas. "Okay, out of the spin out. They look like more fun on TV, in case anyone wonders."

"Where's the Escalade?"

I checked the rearview. Nothing. Checked to the sides. Nothing. "I don't know."

"How do you lose an Escalade?"

"I have no idea." I looked around again, still nothing. I turned front to see the SUV appear out from what I realized was a wash and stop dead in front of me. I screamed and slammed on the brakes. The car stopped two inches from the Escalade. I saw smoke coming out from under the hood. "Bye, Gloria, I have to run away so they can chase me on foot before they kill me. Thanks for being there."

I kicked off my shoes, opened the door, and leaped out. I thought I heard someone who wasn't Gloria shouting my name from the interior speaker, but I was too busy running to stop to say good-bye to the rest of the Emergency Assistance gang.

Running barefoot in the desert is not fun, but it's better than running in four inch stilettos. My dress was a hindrance. I pulled it up, ripped the slit up to the waist seam and kept on running. I could hear someone behind me, breathing hard.

I didn't turn around. Track trained you well about that. Look behind, lose the race. This was a lot like when Alliflash was chasing me, only I'd actually had a hope of survival there. I knew without asking that Reid had nothing pleasant planned for me.

I had no destination other than "away." I had no hope of rescue, I just didn't want to die like this.

Not my choice, of course. Someone grabbed my hair and pulled. It hurt like hell and caused me to fall back, right into whoever was yanking on me. Turned out to be Reid. He looked more reptilian up close, as if he were part snake. I was terrified of snakes.

"You're a lot of work," he snarled. "I hope you'll be worth it." I tried to get away, and he slapped me, hard, and then backhanded me for good measure. I'd locked my jaw closed just in time, but it hurt like hell.

"Isn't this stupid, for you to be out here doing your own dirty work?"

He smiled. I'd thought the Supreme Fugly had been bad, but this man was pure human and pure evil. "Where's the enjoyment in that?" He dragged me back toward the cars. I was happy to note he was still limping. I wondered how he'd caught me, then figured he'd been high on adrenaline.

"You're willing to risk your career by murdering me?"

"Oh, not just murdering you." He flung me to my knees

so I was in the SUV's headlights. Reid jerked his head, and
Shannon got out of the driver's seat, carrying what looked
like a lead pipe and wire cutters. Reid took them from him,
and Shannon looked at me and giggled. It scared me as
much as anything else had.

"You see, it's easy to destroy evidence, if you know what
you're doing." Reid was walking around me, slapping the
pipe into the palm of his hand. "First, you cut off the fingertips at the first knuckle and scatter them for the animals
to eat."

"No fingerprints."

"Correct. Then, you use the pipe to crush all the bones
in the feet. Hard to run. But, just to be sure, I'll break all the
bones in your legs and arms, too." He stopped in front of
me. "Then, well, I'll have some fun." He slid his hand under
the top of my dress. I tried to shove him away but he put
the pipe against my head. He pawed my breasts, doing his
best to be rough. I gritted my teeth.

"You're going to leave your DNA in me? That seems
stupid."

Reid put the pipe in front of my eyes. "No . . . not my
DNA." He let that one hang on the air for a few moments.
"Then, after I've expanded your, heh, horizons, then I'll
break your rib cage. Then, well, then I'll smash your teeth
out. You, of course, will still be alive, oh, and don't worry
about fainting—I've brought plenty of smelling salts."

I didn't say anything. I knew I couldn't talk without crying or sounding terrified.

"Finally, of course, I'll smash your skull. There won't be
much of you left to identify, but a shallow grave out here
should be sufficient. I must thank you for choosing this location. It's excellent."

"No problem." I could talk as long as I kept my teeth
gritted. He was still pawing me. He put the pipe under my
chin and pushed. I got the hint and stood up. He took his
hand out of my top, but only so he could send it under my
skirt.

"Nice," he said as he squeezed my thighs. I clamped them
together. He still pawed me, but through my underwear. I
tried not to think about what he was doing, but the only

thing I could focus on was how when Martini did things like this to me it was never frightening, never painful, never against my will.

I closed my eyes. This didn't sit well with Reid, because he pulled his hand away from my body so he could slap my face again. I went to my hands and knees. My head hurt, and I was dizzy. I didn't want this to be the last thing I remembered of my life. If I ever needed to get to the Happy Place, it was now.

I focused on the happiest memory I had—Cabo with Martini. Swimming in the ocean. Just being together, talking, laughing, making love in our private cabana on the beach. I was crying, partially from fear, some from loss. I'd never go there again, even if I survived tonight. I couldn't go back to Cabo without Martini.

Reid grabbed my left wrist and pulled my hand up in front of me. He had the pipe tucked under his arm and the wire cutters in his hand. "Would you like to beg for mercy?"

"Not really. I would like to know why you're doing this to me, aside from your being a sociopath, I mean." My last shot—if someone was monologuing, then I was still alive.

He cocked his head at me. "You don't know?"

"No freaking idea."

"You, you personally, ruined twenty years' worth of planning in two days. Two days! Centaurion Division was going to be destroyed, and instead you caused the arrest of over three hundred operatives, killed my right-hand man, and stole my secret weapon. Not to mention whatever voodoo you did with the astronauts that has the highest levels of government suddenly kowtowing to that miserable space trash."

"What was your ultimate goal with all this? I'm not clear."

"What do you mean?"

"Why the extensive network of coconspirators, the triple plans going at the same time, all the destabilization attempts? I mean, is it all just an elaborate ruse to cover up a huge heist? Did you just love *Ocean's Eleven* a bit too much?"

He laughed. "Not money. Power. Whoever controls the space trash controls the world."

"Taft said he wanted them to be his slaves."

"A good word. They aren't human; they don't belong here. They use resources; have power and respect in the highest levels of world government. And why? For no reason other than they have some knowledge we don't." He put his face near mine. "Understand me. I will bring them down, under my heel. They will be mine to control, or I will destroy every last one of them."

I slammed my forehead into his nose. It hurt, but my head hurt already, so who cared. He fell back and I wrenched out of his grasp. I rolled and scrambled to my feet.

"Freeze." Shannon's voice. I froze, turned around. Sure enough, he had a gun trained on me. Of course, being shot to death sounded infinitely better than what Reid had planned. I took off to my right.

I heard car doors slam. They were coming after me in the Escalade.

CHAPTER 70

THE SUV WAS ALMOST ON ME, but just before it ran me down, it circled and came at me. Oh, they were playing a new game, Kitty Herding. Fine.

Played this for a bit, spent a lot of time diving one way and then the other. Of course, I was exhausted, and they were going to win. I decided to stop playing. I stood still facing the car. It was heading toward me, full speed ahead. Maybe ACE was watching and would join me into the group consciousness.

I could see Shannon and Reid's faces. I flipped them the bird. And then something hit me, but not the Escalade.

Suddenly I was a mile away, up against a rock hard body I knew well. Martini's arms were wrapped around me, and his hearts were pounding more than I'd ever felt, even after an adrenaline harpoon.

He let go of me and stepped back. His chest was heaving, his shirt was pretty much shredded, and he looked crazy. My ex-boyfriend, the Incredible Hunk. "You couldn't stay around Pueblo Caliente?" he gasped out.

I was going to answer, but the Escalade had found us. "Jeff, we need to run."

"No." He grabbed me and shoved me away, hard. I went flying, but I landed on something soft. I chose to believe he'd aimed me that way. He was in front of the car now, and he wasn't moving.

I screamed as the car hit him. Or at least, as I thought

it hit him. Because from what I could tell, he moved at the last moment, grabbed the side of the bumper and the driver's door handle, and flung the Escalade over to the side, as if it were just a large toy truck. Okay, he *was* the Incredible Hunk.

The SUV landed, bounced, and rolled, ending up on its side about a hundred yards from Martini. I scrambled to my feet and ran to him, but he was heading for the car. He got there and ripped the undercarriage out with his bare hands. I was clear on how he'd gotten out of the restraints in the isolation tank.

Martini grabbed Reid and pulled him out, along with the lead pipe. "I know what you wanted to do to her with this," he snarled.

Reid opened his mouth, and Martini punched it. I saw shattered teeth and blood. Martini took the pipe, slammed it against the back of Reid's neck, and then twisted it as if it were a licorice stick. He pulled it tight, then lifted Reid up like a rag doll, and slammed his head into the body of the Escalade. Repeatedly. I had to look away.

I saw movement. Shannon had climbed out; he was behind Martini, and he had a gun trained on Martini's back. I started running again. "Jeff!" Martini spun, and I threw myself at Shannon, achieving the best tackle of my limited football career. The gun went off, but the bullets missed Martini.

Shannon was attacking me now, and I realized he was using martial arts. Fine, I was tired of not getting to hit back. Kung fu maneuvers all have peace and beauty names, like Tiger Blesses the Sun or Dragon Dances on Air. We had a technique at my studio called Crane Prays to the River that we'd all nicknamed Crane Opens a Can of Whuppass. Shannon was perfectly placed, and it was time to open the can.

I jumped to the side to avoid his punch while blocking with my arms, which threw him off-balance. Kicked out his knee with a side-blade kick; he went down. Hit his temple with a left palm-heel strike, followed by a right palm-heel strike to his face, double right side-blade kicks to the floating ribs and the side of his head. Turned and did the pretty on-guard stance. Watched Shannon burble with his neck at a funny angle. Hey, at my studio, our rule was they went to the ground, and then we'd decide if we let them live or not. I'd chosen not.

Martini still seemed to be channeling the Hulk and Raging Bull at the same time. His body was shaking, and his breathing was heavy. He was staring at me, and he looked close to insane. I wasn't sure if I should say something or run or what. But all I wanted was for him to hold me.

"What did he do to you?" Martini's voice was a menacing growl.

"Not as much as he wanted to."

"He *touched* you." He stalked over to me, and I started to cry. I didn't want to be afraid any more, I wanted it to be over.

He reached for me, and I cringed. "Jeff . . . please . . . I didn't want him to."

Martini's expression changed. He didn't look enraged or out of his mind any more. He looked as though he was going to break down. "I know." He stroked my face, gently, where Reid had hit me. "I'd have been here sooner, but you were actually driving faster than I could run."

"We're a hundred miles from Caliente Base, maybe more. How did you get here?" The aftermath was starting to hit me, and my body began to shake.

"I ran." He slid his hand around to the back of my neck and massaged.

"The whole way?" He put his other hand on my waist and drew me toward him.

"Yeah."

"How?" One hand was at the back of my head and one at my lower back. But our bodies still weren't touching.

"An effect of the drugs they gave me with a massive amount of adrenaline."

I looked down at his inner forearms. It was still dark, but we were close and my eyes were adjusted—I could see needle marks. "Jeff, what did you do to yourself?"

"What I had to."

"Why?"

He gave me a shaky smile. "Because I love you. I always

have, I always will. Even if you never want anything to do with me again." He swallowed. "Baby, can you ever forgive me?"

I started to bawl, buried my face in his chest and wrapped my arms around him. He held me tightly against him. I tried to tell him I was sorry, but the words weren't coming out coherently.

He kissed the top of my head. "It's okay, baby, it's all right. I'm here."

"Don't leave me." It was the only thing I could get out.

Martini squeezed me. "No, not if you don't want me to."

I looked up. "I'm sorry I didn't realize you were sick."

He bent and kissed me—it was deep, powerful, a bit frantic. It was wonderful, and as his tongue twined around mine, my body finally started to relax.

He ended the kiss slowly, slid his hands down my arms, then backed away just a little, but he kept hold of my hands in one of his. "I've . . . been trying. . . . " He stopped, closed his eyes, and took a deep breath. Then he went down on one knee and my chest got tight.

Martini opened his eyes and looked up at me. "Our culture doesn't get engaged or give rings. When we find the person we . . . want to spend the rest of our lives with, we make a declaration, of love, fidelity, and trust." He gulped and put his free hand into his pocket. He opened my hands and laid something across them. "It's called a Unity Necklace. It shows that the person wearing it has accepted someone's declaration. You wear it until you're married." He was shaking, but I didn't think it was from the drugs. "They . . . they're passed down through families, through the male children. This one's been in our family for centuries. The stone and the metal are from our home world."

I stared at it. It was an unusual design, geometric shapes intertwining to create something very lovely and very non-human. The stone in it was dark, I couldn't tell if it would be black, blue, or green in the light.

"Oh, Jeff . . . I can't put this on." His eyes closed and pain washed over his face. "My hands are shaking too much." His eyes opened, and he looked at my expression. "I don't want to lose it."

He gave me a half-smile and stood up. He took the necklace and slid his hands up my body and around my neck. He fastened the necklace, then adjusted it between my breasts. He pulled me into his arms and kissed me, and this time we didn't stop.

We were still kissing when the helicopters arrived.

CHAPTER 71

IT WAS AN IMPRESSIVE ARRAY of choppers. I'd never seen so many other than in the opening credits of *MASH*. They were military ones of different kinds—police, sheriff, and highway patrol, as well as a couple of news helicopters—but there was also one that looked big, sleek, and expensive.

The wind they created was intense, and my skirt was ripped up to my waist. I was doing a Marilyn Monroe in black for the crowd as my hair whipped around Martini and me. I turned in to his chest, and he covered my face with his hand. We both gave up on my dress. I tried not to remember I was wearing black thong underwear and just pretended this wasn't happening.

The blades slowed, and people got out and ran toward us. Christopher reached us first. He didn't say anything, just grabbed us and held on. We group hugged for quite a while but it still ended too soon. "Next time Kitty has a class reunion? I want you both to stay home."

Martini managed a grin. "We'll see."

"Kitty, are you okay?" There were plenty of spotlights now, and I saw Christopher look at my face. "Who hit you?" His tone was furious.

"Reid. He likes—liked to do horrible things to women."

Christopher looked around. "I see two dead bodies. Who killed them?" Martini and I both raised our hands.

"Great. Not that I wanted them alive, but this is going to get ugly fast. Reid's a well-known politician."

"Did they know he was the devil?"

Martini hugged me. "It'll be okay, baby."

I saw my parents getting out of, of all things, one of the news helicopters. I started to leave Martini and Christopher to go to them, but my mother proved she really could run twenty miles with ease. She sprinted to us so fast I didn't have time to do more than get my arms free.

Mom held me in the bear hug, and I didn't mind at all. "You're okay?" I nodded. "Jeff?" I nodded again. "You two back together?"

I pulled away and looked at her. "How did you know about that?"

"Gloria recorded your call, and played it all back for us while we commandeered the Channel Five News Chopper."

My dad reached us now and grabbed me. He was shaking. "I thought we'd never see you again."

"It's okay, Dad. I'm okay."

Dad reached out and pulled Martini to him. "You saved her again."

Martini laughed. "She did most of the saving."

"Yeah, all but the part where Reid was going to run me down with the Escalade. Jeff kind of handled that save."

Mom was hugging Christopher, then she and Dad switched. We were turning into group hug central.

Someone pulled me out of the group and into his arms. "Can I mention that I hate it when you do stuff like this, girlfriend?"

I leaned against Reader's shoulder. As always, a nice place to be. "You know how to solve it."

He laughed. "I thought this might scare me straight. Didn't, but I'm still working at it." He rocked me. "You and Jeff back to normal?" I moved back a little bit and pointed to my chest. "It's a great rack, Kitty, spoken as a gay guy with taste." I rolled my eyes and pointed again. "What? Oh! Really?" He grinned.

"Yeah, really."

"I told you they make great mates."

"Let's hope you're right."

"James, why are you staring at Kitty's chest?" Christopher sounded slightly annoyed. Moving back to normal.

Reader turned me around, put his arms around me, and moved my dress a bit. I saw my parent's eyes go wide, but Christopher gave me a big smile. "I told you I'd fix it."

Martini snorted. "Yeah, thanks for that. I don't think strapping me down in an isolation chamber counts as 'fixing' the situation."

"Nice necklace," my father said. "Why is it and too much of Kitty's chest being shown off?"

"Dad, I show off more in a bikini."

"I didn't need to hear that."

"It means Jeffrey has declared for Katherine, and she's accepted." I wasn't expecting White to be here. He never used my full name, either.

"I didn't think intermarriages were allowed," Mom said.

"Under a variety of circumstances, the Office of the Pontifex has been reconsidering its position." White took me out of Reader's arms and hugged me. "Not tomorrow, but soon," he whispered.

I heard the unmistakable sound of big guns being cocked. I reached out and took Reader's hand, just in case. White took my other hand in his. I saw Martini poised by my father and Christopher by my mother.

"Police! Put your hands in the air!"

We did, though White and Reader didn't drop my hands, and I saw Christopher had Mom's and Martini had Dad's.

A voice boomed out via loudspeaker. "Officers, you are interfering in a federal investigation. Put your weapons down." Sounded like Kevin, really pissed.

None of the guns moved.

A different voice came out via a different loudspeaker. "Officers, this is Colonel Franklin of the United States Air Force. Put your weapons down or we will put them down for you."

"We're pretty popular," I said to White.

"I've always told you to never complain about having extra backup."

"Yes, wise man. No argument. You just tend to roll with a lot more big guns than I ever get to."

"You're impetuous. I'm not." White sighed. "The police seem unwilling to cooperate."

Yet another voice boomed out. "This is Major General Mortimer Katt of the United States Marines. We suggest you listen to Colonel Franklin's orders because you are surrounded and we are getting impatient with your stubbornness."

"Uncle Mort's here?" I hissed to Dad.

"What, you were being pursued by crazed murderers and you didn't think I'd make the call?"

The police still weren't moving.

A man got out of the expensive helicopter. I recognized his shape. He sauntered over to the policeman with the bullhorn and put a badge in his face. "Stand down! Federal officers!" Finally, the guns weren't pointing at us.

Chuckie took the bullhorn. "I want all police, highway patrol, sheriff, and news teams on the ground, by the Escalade, and I want them assembled in three minutes. Can the Marines please ensure that all requested parties comply?" There was a scramble, and a bunch of guys sort of appeared out of the landscape.

"Where the hell were they when I needed them?"

Reader laughed. "From what we could tell, you were breaking land speed records. They were probably just trying to catch up. Just be glad Kevin had the presence of mind to monitor the police bands—it's the only way we had a clue of what was going on."

Chuckie came over to us. "Oh, put your hands down, please. Angela, good to see you."

"Always nice to get a visit from the only C.I.A. bigwig I can stand," Mom said.

"C.I.A.? You said you were in the ET Division!"

Chuckie shrugged. "I am. It's the ET Division of the C.I.A." He grinned. "We don't always see eye-to-eye with Centaurion or the P.T.C.U."

The realization that the "new head guy" at the C.I.A. Martini hadn't wanted me to meet was the guy I'd known since ninth grade was irony I wasn't emotionally up to handling just now.

I almost mentioned that he'd lied to me but decided against it. It was going to be miserable enough explaining to Martini what was going on with Chuckie and me. I didn't need to make it worse.

"Mr. White," Chuckie was addressing Christopher, not Richard. "If you wouldn't mind altering all the footage?"

"Giving us orders as usual?" Christopher snapped.

Chuckie shrugged. "They have far more information on tape than I believe any of our organizations want made available to the public. Please ensure that you show Leventhal Reid to be acting recklessly while under the influence of methamphetamines and in the presence of a known drug dealer." He pointed to Shannon's body. "Since I'm sure the world knows of the high-speed chase by now, just make it good and lurid."

"Why?"

"He's a known user, and it'll make the story fly better through the channels I'll have to send it. Besides, politicians behaving badly goes over well with the media."

Christopher gave Chuckie a curt nod and then signaled toward a couple of the zillion and one helicopters. A bunch of A-Cs poured out and went with him over to the news choppers.

"Big job?" I asked White.

"Worse than when you killed your first superbeing," he said with a chuckle.

"Mr. Martini, is it safe to assume you're not up to memory alterations right now?" Chuckie and Martini were eyeing each other.

"I'm up to whatever I need to be, Reynolds," Martini said, eyes narrowed.

"No insult intended. I'm aware of the . . . ordeal you've been through. And I'd like someone to suggest an alternative scenario to Kitty playing Speed Racer through the Arizona desert in a stolen car. Take your time."

Martini glared at me. "*This* is Mr. My Best Friend? *This* is who proposed to you tonight?" He sounded furious.

I backed up against Reader. "Um. . . . "

"Yeah," Chuckie said. "She said she'd think about it. Means no."

"Um. . . . "

Chuckie looked at me. "Well, it means no if the other guy runs over a hundred miles on foot in time to save you from the vicious sociopath." He looked over at the dead bodies and then back to me. "And then tosses a moving car, rips it apart with his bare hands, wraps a three-inch diameter lead pipe around said sociopath's throat, and proceeds to turn said sociopath's head into pulp. Otherwise, it might have meant maybe."

"Stay away from her," Martini snarled.

Chuckie got up into Martini's face. "You wish. I'll be at the wedding. I'll be watching. Screw up again, and I'll make sure you pay for it." He turned away, came over to me, took my arm, and led me away from the others. I looked back— Martini was glaring at us.

"Chuckie, this is probably a really bad idea."

"He's in control. The drug replicates, as your friend said. However, the counter for the drug is adrenaline." He gave a short laugh. "Martini injected himself with enough adrenaline to kill a horse. It gave him the super strength you saw, tripled or more his regular stamina, and provided faster and stronger regeneration. It won't last. After the first few hours' worth of him acting like the Hulk, the adrenaline will burn out the rest of the drug."

"How do you know that?"

He shrugged. "You told me to help him. I called in some favors and put some Earth scientists who can actually outthink the A-Cs on this. Most of the work had been done, so it was fast."

"Did you tell Jeff?"

Chuckie shook his head. "No. He'd already shot in the adrenaline and was after you before we'd figured it out."

"Then how did he know?"

"I assume he didn't." Chuckie stroked my face. "He did what I would have if I'd been able to, what any man would, if he loved you enough. He took a dangerous risk to have the hope of getting to you in time. It worked." He gave me a bittersweet smile. "You're alive, and you chose him. I break even."

"I would have said yes seven months ago." Or, probably, any time between Vegas and Martini.

"But you didn't say yes in Vegas."

"You weren't joking then?" Horror danced in my mind, laughing at me, but I tried to keep it out of my voice. Wasn't sure I succeeded.

"No. Getting married by an Elvis impersonator seemed like something right to do at the time."

"I thought you were kidding." Horror was joined by its best buddy, Guilt. Both of them pointed out that I was a moron.

"Yeah, I figured you cracking up and suggesting we go visit the white tigers again was sort of a clue."

It was truly official—I was the densest girl on this or any other planet, including when told something point blank. He'd asked me to marry him and I'd laughed. Why had he even spoken to me after that? "Oh, God, Chuckie, please tell me you know I wasn't laughing at you—" My voice was heading to the dog-only register.

He put his finger to my lips. "Hush. I know. I knew then, too. You've never laughed at me, Kitty, or made fun of me, not once since we met. Just one of the many reasons I've always loved you." He shrugged as he took his hand away. "You weren't ready to think of me romantically then. I realized it. Patience is one of my virtues, after all." He gave me another sad smile. "Though, right now, I have to admit I see it as something of a curse."

"Were you in the C.I.A. then?"

"No, I joined up afterward. Your mother recruited me."

"My *mother*?" I wondered if I was the only person I knew whom Mom hadn't helped land a job. Probably.

Chuckie shrugged. "She wanted someone there she could trust."

Something registered. "Mom knew you'd proposed in Vegas?"

"Knew, told me she'd hoped you'd say yes, but when you didn't, decided to, and I quote, let you stay dense and unaware for a while more and put me to useful work."

"Nice." Accurate, of course. "But, the C.I.A., not the P.T.C.U.?"

"The C.I.A. wanted me more, for a variety of reasons, my being independently wealthy at a young age and my brainpower being the two biggest ones. Being, as you always put it, the conspiracy king, helped, too. I went for it not only to help my country but because it seemed like a good way to impress girls."

"They liked that you were into the conspiracy theories?"

He grinned. "They were worried. Because I was always right."

"Not a surprise, really."

"Yeah. They figured I had the means, the brains, and the interest to actually blow a lot of things wide open. Easier to recruit me than to kill me, thankfully. I think your mother had a lot to do with it, too. As I said, she wanted someone there she knew she could trust."

"Figures." No one told me anything until they absolutely had to, did they?

"I didn't want to bring you into this world, but once you were in it . . ." He looked sad, and I ran through all the points in our relationship when, if I'd just noticed, things would have taken at least a slightly different course. There were a lot of them.

"Yeah." I wondered what, ultimately, would have been different if I'd had the brains to comprehend that my best friend was not only in love with me but that I'd been in love with him, too. A lot, probably. Or maybe nothing. One thing was sure—we were never going to know. "Our timing sucks."

"Yeah. You still my friend? Or have I lost that?" He didn't sound suave all of a sudden. He sounded like the guy I'd spotted reading *X-Men Unlimited* the first day of high school. The one who'd been shocked when I plopped down next to him to discuss the merits of Wolverine over Cyclops. The friend who'd always been there for me when I needed him—just like tonight.

I hugged him. "You'll always be my friend, Chuckie."

He held me tightly. "Good. I meant it, I'm coming to your wedding."

"Good."

"Your intended doesn't think so."

I looked up at him. "It'll keep him on his toes."

Chuckie bent and kissed my forehead. He kept his lips against my skin. "If he ever again hurts you, breaks your heart, does anything that makes you feel the way you did earlier today, you come to me." He kissed me again, then pulled away. "I love you."

Then he turned around and walked back to the sleek, black helicopter. He got in and it took off. I watched until it was swallowed by the moonless night.

CHAPTER 72

THE MEMORIES WERE CHANGED AND the videos altered. Leventhal Reid's Wild Ride was heading off to the news media as the top story of the night, made as lurid as requested, since he was shown to be after a bevy of terrified college co-eds. The military took care of cleanup, Kevin and my parents were taking care of anything else, including doing something nice for Gloria and her coworkers, and Centaurion personnel were encouraged to disappear.

My car and my stuff were at the Princess, so I insisted on going there. My car had a note on it from Chuckie saying the C.I.A. had defused and removed the variety of booby traps Reid's people had put on it, but Christopher had a team give it the once-over anyway. While we were waiting, an A-C operative showed up with a rolling bag he handed to Martini.

"What's that?"

Martini shrugged. "Hotel's paid for through the weekend."

"Let's get you registered, then. I no longer have a key." Or shoes, a driver's license, cell phone, or cash. Thank God I'd left my iPod in the room.

Reader handed me my handbag and shoes. "You might want these, girlfriend."

"Wow, how'd you get them?"

He grinned. "Uh, I walked over to the stolen Mazda, extracted your stuff, and asked the Marines to be sure to get the car back in one piece. It was tough, hanging out with all the buff guys in uniform, but you know, anything for you and the cause."

"You're a prince, James."

Martini grunted and took my hand. "Let's go."

"We look like crap. Since we can get in after all, let's just go to the room."

"Nah. I want a key." He still looked like Bruce Banner right before or after the Hulk change, and I looked like Elvira after a week-long bender. This wasn't really a great idea in my book, but he was determined.

We went to the desk, and either the folks at the Princess saw this kind of thing all the time or Martini's money was extra-special, because he was greeted warmly and with no undue concern. No one mentioned how we looked; no one mentioned that I'd stolen a Porsche in front of them, nothing.

"Did you just do a little mind meld or something?" I asked as the elevator arrived.

"Never pays to upset the help." We got inside, hit the button for the top floor, and he pulled me into his arms and ravaged my mouth. He had me up against the wall and our bodies grinding together well before we reached our floor.

We got into the room, and he looked wild again. "Jeff? You okay?"

"Yeah." His voice was low and his breathing heavy. He grabbed my dress and ripped it off me, lifted me up, and slammed my pelvis against his. His mouth covered mine as I moaned, wrapped my legs around him, and got the remains of his shirt off.

We fell onto the bed. It felt so much better lying on it with him on top of me. He pulled away from me for a moment though his lower body still pinned mine. "The reaction's still going on. Time and exertion work it out." His eyes were wild, but they weren't frightening.

I ran my foot along his leg. "We have the time."

He gave me a slow smile. "Sure you don't want to take one of your other offers?"

I slid my hand up his chest, around his neck, and into his hair. "Show me what you have that they don't." I pulled his head to mine and kissed him. He wrapped his arms around me and everything felt right again.

We made wild love in every part of the room and in the shower twice. I found myself wondering if it was wrong to want to have a little of this drug and adrenaline cocktail around, just for special occasions.

Dawn came, and we were still occupied. But I could tell the effects were wearing off. Not that his performance suffered, but his heartbeats and pulse were slowing back to normal, his breathing was calmer, his eyes looked right again.

Somewhere in the morning we fell asleep, my face buried in his chest, wrapped around each other just like the first time he'd ever held me in the night. And just like then, I wasn't frightened because he was holding me.

The room phone rang and woke us both up. I managed to look at the clock. Two in the afternoon. Okay, not an unreasonable time to be calling. Martini growled, searched around for the phone, and got it on the sixth ring. "WHAT? Oh, hi. Yeah, fine. Huh? Uh, sure. Give us an hour. Yeah, just woke up. Okay. Can't wait." He hung up. "I think I liked him better when he was after you."

"Who?"

"Brian. He and Serene are here and want to hang at the pool with us."

"It's more fun to be at these things with someone you know, believe me."

"That why you were so happy to see Reynolds last night?" He rolled out of bed. At first I thought we were headed for a fight, but he picked me up and carried me into the bathroom.

"I was kind of heartbroken, you know."

"I know." He kissed me tenderly. "I felt it, every emotion you had. My powers were so enhanced it was as though I could see you." He held me tightly. "I felt each time you thought about me, and how much it hurt you. I never wanted to hurt you." His voice broke.

I wrapped myself around him. "Jeff, it's okay. It wasn't your fault."

"Yeah, it was. I had that explained to me."

"By whom?"

"ACE. He was very upset because, as he also explained, he realizes he can't take an active role most of the time. But you were in danger, and I think ACE cares more about your safety than Paul's." He turned on the shower.

"Is that why you and Paul got into a fight?"

"Yeah. ACE was letting me have it, and I didn't like it. So they knocked me out, Christopher put me into isolation, and then ACE chatted with me inside my mind. That is the freakiest thing in the world, let me just mention." He was still holding me as he stepped into the shower.

"Yeah, he's done it with me, too."

"Well, I doubt he told you that your rampant jealousy and unwillingness to forget a minor transgression were not only causing massive heartbreak but were potentially going to result in the destruction of every person you cared about, starting with the one you loved the most."

"Um, no. Not so much."

"Yeah. ACE gave me the tip about the adrenaline, too."

What a relief. "Oh, good. So you knew it would react against the drugs and clear them out of your system?"

"No. He told me the only chance I had to get to you in time was to give myself an overdose of adrenaline that would most likely kill me."

I reared back and stared at him. "You were willing to kill yourself?"

"To save you? Yes." His expression was dead serious. I figured ACE had to have known what the real drug reactions would be, so he'd been testing Martini. That wouldn't go against what ACE felt was the prime directive, after all—Martini still had free will to decide what to do. I sent a thank you thought to ACE; I was pretty sure he'd hear it, though he might not let me know all the time.

"I love you, Jeff."

Martini smiled. "I love you, too, baby. Now, let's get cleaned up so I can rub sunscreen all over you." I laughed and he grinned. "Oh, and, just to settle this now, we're honeymooning in Cabo."

"You do know how to close a deal, don't you?"

He kissed me, then gave me an extra signing bonus.

CHAPTER 73

"**NONE OF THESE PEOPLE REALLY** remember you," Martini said in a low voice, as we slow danced to, finally, a song from the nineties, "How do I Live" by LeAnn Rimes. I was thankful they hadn't played this the night before. "And most of the ones who do just sort of remember you, and Brian, as blurred images. Half of them think I went to school with you, too. Why?"

"We haven't seen each other for ten years. I remember Sheila, Amy, and Chuckie because I still see them and keep in touch with them. I mean, come on, Christopher had to tell me who Brian was, and Brian was more important to me than any other person currently in this room."

"I don't understand it."

"I know, baby. But this is what it's like for humans. I didn't expect anything more. It's okay, I'm having fun with you and Brian and Serene."

"Will your college reunion be like this?"

"Maybe better. Keep in mind, Chuckie and I went to A.S.U. together, both majored in Business, and graduated the same year."

"He's coming to our wedding. Like seeing him at the reunion would be worse?"

"From what you both said, you two see each other all the time."

"Yeah, can't wait for when we have to pull you in, which I'm sure he'll insist on immediately."

"Maybe." Chuckie hadn't called me in for six months, after all. Which was proof he'd known what was going on and who I was involved with. And this was another reason he really was an awesome guy—he'd given me time to make the choice about Martini without outside pressure. Not that I was going to share a positive thought about Chuckie with Martini right now. We were having a good time, and I wanted to keep it that way. "It won't matter."

The song finished, and the next one the deejay chose was "Bitch" by Meredith Brooks. Martini grinned. "Better make sure." He swung me into a dance that was like the tango, only faster and sexier. Almost like the one Brian and I had done a long time ago, similar to the one I'd done with Chuckie the night before, but still unique, and far more erotic.

I was in his arms, my chest tight against his, when the dance and the song ended. "What was that?" I was ready to go over the edge, and I knew Martini could tell, by the smile on his face.

"How we tango, alien-style. It's adaptable to any beat."

Another song came on. "Angel" by Aerosmith. "Can we do it to this song?"

"Anything you want, I'll do." Martini kissed me, then led me again through the alien tango. All night long.

Coming in April 2011
The third novel in the Alien series from
Gini Koch

ALIEN IN THE FAMILY

Read on for a sneak preview

CALIENTE BASE WAS THE SMALLEST of all the U.S. Centaurion strongholds. Located just outside Pueblo Caliente, Arizona, it was originally supposed to merely provide a safe access for Centaurion personnel into Arizona, which had a lot of activity.

Until about six months prior, when I'd sort of led a second generation A-C uprising, declared the younger A-Cs who were of age to be political refugees, and had the U.S. government annex Caliente Base as the home base for our refugees. My way with people is legendary.

This had worked out better than it sounds, since Christopher's father, Richard White, the A-C Sovereign Pontifex and therefore reigning religious leader of their large and extended clan had, it turned out, been looking for a smooth political way to allow inter-species marriages, based on my firmly held belief it was going to be better for both humans and A-Cs in the short and the long run.

Most of us had lived at the Dulce Science Center prior to this, and Martini and I continued to keep quarters there, in what I called his Human Lair. But we spent at least half the time in Caliente Base as well, since the younger generation were still considered religious refugees by the American government.

We were in the main conference room in Caliente Base, which was on the tenth floor of the complex. A-C complexes went down, not up, so we were deep underground.

But A-C technology was quite advanced and the lighting made you think you were seeing the sun. Well, in the day. In the wee hours of the morning we were now in, all the lighting did was make you tired.

We had all of Alpha and Airborne teams with us, as well as Kevin Lewis, who was my mom's right-hand man in the P.T.C.U. and assigned to a permanent position within Centaurion Division. He was a gorgeous black guy who looked like he'd been a professional athlete. He had a great smile that included incredible teeth, and he was loaded with bags of charisma. He was also happily married, but that didn't mean I wasn't allowed to look at him. Sometimes I could do it without drooling, too.

With Kevin's addition, it meant there were three women and just an entire roomful of hunky men with us. I loved briefings.

"Can't you people do something about the lighting?" Chuckie asked. We were sitting in the romantic glow I loved when Martini and I were in the midst of an all-night sex-a-thon. Trying to have a meeting like this was, at best, difficult.

"No. Like we've already said." Christopher's snark was on high. "Caliente isn't as sophisticated a base as Dulce."

"Define sophisticated," Chuckie muttered.

"Look, it doesn't matter." My necklace was off my neck and sitting in the middle of the conference table, which I knew upset Martini emotionally, even though he understood the need logically. "We can all see it. It's pretty much an exact match for the light show from earlier tonight."

"So, you really think this means we have visitors coming?" Kevin didn't sound as freaked out as everyone else. Maybe it was because he was already married.

"Yeah, I really think so. The timing works out."

"Very much so," Chuckie agreed. "We just need to know if they're friendly or hostile." I got the distinct impression he didn't believe Martini had no conscious knowledge of what was going on or how this was being accomplished.

"Well, they're from Alpha Centauri, and they exiled us here. I'm betting on hostile." Gower sounded upset, just like everyone else.

"But, why?" This question was from Lorraine, one of our only two other female agents. She was a bit younger than me, and had gotten involved during my first outing with the A-Cs, aka Operation Fugly. Like all A-C women, who I thought of as the Dazzlers, she was beyond gorgeous. She was also beyond nice, and one of my two best girlfriends in the A-C community.

"I'm with Lorraine. I don't see why it's a negative." Claudia was my other A-C female operative and friend. She was about my age, winsome and brunette to Lorraine's buxom blonde, just as nice. They were both also scientifically brilliant and excellent medical technicians. I could sprint and hurdle and do some kung fu. Somehow, they reported to me. And didn't mind.

"Why so?" Kevin asked. He was taking over, subtly, which was okay with everyone in the room other than Chuckie. Technically, the C.I.A. reported dotted line into the P.T.C.U., and we all liked the P.T.C.U. a lot better.

Lorraine shrugged. "So they want to come out for Jeff's wedding. I think it's nice. About time they acknowledged that we're all here and alive and doing the work they should be helping us with."

"They put up the PPB net to keep us from leaving the solar system, hell, to keep us from leaving the inner planets." Martini sounded as angry as he looked. "These people aren't our friends, they're our enemies. It's about time we accepted that."

"Paul? What does ACE think? This is really a time when we need his expertise."

Gower nodded, twitched a bit, and then the ACE voice came out of his mouth. "Jeff is right. But Lorraine is right, too."

Silence. We all looked at each other.

"Um, ACE? That's it?"

"Yes." Gower twitched and blinked. "One day, supposedly the palsy will go away. I think ACE is confused, Kitty. He can't imagine anyone not wanting to meet you."

"Oh, the superconsciousness hero worship," Christopher said as he rolled his eyes. "Can you get through to him that some people don't think Kitty walks on water?"

"Not really. ACE, ah, doesn't like that kind of discussion." Gower looked uncomfortable.

Reader laughed. "Be happy Kitty uses ACE's powers for good. Remember, ACE thinks Kitty thinks right."

There was a lot of good-natured laughing and kidding about this, but I knew it to be true—when ACE had come to Earth, I was the only one who'd understood what was going on. So, I tried to think like ACE would, and figure out why anyone would be coming out from Alpha Centauri for this wedding. I came up with nothing, other than an idea of who might know.

"Jeff, is it normal morning in Florida?"

Martini sighed. "Yes, baby, it is." He pulled out his cell phone and dialed. "Hi, Dad, good morning. No, not yet. Yes, glad you liked the invitations, it took us three weeks to choose them. No, no, I didn't. Because I hate them. No, I'm not joking, I hate, no, make that despise them. You have got to be kidding. Mom has no right to invite anyone to our wedding, let alone them. Argh! Okay, fine! Look, that's not why I'm calling."

He looked over at me and covered the phone. "Against all logic and common sense, my mother invited Barbara and her husband to our wedding."

"Is she high?" Barbara had tried to force Martini to marry her daughter, Doreen. In fact, it was this incident that had caused the younger generation's revolt and mass exodus to Caliente Base.

"Who knows?" Martini went back to the phone. "Thanks for the update. Glad to know everyone's healthy, and could not have lived without the newest babies' pooping, eating, crawling, and walking report. Now, can we get to the reason I called, since we're about to go to a state of national emergency?"

Apparently not. Martini leaned on the conference table, his head on his free hand, without speaking. He grunted occasionally.

"Is every call to them like this?" Chuckie asked me quietly.

"Pretty much."

"No wonder he's always in a bad mood."

Lorraine was on her phone, undoubtedly warning Doreen that her parents were going to be coming to our wedding. She looked at me. "Doreen says she and Irving will be happy to physically prevent her parents from entering."

I managed a laugh. "Tell her thanks and I'll keep it in mind." Irving was a human science geek, meaning he was what every Dazzler under thirty was hoping to bag. Dazzlers really went for brains. If the packaging was decent to look at, that was a bonus, but not what mattered. Once we were all relocated to Caliente Base, I'd had to pass a law that they were not allowed to try to meet Stephen Hawking—they would have killed him with love, and I figured we still needed his brain.

Martini was finally getting a word in edgewise. "Great, Mom. Thanks. Can I please talk to Dad again? National emergency and all that. Yes, I really do think it's more important than the seating arrangements. Yes, more important than the two families meeting. Trust me, that's going to seem like nothing shortly."

We were trying to figure out just how to have our families meet. My parents and my Uncle Mort, the career, high-ranking Marine, all knew the truth about Centaurion Division. And they were the only ones in my entire extended family who did. Since my mother was a former Catholic and my father was Jewish, we were already getting the whole mass versus temple questions coming. I hadn't figured out how to explain that we were going to end up doing neither. I'd done a ton of research into Earth religions to find the one with the closest ceremony to what our A-Cs performed. So far, not a lot of luck.

It appeared Martini had his father on the phone again. "Dad, cutting to the chase here. Do we still have relatives alive on the home world and would they actually think about coming to my wedding?"

He sat up, then he sat back, then he stood up and stepped away from the table. This was never a good sign. I looked at Christopher. He pulled out his phone and dialed. "Dad? Sorry but we need you here, right now. Thanks." He nodded to me. "He'll be here shortly, just needs to dress and get to a gate."

Martini was still on the phone, and I could see his whole

body was tensed. Chuckie could, too. "Okay," he said quietly. "I'm willing to buy that Martini had no idea of what giving you that thing would do."

I felt myself relax a bit. "He wouldn't do something to put me in danger, let alone the entire world. He's spent his whole life protecting it."

Chuckie patted my hand. "I know. But I had to be sure."

"You don't think he's faking it?"

"I see his sarcastic ways are rubbing off on you." Chuckie leaned next to me and spoke softly in my ear, so no one else could hear. "I know they can't lie. I've seen him angry before, more than you, probably. I've also seen him scared. And he's both."

I gave him a dirty look, and whispered into his ear. "You make it sound like Jeff wets himself or something. He's not scared often, if at all."

Chuckie laughed, then did the ear thing again. "I love this, but you're going to get in trouble when he's off the phone. And, I didn't mean it as an insult. Like most of us, he gets scared. But he shows it like, well, I show it, or White shows it—by getting angry, going into an authority mode, and so on." He laughed softly again. "I'm not insinuating your man's a wimp, Kitty. If he was, I'd be running Centaurion already."

I was going to ask him what that meant when Richard White entered the room. He'd used hyperspeed to get dressed and over here, which was sort of a relief. He took a look around. "What's going on?"

Martini looked at me over his shoulder. "Tell him." Then he went back to his phone call.

I took a deep breath. "We have unexpected company coming."

White looked at the necklace. "Oh, my God."

When the head of an entire religious organization says that, any calm left in the room goes running to hide under the covers.

White sat down in the only open chair, which happened to be the one Martini had vacated. It didn't appear to be an issue—Martini was still on the phone with his father, and I got the impression it was going from bad to worse.

"You want to explain this? Keeping in mind we have both the C.I.A. and the P.T.C.U. represented in the room?" White looked shaken enough I felt it necessary to remind him he wasn't with family, only.

He shook his head. "I can't believe it."

"Neither can we. Not that we know what 'it' is, but we're willing to bet we won't believe it, either."

White looked at Chuckie. "Were there lights somewhere?"

"Funny you should ask." Chuckie explained the light pattern, both physical and time-wise, and where they were located. "What about those mountain ranges is significant?"

"Nothing, they're just close and in the right formation." White had his head leaning in one hand. I was prepared for every A-C to do this shortly.

"So that message could have been sent in to any region?" Chuckie was being polite, but I could tell he was getting tired of one-sentence answers.

"No. It went to the nearest formation by the active piece." White indicated the necklace. "How did you realize what it was?"

Chuckie shrugged. "I'm more observant than most people." This I knew to be true. "I've seen that thing around Kitty's neck any time I've seen her for the last six months. It was easy to recognize. Six months ago, the second time I saw it," he added.

"Why didn't you bring this to our attention sooner?" White sounded angry.

Chuckie let the knife show, just a bit. "Because we had to make sure this wasn't some kind of dangerous power play being made by Centaurion personnel." He pointedly looked over at Martini.

"Jeffrey has nothing to do with this," White said, eyes narrowed.

"Bullshit. He has everything to do with it. However, I'm willing to accept that he had no idea what giving that necklace to Kitty was going to trigger."

"Richard, it's sort of creepier than that. The first light manifestation appeared during Operation Fugly." On cue, White winced. "Um, I mean, during the Big Take-down. Or whatever you call it." I never paid attention to their names for offensives—they were always official and boring.

"When Jeff knew he wanted to marry her," Christopher added quietly. "As near as Reynolds has told us, pretty much the same night."

White nodded. "They are tuned to the family, and Jeffrey's the last in Alfred's line." He closed his eyes. "This will happen with you, too, son."

"What?" Christopher looked shocked. "I'm not getting married. And, I'm part of your male line."

"Yes, but it's different for you because of your mother. And, I know you've not declared for anyone yet, but when you do . . ." White's voice trailed off and he looked at me. "Oh, dear."

"This just went to DEFCON Worse, didn't it?"

"Oh, hell." Reader had his head in his hands. It *was* catching.

"What? James, what?"

He looked around. "Oh, well. Not like it's a secret to anyone in this room." He sighed. "Kitty, Jeff wasn't the only one who, ah . . . ?" His voice trailed off and he shot an uncomfortable look toward Christopher.

Who went pale. "Oh, you've got to be kidding! We're past that!" He shot a look at Martini. "Really, we're past that." What we were past was the fact Christopher had also wanted me when we'd first met, and we'd had a brief, wild moment in an elevator. Martini had had a hard enough time letting the incident go, but Christopher and I had been very careful since then and hadn't done anything remotely romantic, and in fact, acted like opposing magnets when something potentially romantic loomed.

"Yeah, yeah, doesn't matter," Martini shot back. "Reynolds is going to be a bigger problem."

"Me? Why?" Chuckie sounded confused for the first time.

Martini spun around. "Because you still want to marry her if you can. It's complex, and it's not pretty, and I need to get the rest of the details." He looked at Gower. "We need everyone on high alert. Everyone's going to have to be briefed, in shifts, key personnel first. But down to the youngest child who's of age to know why we're all really here. Oh, and all of my family, and I do mean all, down to the youngest kids who can communicate verbally or mentally." He went back to his corner.

We all looked at each other. "Richard, you mind telling us what's going on? I mean, it's that, or we all just go running off screaming into the streets."

White took a deep breath and let it out slowly. "Alfred and my late wife were cousins, not as close as Christopher and Jeffrey are, about as close as Jeffrey and Paul, and Michael, are."

Interesting, hadn't known that. "Okay ... so, cousins married a brother and sister. Not totally unusual."

"No, not at all, on either one of our worlds." White didn't want to go on, it was obvious.

Michael, who'd been uncharacteristically quiet this entire time, spoke up. "You want me to explain it?" He was a smaller version of his older brother—big, black, bald, and gorgeous. He was also a major womanizer, but I doubted that had relevance here.

"How do you know?" White sounded shocked. Gower looked as shocked as White sounded.

Michael shrugged. "My mother told me about it. She was ... concerned I would use our Unity Necklace ... inappropriately." Oh, wow, so him being a womanizer *was* relevant. Double interesting.

"What did she tell you?" White sounded guarded.

"That we were close enough from a blood standpoint that it could affect us."

"What could affect you?" I figured the rest of us were getting as impatient as I was.

Michael gave me a wry smile. "Jeff and Christopher are part of the Alpha Centaurion Royal Family."

Gini Koch lives in the American Southwest, works her butt off (sadly, not literally) by day, and writes by night with the rest of the beautiful people. She lives with her husband and daughter, three dogs (aka The Canine Death Squad), and two cats (aka The Killer Kitties). When she's not writing, Gini spends her time going to rock concerts with her daughter, teaching her pets to "bring it," and driving her husband insane asking, "Have I told you about this story idea yet?"

You can reach her via:
her website (www.ginikoch.com),
email (gini@ginikoch.com),
Twitter (@GiniKoch), or
Facebook (www.facebook.com/Gini.Koch).